Eighteenth Period: Haruaki-sensei's Morning Discipline Patrol!

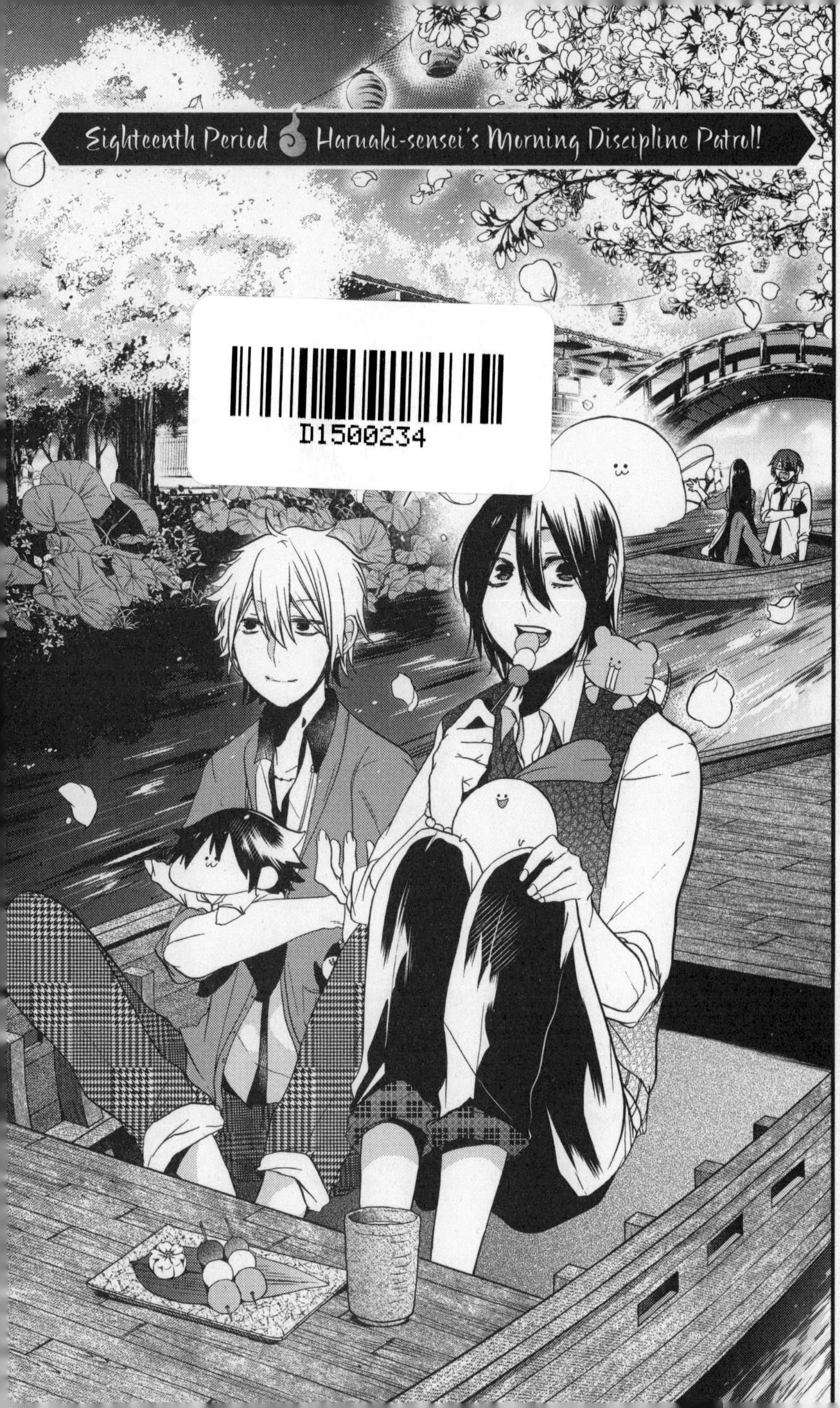

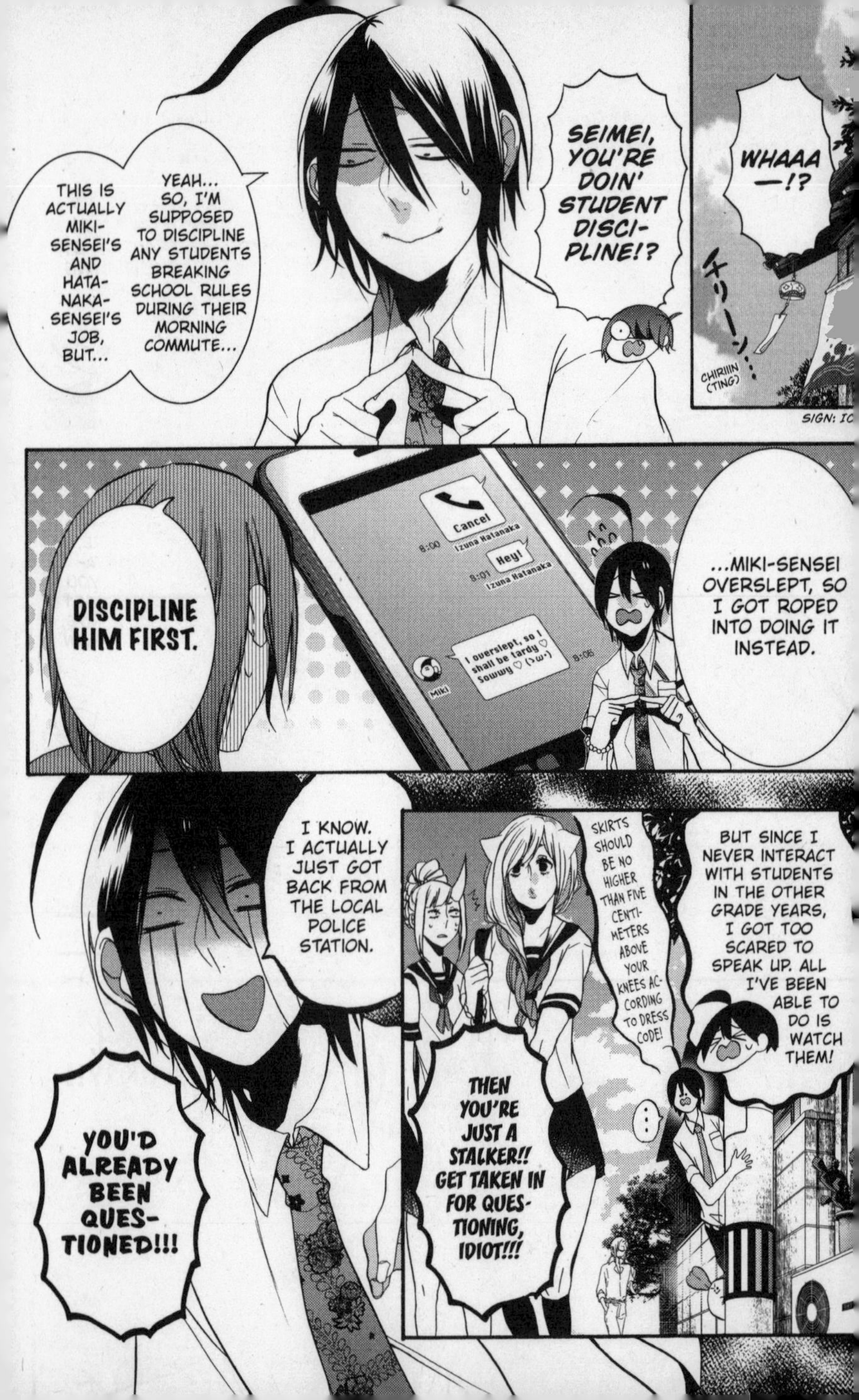
WHAAAA—!?
チリーン…
CHIRIIIN (TING)
SIGN: IC
SEIMEI, YOU'RE DOIN' STUDENT DISCI-PLINE!?
YEAH... SO, I'M SUPPOSED TO DISCIPLINE ANY STUDENTS BREAKING SCHOOL RULES DURING THEIR MORNING COMMUTE...
THIS IS ACTUALLY MIKI-SENSEI'S AND HATA-NAKA-SENSEI'S JOB, BUT...
...MIKI-SENSEI OVERSLEPT, SO I GOT ROPED INTO DOING IT INSTEAD.
Cancel
8:00 Izuna Hatanaka
Hey!
8:01 Izuna Hatanaka
I overslept, so I shall be tardy♡ Sowwy♡ (>w•)
8:05
MIKI
DISCIPLINE HIM FIRST.
BUT SINCE I NEVER INTERACT WITH STUDENTS IN THE OTHER GRADE YEARS, I GOT TOO SCARED TO SPEAK UP. ALL I'VE BEEN ABLE TO DO IS WATCH THEM!
SKIRTS SHOULD BE NO HIGHER THAN FIVE CENTI-METERS ABOVE YOUR KNEES AC-CORDING TO DRESS CODE!
...
THEN YOU'RE JUST A STALKER!! GET TAKEN IN FOR QUES-TIONING, IDIOT!!!
I KNOW. I ACTUALLY JUST GOT BACK FROM THE LOCAL POLICE STATION.
YOU'D ALREADY BEEN QUES-TIONED!!!

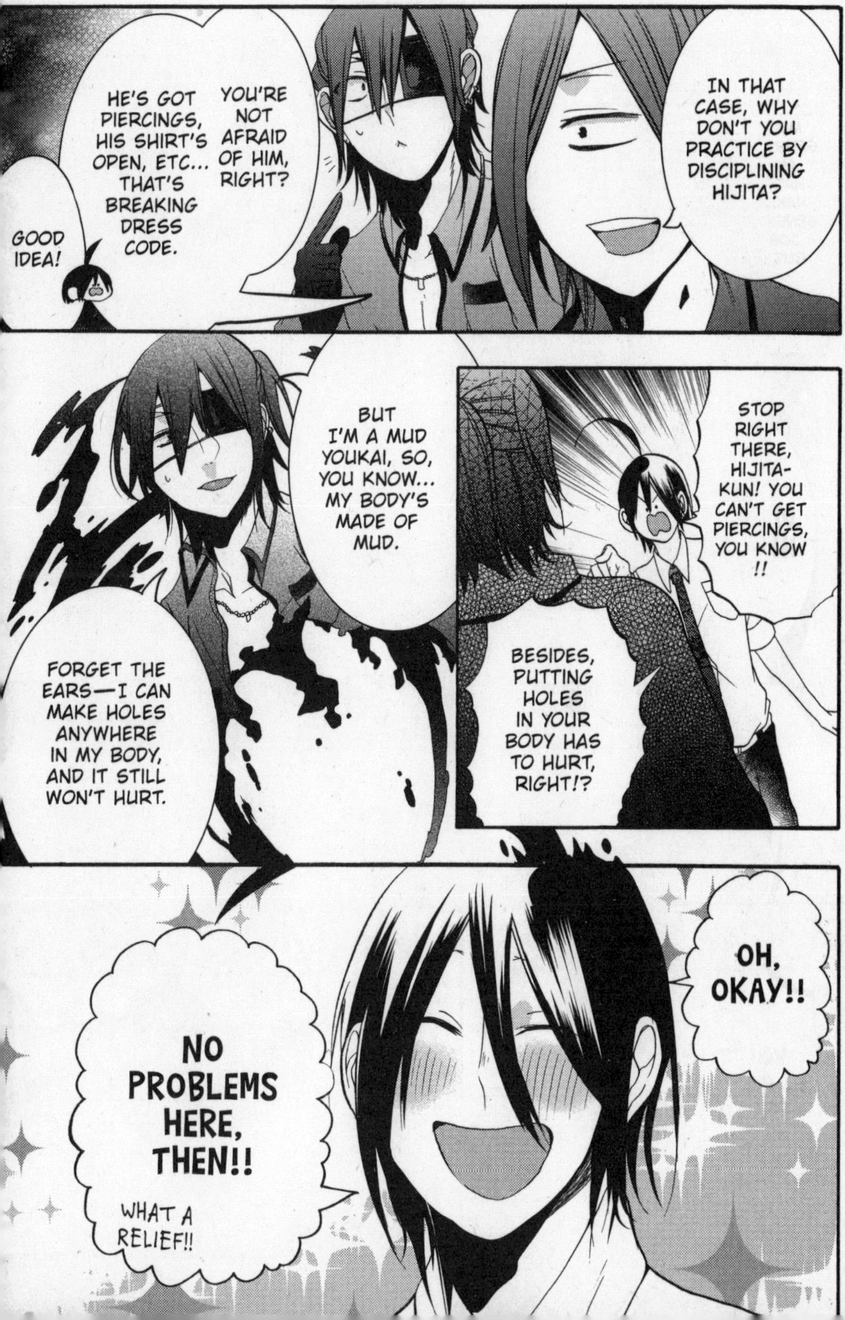
IN THAT CASE, WHY DON'T YOU PRACTICE BY DISCIPLINING HIJITA?
YOU'RE NOT AFRAID OF HIM, RIGHT?
HE'S GOT PIERCINGS, HIS SHIRT'S OPEN, ETC... THAT'S BREAKING DRESS CODE.
GOOD IDEA!
STOP RIGHT THERE, HIJITA-KUN! YOU CAN'T GET PIERCINGS, YOU KNOW!!
BESIDES, PUTTING HOLES IN YOUR BODY HAS TO HURT, RIGHT!?
BUT I'M A MUD YOUKAI, SO, YOU KNOW... MY BODY'S MADE OF MUD.
FORGET THE EARS—I CAN MAKE HOLES ANYWHERE IN MY BODY, AND IT STILL WON'T HURT.
OH, OKAY!!
NO PROBLEMS HERE, THEN!!
WHAT A RELIEF!!

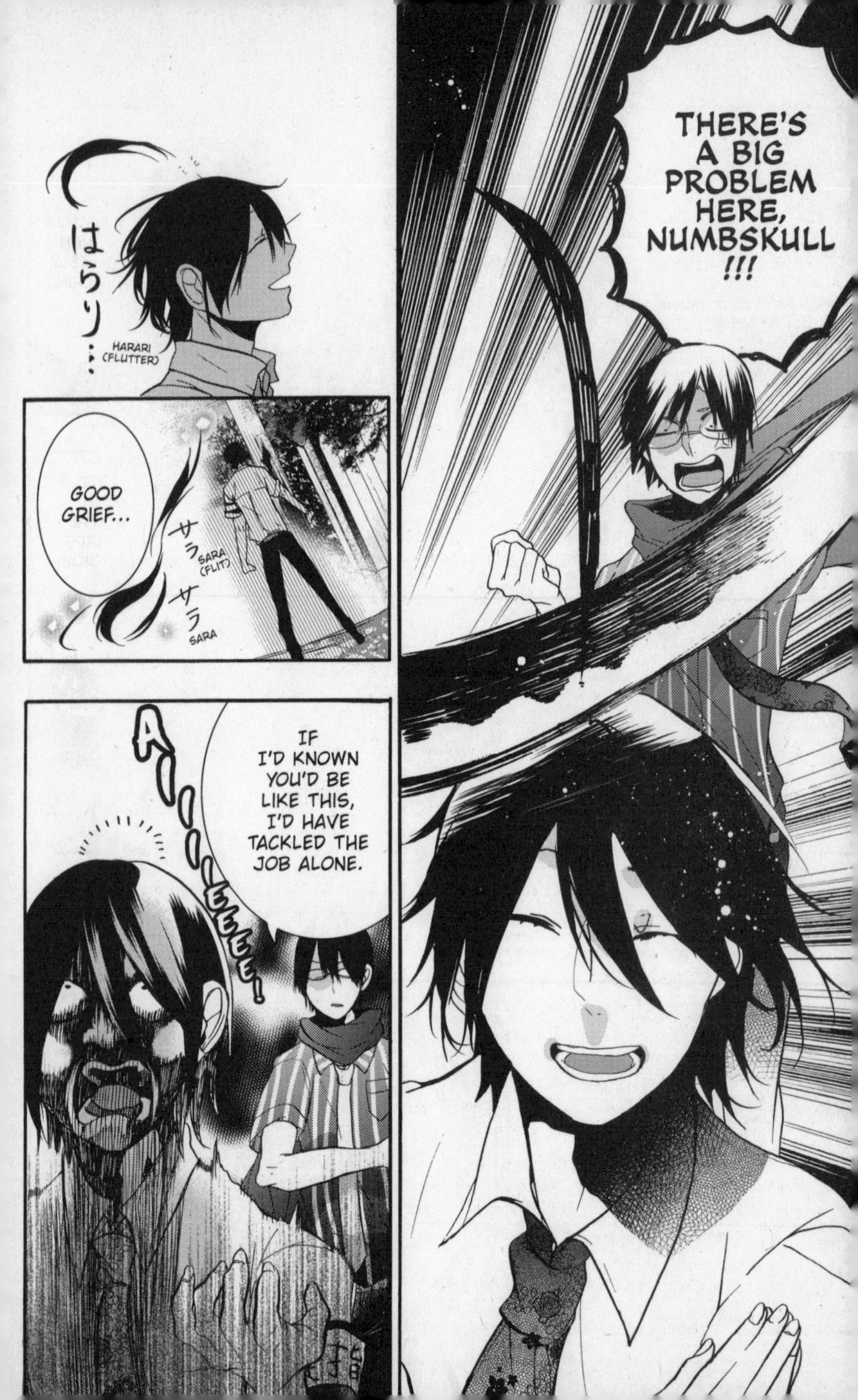
THERE'S A BIG PROBLEM HERE, NUMBSKULL!!!
はらり…
HARARI (FLUTTER)
GOOD GRIEF...
サラ
SARA (FLIT)
サラ
SARA
IF I'D KNOWN YOU'D BE LIKE THIS, I'D HAVE TACKLED THE JOB ALONE.
AIIIIIEEEEE!

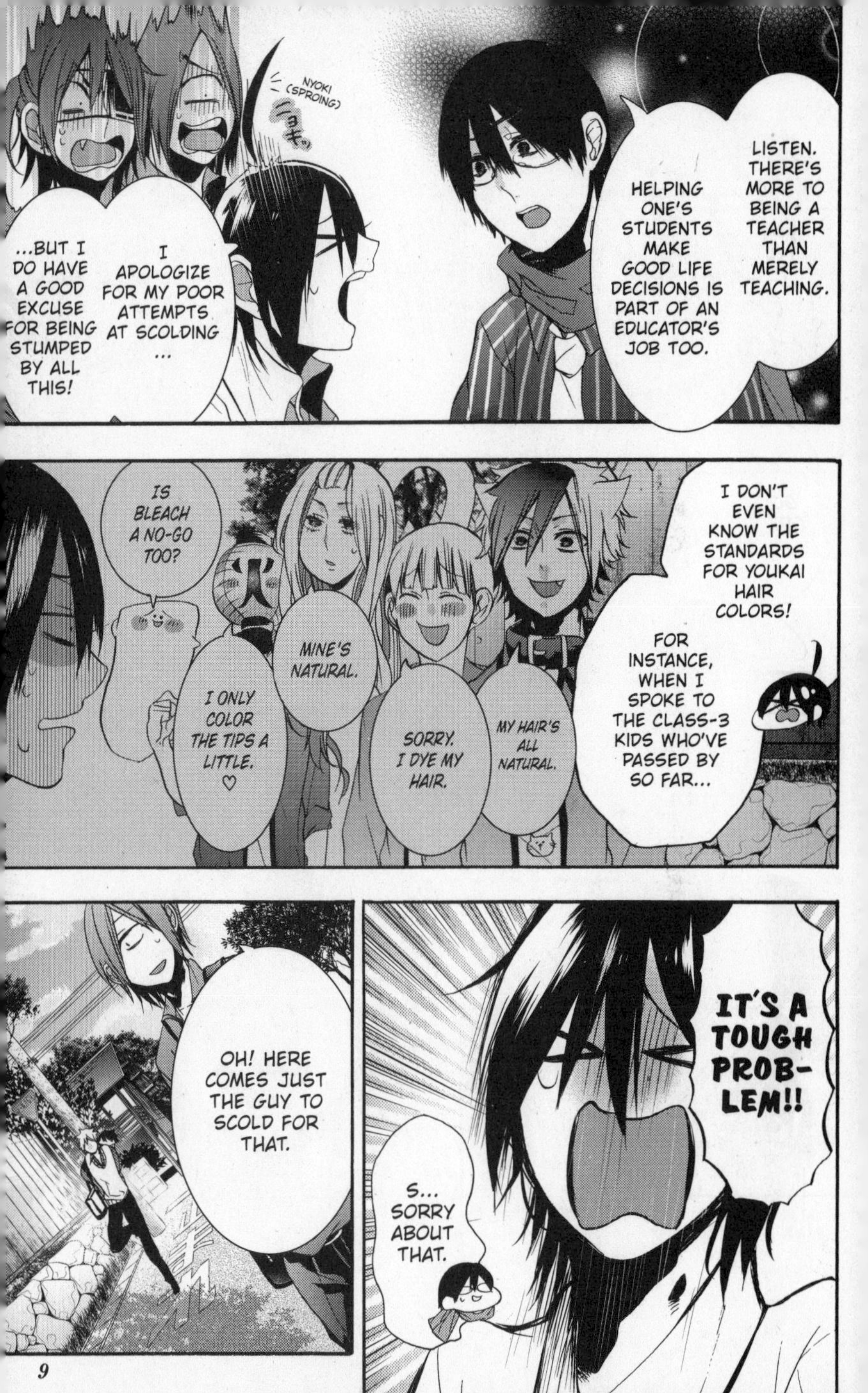
LISTEN. THERE'S MORE TO BEING A TEACHER THAN MERELY TEACHING.
HELPING ONE'S STUDENTS MAKE GOOD LIFE DECISIONS IS PART OF AN EDUCATOR'S JOB TOO.
NYOKI (SPROING)
I APOLOGIZE FOR MY POOR ATTEMPTS AT SCOLDING...
...BUT I DO HAVE A GOOD EXCUSE FOR BEING STUMPED BY ALL THIS!
I DON'T EVEN KNOW THE STANDARDS FOR YOUKAI HAIR COLORS!
FOR INSTANCE, WHEN I SPOKE TO THE CLASS-3 KIDS WHO'VE PASSED BY SO FAR...
MY HAIR'S ALL NATURAL.
SORRY. I DYE MY HAIR.
MINE'S NATURAL.
I ONLY COLOR THE TIPS A LITTLE. ♡
IS BLEACH A NO-GO TOO?
IT'S A TOUGH PROB-LEM!!
S... SORRY ABOUT THAT.
OH! HERE COMES JUST THE GUY TO SCOLD FOR THAT.

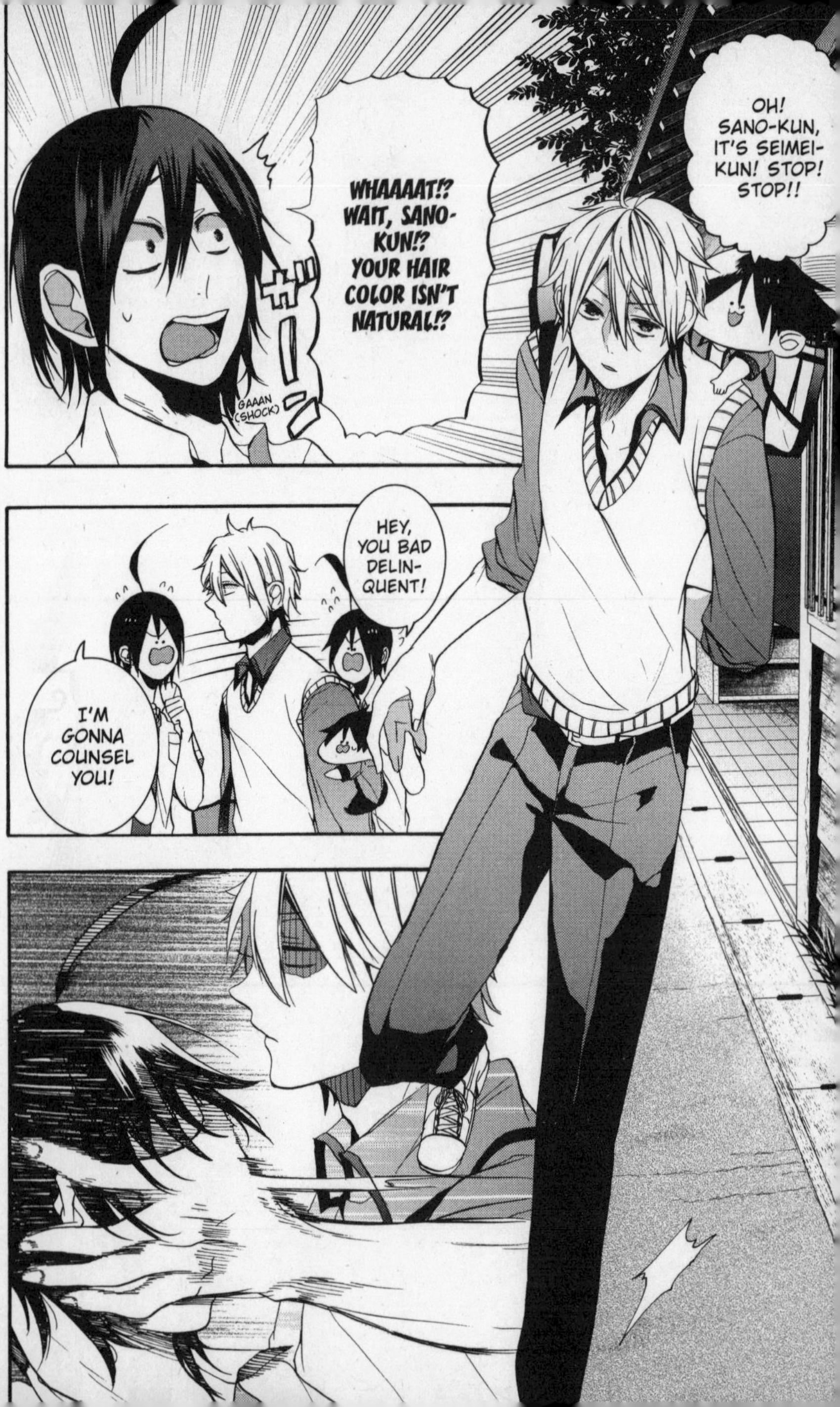
OH! SANO-KUN, IT'S SEIMEI-KUN! STOP! STOP!!
WHAAAAT!? WAIT, SANO-KUN!? YOUR HAIR COLOR ISN'T NATURAL!?
GAAAN (SHOCK)
HEY, YOU BAD DELIN-QUENT!
I'M GONNA COUNSEL YOU!

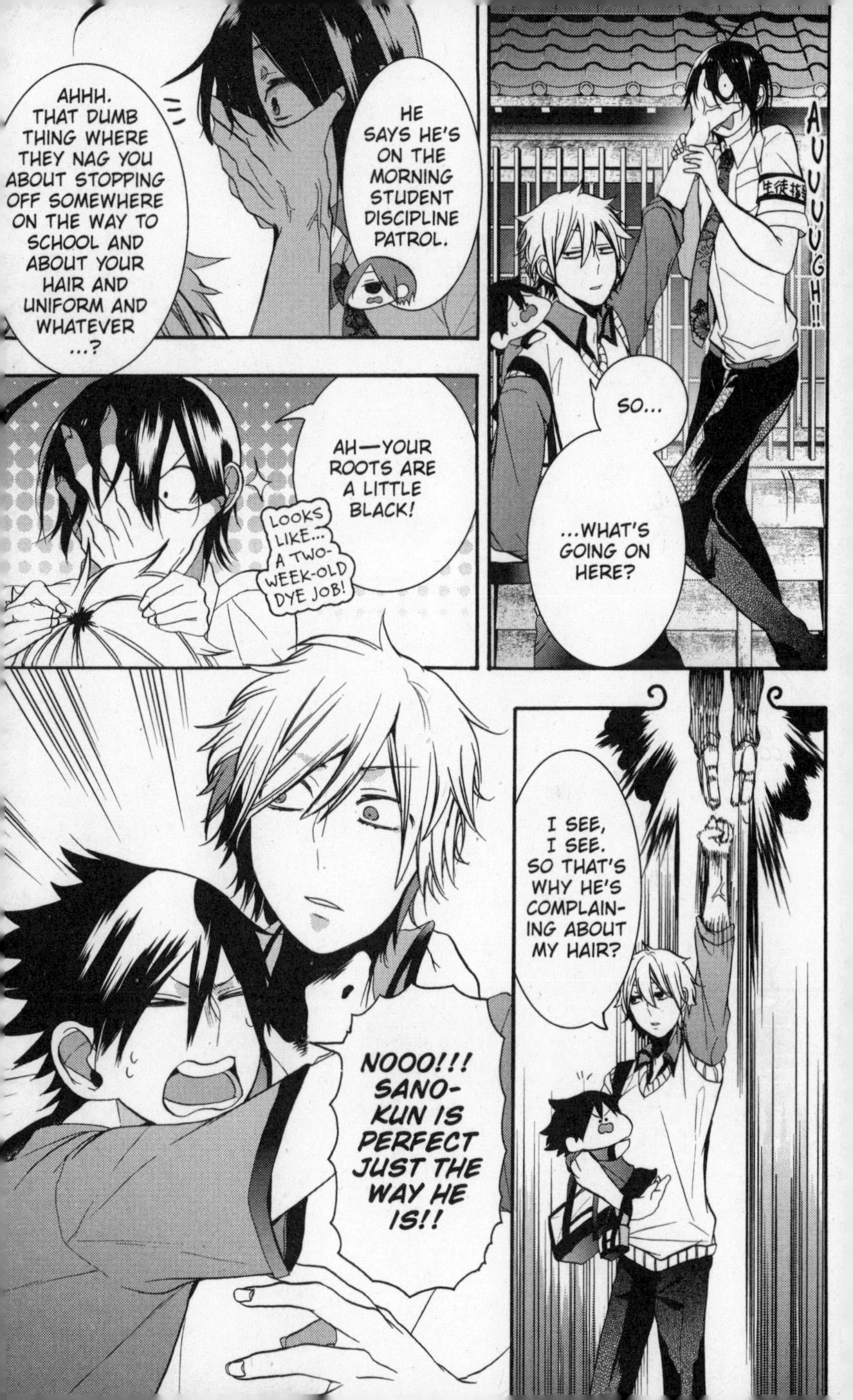
AUUUUGH!!
SO...
...WHAT'S GOING ON HERE?
HE SAYS HE'S ON THE MORNING STUDENT DISCIPLINE PATROL.
AHHH. THAT DUMB THING WHERE THEY NAG YOU ABOUT STOPPING OFF SOMEWHERE ON THE WAY TO SCHOOL AND ABOUT YOUR HAIR AND UNIFORM AND WHATEVER ...?
AH—YOUR ROOTS ARE A LITTLE BLACK!
LOOKS LIKE... A TWO-WEEK-OLD DYE JOB!
I SEE, I SEE. SO THAT'S WHY HE'S COMPLAINING ABOUT MY HAIR?
NOOO!!! SANO-KUN IS PERFECT JUST THE WAY HE IS!!

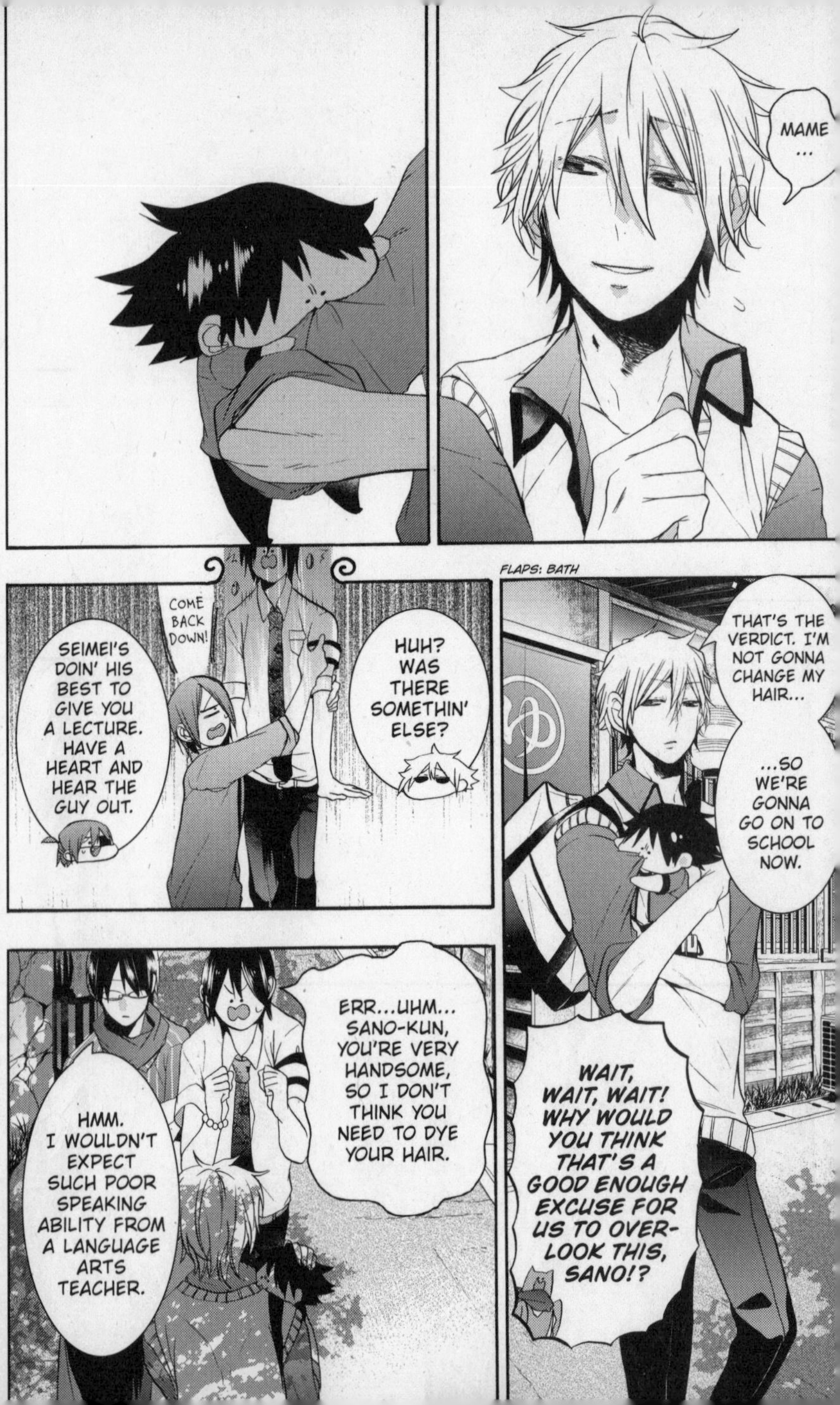
MAME ...
FLAPS: BATH
THAT'S THE VERDICT. I'M NOT GONNA CHANGE MY HAIR...
...SO WE'RE GONNA GO ON TO SCHOOL NOW.
WAIT, WAIT, WAIT! WHY WOULD YOU THINK THAT'S A GOOD ENOUGH EXCUSE FOR US TO OVER-LOOK THIS, SANO!?
HUH? WAS THERE SOMETHIN' ELSE?
COME BACK DOWN!
SEIMEI'S DOIN' HIS BEST TO GIVE YOU A LECTURE. HAVE A HEART AND HEAR THE GUY OUT.
ERR...UHM... SANO-KUN, YOU'RE VERY HANDSOME, SO I DON'T THINK YOU NEED TO DYE YOUR HAIR.
HMM. I WOULDN'T EXPECT SUCH POOR SPEAKING ABILITY FROM A LANGUAGE ARTS TEACHER.

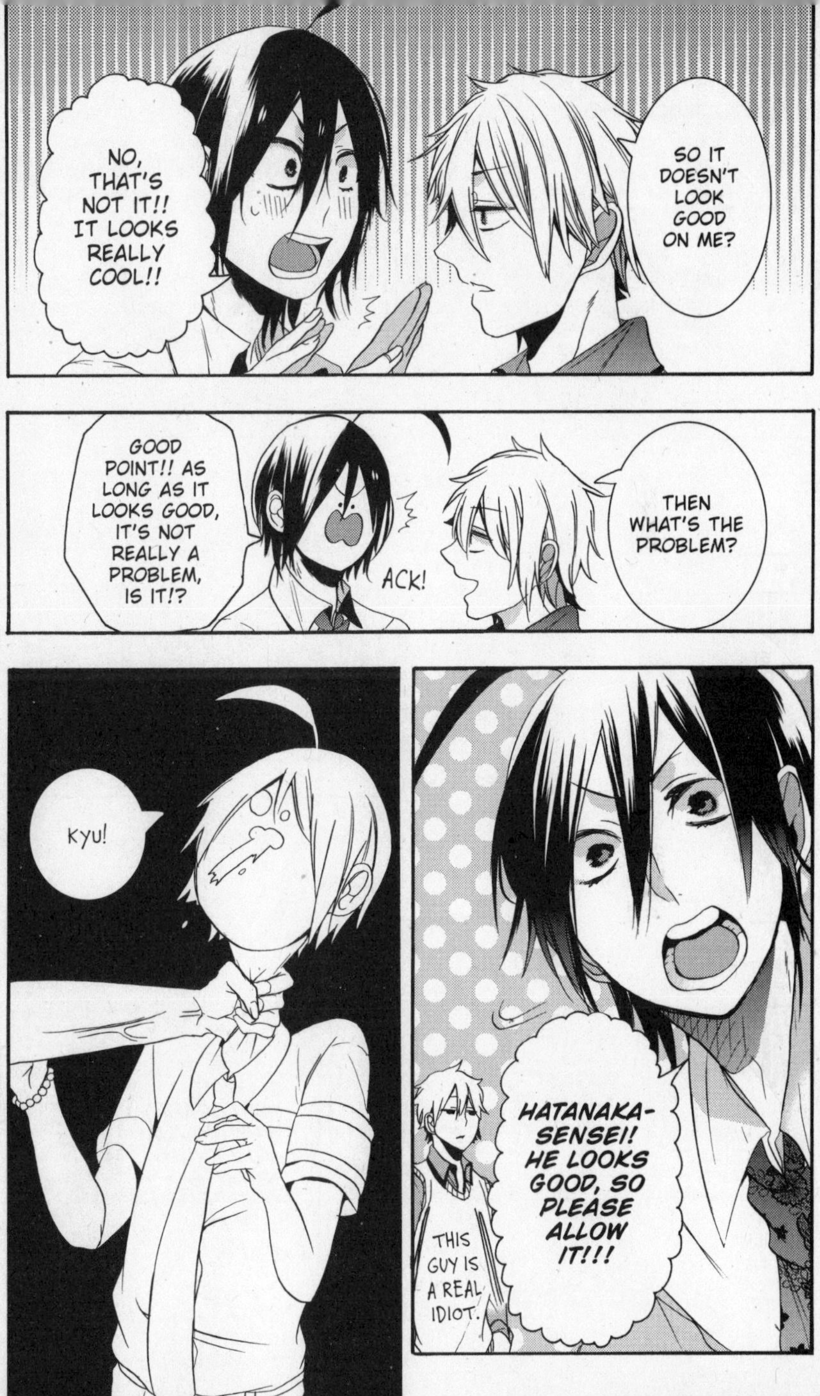
SO IT DOESN'T LOOK GOOD ON ME?
NO, THAT'S NOT IT!! IT LOOKS REALLY COOL!!
THEN WHAT'S THE PROBLEM?
ACK!
GOOD POINT!! AS LONG AS IT LOOKS GOOD, IT'S NOT REALLY A PROBLEM, IS IT!?
HATANAKA-SENSEI! HE LOOKS GOOD, SO PLEASE ALLOW IT!!!
THIS GUY IS A REAL IDIOT.
KYU!

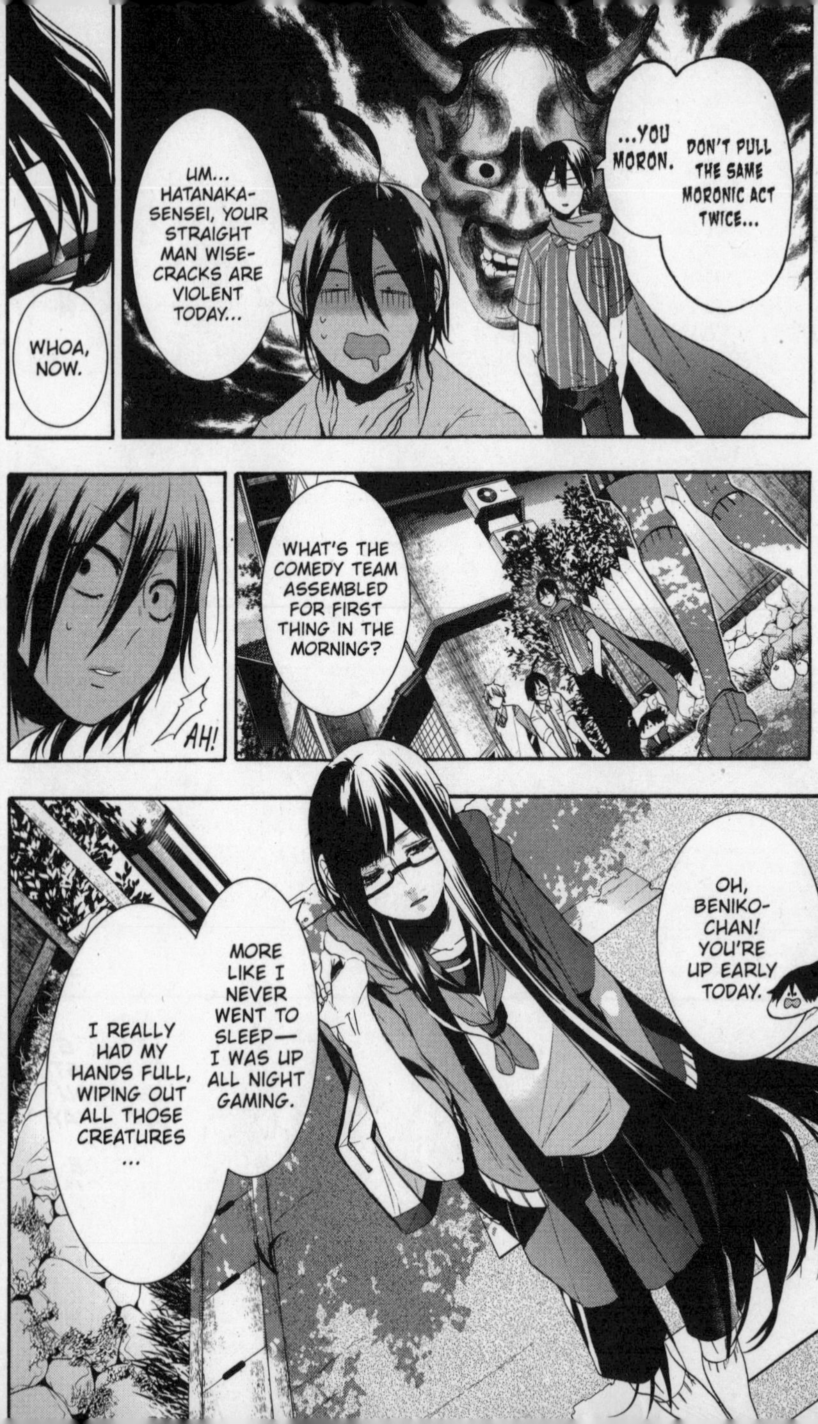
...YOU MORON.
DON'T PULL THE SAME MORONIC ACT TWICE...
UM... HATANAKA-SENSEI, YOUR STRAIGHT MAN WISE-CRACKS ARE VIOLENT TODAY...
WHOA, NOW.
WHAT'S THE COMEDY TEAM ASSEMBLED FOR FIRST THING IN THE MORNING?
AH!
OH, BENIKO-CHAN! YOU'RE UP EARLY TODAY.
MORE LIKE I NEVER WENT TO SLEEP— I WAS UP ALL NIGHT GAMING.
I REALLY HAD MY HANDS FULL, WIPING OUT ALL THOSE CREATURES ...

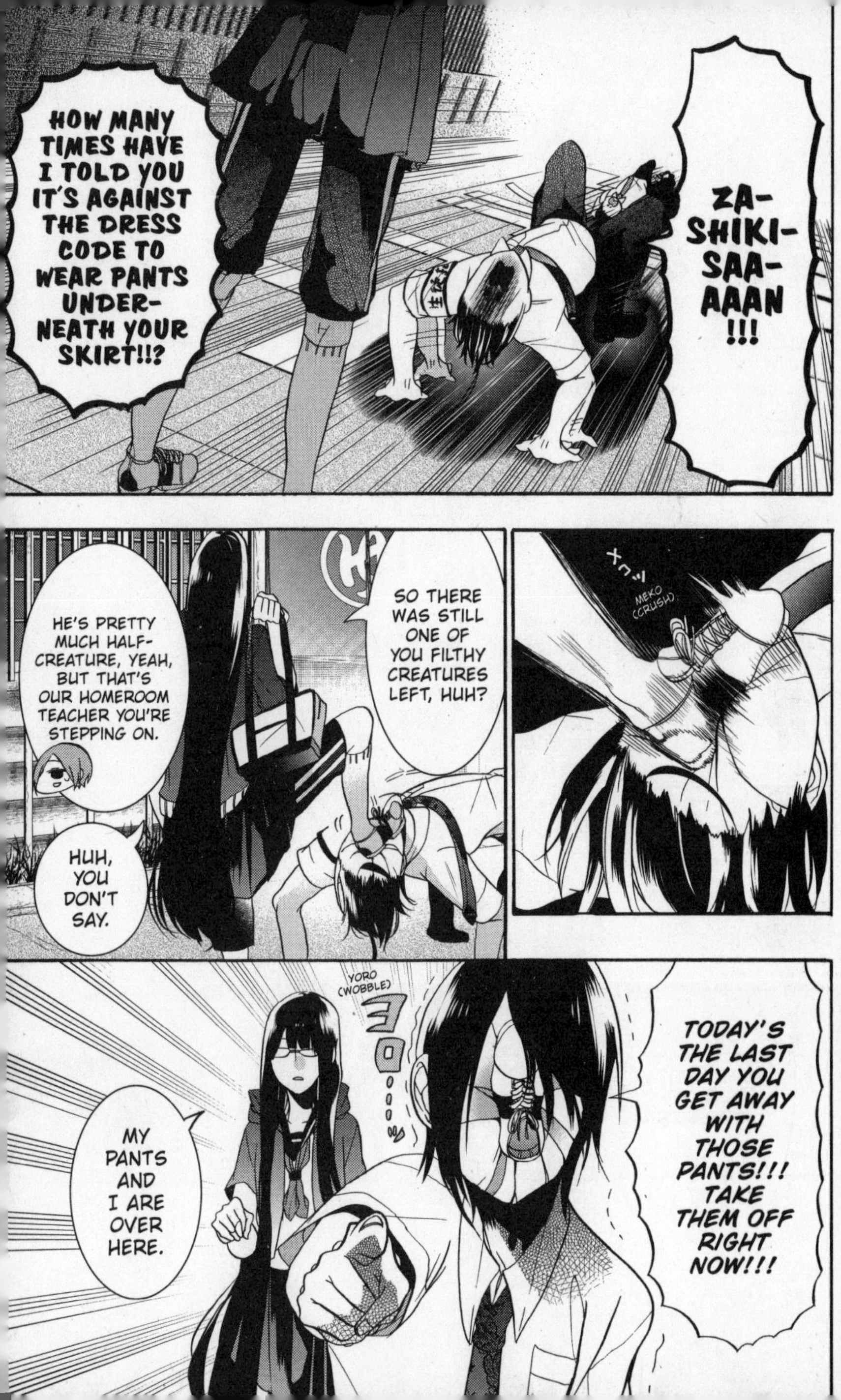
ZA-SHIKI-SAAAAAN!!!
HOW MANY TIMES HAVE I TOLD YOU IT'S AGAINST THE DRESS CODE TO WEAR PANTS UNDERNEATH YOUR SKIRT!!?
メコッ
MEKO (CRUSH)
SO THERE WAS STILL ONE OF YOU FILTHY CREATURES LEFT, HUH?
HE'S PRETTY MUCH HALF-CREATURE, YEAH, BUT THAT'S OUR HOMEROOM TEACHER YOU'RE STEPPING ON.
HUH, YOU DON'T SAY.
TODAY'S THE LAST DAY YOU GET AWAY WITH THOSE PANTS!!! TAKE THEM OFF RIGHT NOW!!!
YORO (WOBBLE)
ヨロ
MY PANTS AND I ARE OVER HERE.

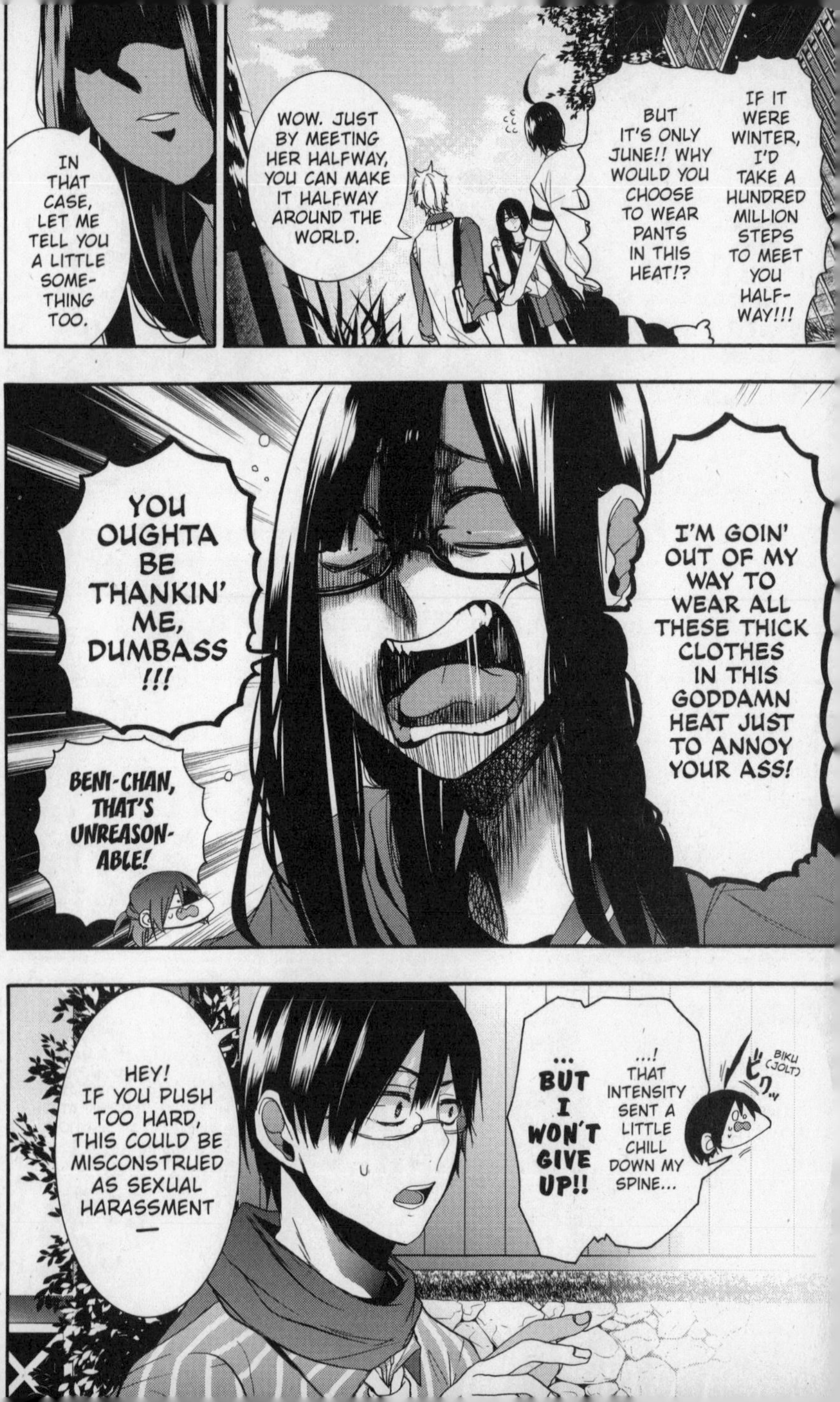
IF IT WERE WINTER, I'D TAKE A HUNDRED MILLION STEPS TO MEET YOU HALF-WAY!!!
BUT IT'S ONLY JUNE!! WHY WOULD YOU CHOOSE TO WEAR PANTS IN THIS HEAT!?
WOW. JUST BY MEETING HER HALFWAY, YOU CAN MAKE IT HALFWAY AROUND THE WORLD.
IN THAT CASE, LET ME TELL YOU A LITTLE SOME-THING TOO.
I'M GOIN' OUT OF MY WAY TO WEAR ALL THESE THICK CLOTHES IN THIS GODDAMN HEAT JUST TO ANNOY YOUR ASS!
YOU OUGHTA BE THANKIN' ME, DUMBASS!!!
BENI-CHAN, THAT'S UNREASON-ABLE!
BIKU (JOLT)
...! THAT INTENSITY SENT A LITTLE CHILL DOWN MY SPINE...
... BUT I WON'T GIVE UP!!
HEY! IF YOU PUSH TOO HARD, THIS COULD BE MISCONSTRUED AS SEXUAL HARASSMENT—

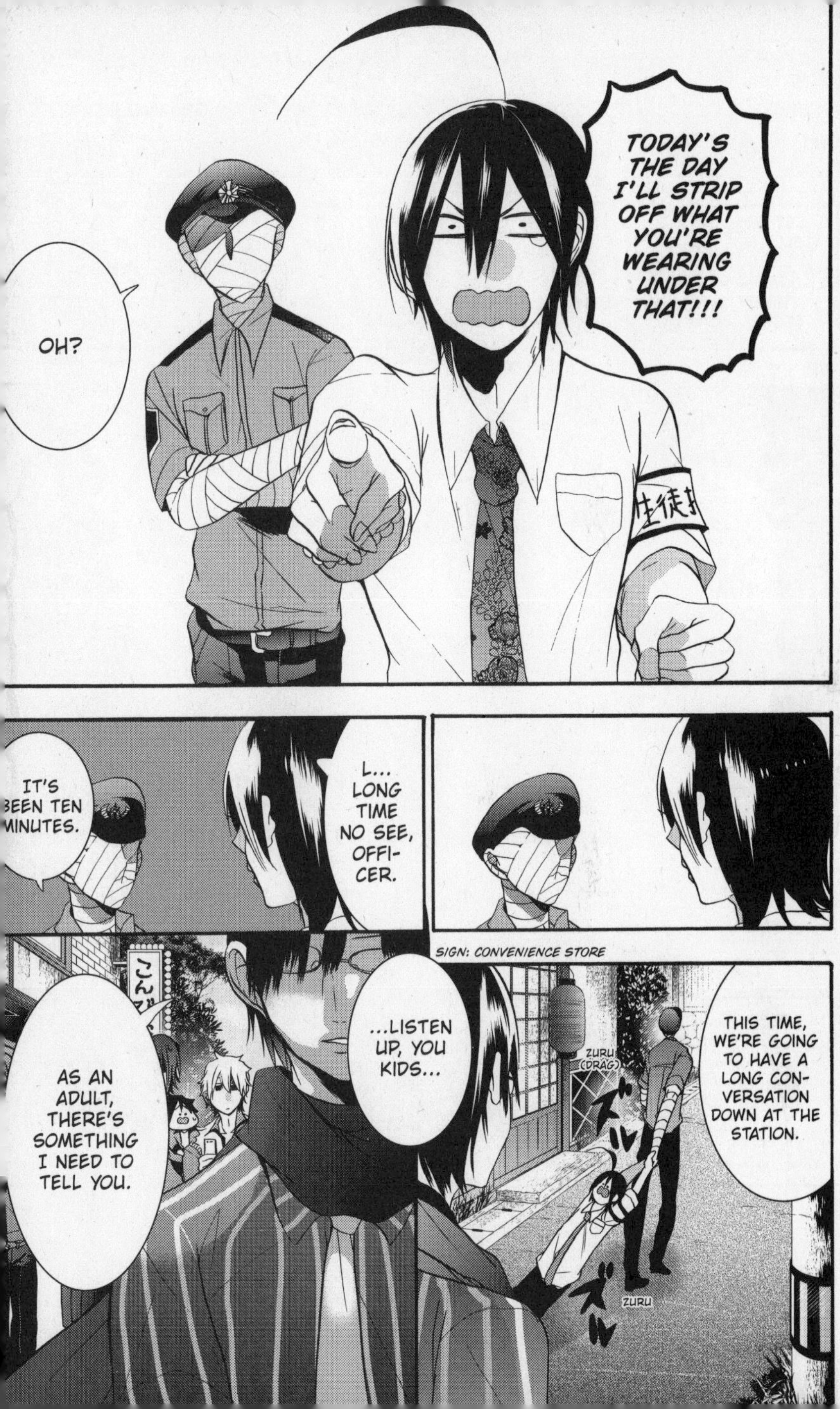
TODAY'S THE DAY I'LL STRIP OFF WHAT YOU'RE WEARING UNDER THAT!!!
OH?
L... LONG TIME NO SEE, OFFI-CER.
IT'S BEEN TEN MINUTES.
THIS TIME, WE'RE GOING TO HAVE A LONG CON-VERSATION DOWN AT THE STATION.
ZURU (DRAG)
ZURU
SIGN: CONVENIENCE STORE
...LISTEN UP, YOU KIDS...
AS AN ADULT, THERE'S SOMETHING I NEED TO TELL YOU.

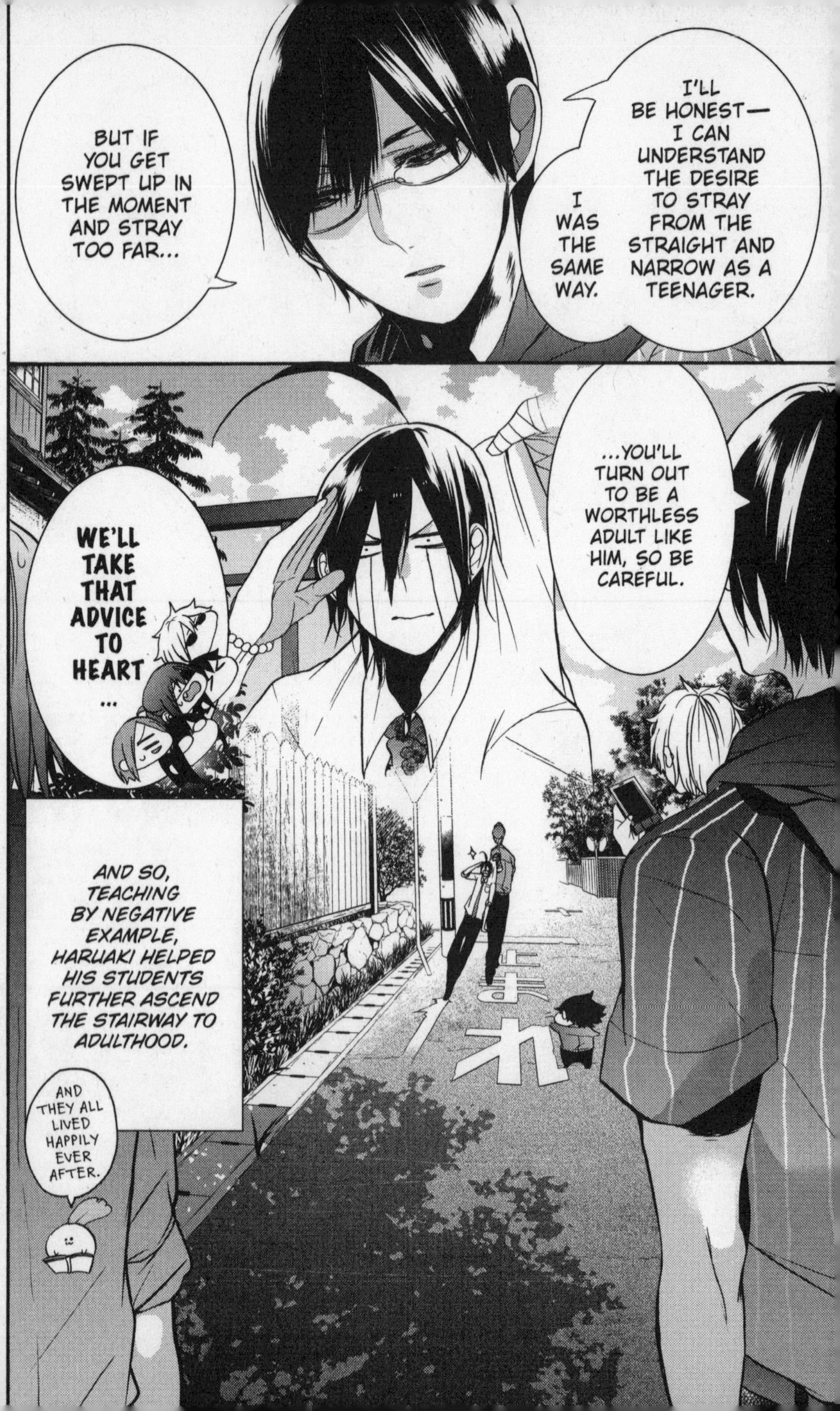
I'LL BE HONEST— I CAN UNDERSTAND THE DESIRE TO STRAY FROM THE STRAIGHT AND NARROW AS A TEENAGER.
I WAS THE SAME WAY.
BUT IF YOU GET SWEPT UP IN THE MOMENT AND STRAY TOO FAR...
...YOU'LL TURN OUT TO BE A WORTHLESS ADULT LIKE HIM, SO BE CAREFUL.
WE'LL TAKE THAT ADVICE TO HEART...
AND SO, TEACHING BY NEGATIVE EXAMPLE, HARUAKI HELPED HIS STUDENTS FURTHER ASCEND THE STAIRWAY TO ADULTHOOD.
AND THEY ALL LIVED HAPPILY EVER AFTER.

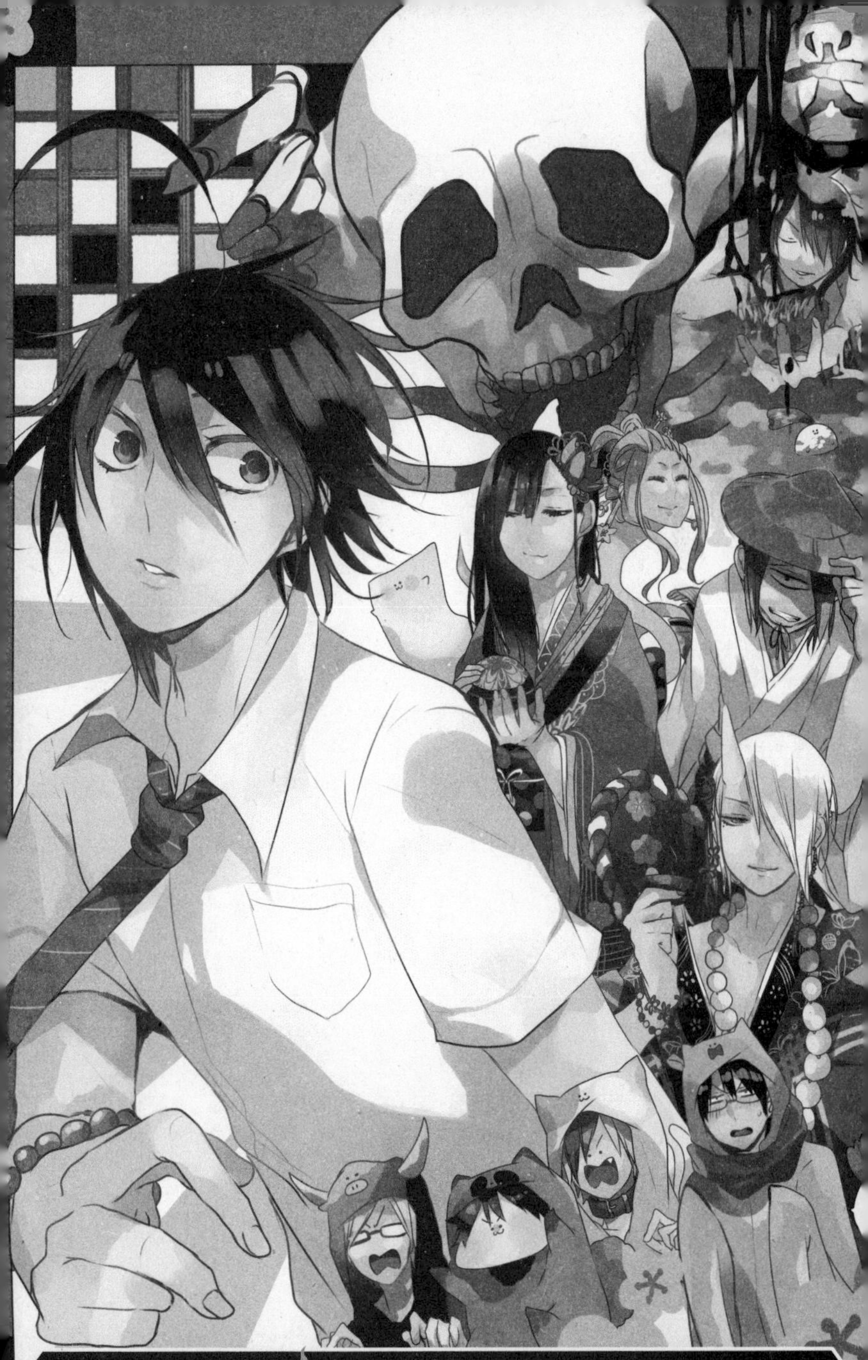

Nineteenth Period — Teachers Vs. Students!? A Midnight Melee!

A Terrified Teacher
at Ghoul School!

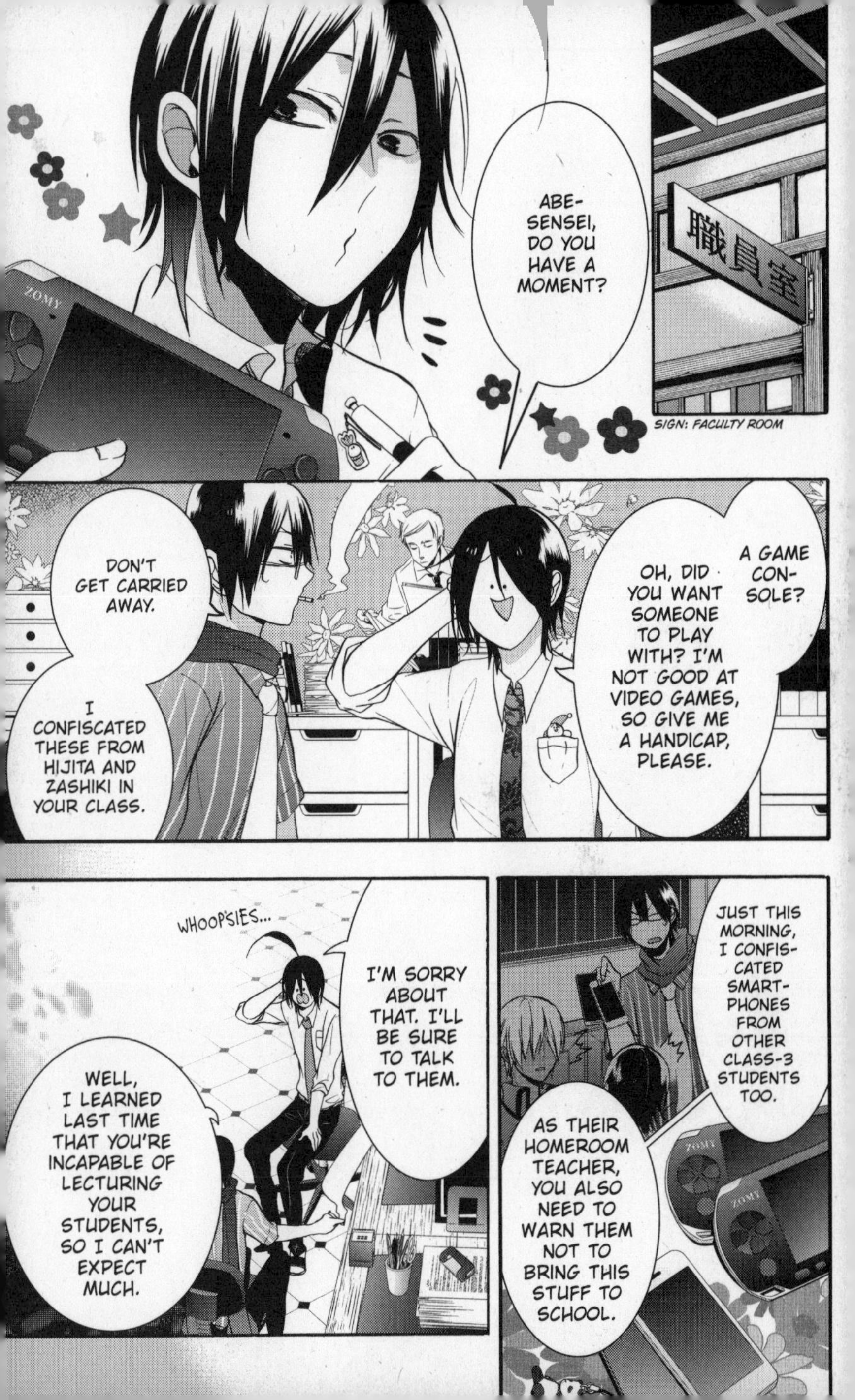
職員室
SIGN: FACULTY ROOM
ZOMY
ABE-SENSEI, DO YOU HAVE A MOMENT?
A GAME CONSOLE?
OH, DID YOU WANT SOMEONE TO PLAY WITH? I'M NOT GOOD AT VIDEO GAMES, SO GIVE ME A HANDICAP, PLEASE.
DON'T GET CARRIED AWAY.
I CONFISCATED THESE FROM HIJITA AND ZASHIKI IN YOUR CLASS.
JUST THIS MORNING, I CONFISCATED SMARTPHONES FROM OTHER CLASS-3 STUDENTS TOO.
AS THEIR HOMEROOM TEACHER, YOU ALSO NEED TO WARN THEM NOT TO BRING THIS STUFF TO SCHOOL.
I'M SORRY ABOUT THAT. I'LL BE SURE TO TALK TO THEM.
WHOOPSIES...
WELL, I LEARNED LAST TIME THAT YOU'RE INCAPABLE OF LECTURING YOUR STUDENTS, SO I CAN'T EXPECT MUCH.

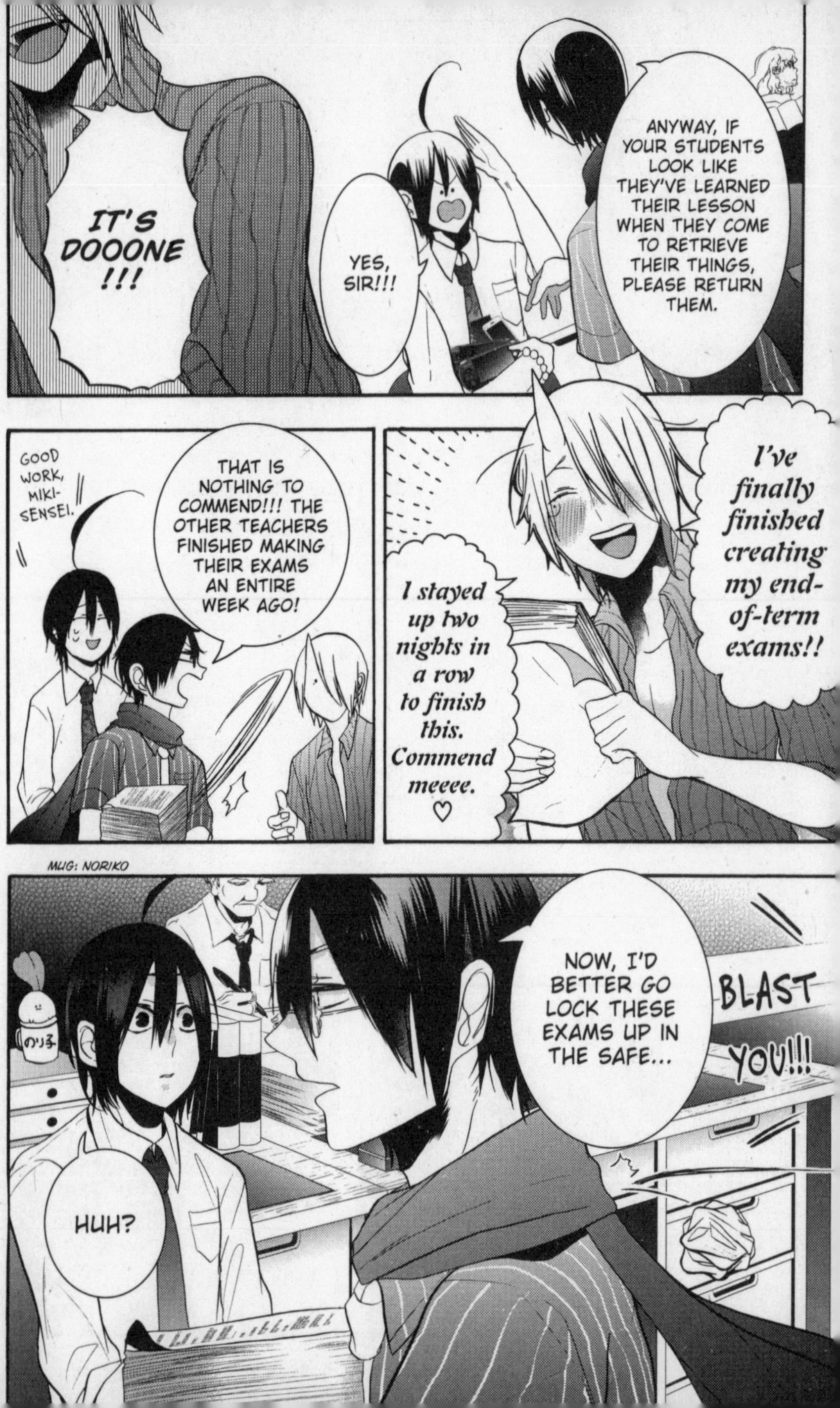
ANYWAY, IF YOUR STUDENTS LOOK LIKE THEY'VE LEARNED THEIR LESSON WHEN THEY COME TO RETRIEVE THEIR THINGS, PLEASE RETURN THEM.
YES, SIR!!!
IT'S DOOONE!!!
I've finally finished creating my end-of-term exams!!
I stayed up two nights in a row to finish this. Commend meeee. ♡
THAT IS NOTHING TO COMMEND!!! THE OTHER TEACHERS FINISHED MAKING THEIR EXAMS AN ENTIRE WEEK AGO!
GOOD WORK, MIKI-SENSEI.
MUG: NORIKO
NOW, I'D BETTER GO LOCK THESE EXAMS UP IN THE SAFE...
BLAST YOU!!!
のり子
HUH?

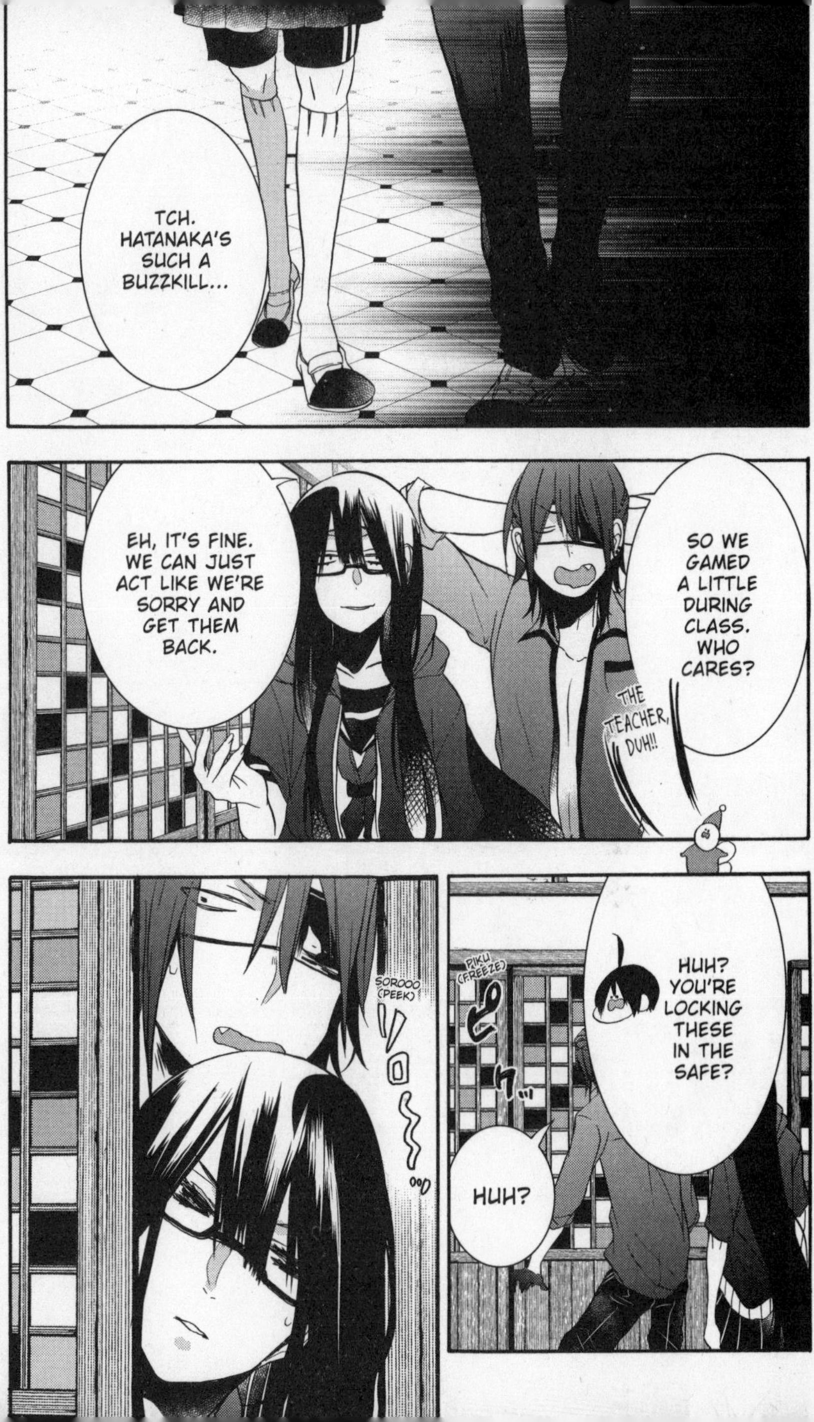
TCH. HATANAKA'S SUCH A BUZZKILL...
SO WE GAMED A LITTLE DURING CLASS. WHO CARES?
THE TEACHER, DUH!!
EH, IT'S FINE. WE CAN JUST ACT LIKE WE'RE SORRY AND GET THEM BACK.
HUH? YOU'RE LOCKING THESE IN THE SAFE?
PIKU (FREEZE)
HUH?
SOROOO (PEEK)

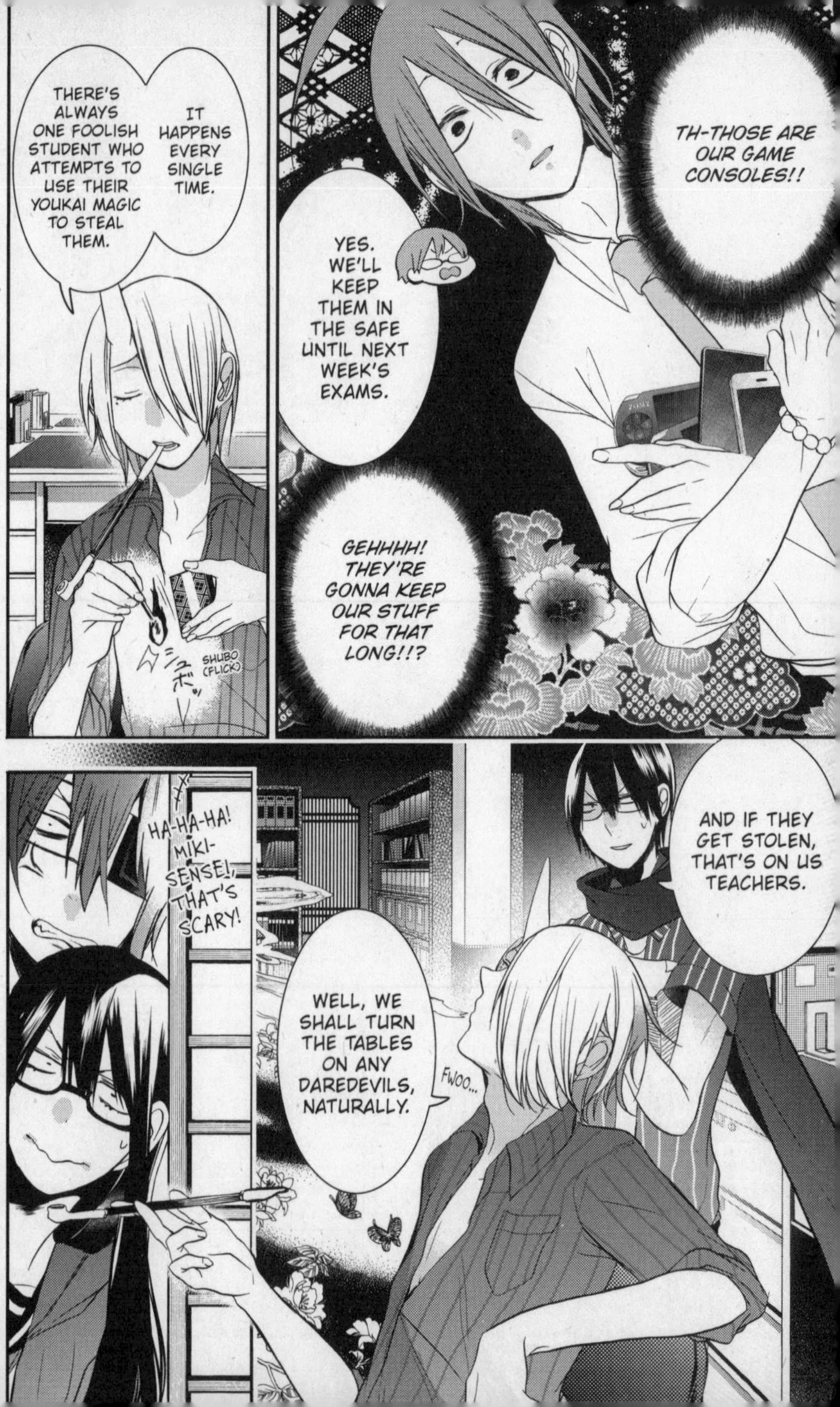
TH-THOSE ARE OUR GAME CONSOLES!!
YES. WE'LL KEEP THEM IN THE SAFE UNTIL NEXT WEEK'S EXAMS.
GEHHHH! THEY'RE GONNA KEEP OUR STUFF FOR THAT LONG!!?
IT HAPPENS EVERY SINGLE TIME.
THERE'S ALWAYS ONE FOOLISH STUDENT WHO ATTEMPTS TO USE THEIR YOUKAI MAGIC TO STEAL THEM.
SHUBO (FLICK)
AND IF THEY GET STOLEN, THAT'S ON US TEACHERS.
WELL, WE SHALL TURN THE TABLES ON ANY DAREDEVILS, NATURALLY.
FWOO...
HA-HA-HA! MIKI-SENSEI, THAT'S SCARY!

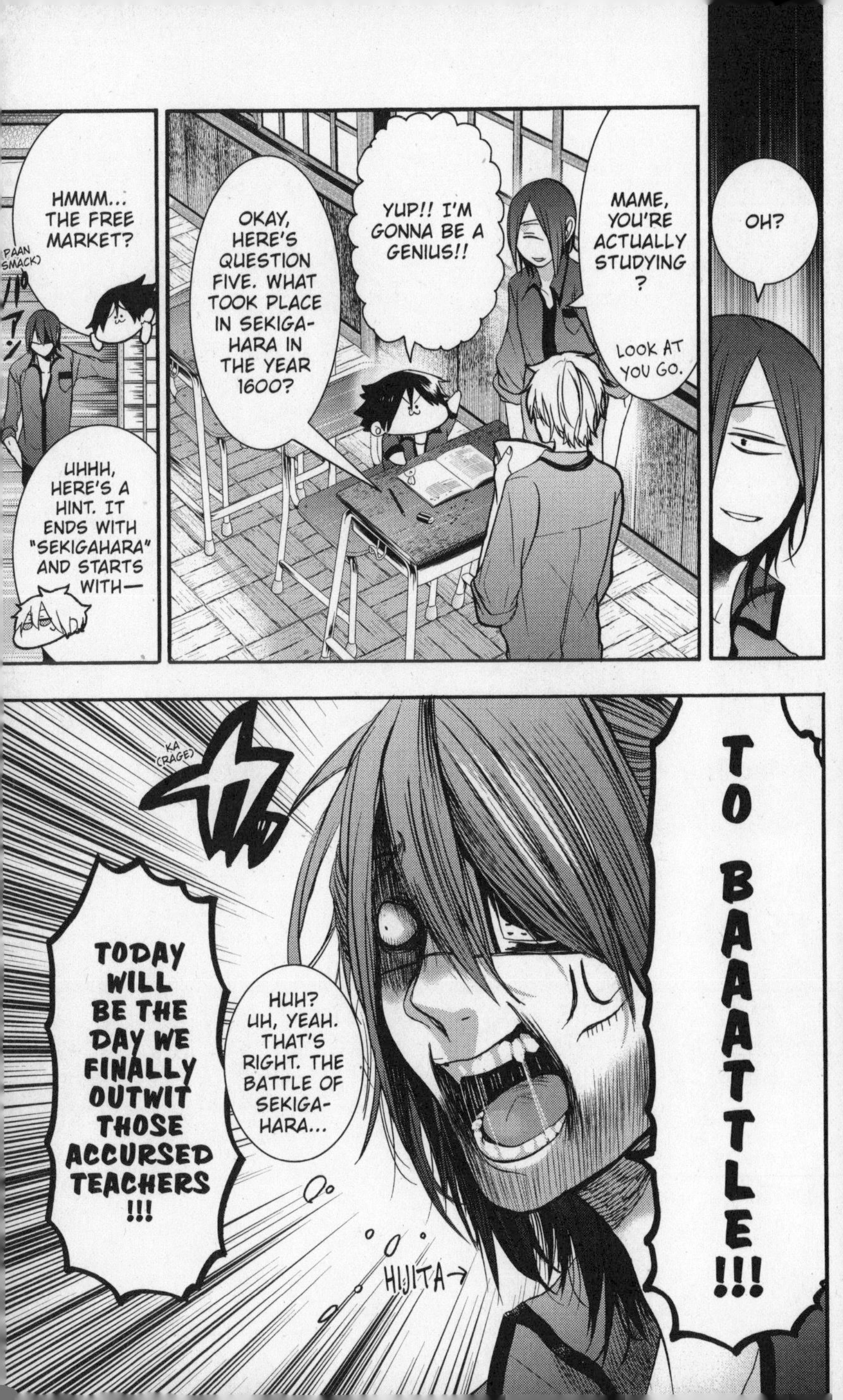
OH?
MAME, YOU'RE ACTUALLY STUDYING?
LOOK AT YOU GO.
YUP!! I'M GONNA BE A GENIUS!!
OKAY, HERE'S QUESTION FIVE. WHAT TOOK PLACE IN SEKIGA-HARA IN THE YEAR 1600?
HMMM... THE FREE MARKET?
(PAAN SMACK)
UHHH, HERE'S A HINT. IT ENDS WITH "SEKIGAHARA" AND STARTS WITH—
TO BAAATTLE!!!
HUH? UH, YEAH. THAT'S RIGHT. THE BATTLE OF SEKIGA-HARA...
KA (RAGE)
TODAY WILL BE THE DAY WE FINALLY OUTWIT THOSE ACCURSED TEACHERS!!!
HIJITA→

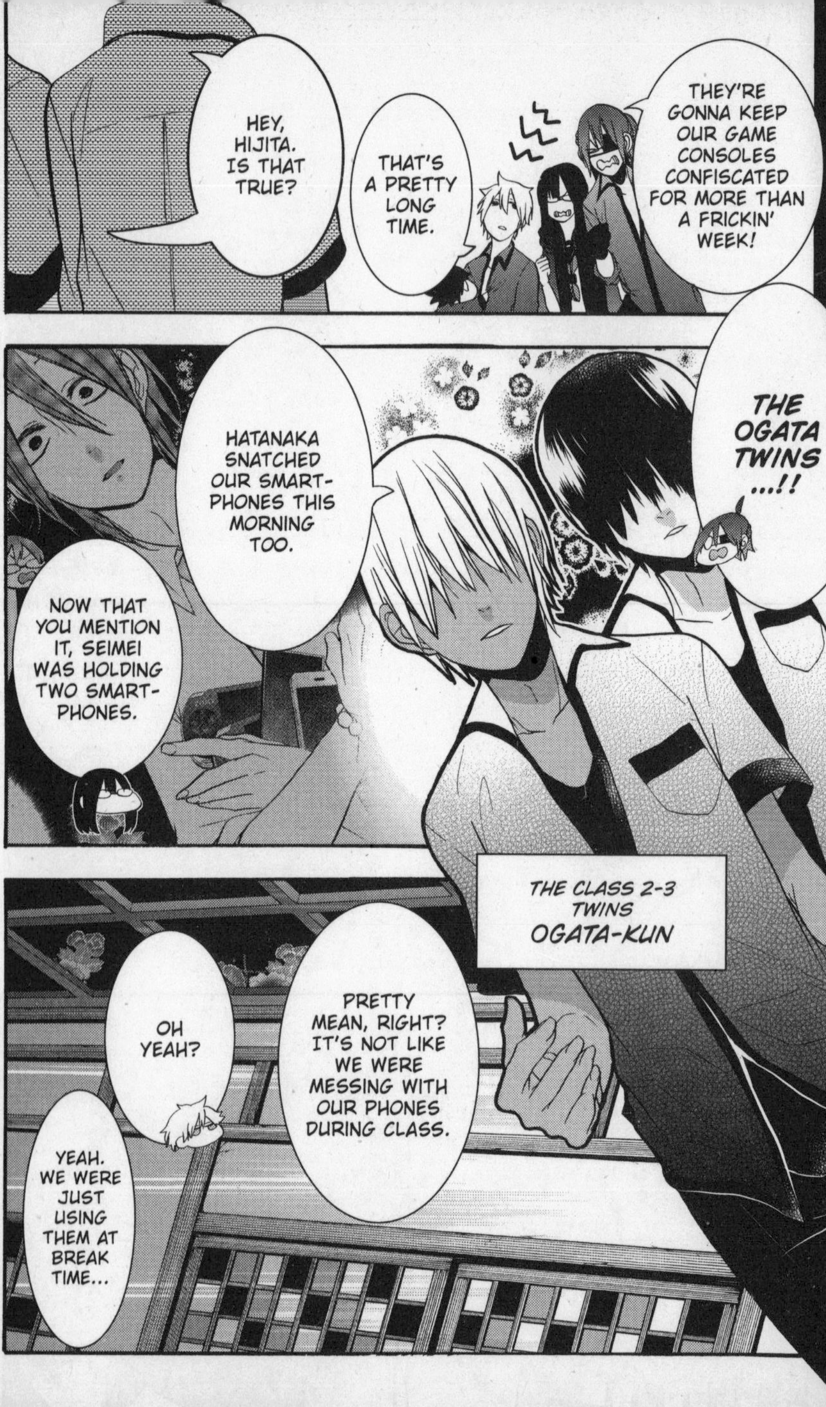
THEY'RE GONNA KEEP OUR GAME CONSOLES CONFISCATED FOR MORE THAN A FRICKIN' WEEK!
THAT'S A PRETTY LONG TIME.
HEY, HIJITA. IS THAT TRUE?
THE OGATA TWINS ...!!
HATANAKA SNATCHED OUR SMART-PHONES THIS MORNING TOO.
NOW THAT YOU MENTION IT, SEIMEI WAS HOLDING TWO SMART-PHONES.
THE CLASS 2-3 TWINS OGATA-KUN
PRETTY MEAN, RIGHT? IT'S NOT LIKE WE WERE MESSING WITH OUR PHONES DURING CLASS.
OH YEAH?
YEAH. WE WERE JUST USING THEM AT BREAK TIME...

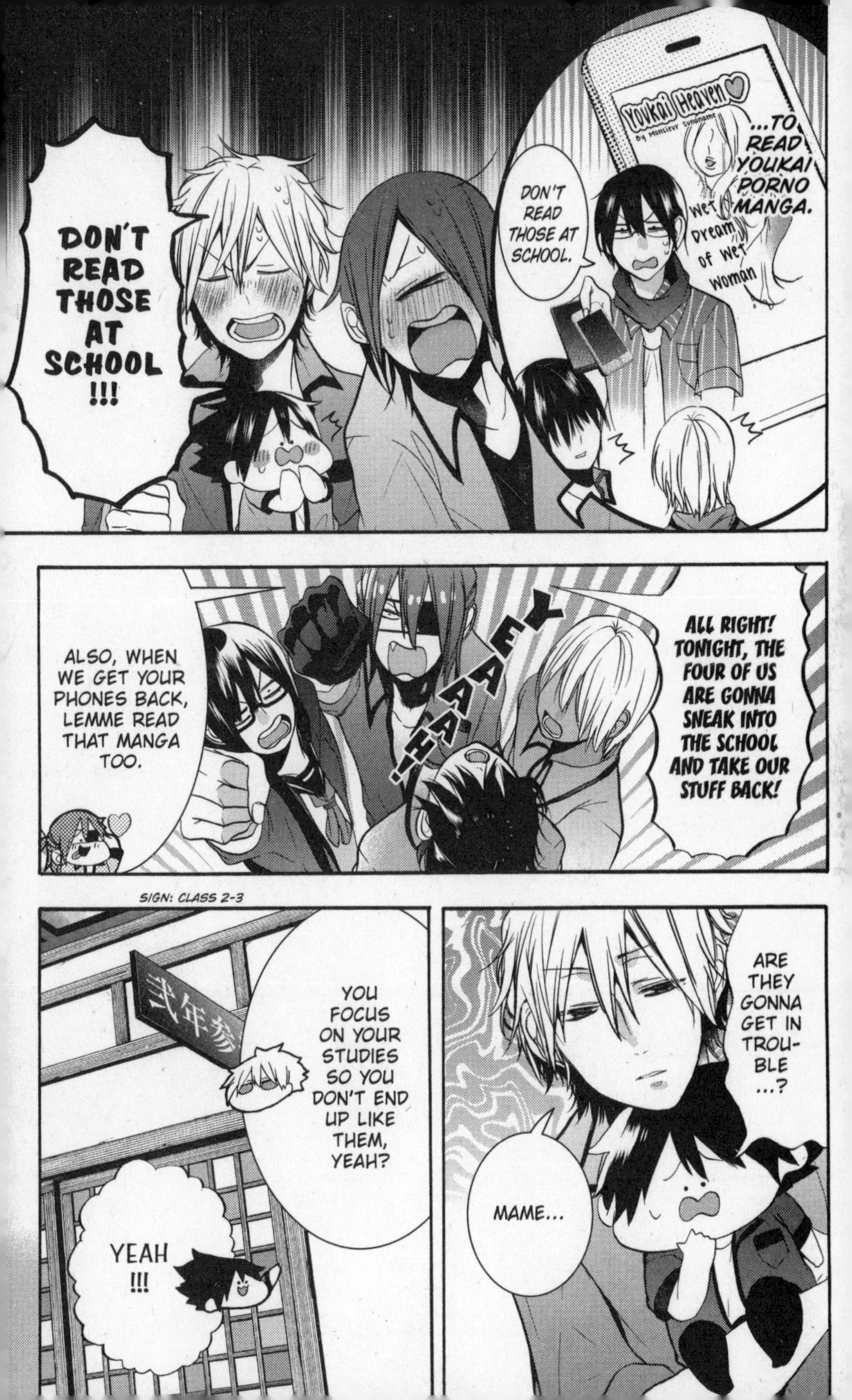
Youkai Heaven
By Monsieur Synoname
...TO READ YOUKAI PORNO MANGA.
Wet Dream of Wet Woman
DON'T READ THOSE AT SCHOOL.
DON'T READ THOSE AT SCHOOL!!!
ALL RIGHT! TONIGHT, THE FOUR OF US ARE GONNA SNEAK INTO THE SCHOOL AND TAKE OUR STUFF BACK!
YEAAAAH!
ALSO, WHEN WE GET YOUR PHONES BACK, LEMME READ THAT MANGA TOO.
SIGN: CLASS 2-3
ARE THEY GONNA GET IN TROU-BLE ...?
MAME...
弐年参
YOU FOCUS ON YOUR STUDIES SO YOU DON'T END UP LIKE THEM, YEAH?
YEAH !!!

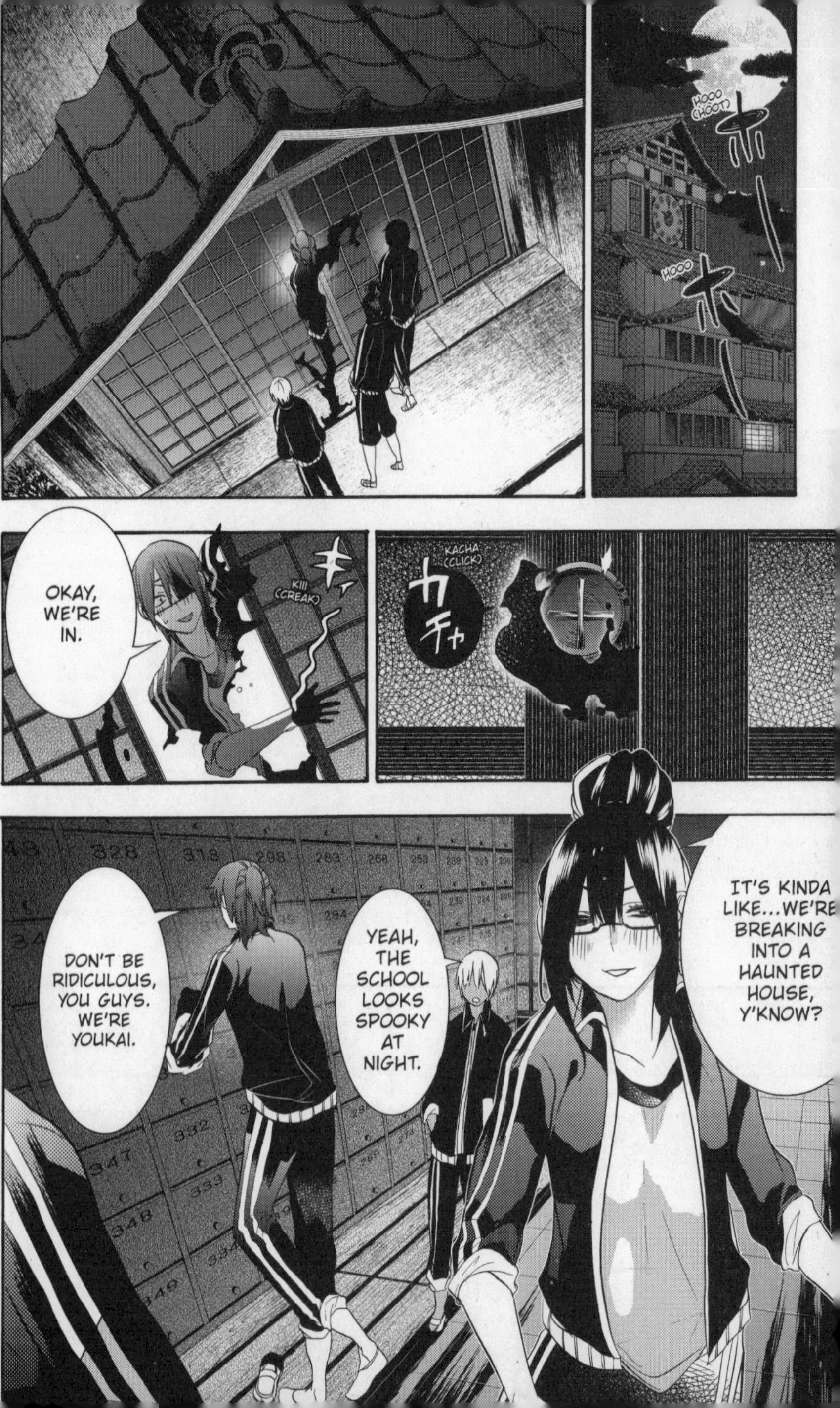

HOOO (HOOT)
HOOO
KACHA (CLICK)
KIII (CREAK)
OKAY, WE'RE IN.
IT'S KINDA LIKE...WE'RE BREAKING INTO A HAUNTED HOUSE, Y'KNOW?
YEAH, THE SCHOOL LOOKS SPOOKY AT NIGHT.
DON'T BE RIDICULOUS, YOU GUYS. WE'RE YOUKAI.

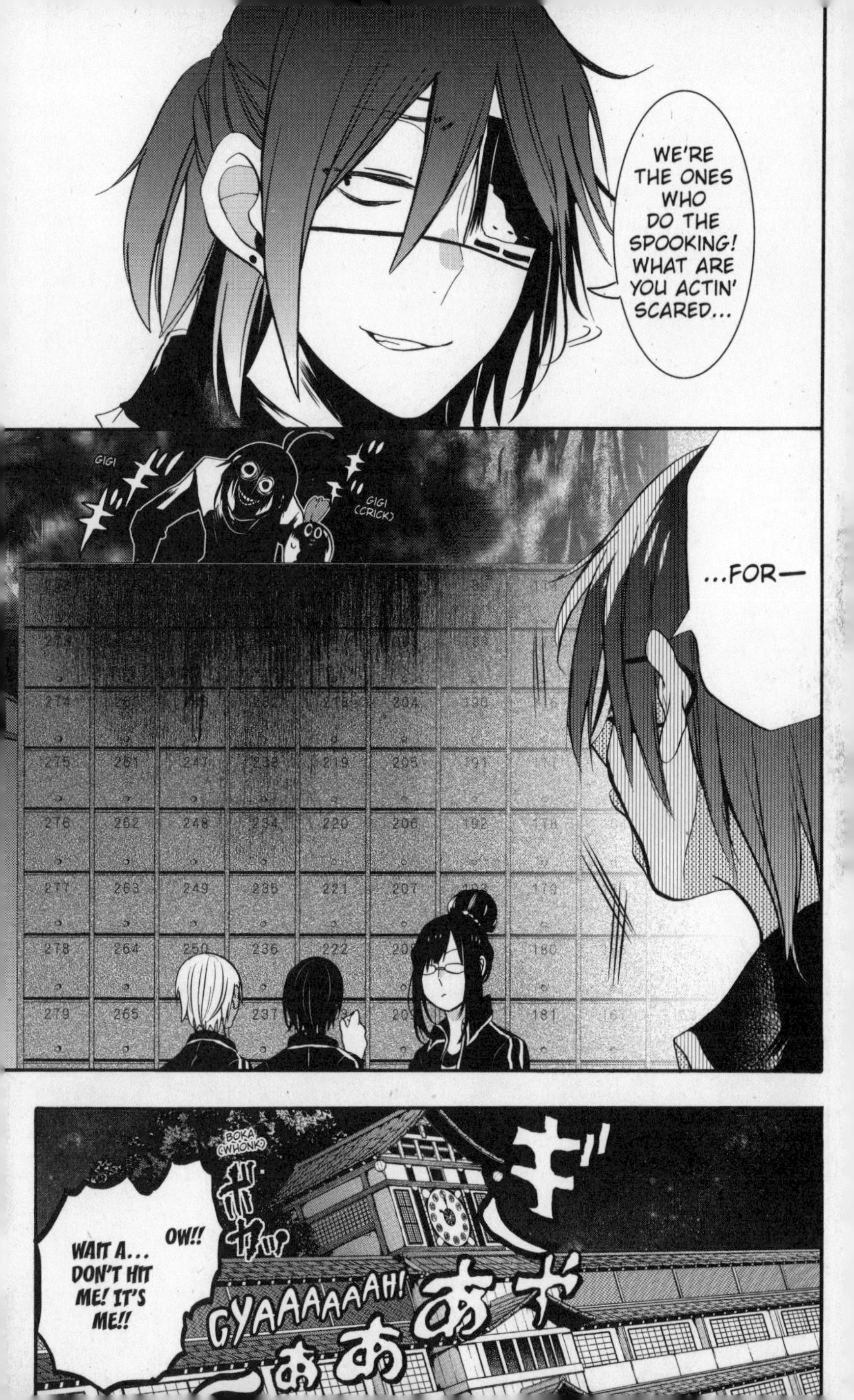
WE'RE THE ONES WHO DO THE SPOOKING! WHAT ARE YOU ACTIN' SCARED...
...FOR—
GIGI (CRICK)
GIGI
GYAAAAAAH!
BOKA (WHONK)
OW!!
WAIT A... DON'T HIT ME! IT'S ME!!

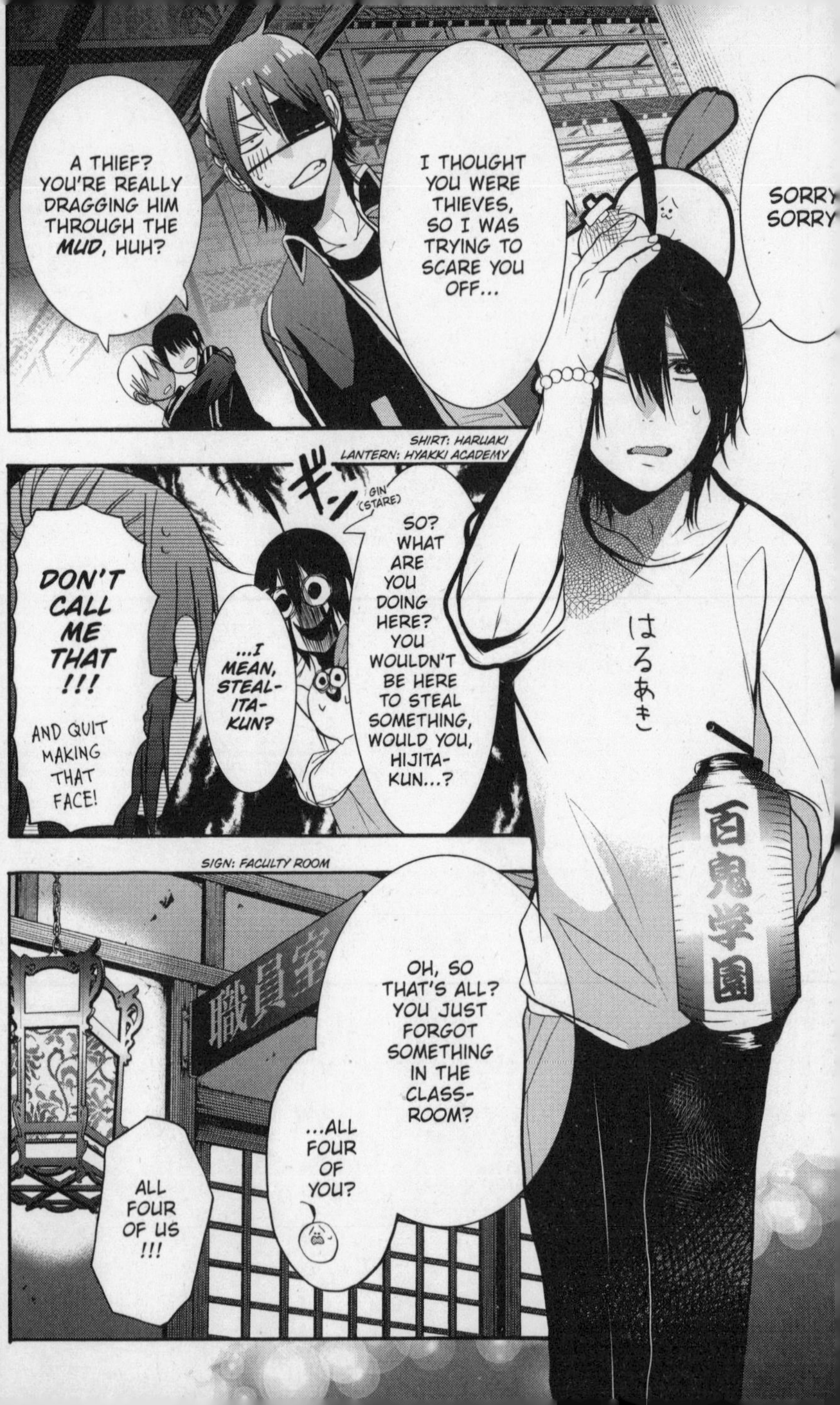
SORRY SORRY
I THOUGHT YOU WERE THIEVES, SO I WAS TRYING TO SCARE YOU OFF...
はるあき
百鬼学園
SO? WHAT ARE YOU DOING HERE? YOU WOULDN'T BE HERE TO STEAL SOMETHING, WOULD YOU, HIJITA-KUN...?
OH, SO THAT'S ALL? YOU JUST FORGOT SOMETHING IN THE CLASS-ROOM?
...ALL FOUR OF YOU?
A THIEF? YOU'RE REALLY DRAGGING HIM THROUGH THE MUD, HUH?
SHIRT: HARUAKI
LANTERN: HYAKKI ACADEMY
ギン
GIN (STARE)
...I MEAN, STEAL-ITA-KUN?
DON'T CALL ME THAT!!!
AND QUIT MAKING THAT FACE!
SIGN: FACULTY ROOM
職員室
ALL FOUR OF US!!!

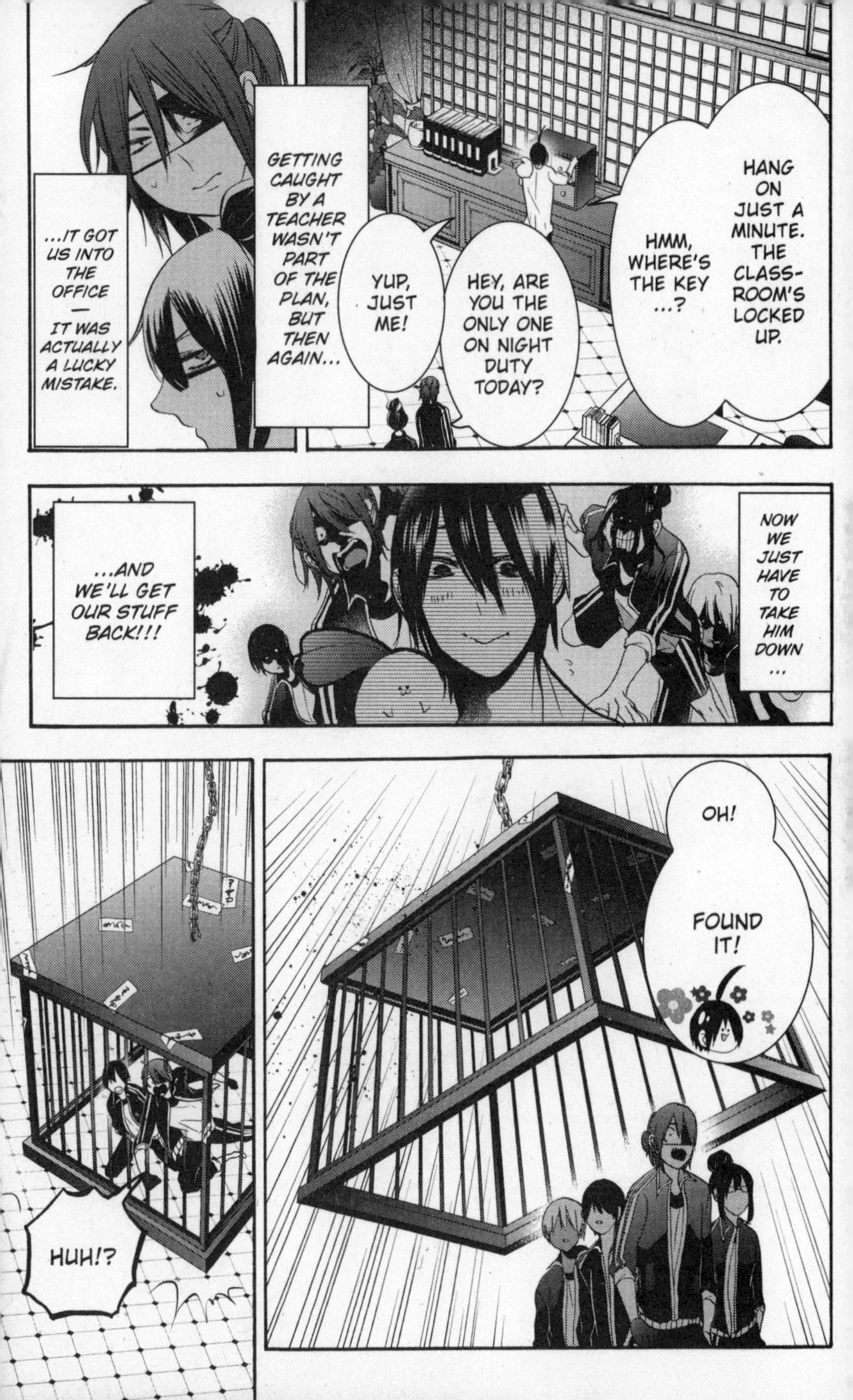
HANG ON JUST A MINUTE. THE CLASS-ROOM'S LOCKED UP.
HMM, WHERE'S THE KEY ...?
HEY, ARE YOU THE ONLY ONE ON NIGHT DUTY TODAY?
YUP, JUST ME!
GETTING CAUGHT BY A TEACHER WASN'T PART OF THE PLAN, BUT THEN AGAIN...
...IT GOT US INTO THE OFFICE — IT WAS ACTUALLY A LUCKY MISTAKE.
NOW WE JUST HAVE TO TAKE HIM DOWN ...
...AND WE'LL GET OUR STUFF BACK!!!
OH!
FOUND IT!
HUH!?

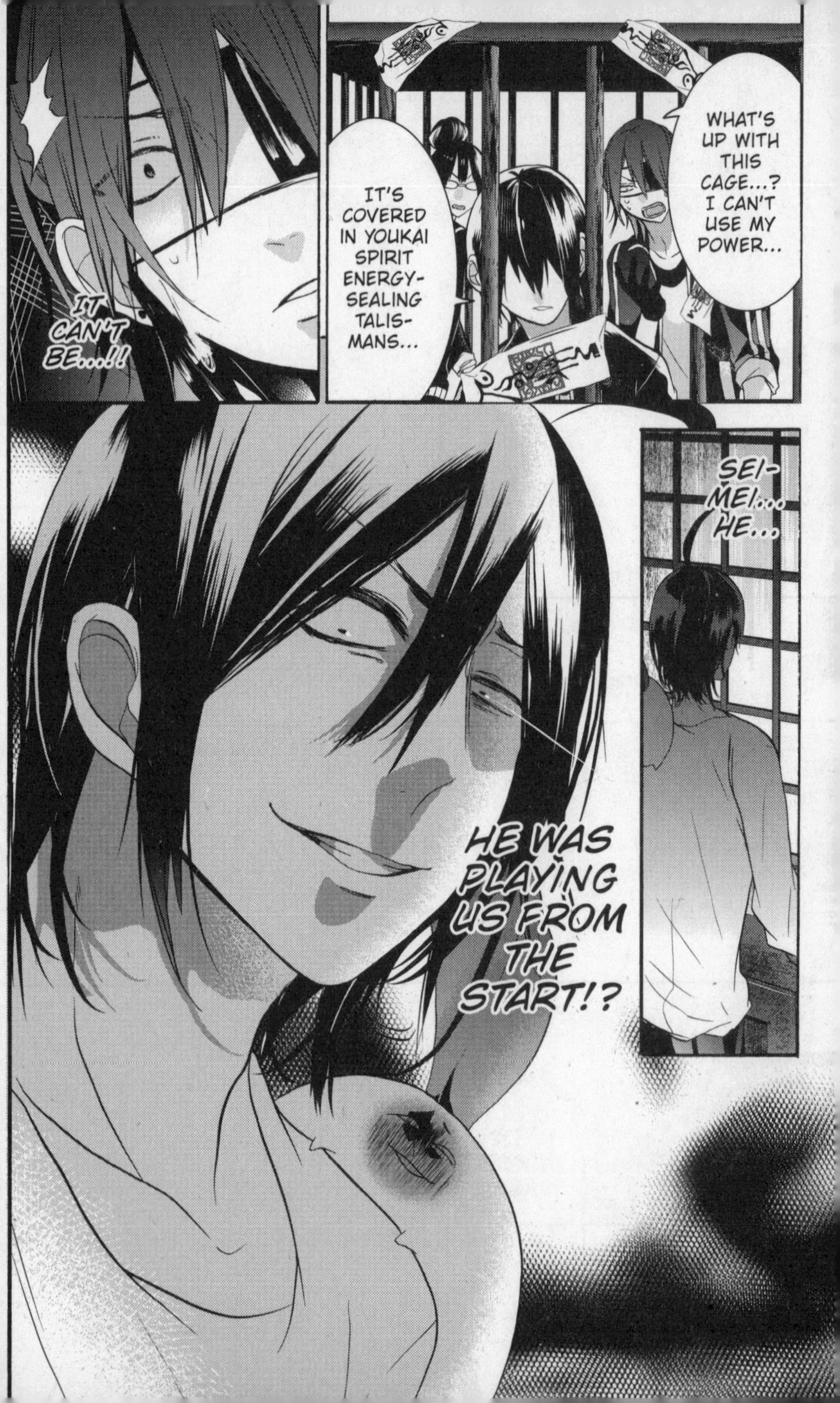
WHAT'S UP WITH THIS CAGE...? I CAN'T USE MY POWER...
IT'S COVERED IN YOUKAI SPIRIT ENERGY-SEALING TALISMANS...
IT CAN'T BE...!!
SEI-MEI... HE...
HE WAS PLAYING US FROM THE START!?

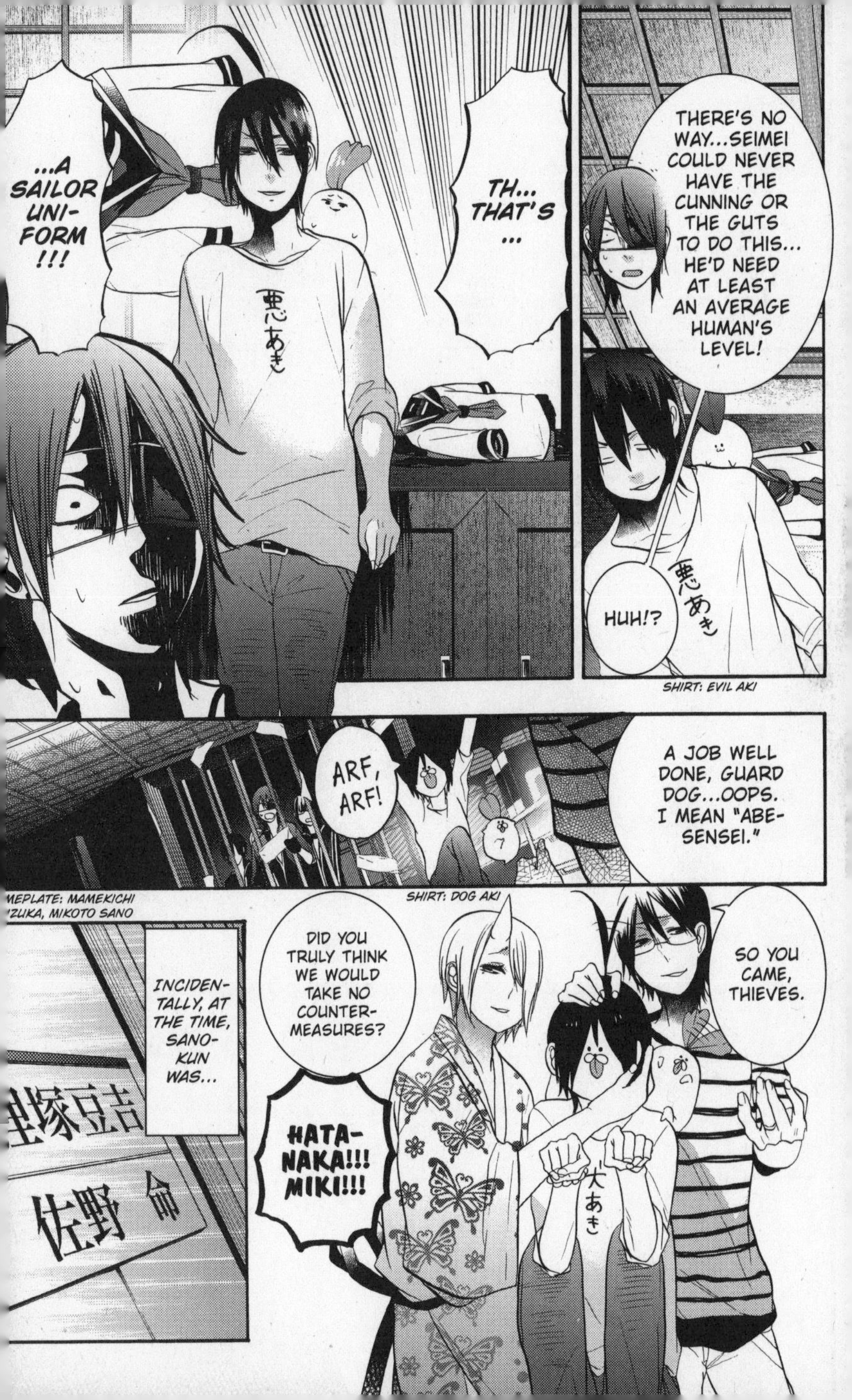
THERE'S NO WAY...SEIMEI COULD NEVER HAVE THE CUNNING OR THE GUTS TO DO THIS... HE'D NEED AT LEAST AN AVERAGE HUMAN'S LEVEL!
HUH!?
悪あき
SHIRT: EVIL AKI
TH... THAT'S ...
...A SAILOR UNI-FORM!!!
悪あき
A JOB WELL DONE, GUARD DOG...OOPS. I MEAN "ABE-SENSEI."
ARF, ARF!
SHIRT: DOG AKI
MEPLATE: MAMEKICHI
ZUKA, MIKOTO SANO
SO YOU CAME, THIEVES.
DID YOU TRULY THINK WE WOULD TAKE NO COUNTER-MEASURES?
HATA-NAKA!!! MIKI!!!
犬あき
INCIDEN-TALLY, AT THE TIME, SANO-KUN WAS...
塚豆吉
佐野 命

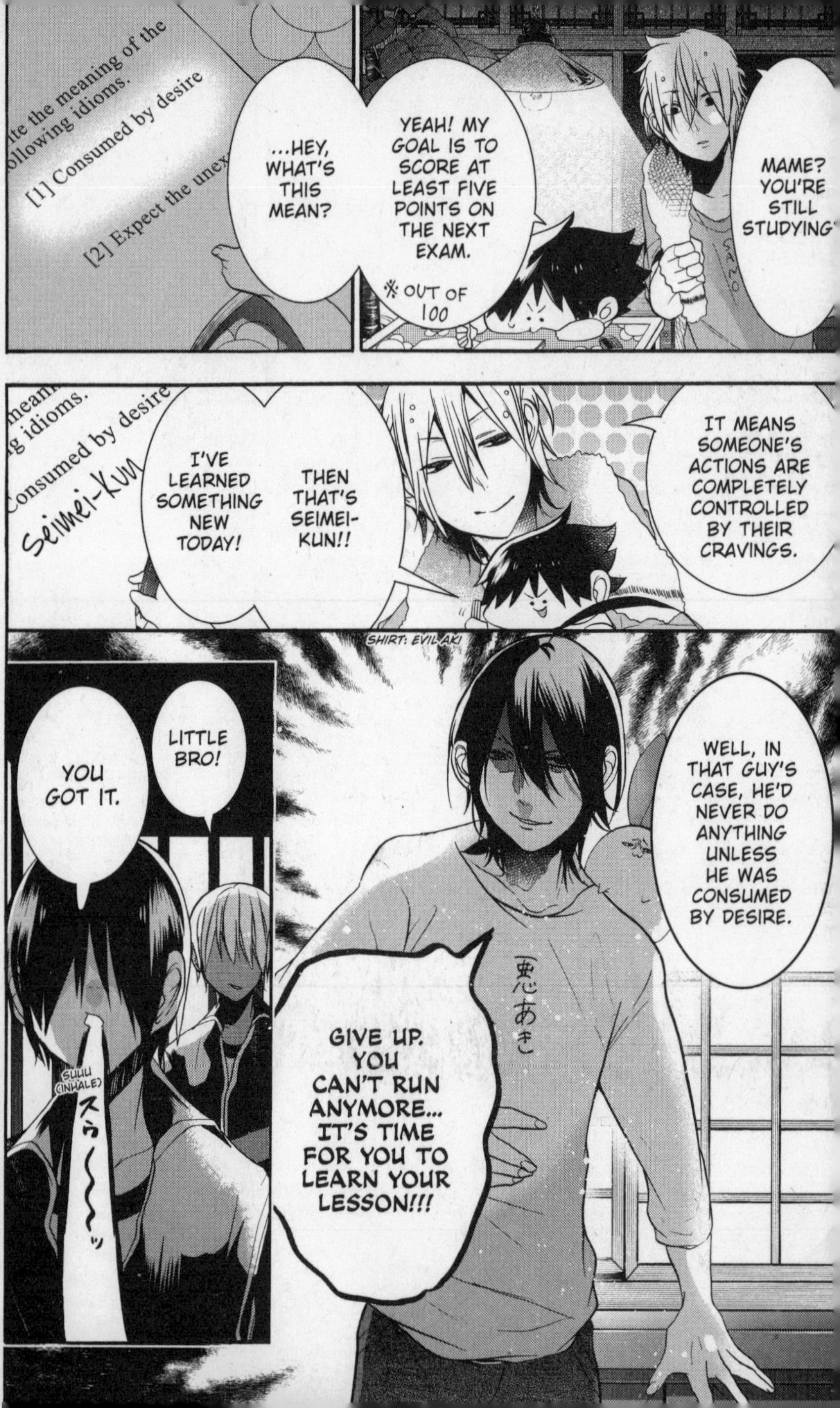
MAME? YOU'RE STILL STUDYING?
YEAH! MY GOAL IS TO SCORE AT LEAST FIVE POINTS ON THE NEXT EXAM.
※OUT OF 100
...HEY, WHAT'S THIS MEAN?
ite the meaning of the
ollowing idioms.
[1] Consumed by desire
[2] Expect the unex
IT MEANS SOMEONE'S ACTIONS ARE COMPLETELY CONTROLLED BY THEIR CRAVINGS.
THEN THAT'S SEIMEI-KUN!!
I'VE LEARNED SOMETHING NEW TODAY!
meani
g idioms.
Consumed by desire
Seimei-Kun
SHIRT: EVIL AKI
WELL, IN THAT GUY'S CASE, HE'D NEVER DO ANYTHING UNLESS HE WAS CONSUMED BY DESIRE.
悪あき
GIVE UP. YOU CAN'T RUN ANYMORE... IT'S TIME FOR YOU TO LEARN YOUR LESSON!!!
LITTLE BRO!
YOU GOT IT.
SUUU (INHALE)
スゥ〜〜ッ

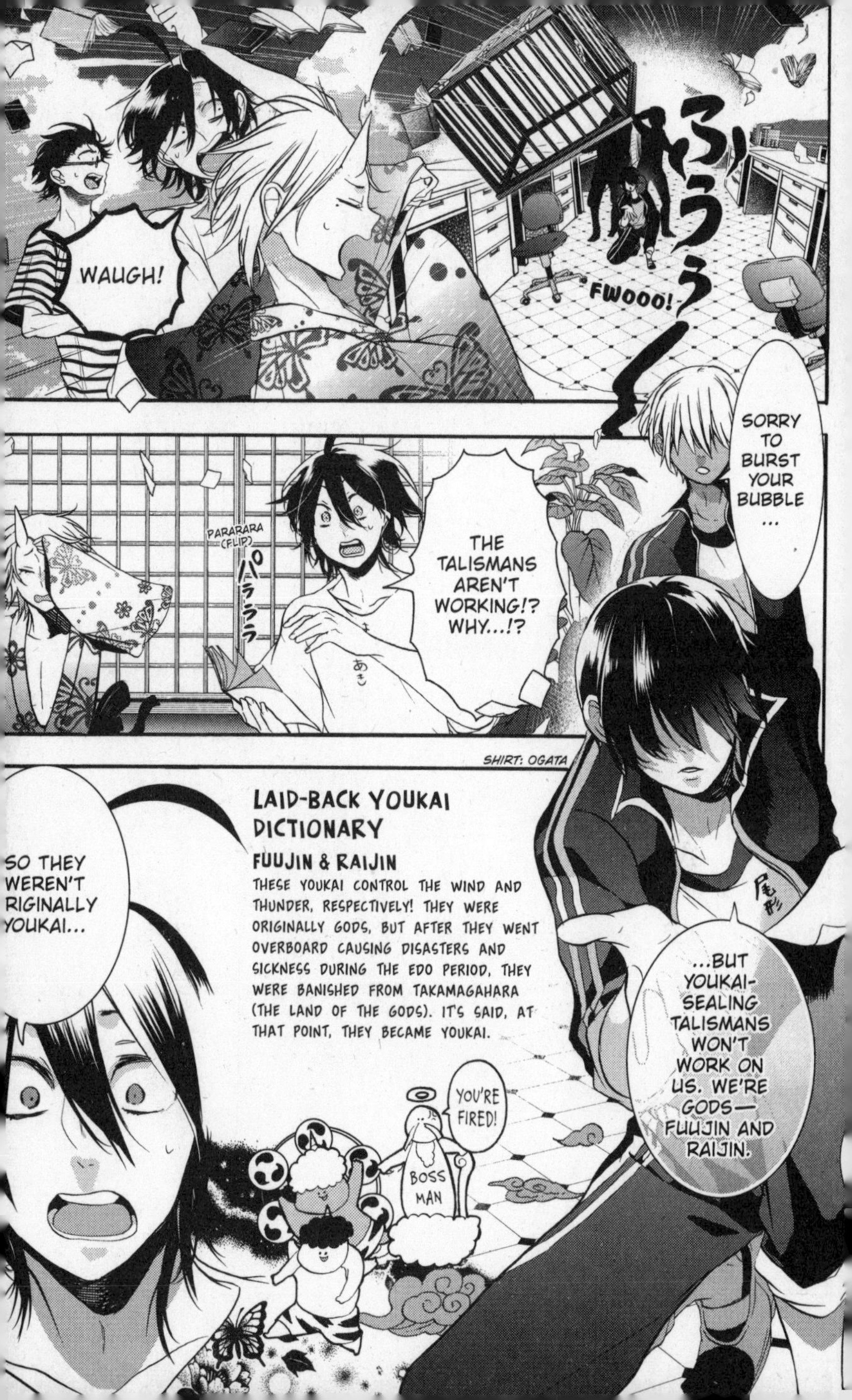
WAUGH!
FWOOO!
SORRY TO BURST YOUR BUBBLE...
...BUT YOUKAI-SEALING TALISMANS WON'T WORK ON US. WE'RE GODS—FUUJIN AND RAIJIN.
THE TALISMANS AREN'T WORKING!? WHY...!?
PARARARA (FLIP)
パラララ
SHIRT: OGATA
SO THEY WEREN'T RIGINALLY YOUKAI...
LAID-BACK YOUKAI DICTIONARY
FUUJIN & RAIJIN
THESE YOUKAI CONTROL THE WIND AND THUNDER, RESPECTIVELY! THEY WERE ORIGINALLY GODS, BUT AFTER THEY WENT OVERBOARD CAUSING DISASTERS AND SICKNESS DURING THE EDO PERIOD, THEY WERE BANISHED FROM TAKAMAGAHARA (THE LAND OF THE GODS). IT'S SAID, AT THAT POINT, THEY BECAME YOUKAI.
YOU'RE FIRED!
BOSS MAN

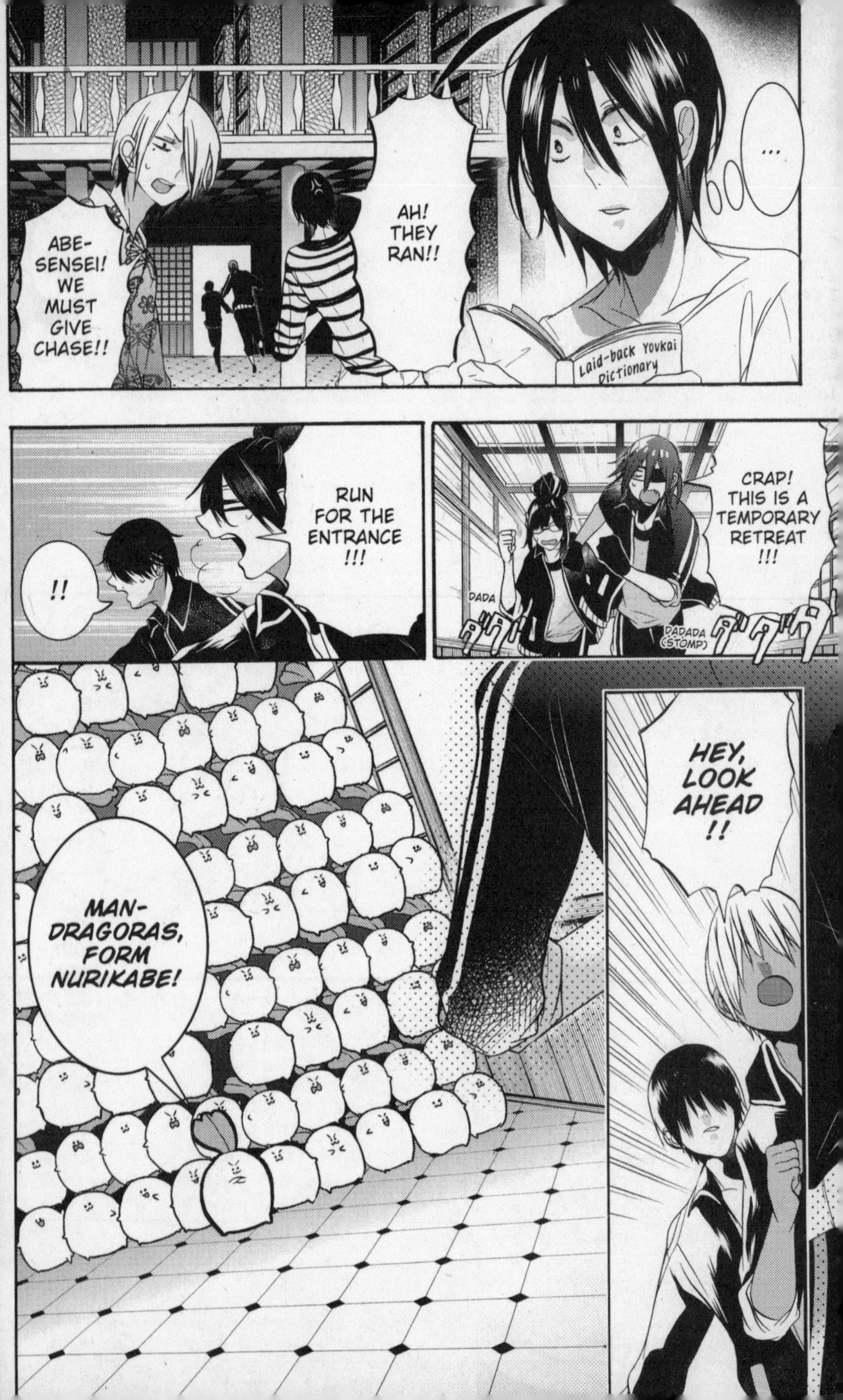
...
AH! THEY RAN!!
Laid-back Youkai Dictionary
ABE-SENSEI! WE MUST GIVE CHASE!!
CRAP! THIS IS A TEMPORARY RETREAT!!!
DADADA (STOMP)
DADA
RUN FOR THE ENTRANCE!!!
!!
HEY, LOOK AHEAD!!
MAN-DRAGORAS, FORM NURIKABE!

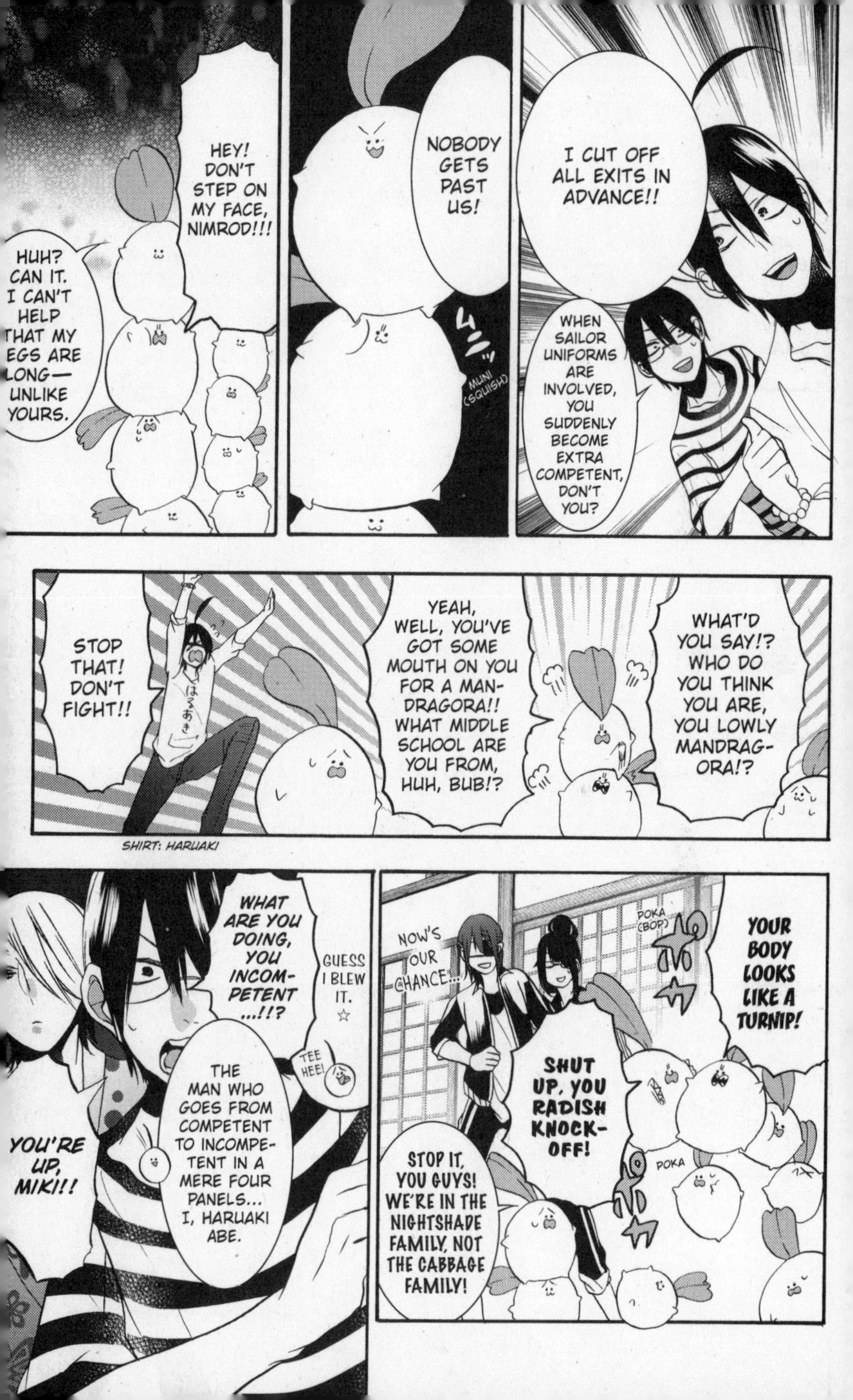
I CUT OFF ALL EXITS IN ADVANCE!!
WHEN SAILOR UNIFORMS ARE INVOLVED, YOU SUDDENLY BECOME EXTRA COMPETENT, DON'T YOU?
NOBODY GETS PAST US!
MUNI (SQUISH)
HEY! DON'T STEP ON MY FACE, NIMROD!!!
HUH? CAN IT. I CAN'T HELP THAT MY EGS ARE LONG— UNLIKE YOURS.
WHAT'D YOU SAY!? WHO DO YOU THINK YOU ARE, YOU LOWLY MANDRAG-ORA!?
YEAH, WELL, YOU'VE GOT SOME MOUTH ON YOU FOR A MAN-DRAGORA!! WHAT MIDDLE SCHOOL ARE YOU FROM, HUH, BUB!?
STOP THAT! DON'T FIGHT!!
はるあき
SHIRT: HARUAKI
YOUR BODY LOOKS LIKE A TURNIP!
POKA (BOP)
NOW'S OUR CHANCE...
SHUT UP, YOU RADISH KNOCK-OFF!
POKA
STOP IT, YOU GUYS! WE'RE IN THE NIGHTSHADE FAMILY, NOT THE CABBAGE FAMILY!
WHAT ARE YOU DOING, YOU INCOM-PETENT ...!!?
GUESS I BLEW IT. ☆
TEE HEE!
THE MAN WHO GOES FROM COMPETENT TO INCOMPE-TENT IN A MERE FOUR PANELS... I, HARUAKI ABE.
YOU'RE UP, MIKI!!

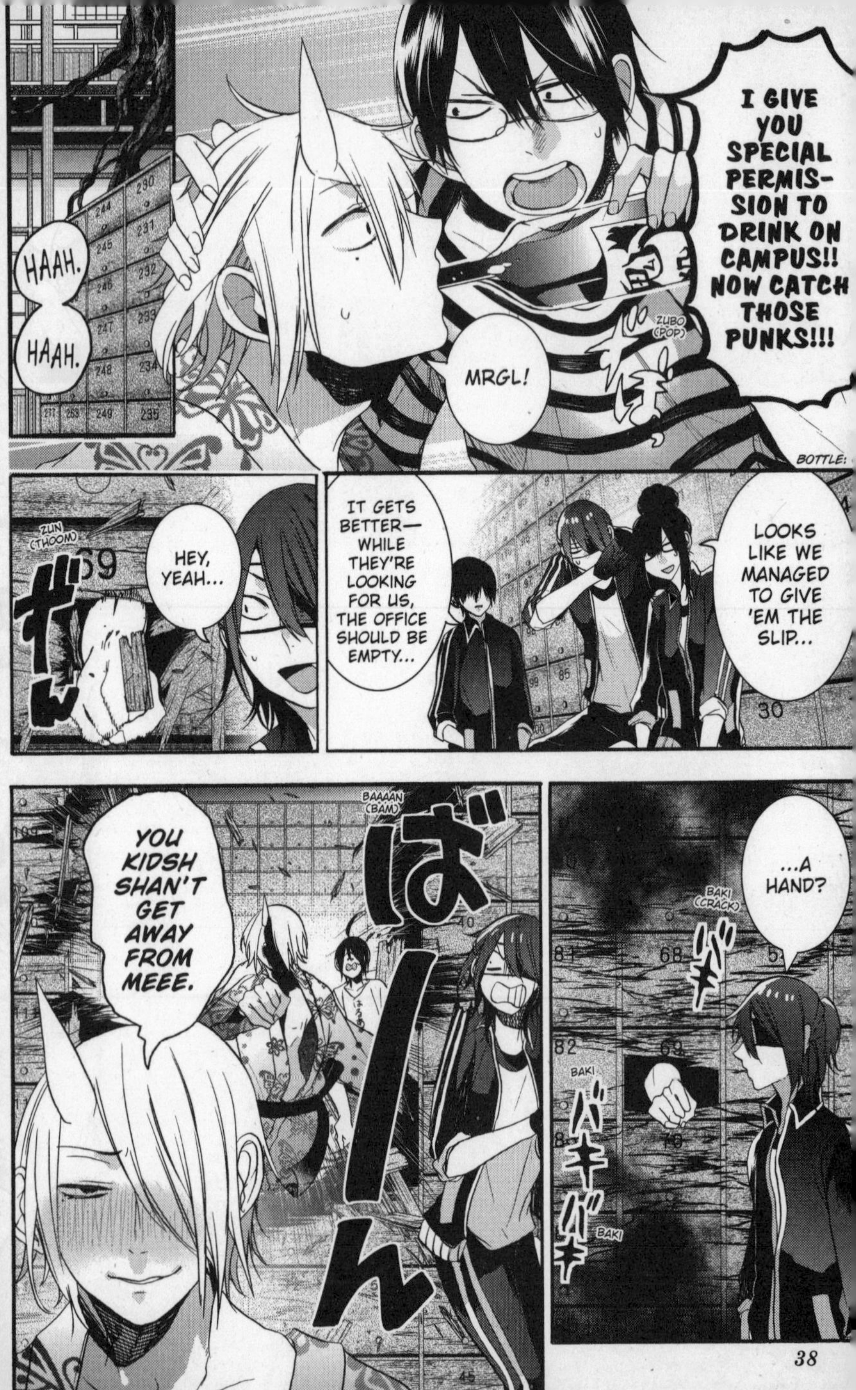
I GIVE YOU SPECIAL PERMISSION TO DRINK ON CAMPUS!! NOW CATCH THOSE PUNKS!!!
ZUBO (POP)
BOTTLE:
MRGL!
HAAH.
HAAH.
LOOKS LIKE WE MANAGED TO GIVE 'EM THE SLIP...
IT GETS BETTER— WHILE THEY'RE LOOKING FOR US, THE OFFICE SHOULD BE EMPTY...
ZUN (THOOM)
HEY, YEAH...
...A HAND?
BAKI (CRACK)
BAKI
BAKI
BAAAAN (BAM)
YOU KIDSH SHAN'T GET AWAY FROM MEEE.

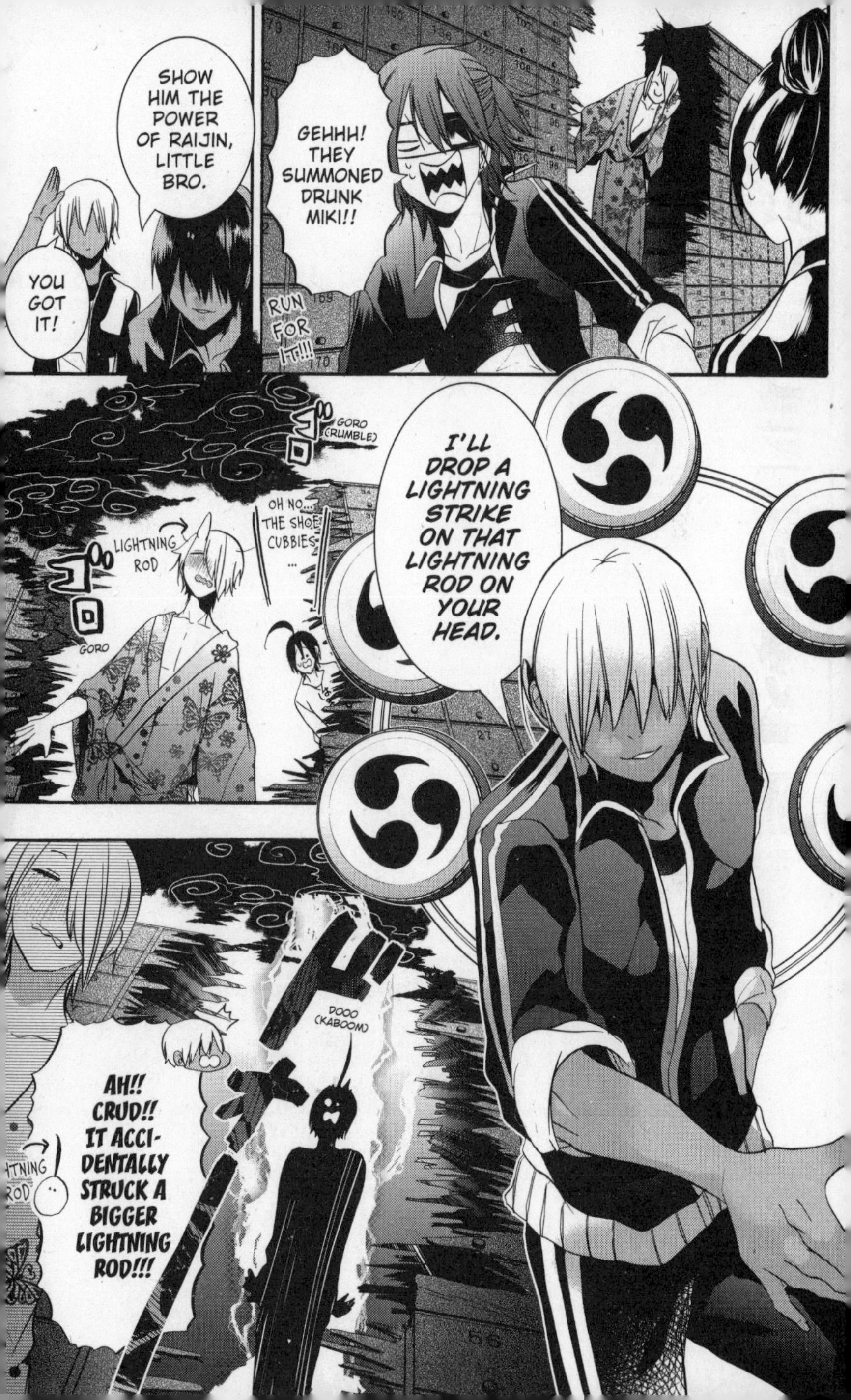
GEHHH! THEY SUMMONED DRUNK MIKI!!
RUN FOR IT!!!
SHOW HIM THE POWER OF RAIJIN, LITTLE BRO.
YOU GOT IT!
I'LL DROP A LIGHTNING STRIKE ON THAT LIGHTNING ROD ON YOUR HEAD.
GORO (RUMBLE)
OH NO... THE SHOE CUBBIES...
LIGHTNING ROD
GORO
DOOO (KABOOM)
AH!! CRUD!! IT ACCI-DENTALLY STRUCK A BIGGER LIGHTNING ROD!!!

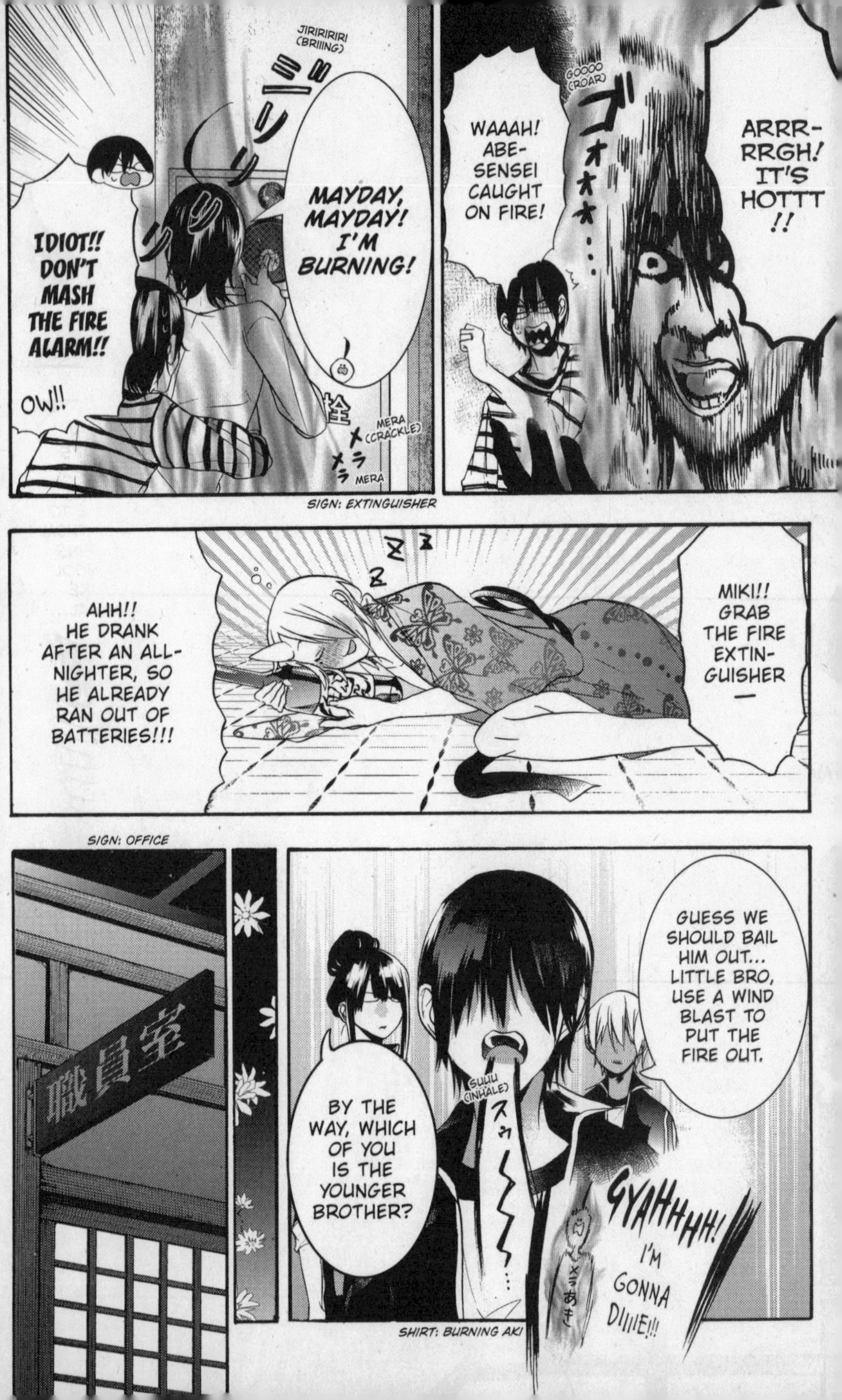
ARRR-RRGH! IT'S HOTTT!!
GOOOO (ROAR)
WAAAH! ABE-SENSEI CAUGHT ON FIRE!
JIRIRIRIRI (BRIIING)
MAYDAY, MAYDAY! I'M BURNING!
IDIOT!! DON'T MASH THE FIRE ALARM!!
OW!!
MERA (CRACKLE) MERA
SIGN: EXTINGUISHER
MIKI!! GRAB THE FIRE EXTIN-GUISHER—
AHH!! HE DRANK AFTER AN ALL-NIGHTER, SO HE ALREADY RAN OUT OF BATTERIES!!!
GUESS WE SHOULD BAIL HIM OUT... LITTLE BRO, USE A WIND BLAST TO PUT THE FIRE OUT.
BY THE WAY, WHICH OF YOU IS THE YOUNGER BROTHER?
SUUU (INHALE)
GYAHHHH! I'M GONNA DIIIE!!!
SHIRT: BURNING AKI
SIGN: OFFICE

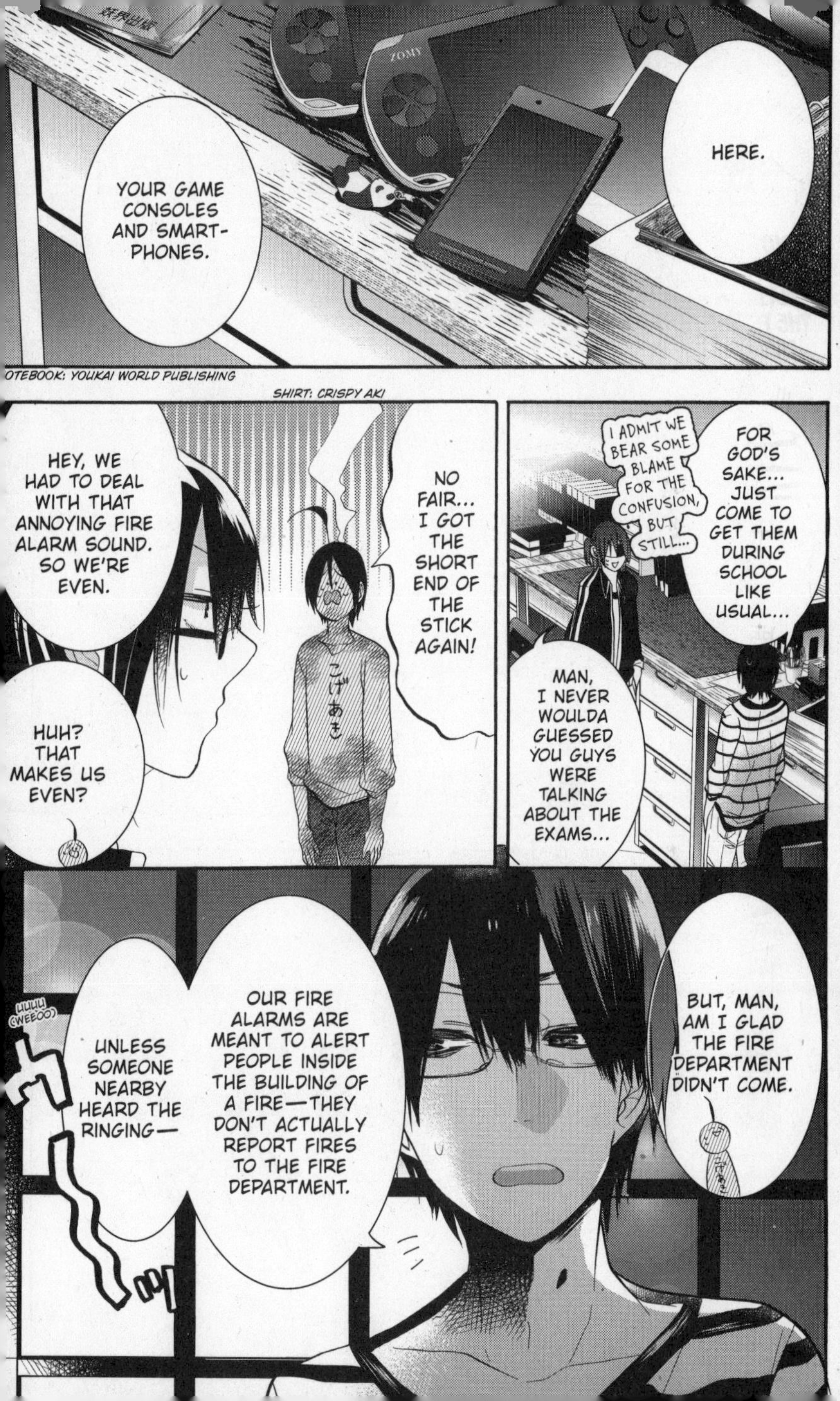
HERE.
YOUR GAME CONSOLES AND SMART-PHONES.
OTEBOOK: YOUKAI WORLD PUBLISHING
SHIRT: CRISPY AKI
FOR GOD'S SAKE... JUST COME TO GET THEM DURING SCHOOL LIKE USUAL...
I ADMIT WE BEAR SOME BLAME FOR THE CONFUSION, BUT STILL...
MAN, I NEVER WOULDA GUESSED YOU GUYS WERE TALKING ABOUT THE EXAMS...
NO FAIR... I GOT THE SHORT END OF THE STICK AGAIN!
こげあき
HEY, WE HAD TO DEAL WITH THAT ANNOYING FIRE ALARM SOUND. SO WE'RE EVEN.
HUH? THAT MAKES US EVEN?
BUT, MAN, AM I GLAD THE FIRE DEPARTMENT DIDN'T COME.
OUR FIRE ALARMS ARE MEANT TO ALERT PEOPLE INSIDE THE BUILDING OF A FIRE—THEY DON'T ACTUALLY REPORT FIRES TO THE FIRE DEPARTMENT.
UNLESS SOMEONE NEARBY HEARD THE RINGING—
UUUU (WEEOO)

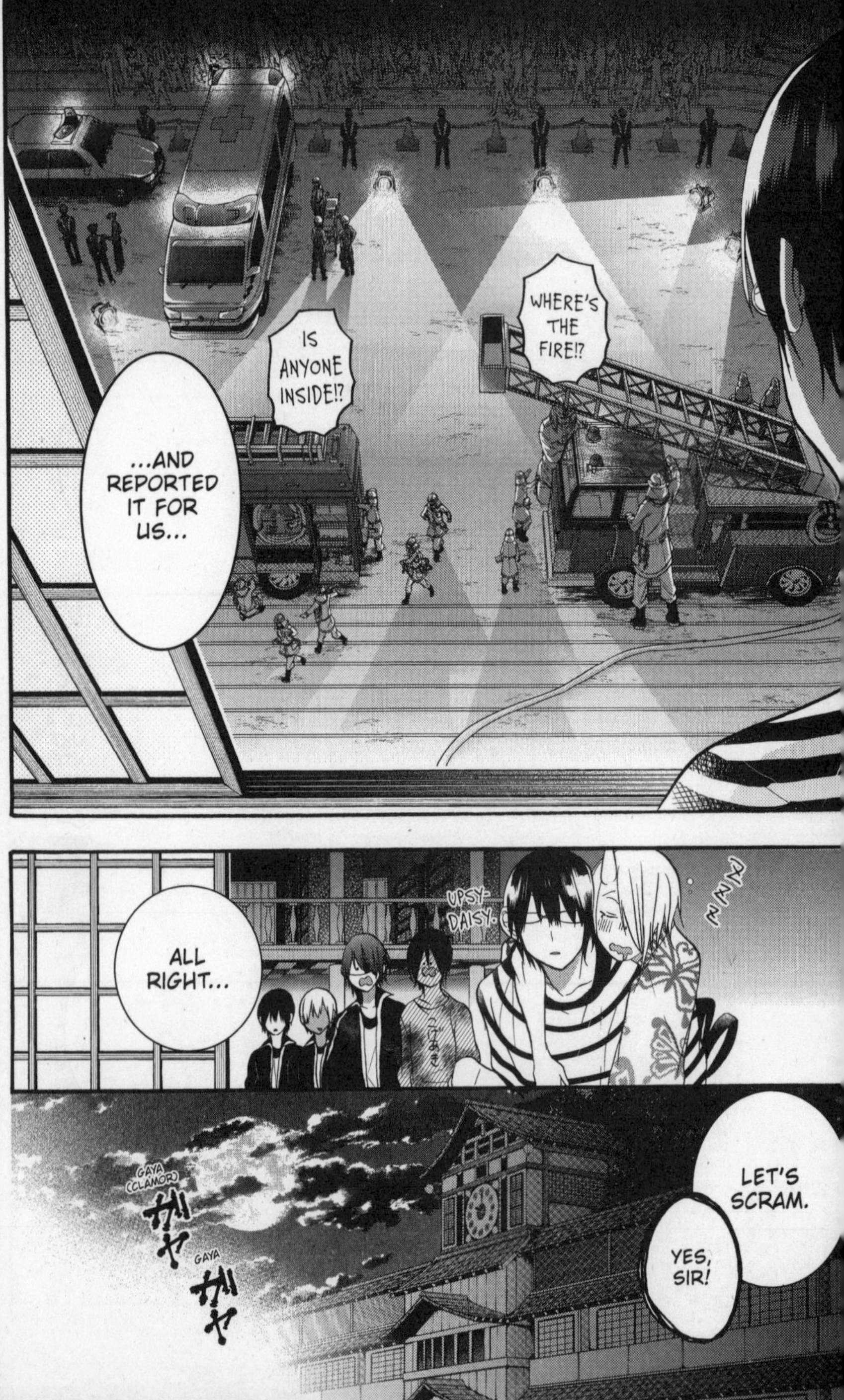
WHERE'S THE FIRE!?
IS ANYONE INSIDE!?
...AND REPORTED IT FOR US...
UPSY-DAISY.
ALL RIGHT...
LET'S SCRAM.
YES, SIR!
GAYA (CLAMOR)
GAYA

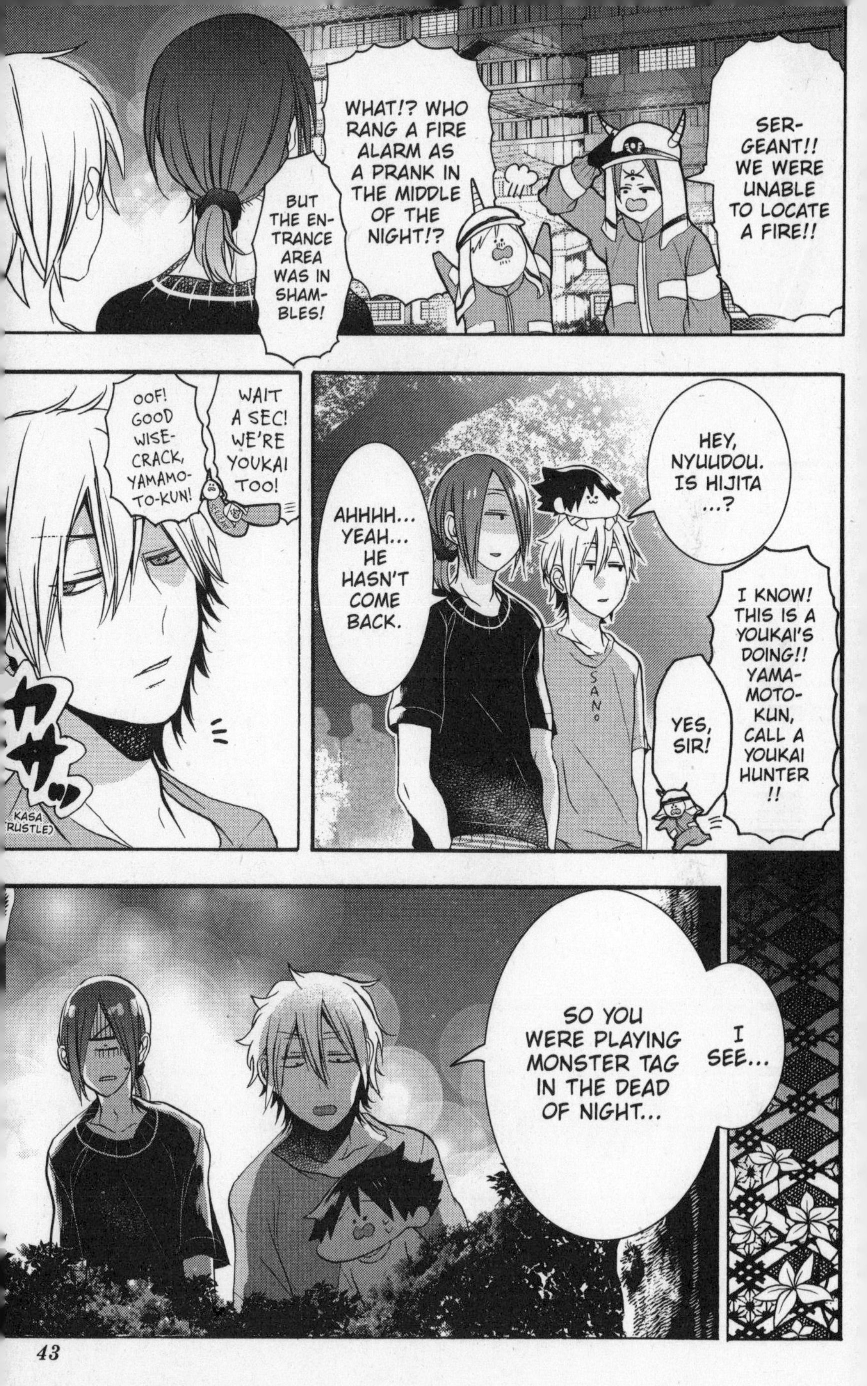
SERGEANT!! WE WERE UNABLE TO LOCATE A FIRE!!
WHAT!? WHO RANG A FIRE ALARM AS A PRANK IN THE MIDDLE OF THE NIGHT!?
BUT THE ENTRANCE AREA WAS IN SHAMBLES!
HEY, NYUUDOU. IS HIJITA ...?
AHHHH... YEAH... HE HASN'T COME BACK.
I KNOW! THIS IS A YOUKAI'S DOING!! YAMAMOTO-KUN, CALL A YOUKAI HUNTER!!
YES, SIR!
WAIT A SEC! WE'RE YOUKAI TOO!
OOF! GOOD WISECRACK, YAMAMOTO-KUN!
KASA (RUSTLE)
I SEE...
SO YOU WERE PLAYING MONSTER TAG IN THE DEAD OF NIGHT...

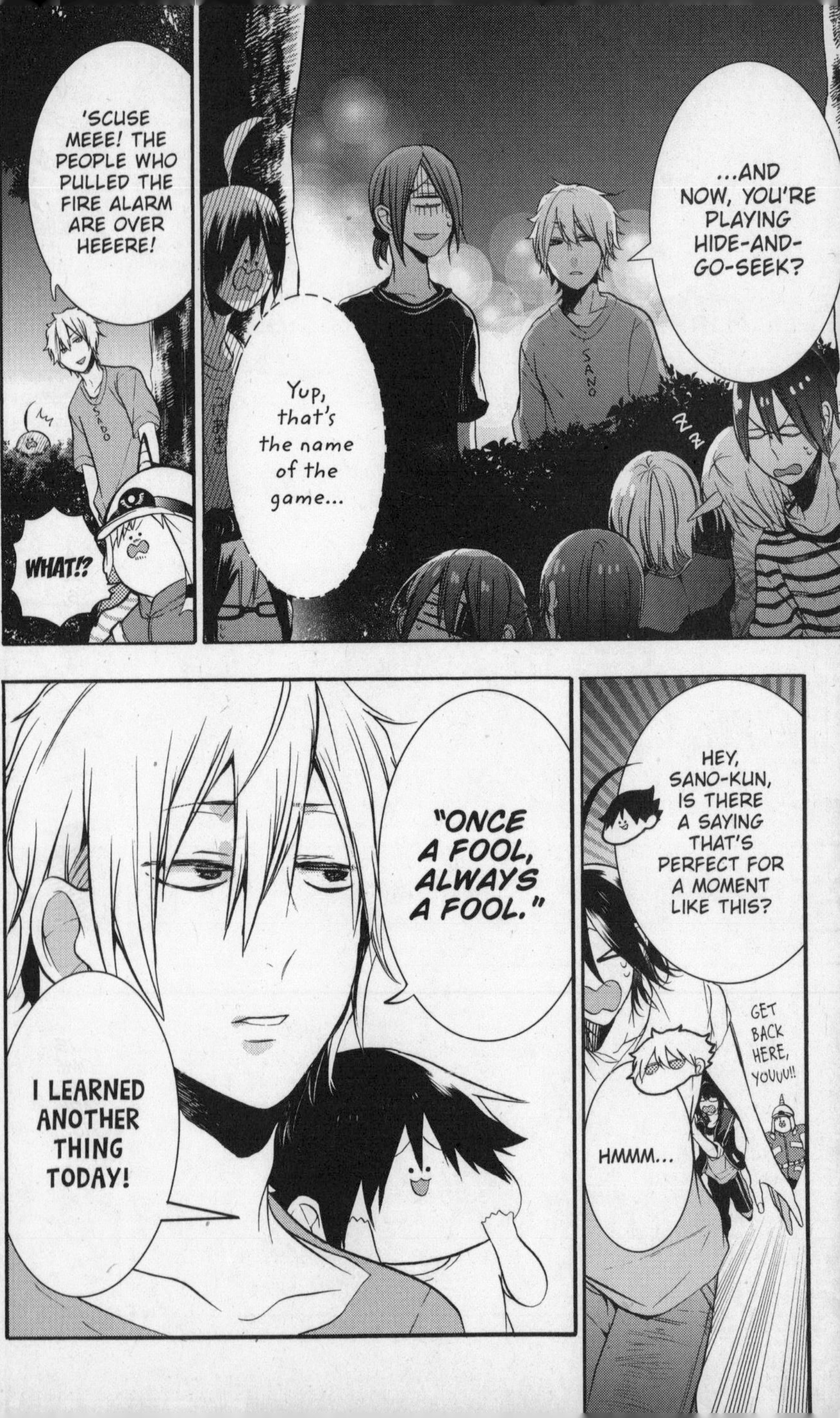
...AND NOW, YOU'RE PLAYING HIDE-AND-GO-SEEK?
Yup, that's the name of the game...
'SCUSE MEEE! THE PEOPLE WHO PULLED THE FIRE ALARM ARE OVER HEEERE!
WHAT!?
HEY, SANO-KUN, IS THERE A SAYING THAT'S PERFECT FOR A MOMENT LIKE THIS?
GET BACK HERE, YOUUU!!
HMMM...
"ONCE A FOOL, ALWAYS A FOOL."
I LEARNED ANOTHER THING TODAY!

Twentieth Period

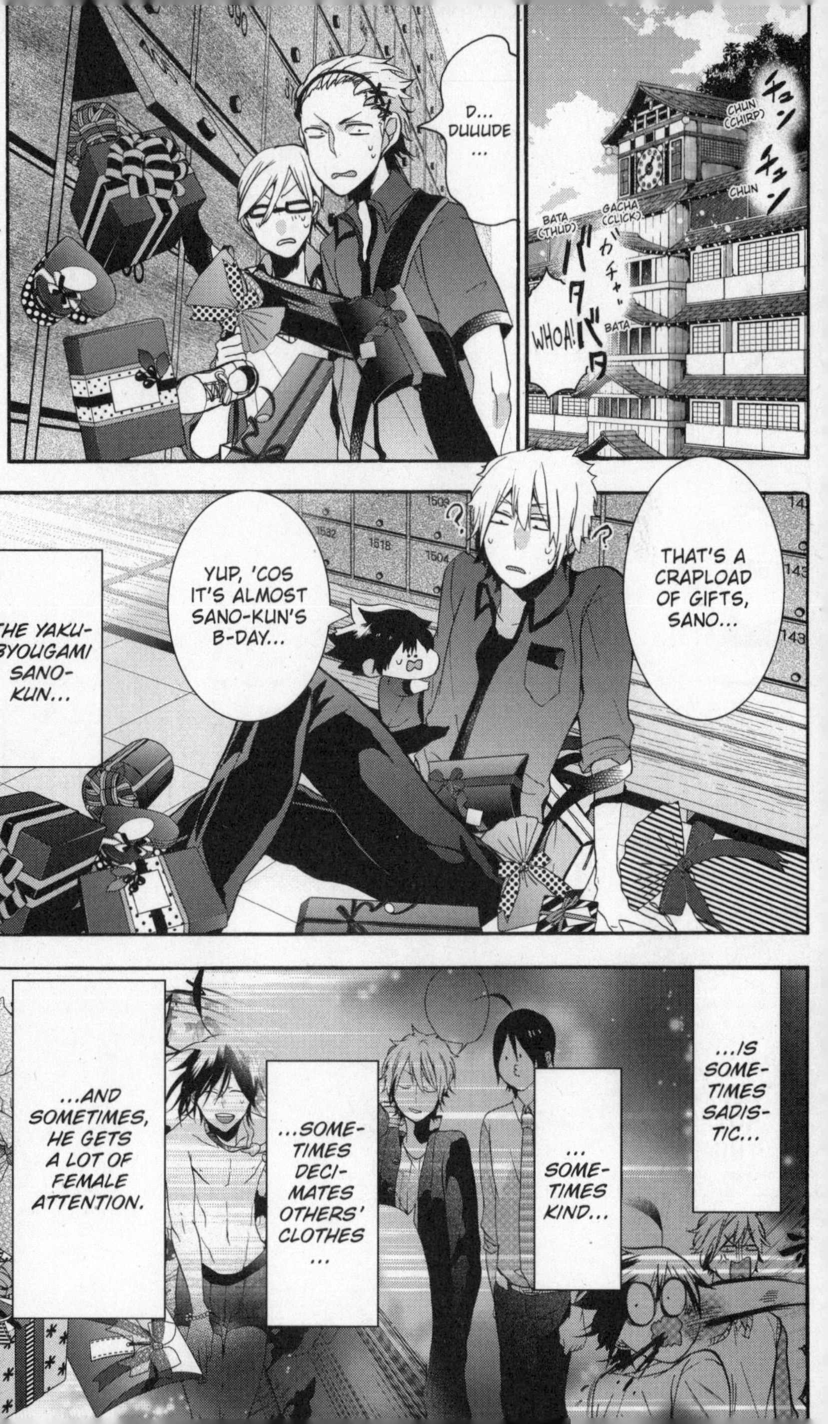
チュン
CHUN (CHIRP)
チュン
CHUN
ガチャ
GACHA (CLICK)
バタ
BATA (THUD)
バタ
BATA
WHOA!
D... DUUUDE...
THAT'S A CRAPLOAD OF GIFTS, SANO...
YUP, 'COS IT'S ALMOST SANO-KUN'S B-DAY...
THE YAKU-BYOUGAMI SANO-KUN...
...IS SOME-TIMES SADIS-TIC...
...SOME-TIMES KIND...
...SOME-TIMES DECI-MATES OTHERS' CLOTHES...
...AND SOMETIMES, HE GETS A LOT OF FEMALE ATTENTION.

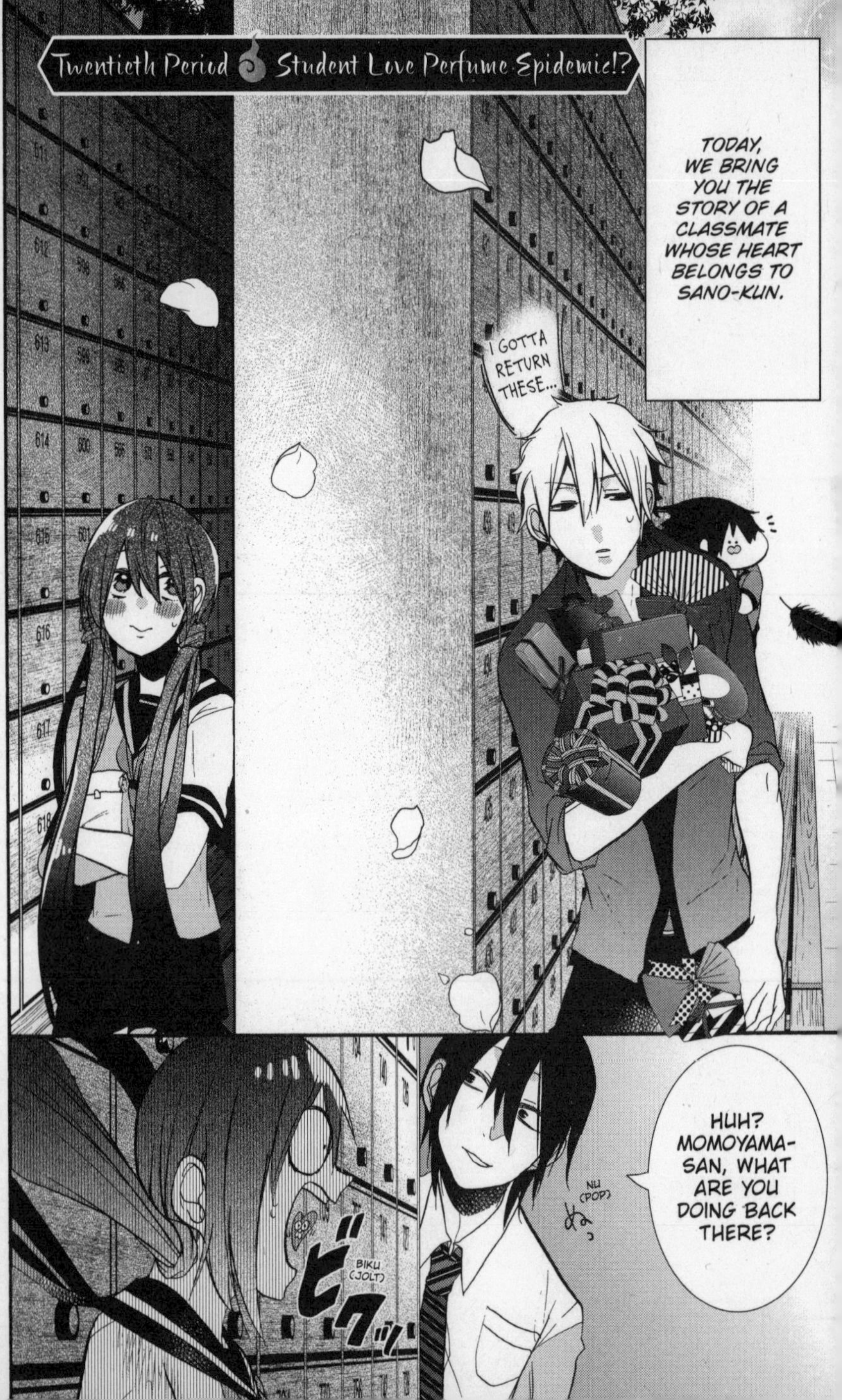

Twentieth Period Student Love Perfume Epidemic!?
TODAY, WE BRING YOU THE STORY OF A CLASSMATE WHOSE HEART BELONGS TO SANO-KUN.
I GOTTA RETURN THESE...
HUH? MOMOYAMA-SAN, WHAT ARE YOU DOING BACK THERE?
NU (POP)
BIKU (JOLT)

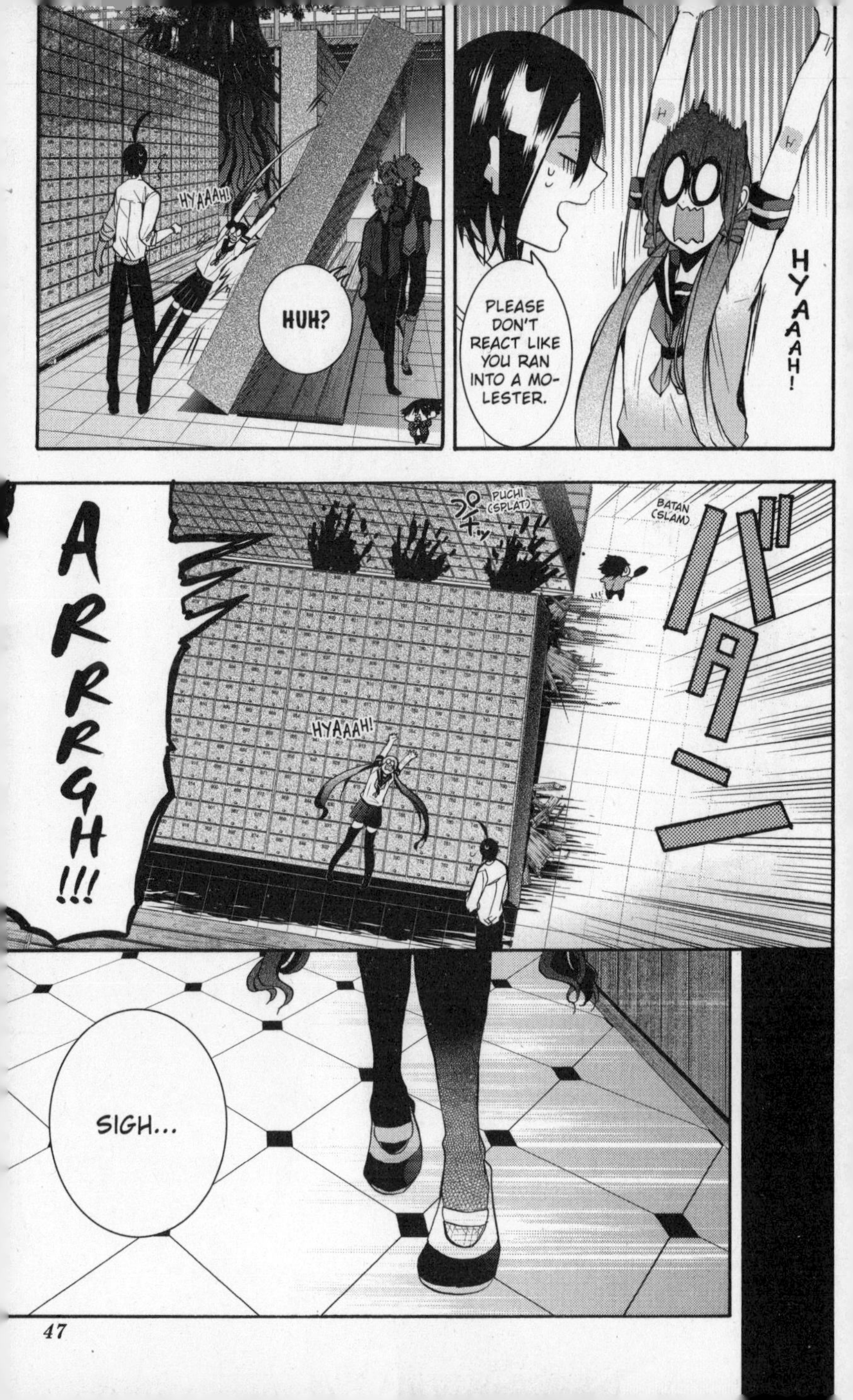

HYAAAH!
PLEASE DON'T REACT LIKE YOU RAN INTO A MO-LESTER.
HYAAAH!
HUH?
BATAN (SLAM)
PUCHI (SPLAT)
HYAAAH!
ARRRRGH!!!
SIGH...

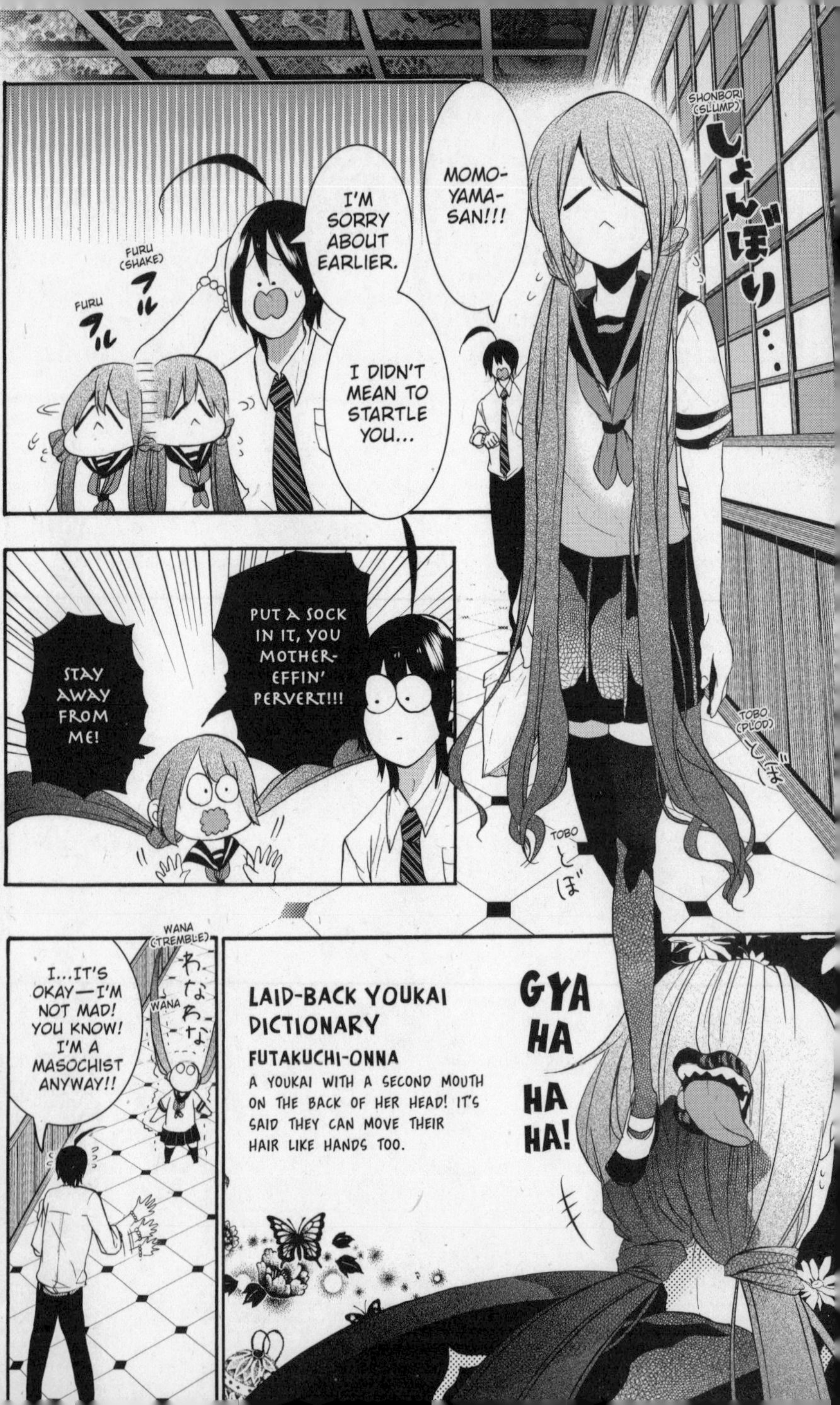

SHONBORI (SLUMP)
しょんぼり
...
MOMO-YAMA-SAN!!!
I'M SORRY ABOUT EARLIER.
I DIDN'T MEAN TO STARTLE YOU...
TOBO (PLOD)
とぼ
TOBO
とぼ
FURU (SHAKE)
フル
FURU
フル
PUT A SOCK IN IT, YOU MOTHER-EFFIN' PERVERT!!!
STAY AWAY FROM ME!
GYA HA HA HA!
LAID-BACK YOUKAI DICTIONARY
FUTAKUCHI-ONNA
A YOUKAI WITH A SECOND MOUTH ON THE BACK OF HER HEAD! IT'S SAID THEY CAN MOVE THEIR HAIR LIKE HANDS TOO.
WANA (TREMBLE)
わな
WANA
わな
I...IT'S OKAY—I'M NOT MAD! YOU KNOW! I'M A MASOCHIST ANYWAY!!

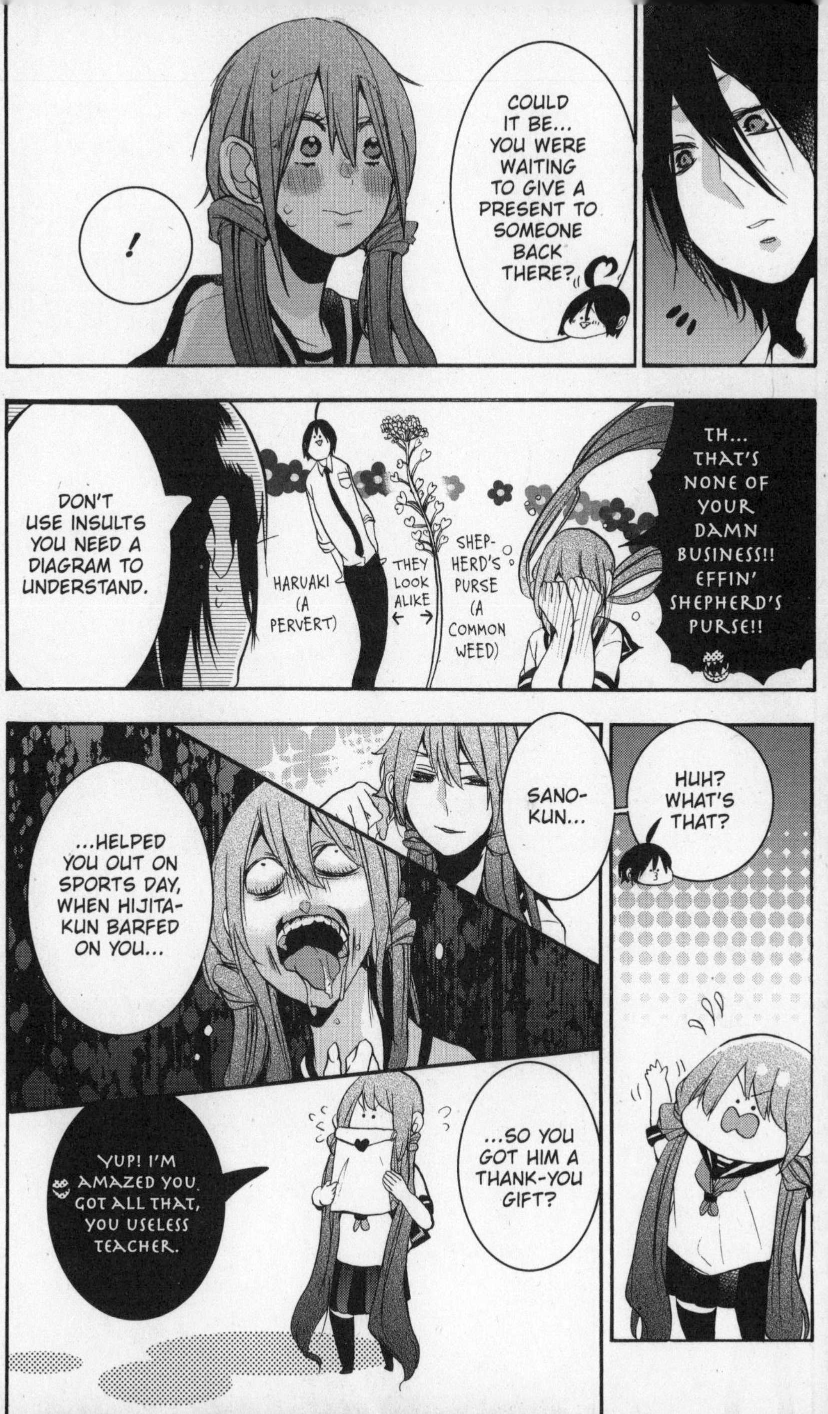

COULD IT BE... YOU WERE WAITING TO GIVE A PRESENT TO SOMEONE BACK THERE?
!
TH... THAT'S NONE OF YOUR DAMN BUSINESS!! EFFIN' SHEPHERD'S PURSE!!
SHEPHERD'S PURSE (A COMMON WEED)
THEY LOOK ALIKE
HARUAKI (A PERVERT)
DON'T USE INSULTS YOU NEED A DIAGRAM TO UNDERSTAND.
HUH? WHAT'S THAT?
SANO-KUN...
...HELPED YOU OUT ON SPORTS DAY, WHEN HIJITA-KUN BARFED ON YOU...
...SO YOU GOT HIM A THANK-YOU GIFT?
YUP! I'M AMAZED YOU GOT ALL THAT, YOU USELESS TEACHER.

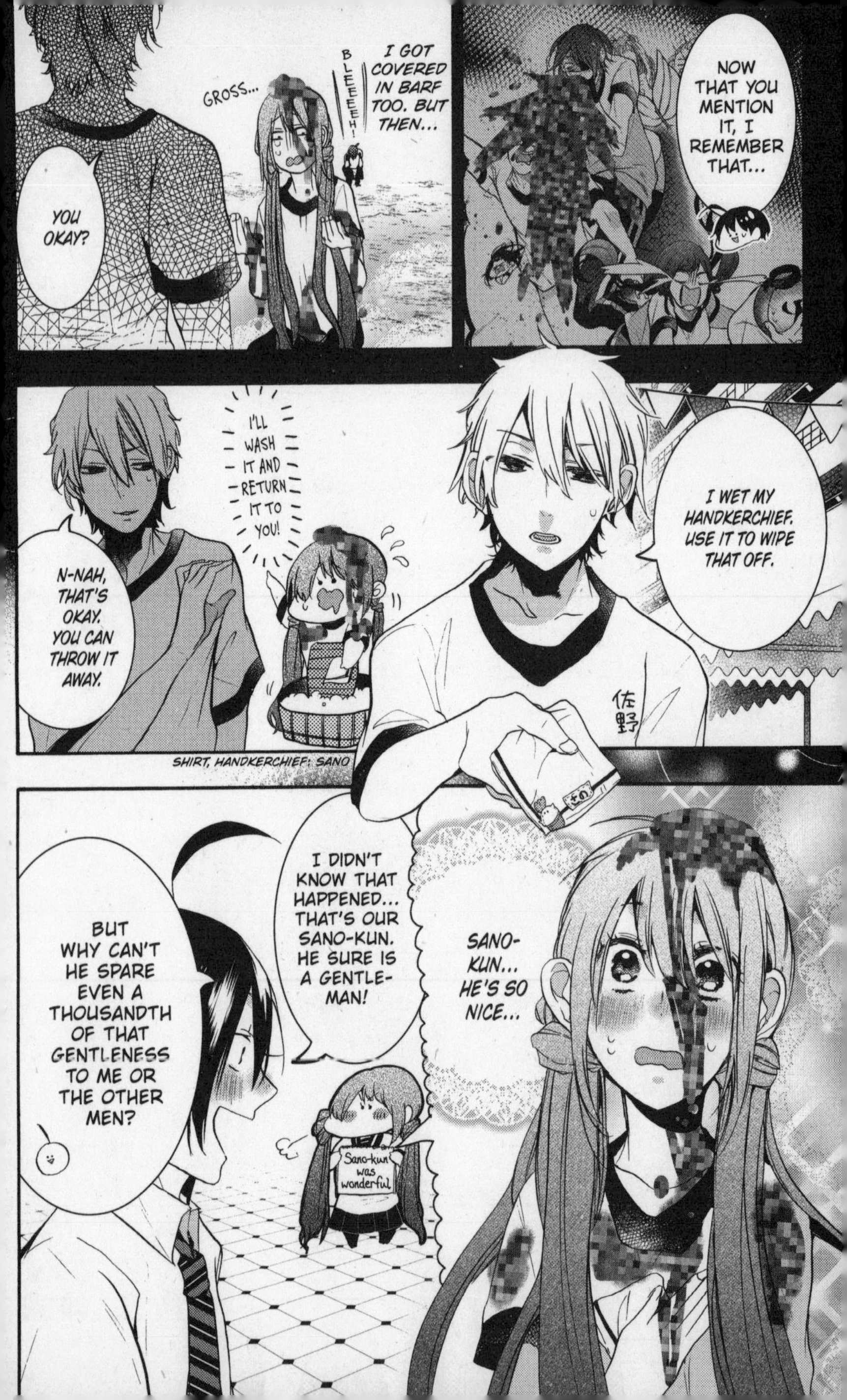
NOW THAT YOU MENTION IT, I REMEMBER THAT...
I GOT COVERED IN BARF TOO. BUT THEN...
BLEEEEEH!
GROSS...
YOU OKAY?
I WET MY HANDKERCHIEF. USE IT TO WIPE THAT OFF.
佐野
I'LL WASH IT AND RETURN IT TO YOU!
N-NAH, THAT'S OKAY. YOU CAN THROW IT AWAY.
SHIRT, HANDKERCHIEF: SANO
SANO-KUN... HE'S SO NICE...
I DIDN'T KNOW THAT HAPPENED... THAT'S OUR SANO-KUN. HE SURE IS A GENTLE-MAN!
Sano-kun was wonderful
BUT WHY CAN'T HE SPARE EVEN A THOUSANDTH OF THAT GENTLENESS TO ME OR THE OTHER MEN?

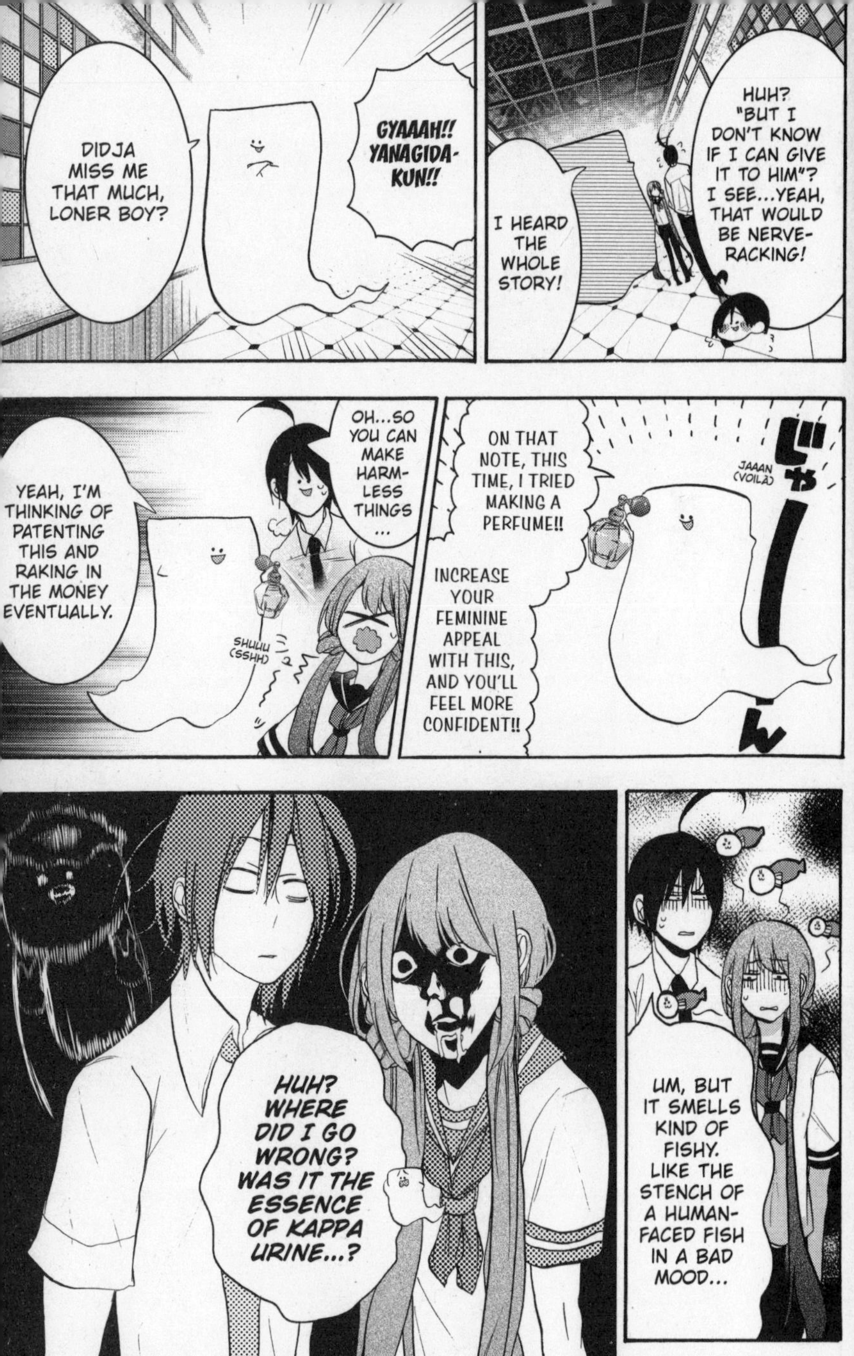
HUH? "BUT I DON'T KNOW IF I CAN GIVE IT TO HIM"? I SEE...YEAH, THAT WOULD BE NERVE-RACKING!
I HEARD THE WHOLE STORY!
GYAAAH!! YANAGIDA-KUN!!
DIDJA MISS ME THAT MUCH, LONER BOY?
じゃーん
JAAAN (VOILÀ)
ON THAT NOTE, THIS TIME, I TRIED MAKING A PERFUME!!
INCREASE YOUR FEMININE APPEAL WITH THIS, AND YOU'LL FEEL MORE CONFIDENT!!
OH...SO YOU CAN MAKE HARMLESS THINGS...
SHUUU (SSHH)
YEAH, I'M THINKING OF PATENTING THIS AND RAKING IN THE MONEY EVENTUALLY.
UM, BUT IT SMELLS KIND OF FISHY. LIKE THE STENCH OF A HUMAN-FACED FISH IN A BAD MOOD...
HUH? WHERE DID I GO WRONG? WAS IT THE ESSENCE OF KAPPA URINE...?

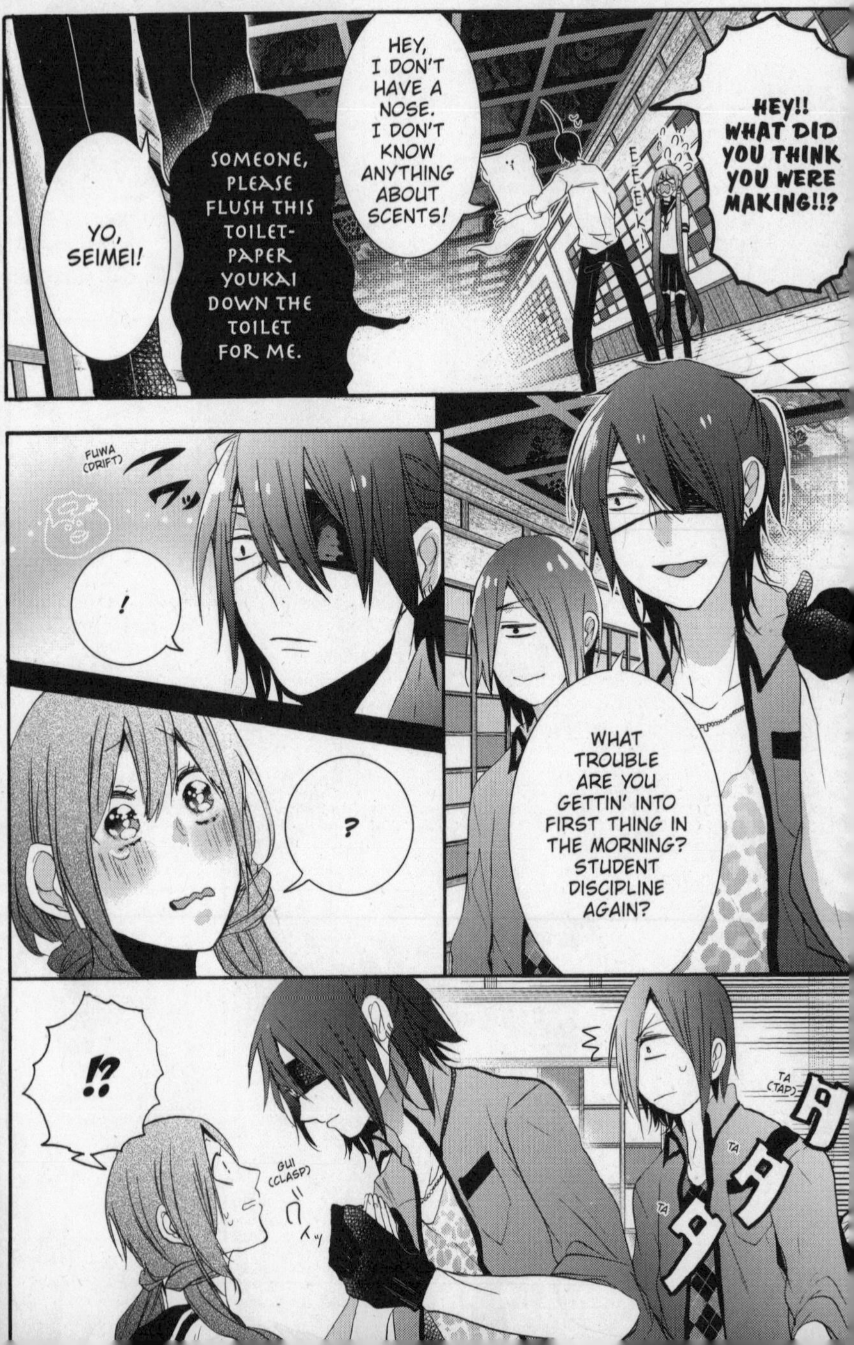
HEY!! WHAT DID YOU THINK YOU WERE MAKING!!?
EEEEK!
HEY, I DON'T HAVE A NOSE. I DON'T KNOW ANYTHING ABOUT SCENTS!
SOMEONE, PLEASE FLUSH THIS TOILET-PAPER YOUKAI DOWN THE TOILET FOR ME.
YO, SEIMEI!
WHAT TROUBLE ARE YOU GETTIN' INTO FIRST THING IN THE MORNING? STUDENT DISCIPLINE AGAIN?
FUWA (DRIFT)
!
?
TA (TAP)
TA
TA
GUI (CLASP)
!?

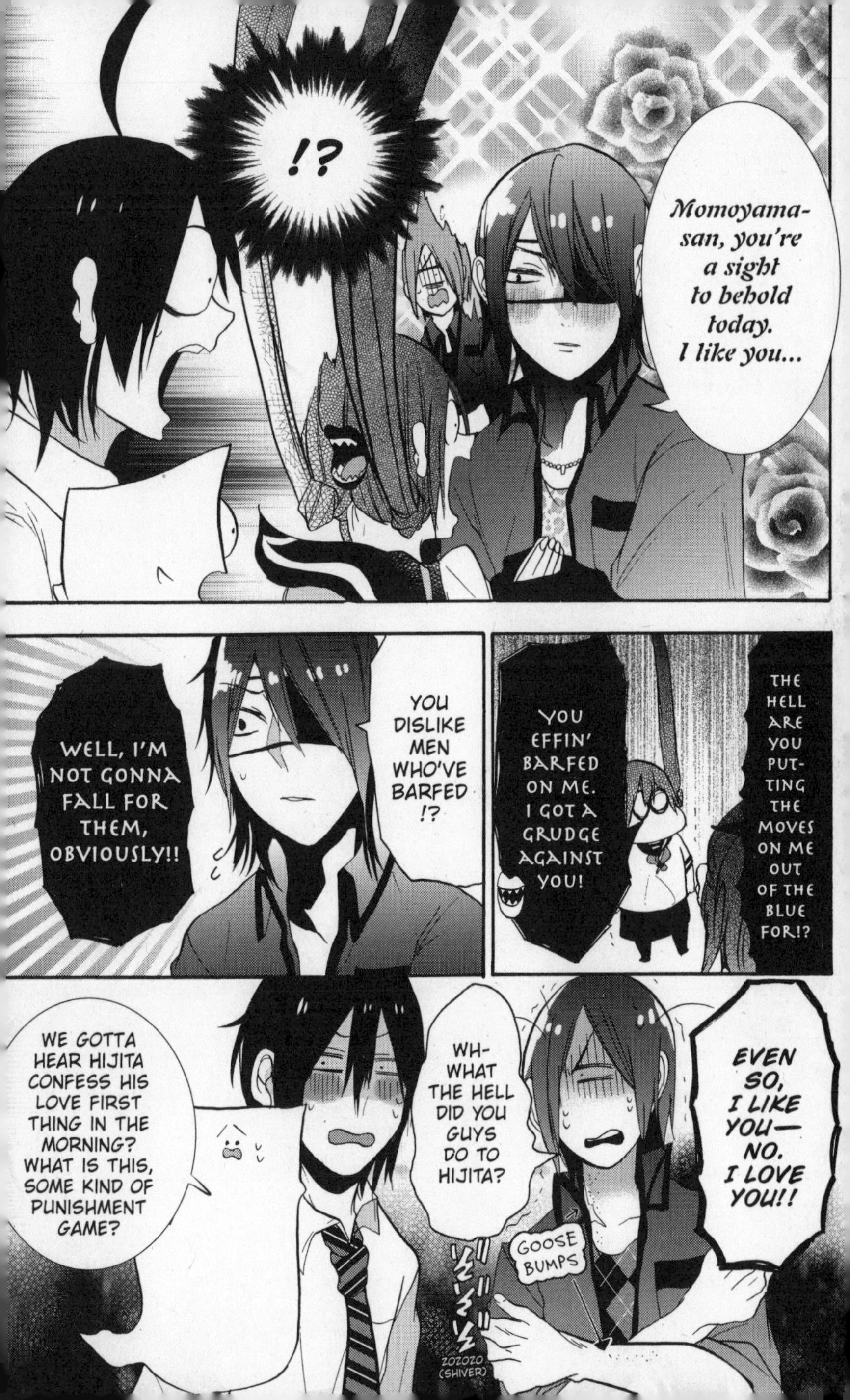

Momoyama-san, you're a sight to behold today. I like you...
!?
THE HELL ARE YOU PUTTING THE MOVES ON ME OUT OF THE BLUE FOR!?
YOU EFFIN' BARFED ON ME. I GOT A GRUDGE AGAINST YOU!
YOU DISLIKE MEN WHO'VE BARFED !?
WELL, I'M NOT GONNA FALL FOR THEM, OBVIOUSLY!!
EVEN SO, I LIKE YOU— NO. I LOVE YOU!!
GOOSE BUMPS
ZOZOZO (SHIVER)
WH-WHAT THE HELL DID YOU GUYS DO TO HIJITA?
WE GOTTA HEAR HIJITA CONFESS HIS LOVE FIRST THING IN THE MORNING? WHAT IS THIS, SOME KIND OF PUNISHMENT GAME?

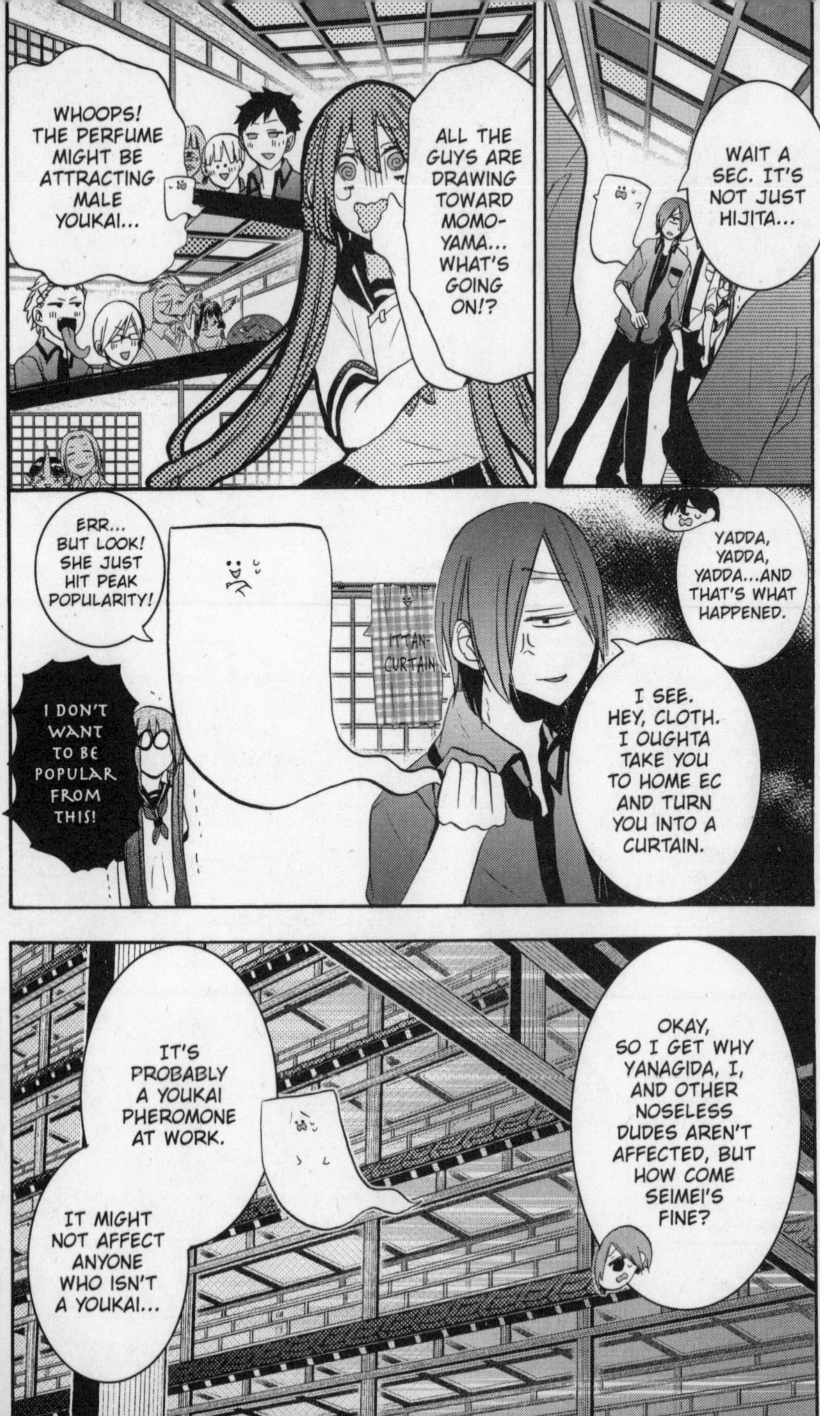
WAIT A SEC. IT'S NOT JUST HIJITA...
ALL THE GUYS ARE DRAWING TOWARD MOMO-YAMA... WHAT'S GOING ON!?
WHOOPS! THE PERFUME MIGHT BE ATTRACTING MALE YOUKAI...
YADDA, YADDA, YADDA...AND THAT'S WHAT HAPPENED.
I SEE. HEY, CLOTH. I OUGHTA TAKE YOU TO HOME EC AND TURN YOU INTO A CURTAIN.
ITTAN-CURTAIN
ERR... BUT LOOK! SHE JUST HIT PEAK POPULARITY!
I DON'T WANT TO BE POPULAR FROM THIS!
OKAY, SO I GET WHY YANAGIDA, I, AND OTHER NOSELESS DUDES AREN'T AFFECTED, BUT HOW COME SEIMEI'S FINE?
IT'S PROBABLY A YOUKAI PHEROMONE AT WORK.
IT MIGHT NOT AFFECT ANYONE WHO ISN'T A YOUKAI...

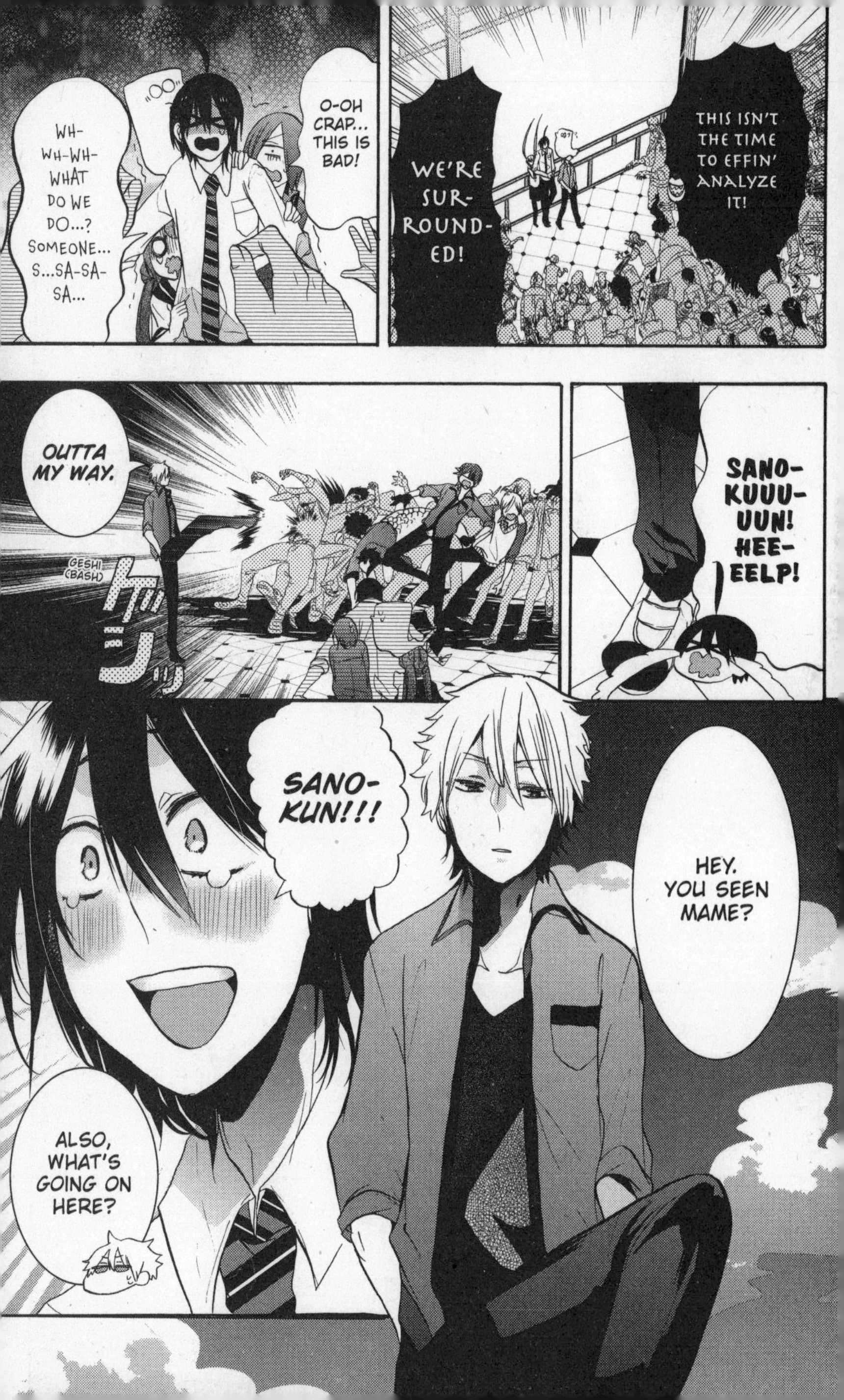
THIS ISN'T THE TIME TO EFFIN' ANALYZE IT!
WE'RE SUR-ROUND-ED!
O-OH CRAP... THIS IS BAD!
WH-WH-WH-WHAT DO WE DO...? SOMEONE... S...SA-SA-SA...
SANO-KUUUU-UUN! HEE-EELP!
OUTTA MY WAY.
GESHI (BASH)
SANO-KUN!!!
HEY. YOU SEEN MAME?
ALSO, WHAT'S GOING ON HERE?

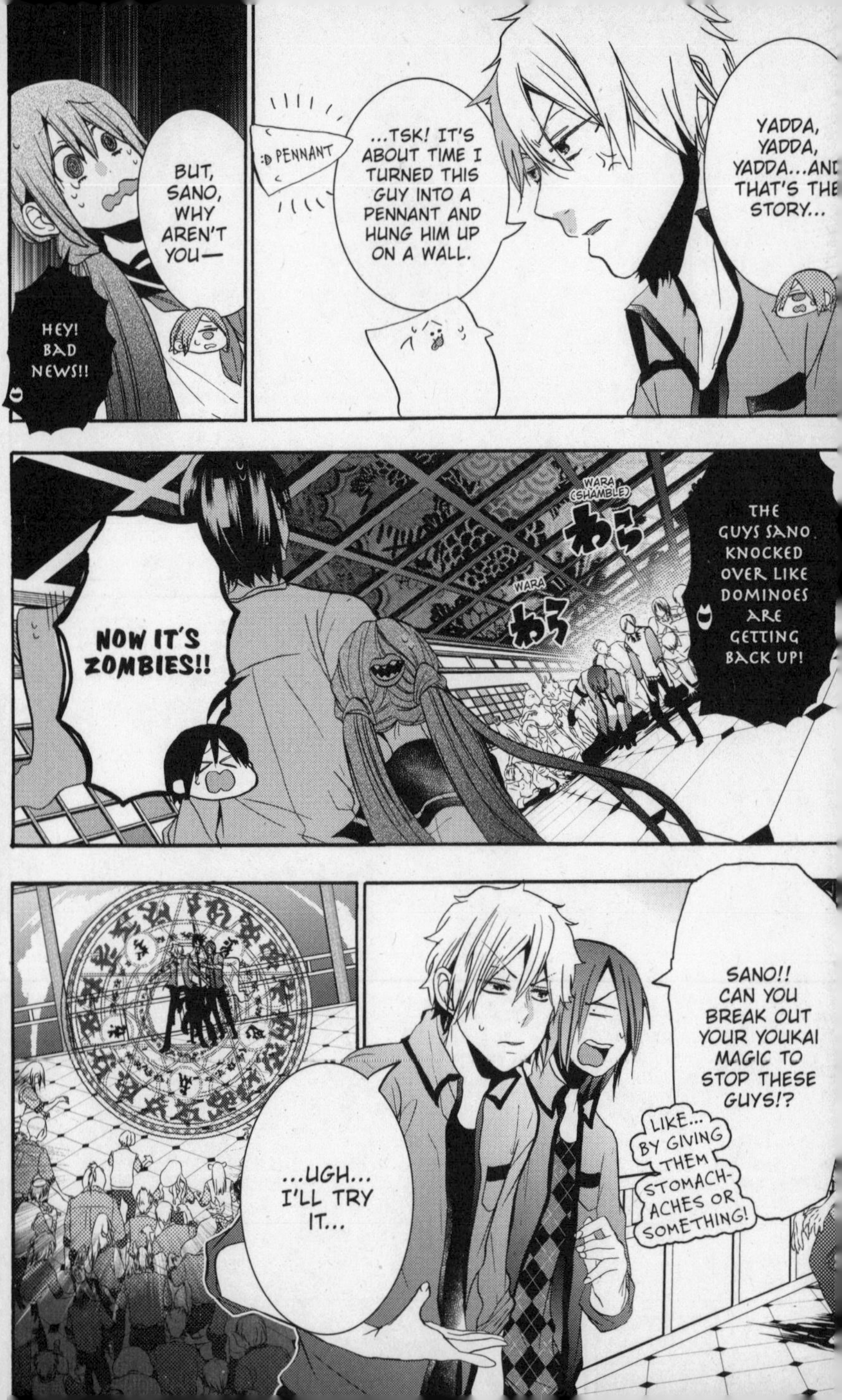
YADDA, YADDA, YADDA...AND THAT'S THE STORY...
...TSK! IT'S ABOUT TIME I TURNED THIS GUY INTO A PENNANT AND HUNG HIM UP ON A WALL.
:D PENNANT
BUT, SANO, WHY AREN'T YOU—
HEY! BAD NEWS!!
THE GUYS SANO KNOCKED OVER LIKE DOMINOES ARE GETTING BACK UP!
WARA (SHAMBLE)
WARA
NOW IT'S ZOMBIES!!
SANO!! CAN YOU BREAK OUT YOUR YOUKAI MAGIC TO STOP THESE GUYS!?
LIKE... BY GIVING THEM STOMACH-ACHES OR SOMETHING!
...UGH... I'LL TRY IT...

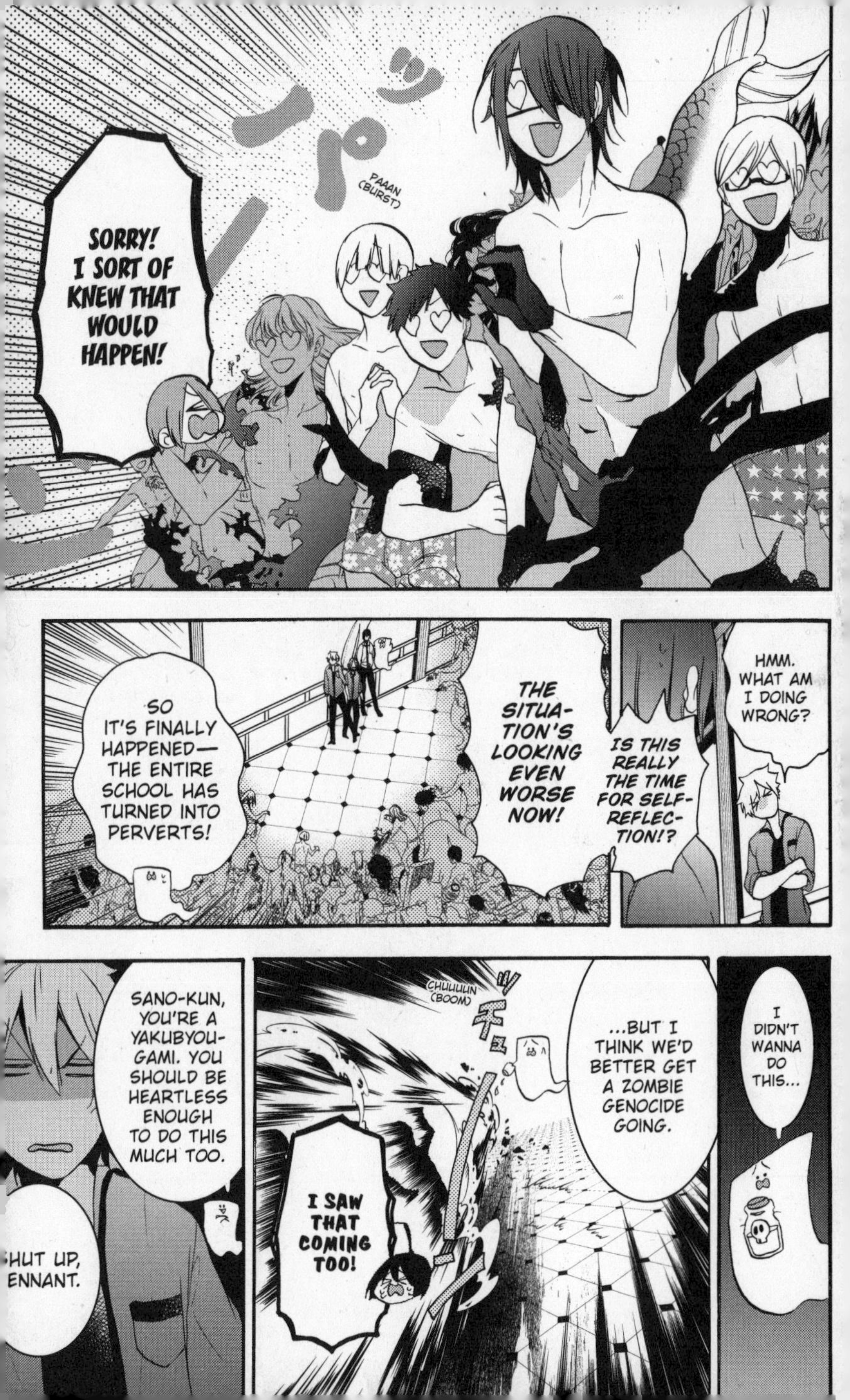
PAAAN (BURST)
SORRY! I SORT OF KNEW THAT WOULD HAPPEN!
HMM. WHAT AM I DOING WRONG?
IS THIS REALLY THE TIME FOR SELF-REFLECTION!?
THE SITUATION'S LOOKING EVEN WORSE NOW!
SO IT'S FINALLY HAPPENED— THE ENTIRE SCHOOL HAS TURNED INTO PERVERTS!
I DIDN'T WANNA DO THIS...
...BUT I THINK WE'D BETTER GET A ZOMBIE GENOCIDE GOING.
CHUUUUN (BOOM)
I SAW THAT COMING TOO!
SANO-KUN, YOU'RE A YAKUBYOU-GAMI. YOU SHOULD BE HEARTLESS ENOUGH TO DO THIS MUCH TOO.
SHUT UP, ENNANT.

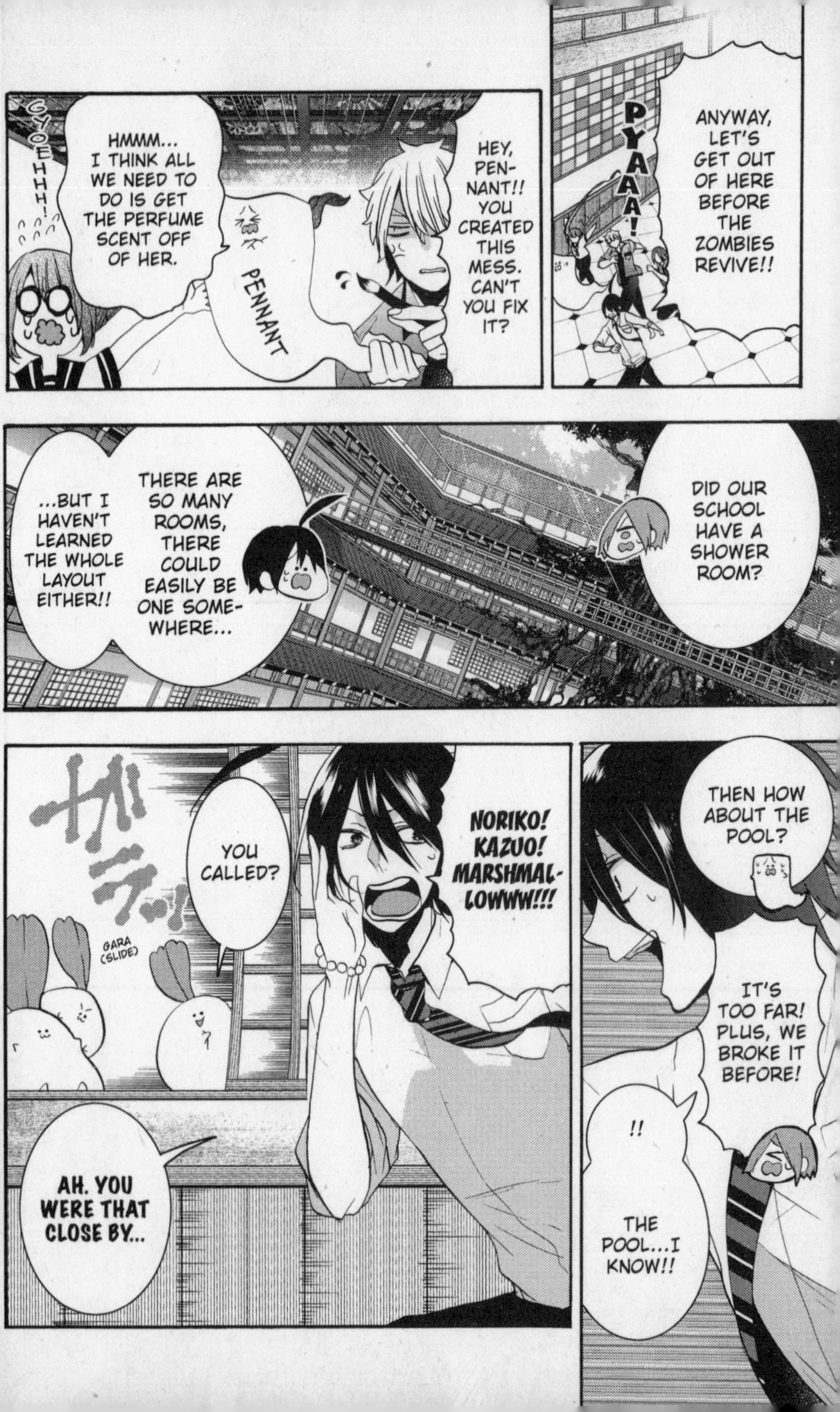
ANYWAY, LET'S GET OUT OF HERE BEFORE THE ZOMBIES REVIVE!!
PYAAA!
HEY, PEN-NANT!! YOU CREATED THIS MESS. CAN'T YOU FIX IT?
PENNANT
HMMM... I THINK ALL WE NEED TO DO IS GET THE PERFUME SCENT OFF OF HER.
GYOEHHH!
DID OUR SCHOOL HAVE A SHOWER ROOM?
THERE ARE SO MANY ROOMS, THERE COULD EASILY BE ONE SOME-WHERE...
...BUT I HAVEN'T LEARNED THE WHOLE LAYOUT EITHER!!
THEN HOW ABOUT THE POOL?
IT'S TOO FAR! PLUS, WE BROKE IT BEFORE!
!!
THE POOL...I KNOW!!
NORIKO! KAZUO! MARSHMAL-LOWWW!!!
YOU CALLED?
GARA (SLIDE)
AH. YOU WERE THAT CLOSE BY...

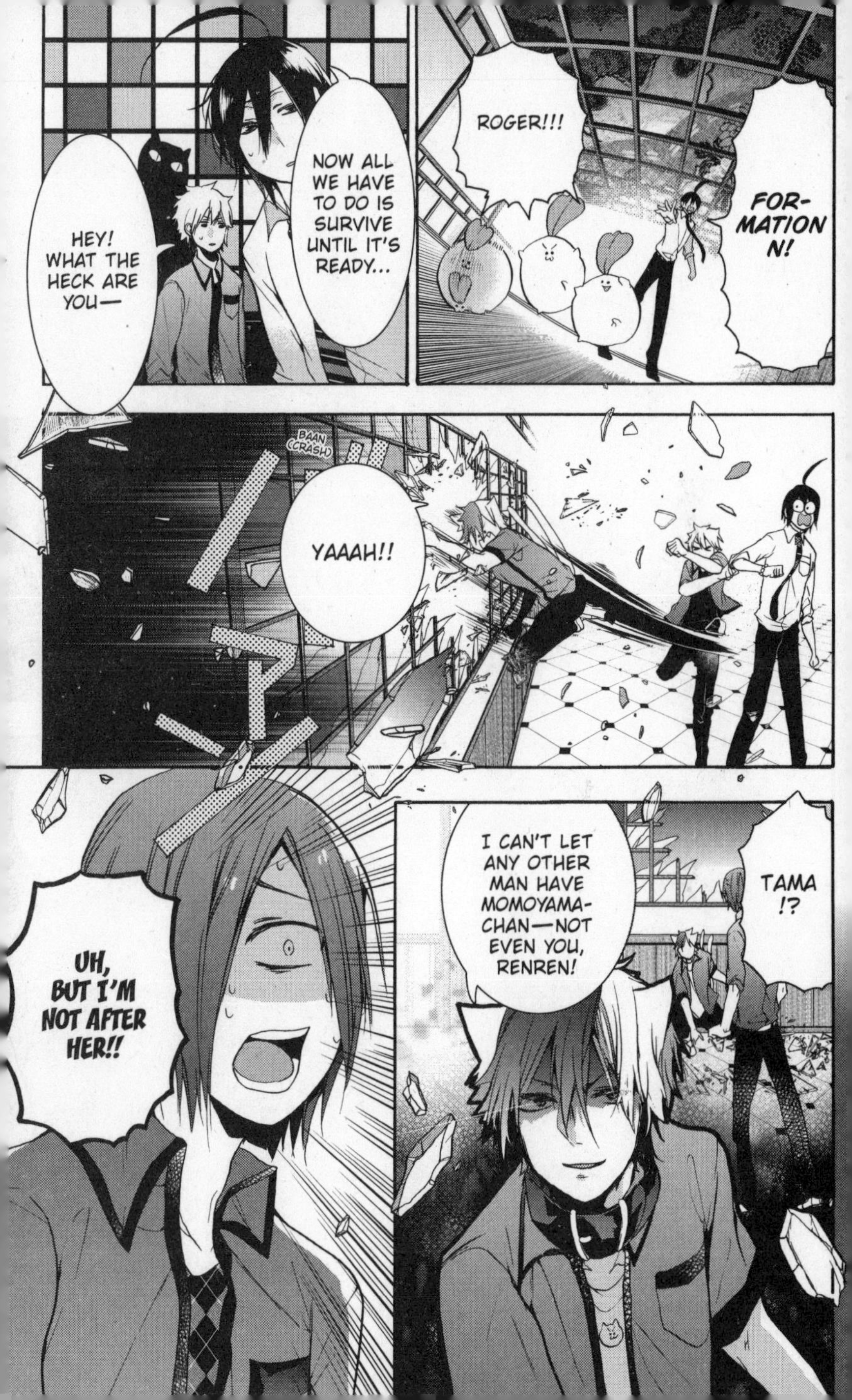
FOR-MATION N!
ROGER!!!
NOW ALL WE HAVE TO DO IS SURVIVE UNTIL IT'S READY...
HEY! WHAT THE HECK ARE YOU—
BAAN (CRASH)
YAAAH!!
TAMA!?
I CAN'T LET ANY OTHER MAN HAVE MOMOYAMA-CHAN—NOT EVEN YOU, RENREN!
UH, BUT I'M NOT AFTER HER!!

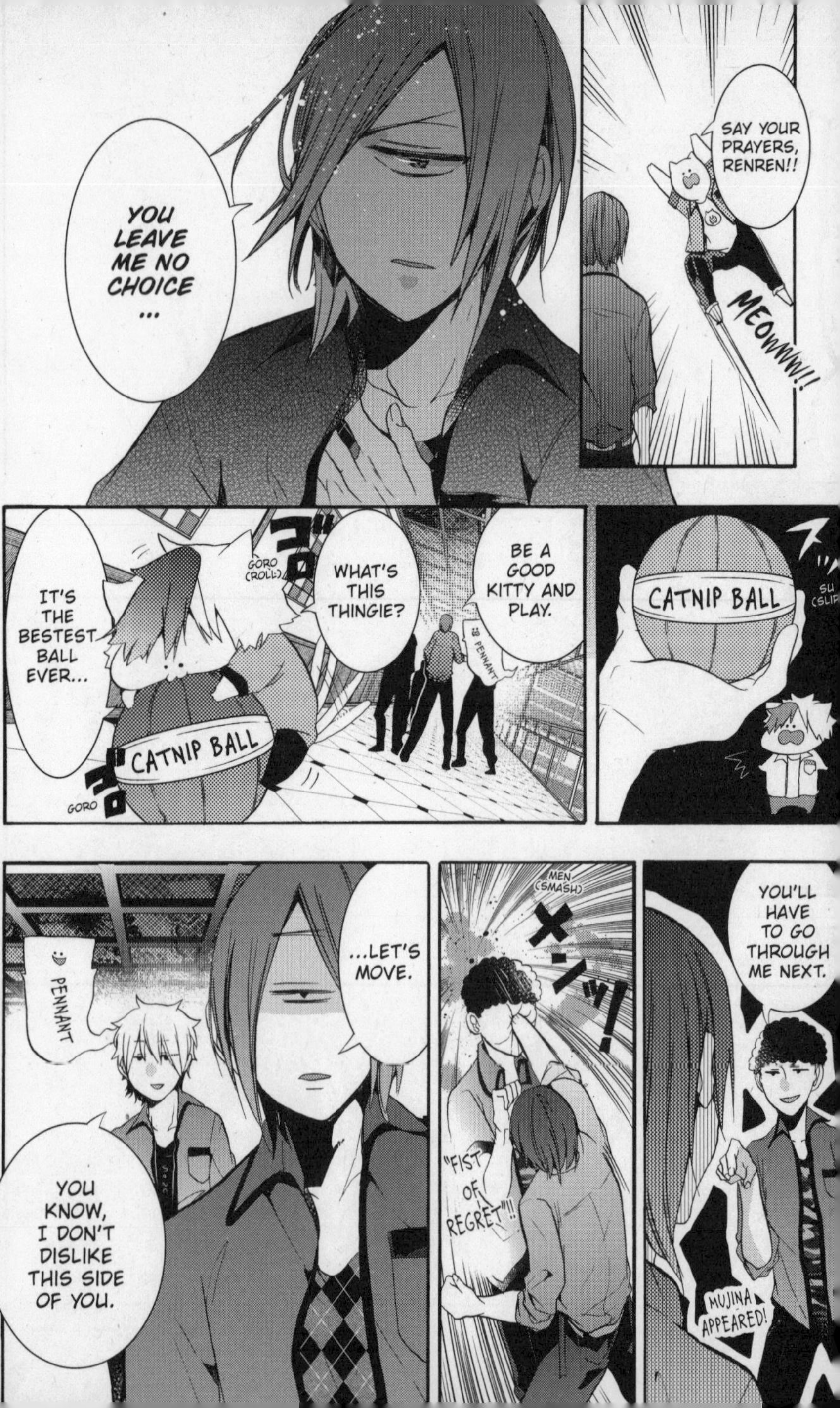
SAY YOUR PRAYERS, RENREN!!
MEOWWW!!
YOU LEAVE ME NO CHOICE...
SU (SLIP
CATNIP BALL
BE A GOOD KITTY AND PLAY.
PENNANT
WHAT'S THIS THINGIE?
GORO (ROLL)
IT'S THE BESTEST BALL EVER...
CATNIP BALL
GORO
YOU'LL HAVE TO GO THROUGH ME NEXT.
MUJINA APPEARED!
MEN (SMASH)
"FIST OF REGRET"!!
...LET'S MOVE.
PENNANT
YOU KNOW, I DON'T DISLIKE THIS SIDE OF YOU.

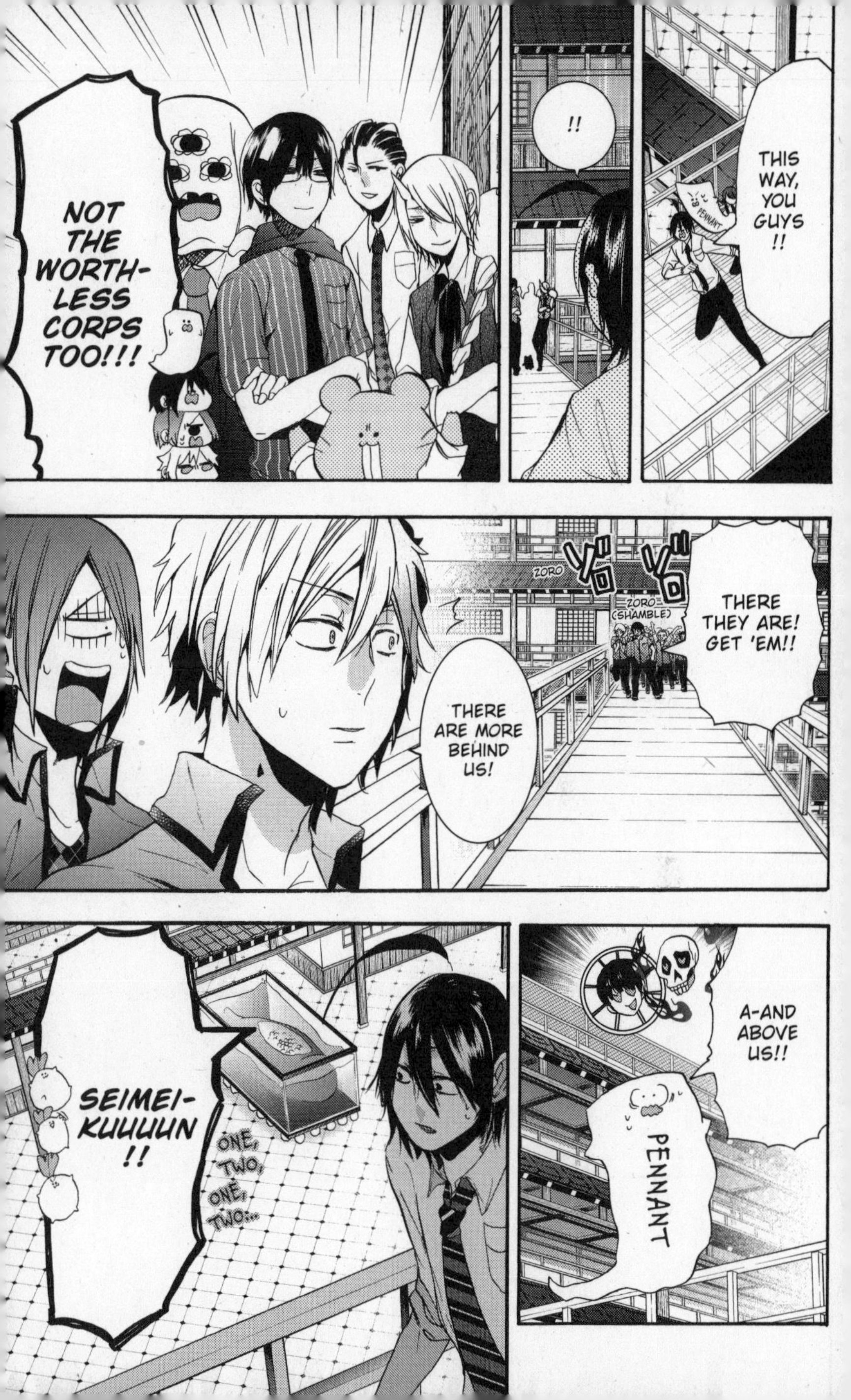
THIS WAY, YOU GUYS!!
PENNANT
!!
NOT THE WORTHLESS CORPS TOO!!!
THERE THEY ARE! GET 'EM!!
ZORO
ZORO (SHAMBLE)
THERE ARE MORE BEHIND US!
A-AND ABOVE US!!
PENNANT
SEIMEI-KUUUUN!!
ONE, TWO, ONE, TWO...

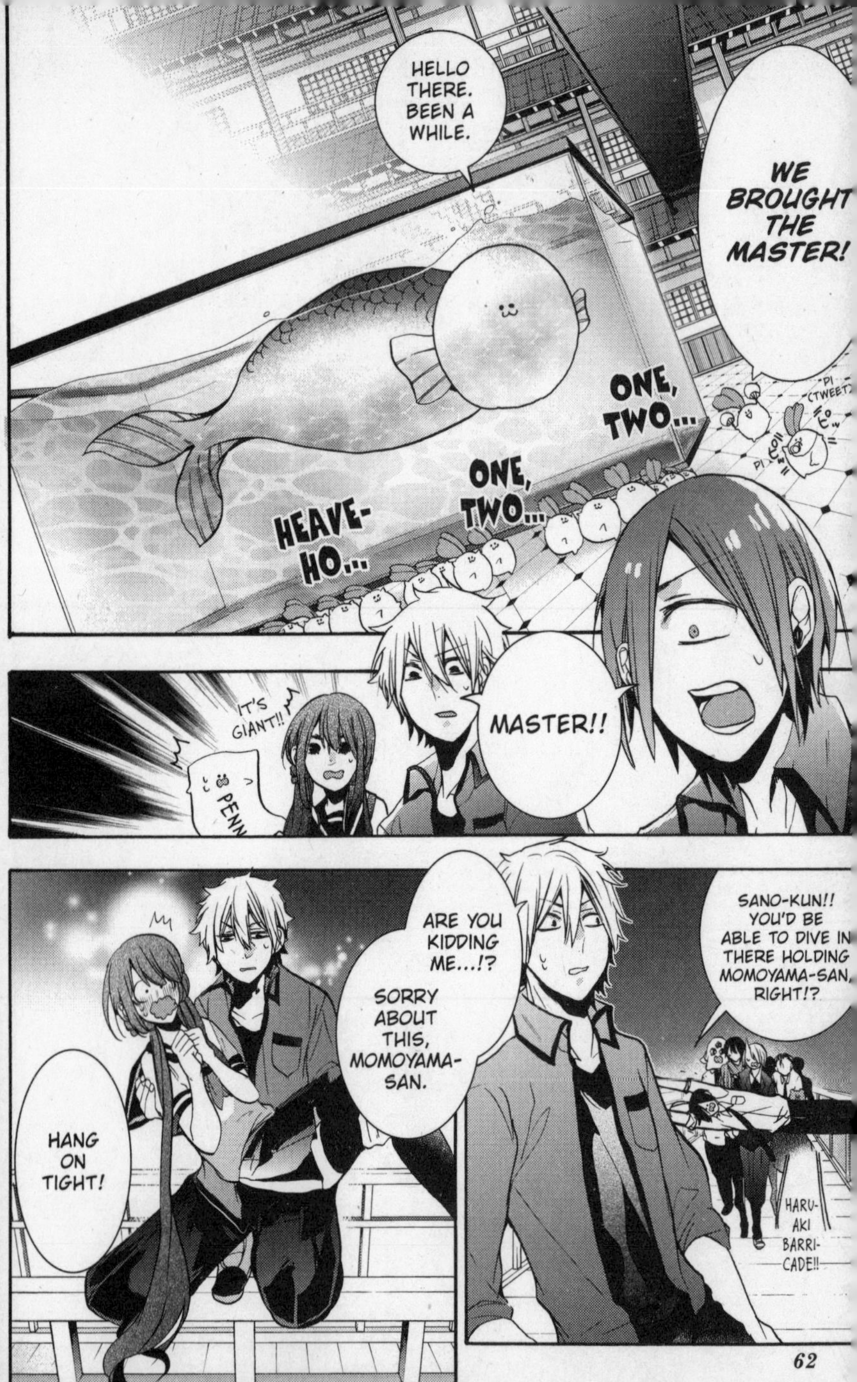

WE BROUGHT THE MASTER!
PI (TWEET)
ONE, TWO...
ONE, TWO...
HEAVE-HO...
HELLO THERE. BEEN A WHILE.
MASTER!!
IT'S GIANT!!
PENN
SANO-KUN!! YOU'D BE ABLE TO DIVE IN THERE HOLDING MOMOYAMA-SAN, RIGHT!?
HARU-AKI BARRI-CADE!!
ARE YOU KIDDING ME...!?
SORRY ABOUT THIS, MOMOYAMA-SAN.
HANG ON TIGHT!

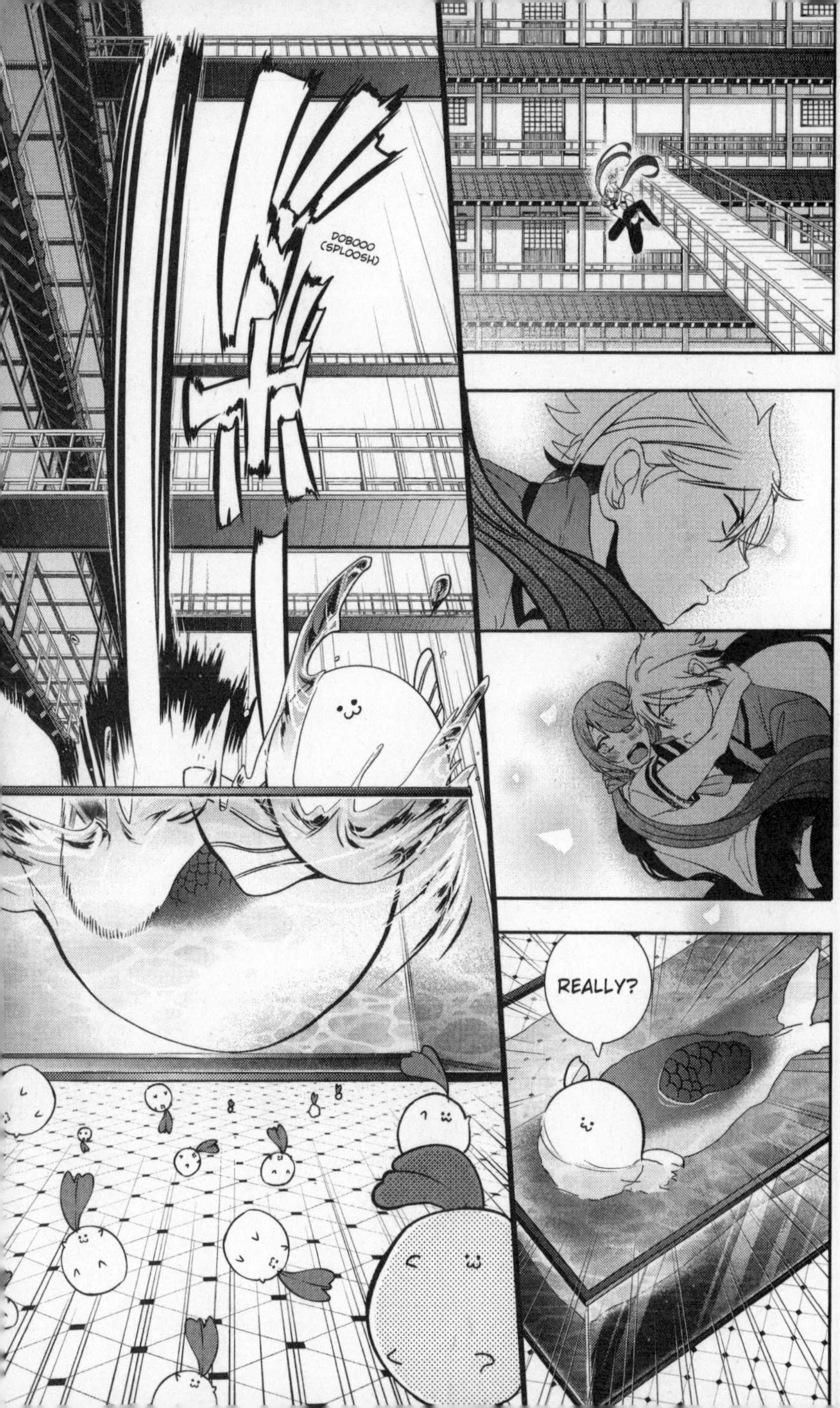
DOBOOO
(SPLOOSH)
REALLY?

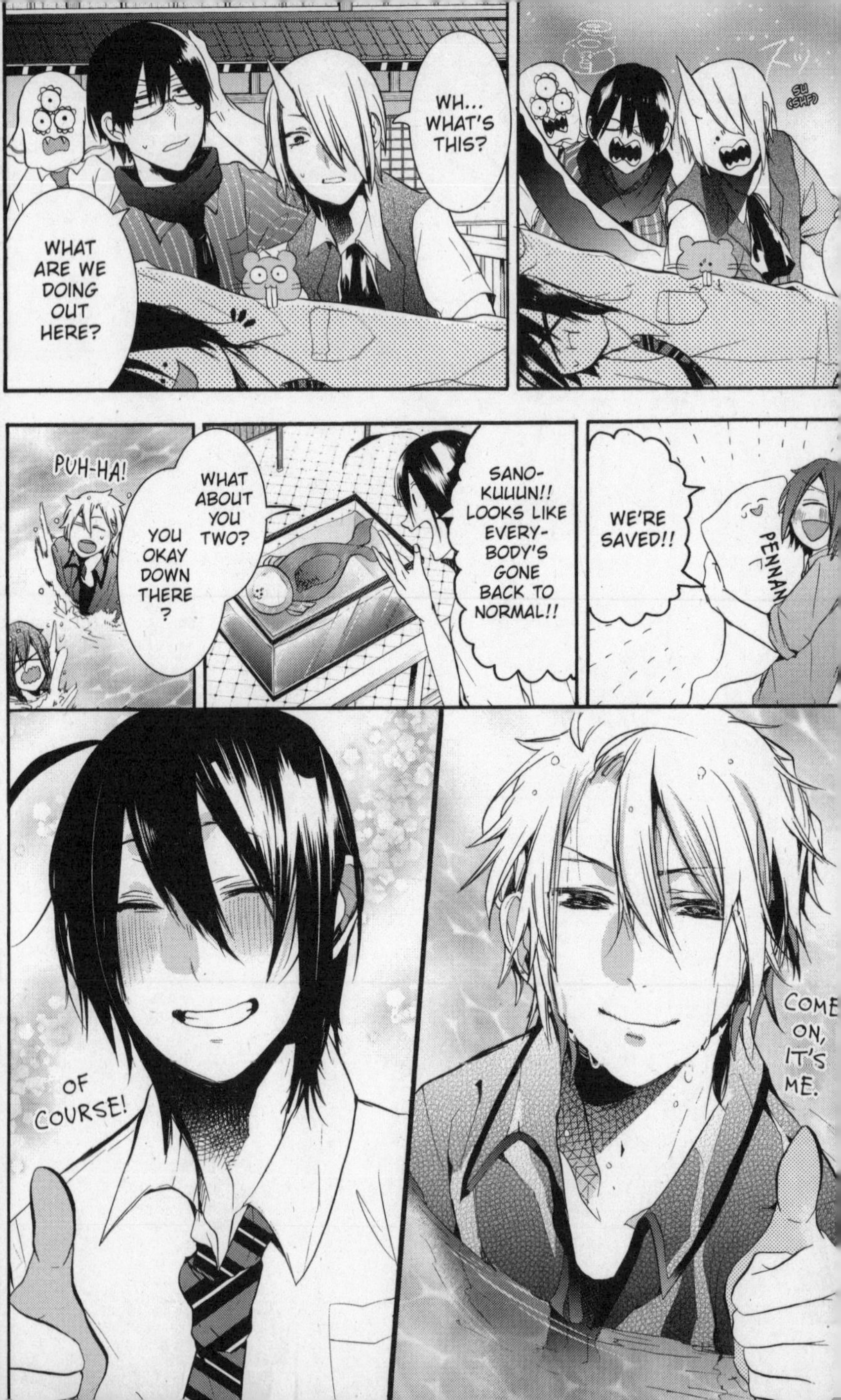

スッ
SU (SHF)
WH... WHAT'S THIS?
WHAT ARE WE DOING OUT HERE?
WE'RE SAVED!!
PENNAN
SANO-KUUUN!! LOOKS LIKE EVERY-BODY'S GONE BACK TO NORMAL!!
PUH-HA!
WHAT ABOUT YOU TWO?
YOU OKAY DOWN THERE?
COME ON, IT'S ME.
OF COURSE!

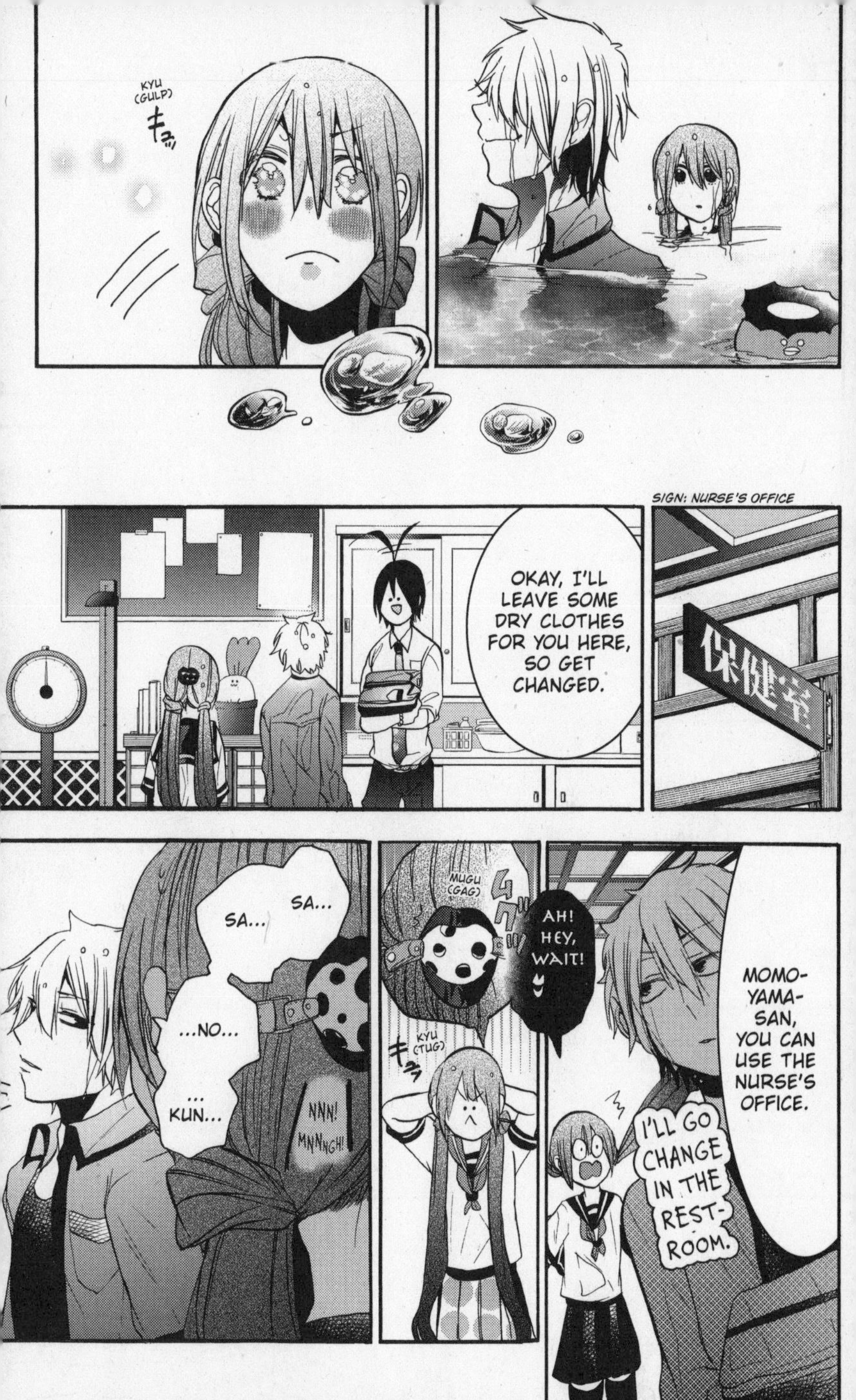
KYU (GULP)
SIGN: NURSE'S OFFICE
OKAY, I'LL LEAVE SOME DRY CLOTHES FOR YOU HERE, SO GET CHANGED.
MOMO-YAMA-SAN, YOU CAN USE THE NURSE'S OFFICE.
I'LL GO CHANGE IN THE REST-ROOM.
MUGU (GAG)
AH! HEY, WAIT!
KYU (TUG)
SA...
SA...
...NO...
...KUN...
NNN! MNNNGH!

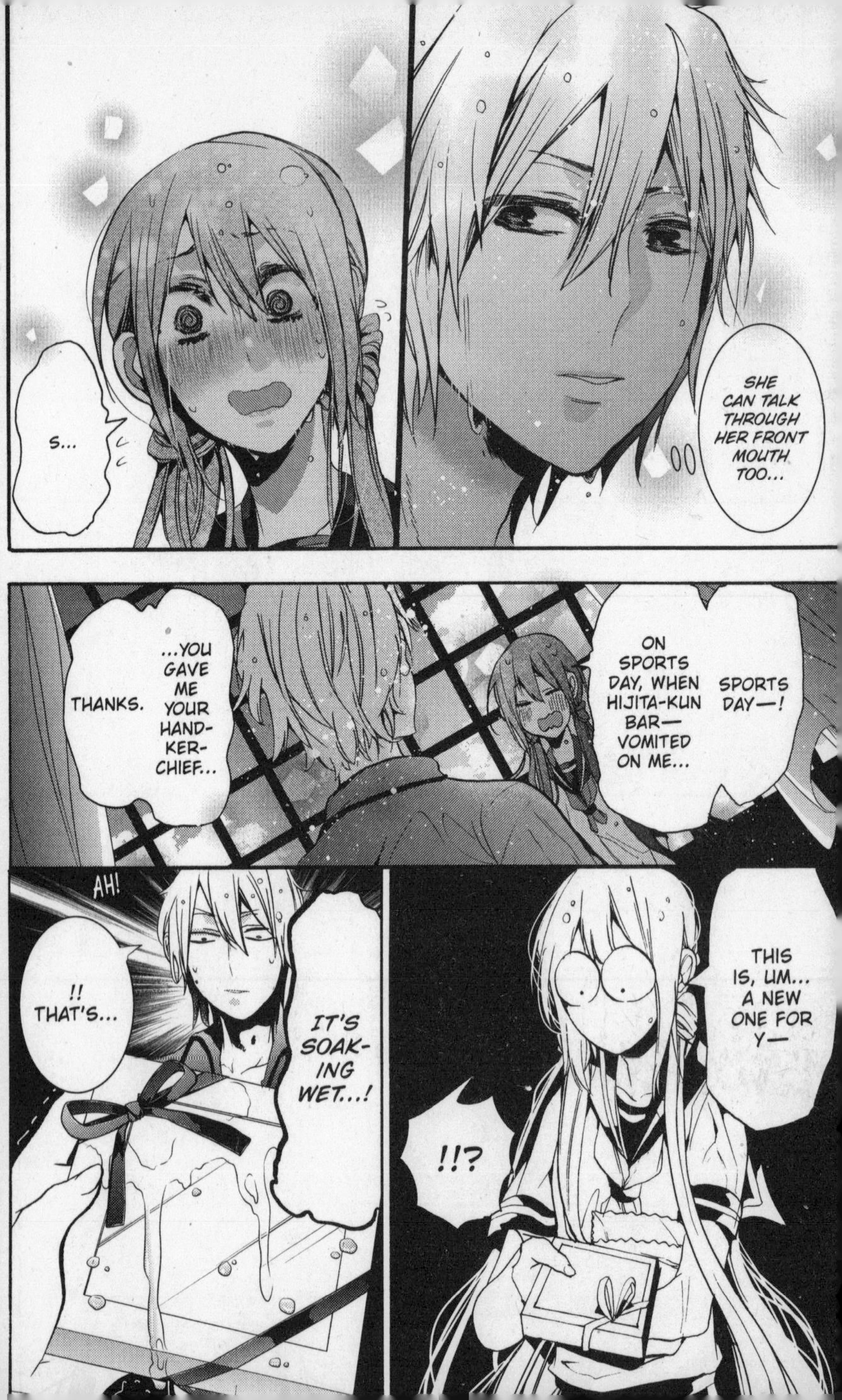

SHE CAN TALK THROUGH HER FRONT MOUTH TOO...
S...
SPORTS DAY—!
ON SPORTS DAY, WHEN HIJITA-KUN BAR— VOMITED ON ME...
...YOU GAVE ME YOUR HAND-KER-CHIEF...
THANKS.
THIS IS, UM... A NEW ONE FOR Y—
!!?
AH!
!! THAT'S...
IT'S SOAK-ING WET...!

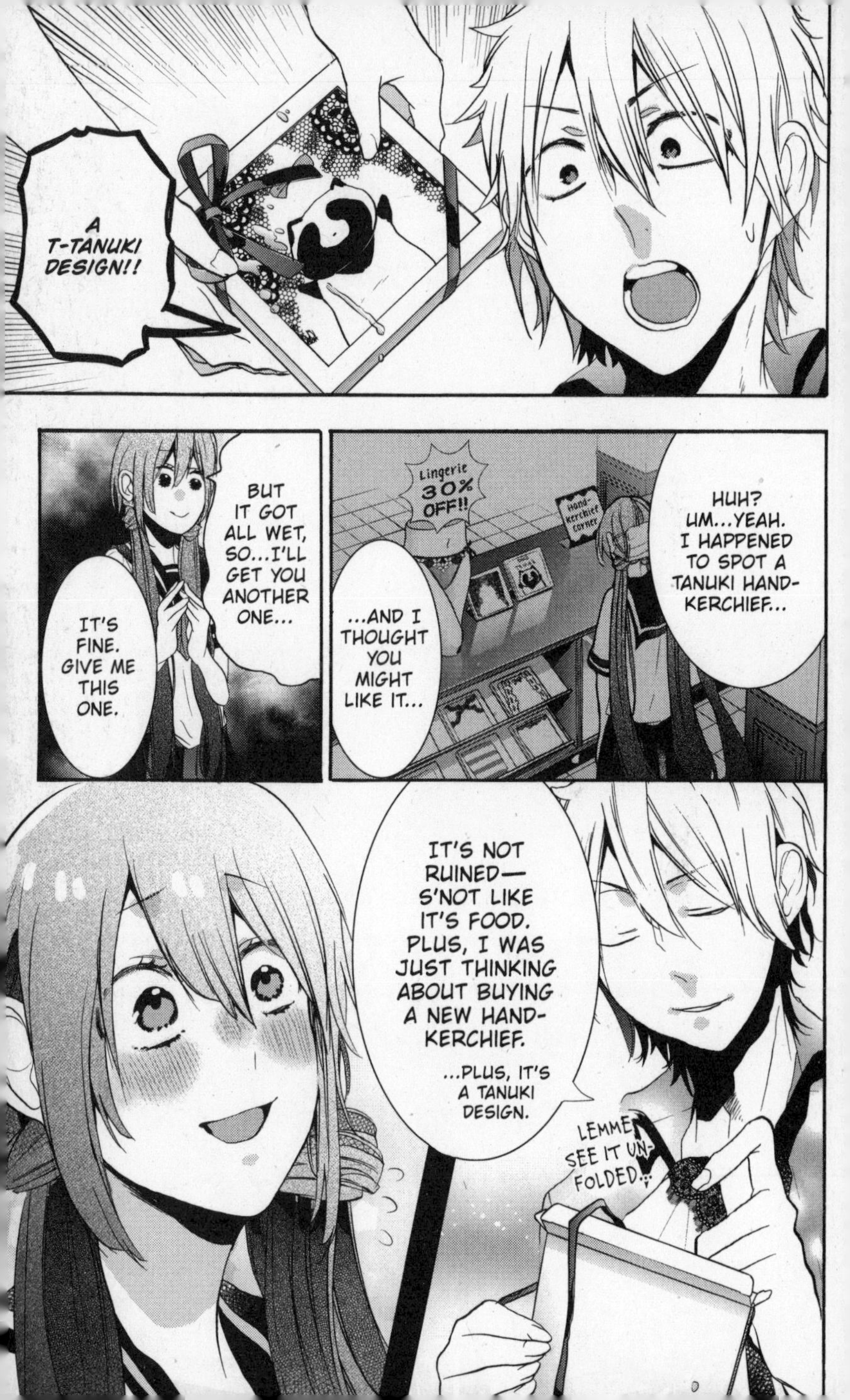
A T-TANUKI DESIGN!!
HUH? UM...YEAH. I HAPPENED TO SPOT A TANUKI HAND-KERCHIEF...
Lingerie 30% OFF!!
Hand-kerchief Corner
...AND I THOUGHT YOU MIGHT LIKE IT...
BUT IT GOT ALL WET, SO...I'LL GET YOU ANOTHER ONE...
IT'S FINE. GIVE ME THIS ONE.
IT'S NOT RUINED— S'NOT LIKE IT'S FOOD. PLUS, I WAS JUST THINKING ABOUT BUYING A NEW HAND-KERCHIEF.
...PLUS, IT'S A TANUKI DESIGN.
LEMME SEE IT UN-FOLDED...

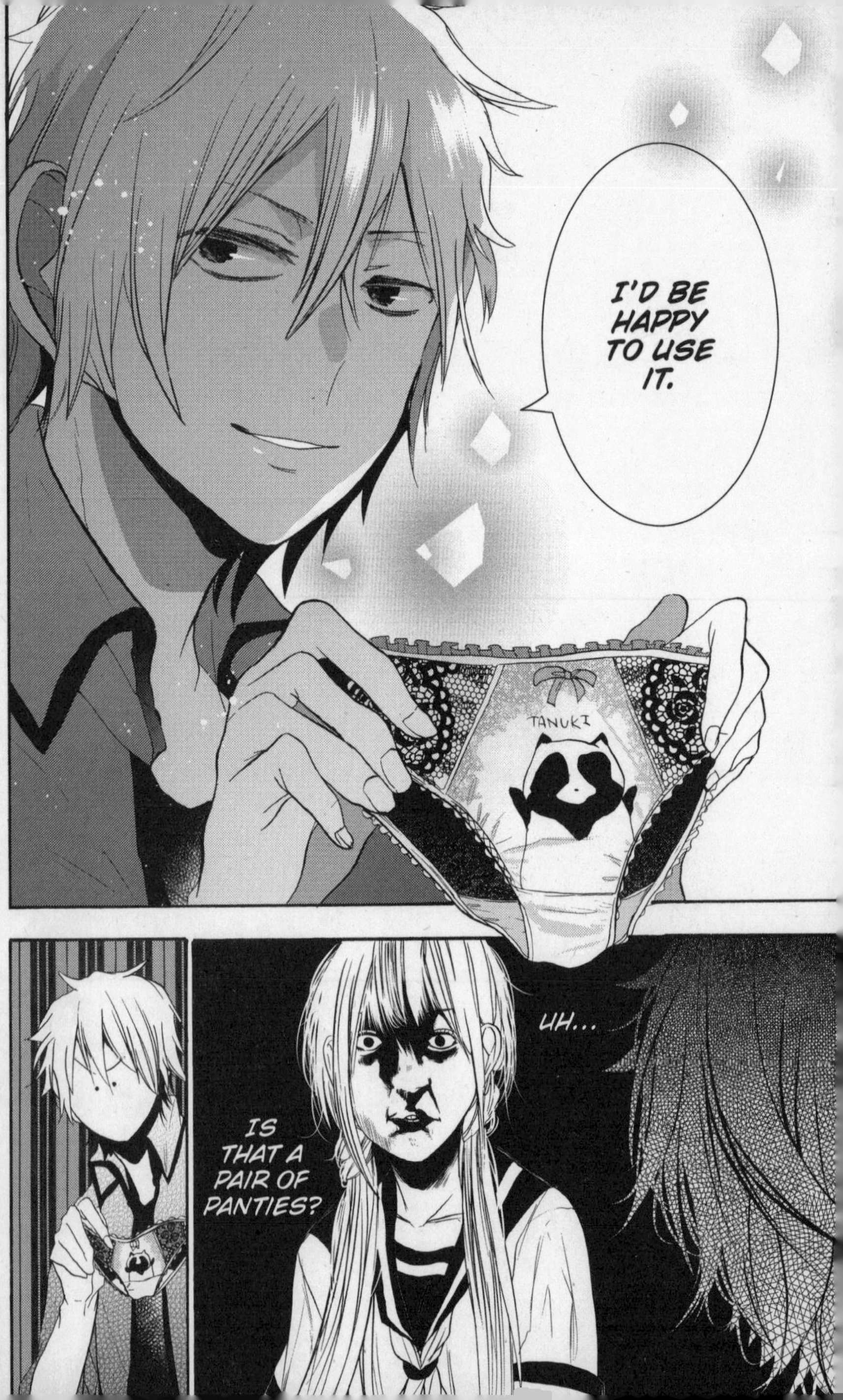
I'D BE HAPPY TO USE IT.
TANUKI
UH...
IS THAT A PAIR OF PANTIES?

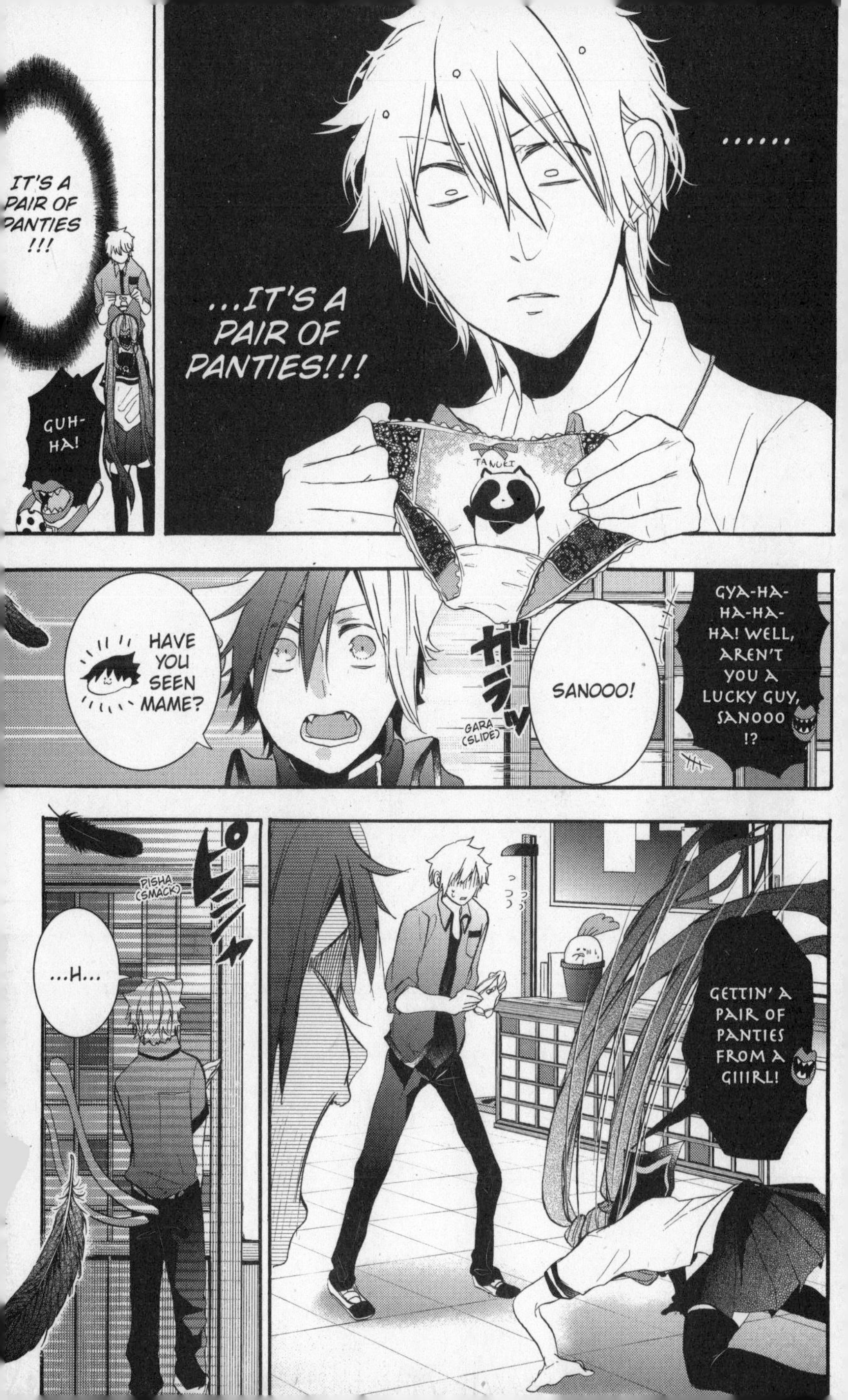
......
...IT'S A PAIR OF PANTIES!!!
TANUKI
IT'S A PAIR OF PANTIES !!!
GUH-HA!
GYA-HA-HA-HA! WELL, AREN'T YOU A LUCKY GUY, SANOOO !?
SANOOO!
GARA (SLIDE)
HAVE YOU SEEN MAME?
GETTIN' A PAIR OF PANTIES FROM A GIIIRL!
PISHA (SMACK)
...H...

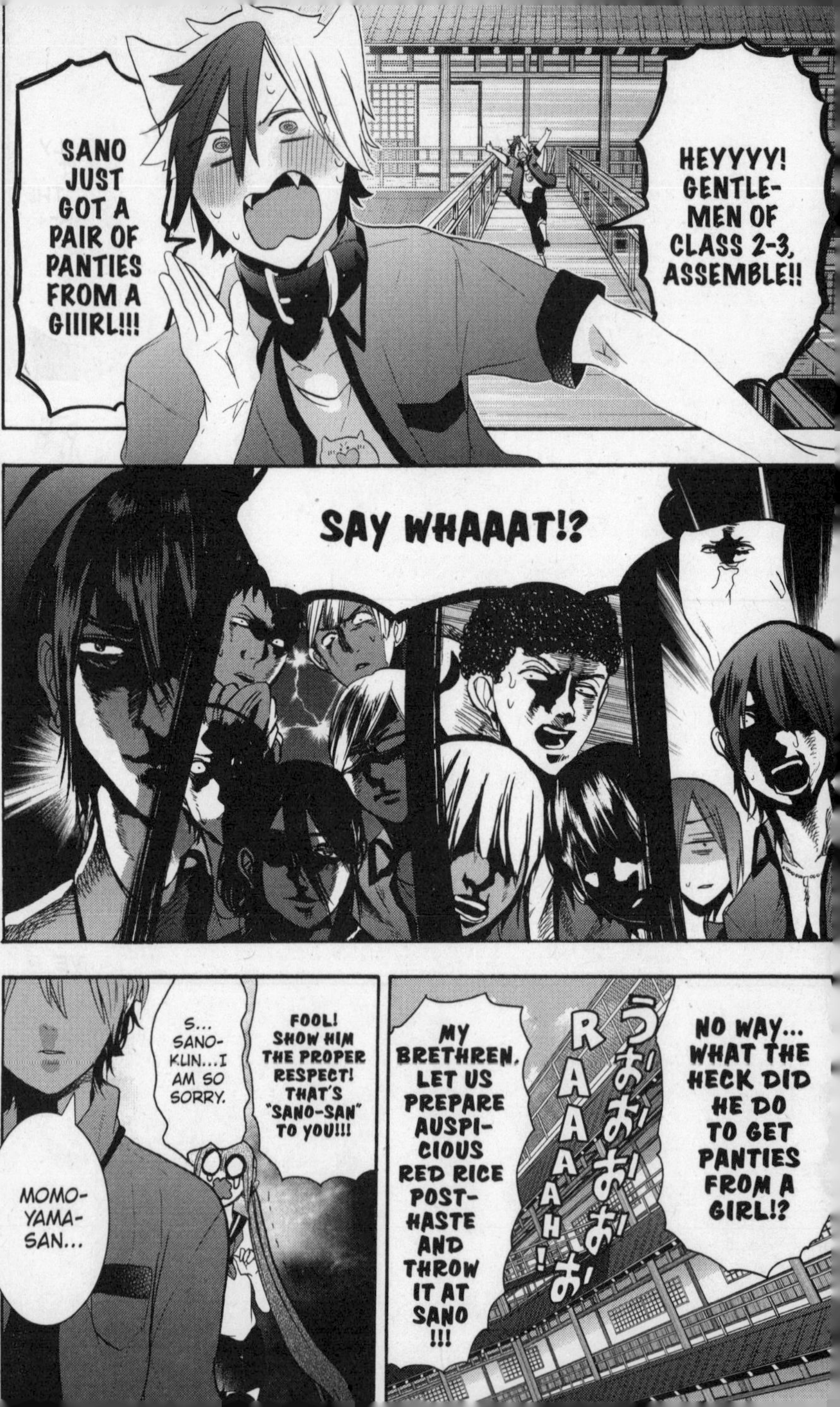
HEYYYY! GENTLEMEN OF CLASS 2-3, ASSEMBLE!!
SANO JUST GOT A PAIR OF PANTIES FROM A GIIIRL!!!
SAY WHAAAT!?
NO WAY... WHAT THE HECK DID HE DO TO GET PANTIES FROM A GIRL!?
うおおおお
RAAAAAH!
MY BRETHREN, LET US PREPARE AUSPICIOUS RED RICE POST-HASTE AND THROW IT AT SANO!!!
FOOL! SHOW HIM THE PROPER RESPECT! THAT'S "SANO-SAN" TO YOU!!!
S... SANO-KUN... I AM SO SORRY.
MOMO-YAMA-SAN...

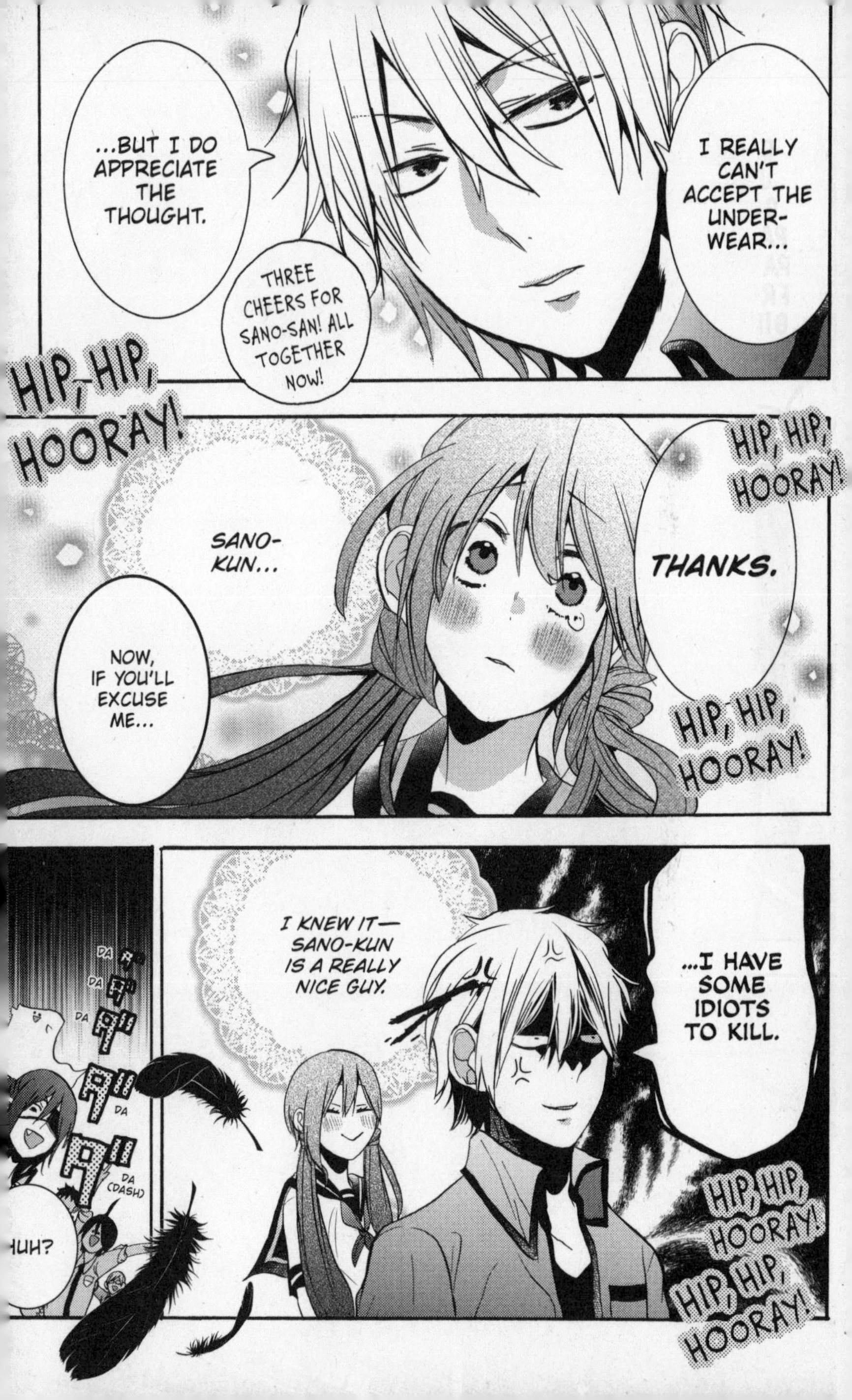
I REALLY CAN'T ACCEPT THE UNDER-WEAR...
...BUT I DO APPRECIATE THE THOUGHT.
THREE CHEERS FOR SANO-SAN! ALL TOGETHER NOW!
HIP, HIP, HOORAY!
HIP, HIP, HOORAY!
THANKS.
SANO-KUN...
NOW, IF YOU'LL EXCUSE ME...
HIP, HIP, HOORAY!
...I HAVE SOME IDIOTS TO KILL.
I KNEW IT—SANO-KUN IS A REALLY NICE GUY.
HIP, HIP, HOORAY!
HIP, HIP, HOORAY!
DA DA DA DA DA (DASH)
HUH?

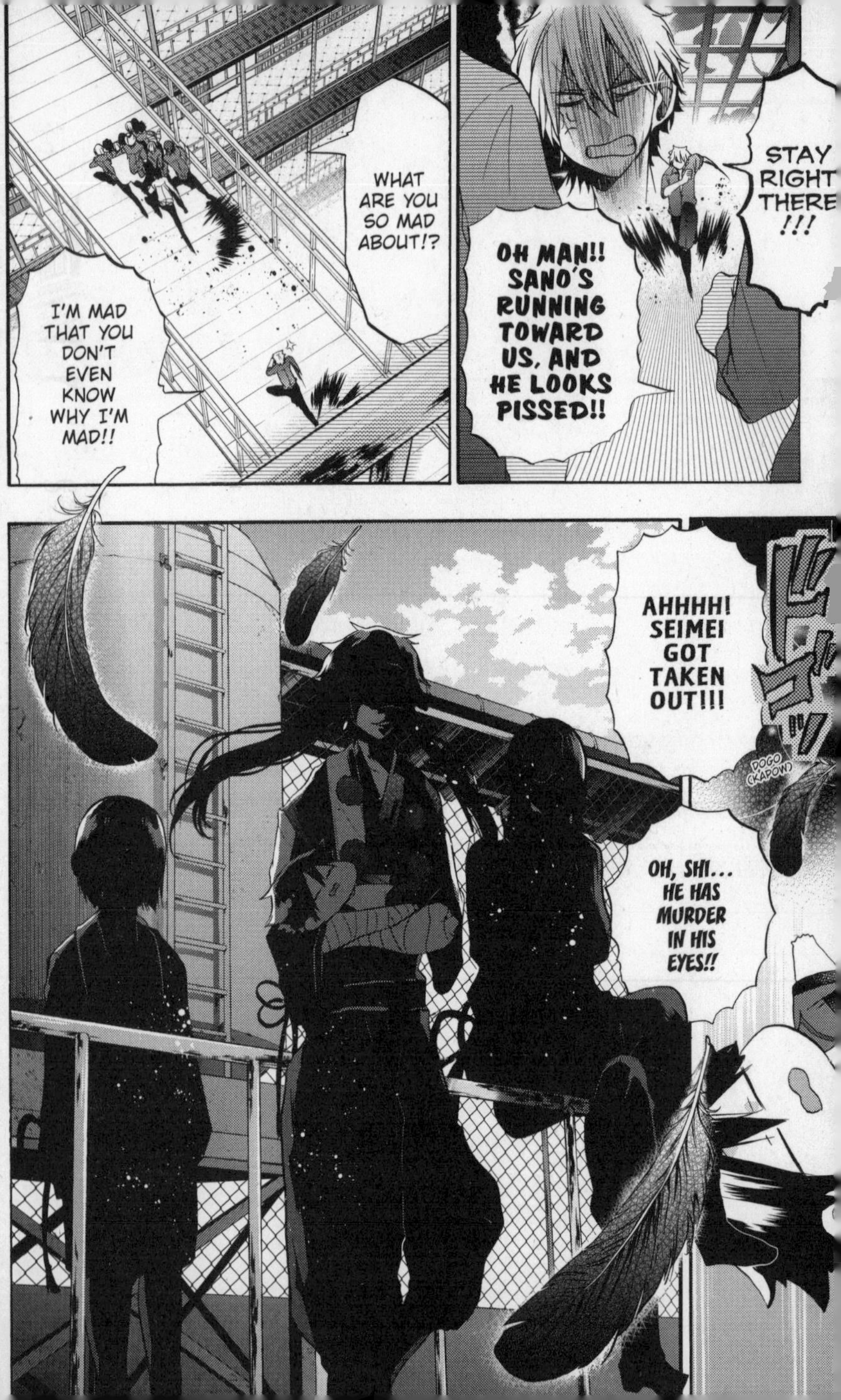
STAY RIGHT THERE!!!
OH MAN!! SANO'S RUNNING TOWARD US, AND HE LOOKS PISSED!!
WHAT ARE YOU SO MAD ABOUT!?
I'M MAD THAT YOU DON'T EVEN KNOW WHY I'M MAD!!
AHHHH! SEIMEI GOT TAKEN OUT!!!
DOGO (KAPOW)
OH, SHI... HE HAS MURDER IN HIS EYES!!

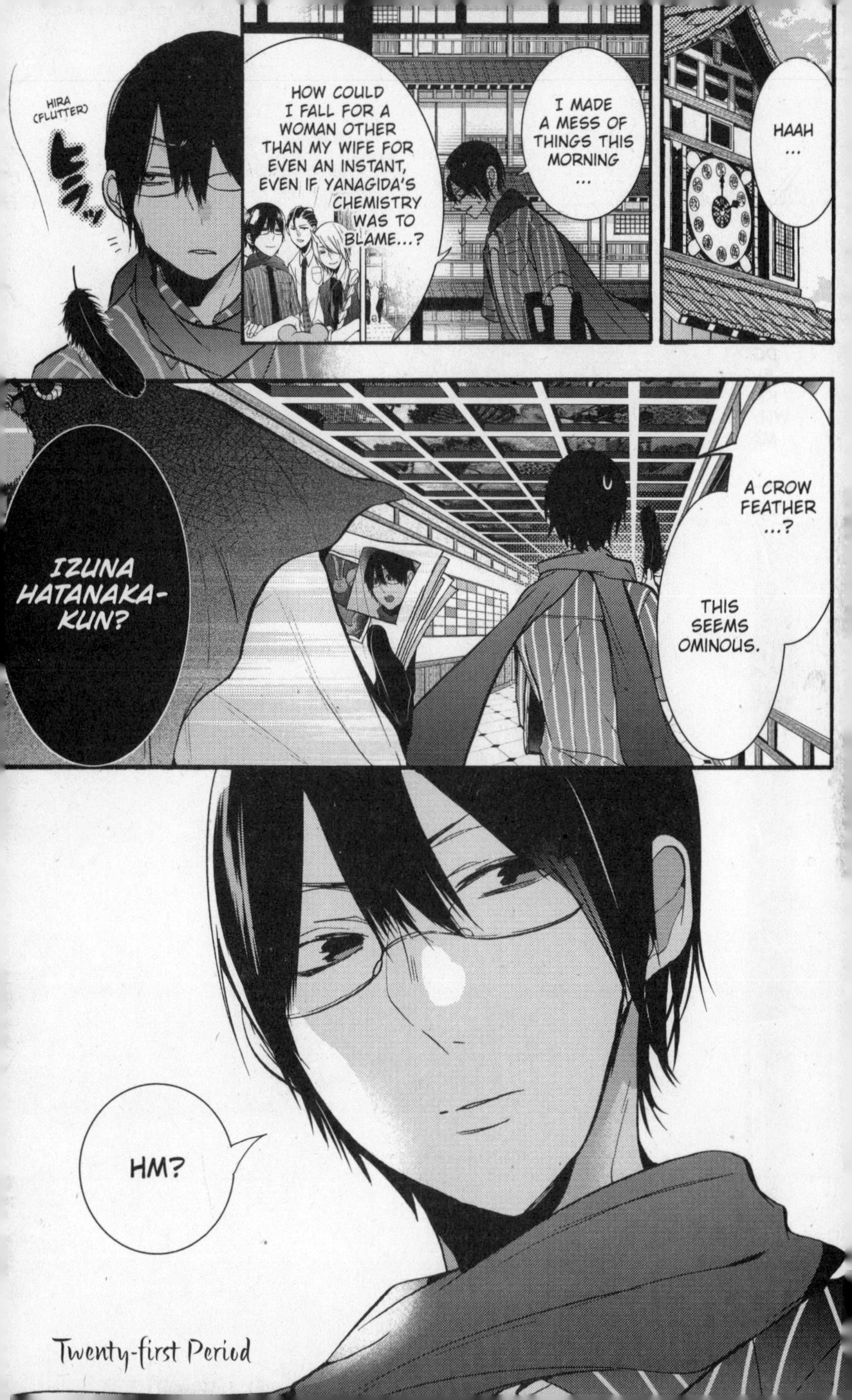
HAAH ...
I MADE A MESS OF THINGS THIS MORNING ...
HOW COULD I FALL FOR A WOMAN OTHER THAN MY WIFE FOR EVEN AN INSTANT, EVEN IF YANAGIDA'S CHEMISTRY WAS TO BLAME...?
HIRA (FLUTTER)
ヒラッ
A CROW FEATHER ...?
THIS SEEMS OMINOUS.
IZUNA HATANAKA-KUN?
HM?
Twenty-first Period

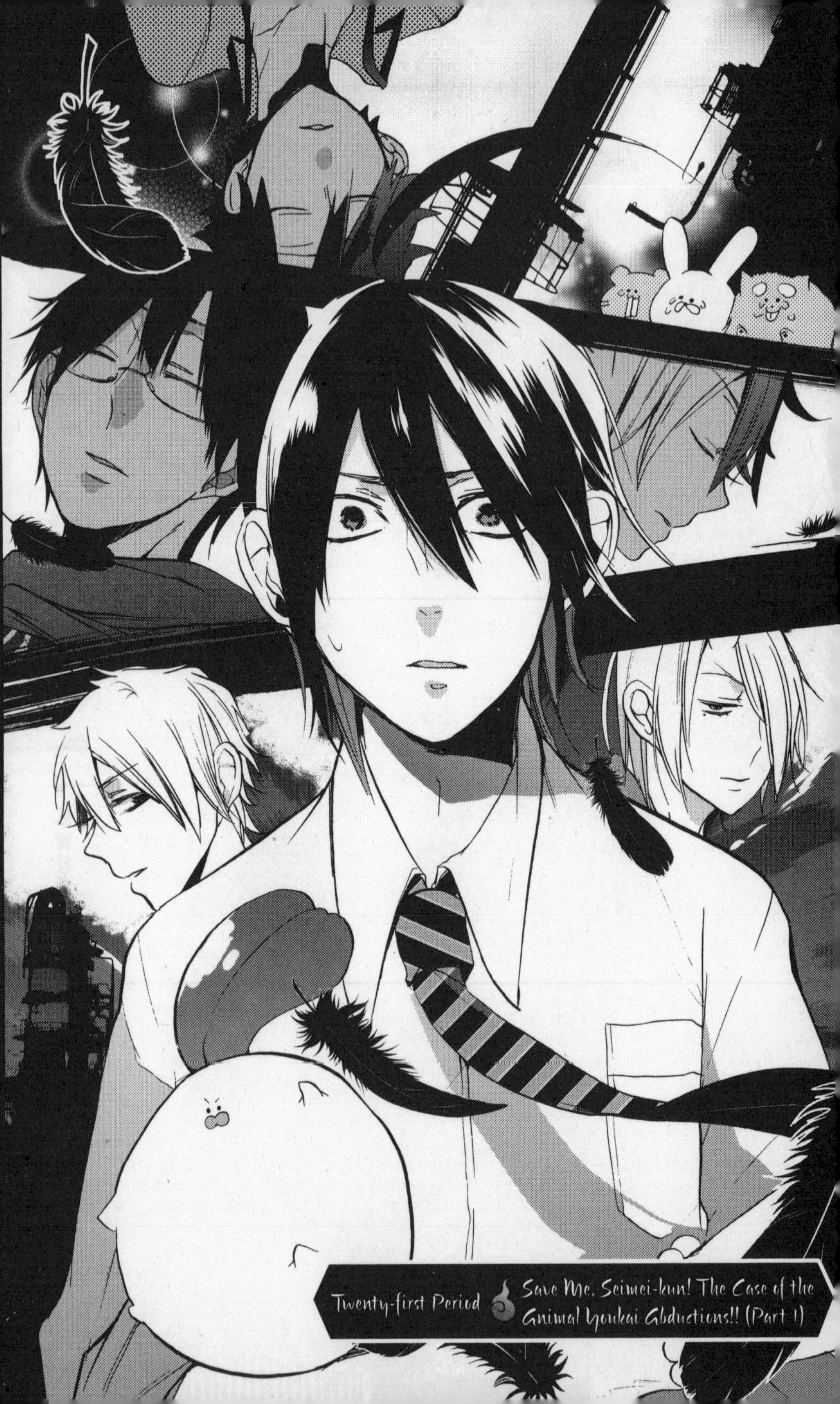
Twenty-first Period
Save Me, Seimei-kun! The Case of the Animal Youkai Abductions!! (Part 1)

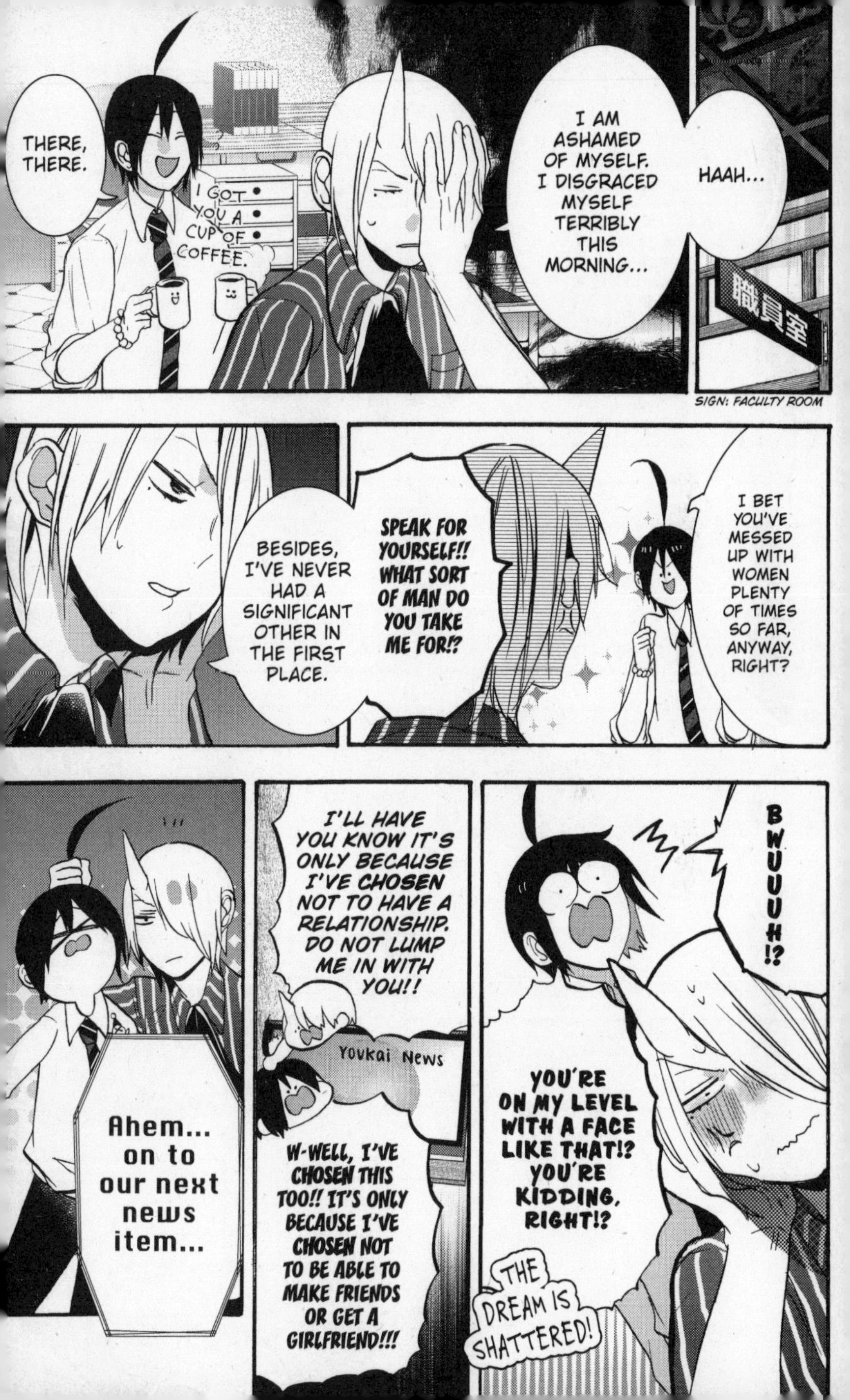
職員室
SIGN: FACULTY ROOM
HAAH...
I AM ASHAMED OF MYSELF. I DISGRACED MYSELF TERRIBLY THIS MORNING...
I GOT YOU A CUP OF COFFEE.
THERE, THERE.
I BET YOU'VE MESSED UP WITH WOMEN PLENTY OF TIMES SO FAR, ANYWAY, RIGHT?
SPEAK FOR YOURSELF!! WHAT SORT OF MAN DO YOU TAKE ME FOR!?
BESIDES, I'VE NEVER HAD A SIGNIFICANT OTHER IN THE FIRST PLACE.
BWUUUUH!?
YOU'RE ON MY LEVEL WITH A FACE LIKE THAT!? YOU'RE KIDDING, RIGHT!?
THE DREAM IS SHATTERED!
I'LL HAVE YOU KNOW IT'S ONLY BECAUSE I'VE CHOSEN NOT TO HAVE A RELATIONSHIP. DO NOT LUMP ME IN WITH YOU!!
Youkai News
W-WELL, I'VE CHOSEN THIS TOO!! IT'S ONLY BECAUSE I'VE CHOSEN NOT TO BE ABLE TO MAKE FRIENDS OR GET A GIRLFRIEND!!!
Ahem... on to our next news item...

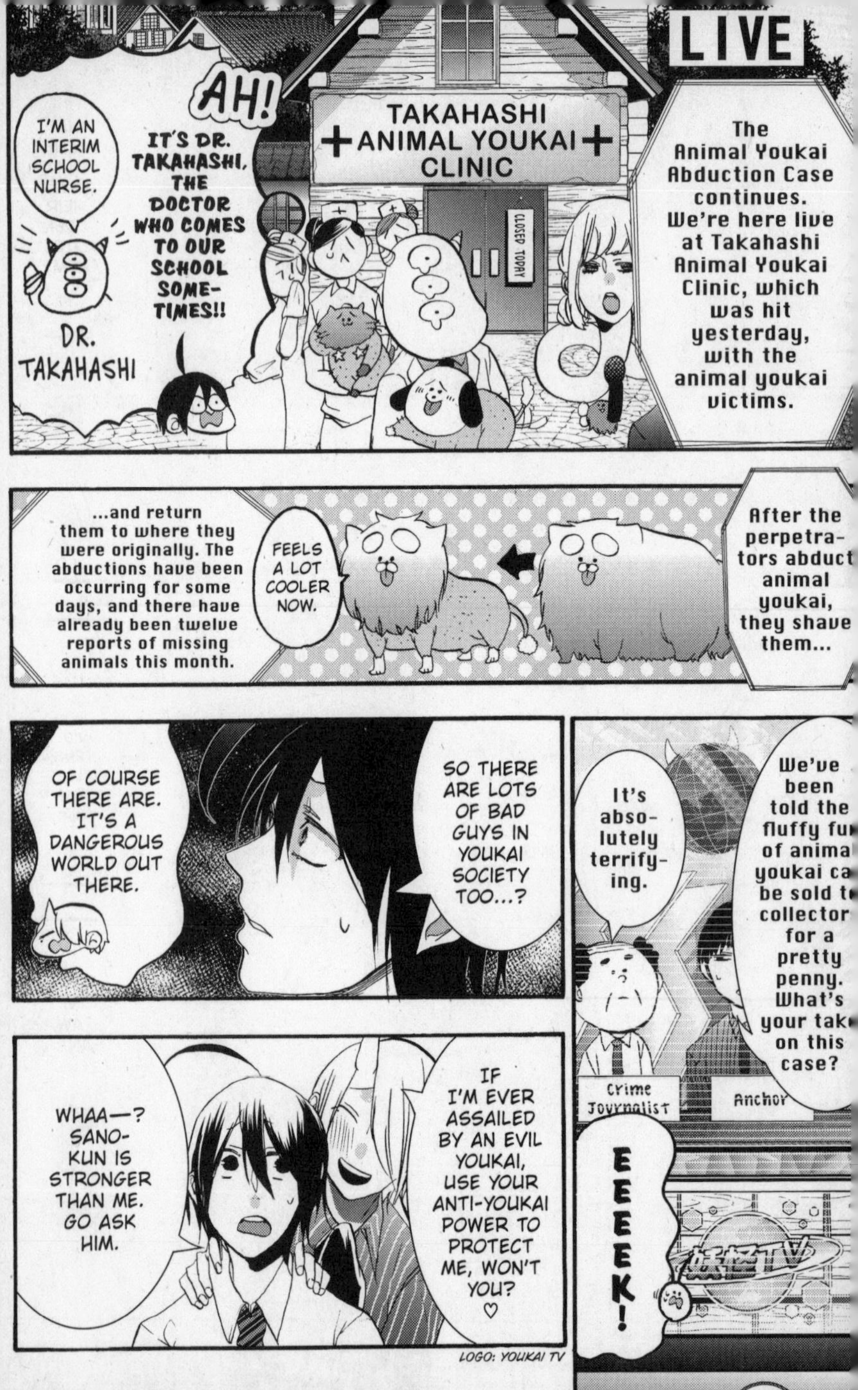
LIVE
The Animal Youkai Abduction Case continues. We're here live at Takahashi Animal Youkai Clinic, which was hit yesterday, with the animal youkai victims.
TAKAHASHI ANIMAL YOUKAI CLINIC
CLOSED TODAY
AH!
IT'S DR. TAKAHASHI, THE DOCTOR WHO COMES TO OUR SCHOOL SOME-TIMES!!
I'M AN INTERIM SCHOOL NURSE.
DR. TAKAHASHI
After the perpetra-tors abduct animal youkai, they shave them...
FEELS A LOT COOLER NOW.
...and return them to where they were originally. The abductions have been occurring for some days, and there have already been twelve reports of missing animals this month.
We've been told the fluffy fu of anima youkai ca be sold t collector for a pretty penny. What's your tak on this case?
It's abso-lutely terrify-ing.
Crime Journalist
Anchor
EEEEK!
SO THERE ARE LOTS OF BAD GUYS IN YOUKAI SOCIETY TOO...?
OF COURSE THERE ARE. IT'S A DANGEROUS WORLD OUT THERE.
IF I'M EVER ASSAILED BY AN EVIL YOUKAI, USE YOUR ANTI-YOUKAI POWER TO PROTECT ME, WON'T YOU? ♡
WHAA—? SANO-KUN IS STRONGER THAN ME. GO ASK HIM.

LOGO: YOUKAI TV

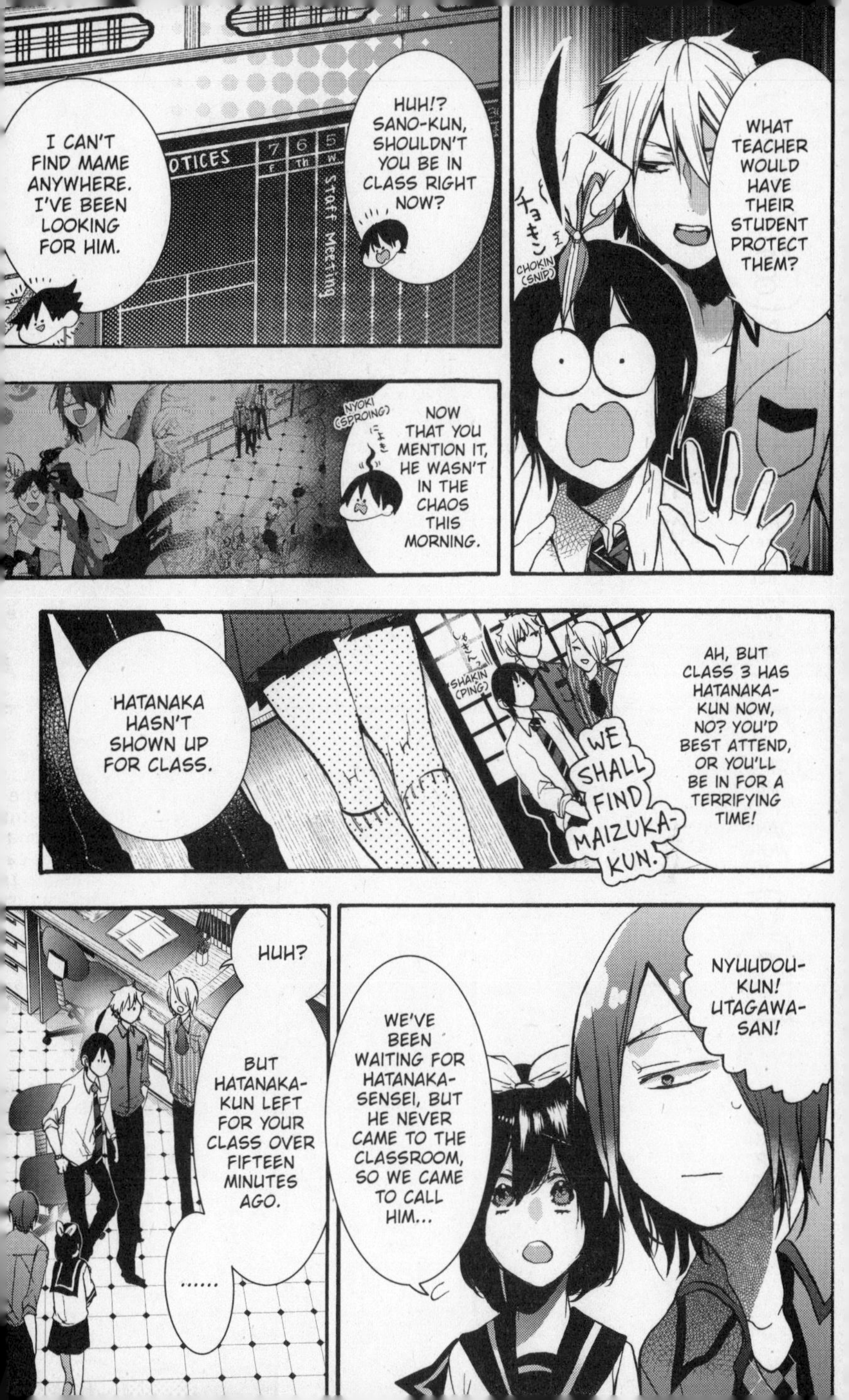
WHAT TEACHER WOULD HAVE THEIR STUDENT PROTECT THEM?
チョキン
CHOKIN (SNIP)
HUH!? SANO-KUN, SHOULDN'T YOU BE IN CLASS RIGHT NOW?
NOTICES
Staff Meeting
I CAN'T FIND MAME ANYWHERE. I'VE BEEN LOOKING FOR HIM.
NYOKI (SPROING)
にょき
NOW THAT YOU MENTION IT, HE WASN'T IN THE CHAOS THIS MORNING.
AH, BUT CLASS 3 HAS HATANAKA-KUN NOW, NO? YOU'D BEST ATTEND, OR YOU'LL BE IN FOR A TERRIFYING TIME!
WE SHALL FIND MAIZUKA-KUN!
しゃきーん
SHAKIN (PING)
HATANAKA HASN'T SHOWN UP FOR CLASS.
NYUUDOU-KUN! UTAGAWA-SAN!
WE'VE BEEN WAITING FOR HATANAKA-SENSEI, BUT HE NEVER CAME TO THE CLASSROOM, SO WE CAME TO CALL HIM...
HUH?
BUT HATANAKA-KUN LEFT FOR YOUR CLASS OVER FIFTEEN MINUTES AGO.
......

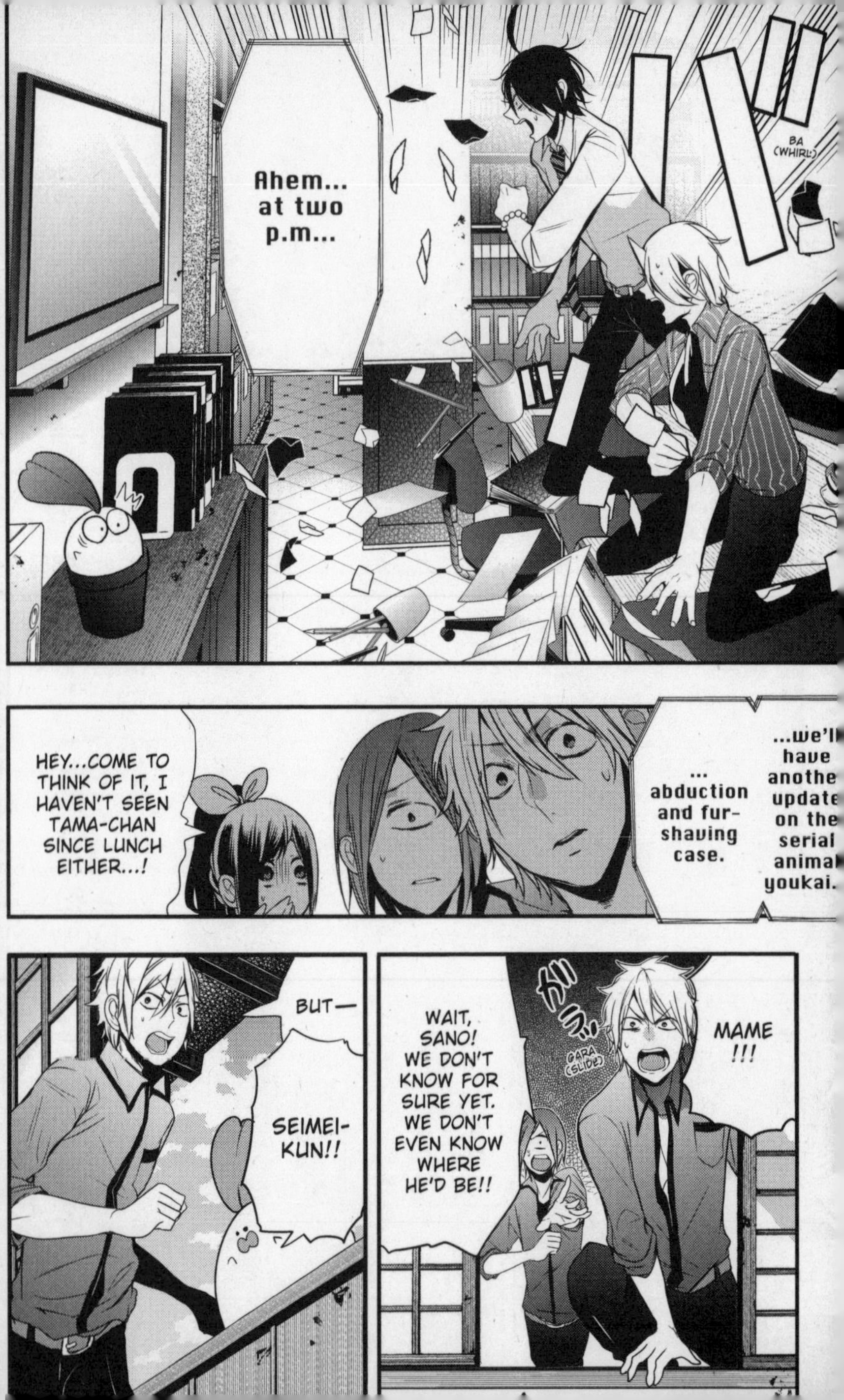

BA (WHIRL)
Ahem... at two p.m...
...we'l have anothe update on the serial anima youkai.
... abduction and fur-shaving case.
HEY...COME TO THINK OF IT, I HAVEN'T SEEN TAMA-CHAN SINCE LUNCH EITHER...!
MAME !!!
GARA (SLIDE)
WAIT, SANO! WE DON'T KNOW FOR SURE YET. WE DON'T EVEN KNOW WHERE HE'D BE!!
BUT—
SEIMEI-KUN!!

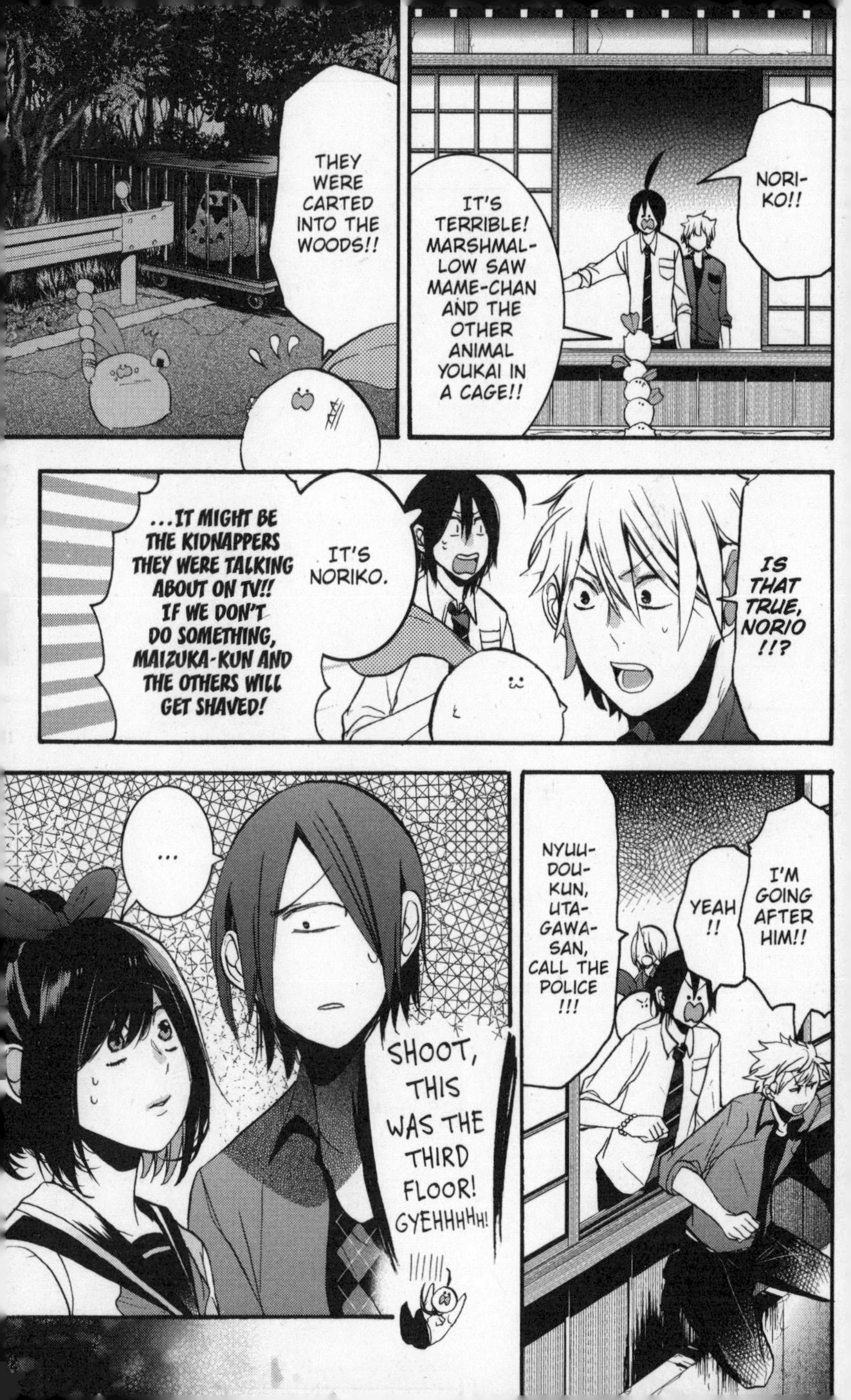
NORI-KO!!
IT'S TERRIBLE! MARSHMAL-LOW SAW MAME-CHAN AND THE OTHER ANIMAL YOUKAI IN A CAGE!!
THEY WERE CARTED INTO THE WOODS!!
IS THAT TRUE, NORIO!!?
IT'S NORIKO.
...IT MIGHT BE THE KIDNAPPERS THEY WERE TALKING ABOUT ON TV!! IF WE DON'T DO SOMETHING, MAIZUKA-KUN AND THE OTHERS WILL GET SHAVED!
I'M GOING AFTER HIM!!
YEAH!!
NYUU-DOU-KUN, UTA-GAWA-SAN, CALL THE POLICE!!!
...
SHOOT, THIS WAS THE THIRD FLOOR! GYEHHHHH!

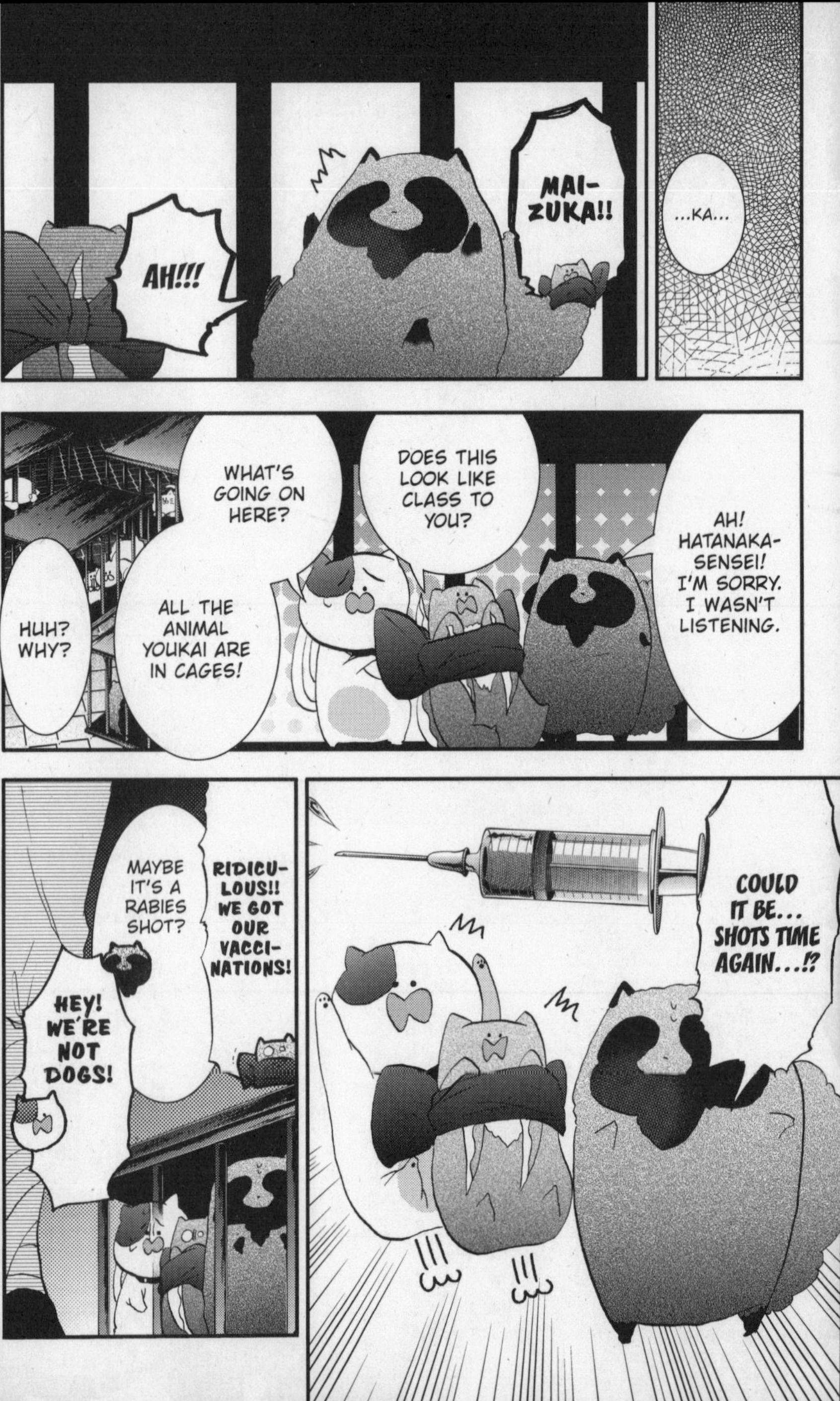
...KA...
MAI-ZUKA!!
AH!!!
AH! HATANAKA-SENSEI! I'M SORRY. I WASN'T LISTENING.
DOES THIS LOOK LIKE CLASS TO YOU?
WHAT'S GOING ON HERE?
ALL THE ANIMAL YOUKAI ARE IN CAGES!
HUH? WHY?
COULD IT BE... SHOTS TIME AGAIN...!?
MAYBE IT'S A RABIES SHOT?
RIDICU-LOUS!! WE GOT OUR VACCI-NATIONS!
HEY! WE'RE NOT DOGS!

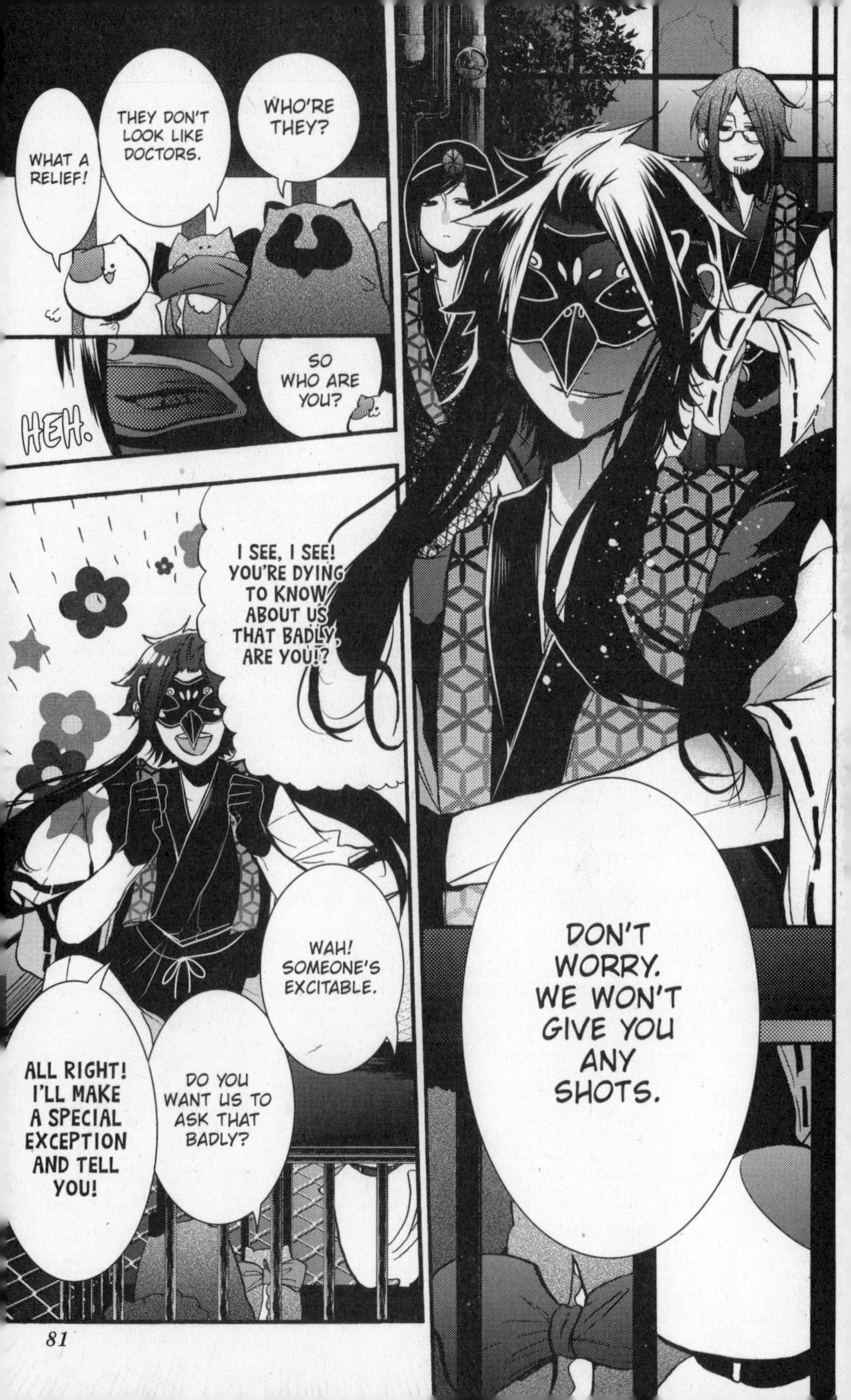
DON'T WORRY. WE WON'T GIVE YOU ANY SHOTS.
WHO'RE THEY?
THEY DON'T LOOK LIKE DOCTORS.
WHAT A RELIEF!
SO WHO ARE YOU?
HEH.
I SEE, I SEE! YOU'RE DYING TO KNOW ABOUT US THAT BADLY, ARE YOU!?
WAH! SOMEONE'S EXCITABLE.
DO YOU WANT US TO ASK THAT BADLY?
ALL RIGHT! I'LL MAKE A SPECIAL EXCEPTION AND TELL YOU!

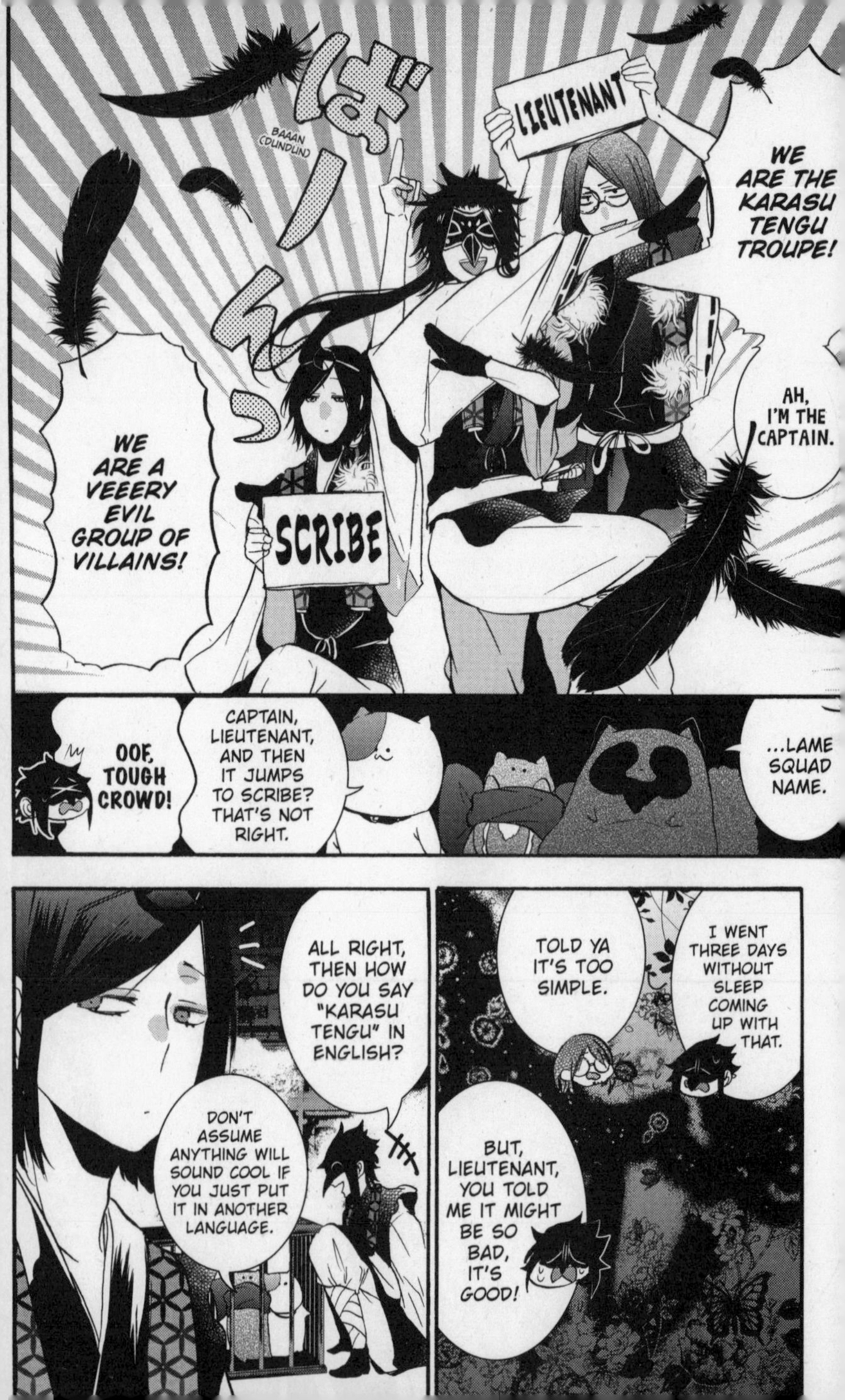
WE ARE THE KARASU TENGU TROUPE!
AH, I'M THE CAPTAIN.
LIEUTENANT
BAAAN (DUNDUN)
SCRIBE
WE ARE A VEEERY EVIL GROUP OF VILLAINS!
...LAME SQUAD NAME.
CAPTAIN, LIEUTENANT, AND THEN IT JUMPS TO SCRIBE? THAT'S NOT RIGHT.
OOF, TOUGH CROWD!
I WENT THREE DAYS WITHOUT SLEEP COMING UP WITH THAT.
TOLD YA IT'S TOO SIMPLE.
BUT, LIEUTENANT, YOU TOLD ME IT MIGHT BE SO BAD, IT'S GOOD!
ALL RIGHT, THEN HOW DO YOU SAY "KARASU TENGU" IN ENGLISH?
DON'T ASSUME ANYTHING WILL SOUND COOL IF YOU JUST PUT IT IN ANOTHER LANGUAGE.

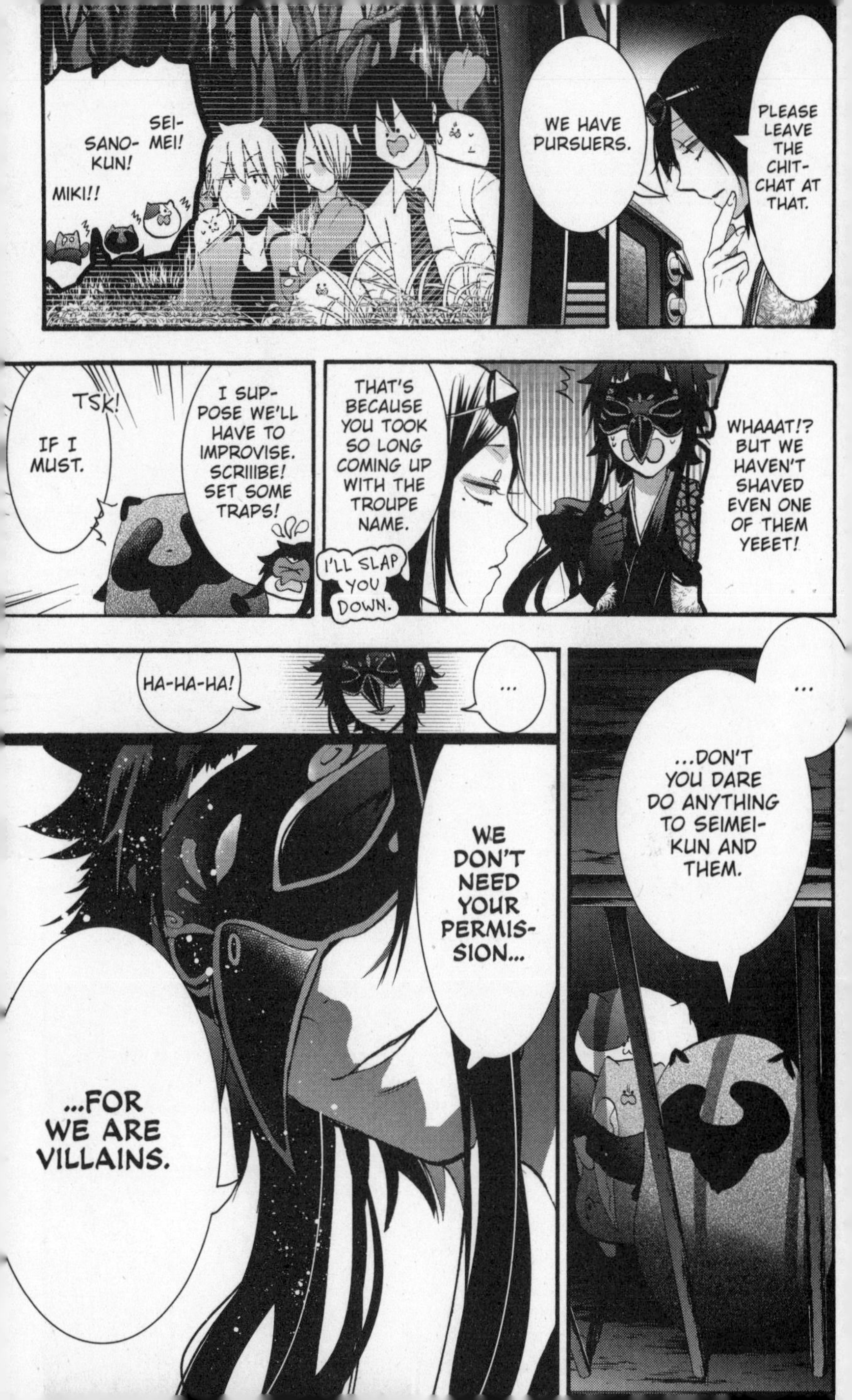
PLEASE LEAVE THE CHIT-CHAT AT THAT.
WE HAVE PURSUERS.
SEI-MEI!
SANO-KUN!
MIKI!!
WHAAAT!? BUT WE HAVEN'T SHAVED EVEN ONE OF THEM YEEET!
THAT'S BECAUSE YOU TOOK SO LONG COMING UP WITH THE TROUPE NAME.
I'LL SLAP YOU DOWN.
I SUPPOSE WE'LL HAVE TO IMPROVISE. SCRIIIBE! SET SOME TRAPS!
TSK!
IF I MUST.
...
...DON'T YOU DARE DO ANYTHING TO SEIMEI-KUN AND THEM.
...
HA-HA-HA!
WE DON'T NEED YOUR PERMISSION...
...FOR WE ARE VILLAINS.

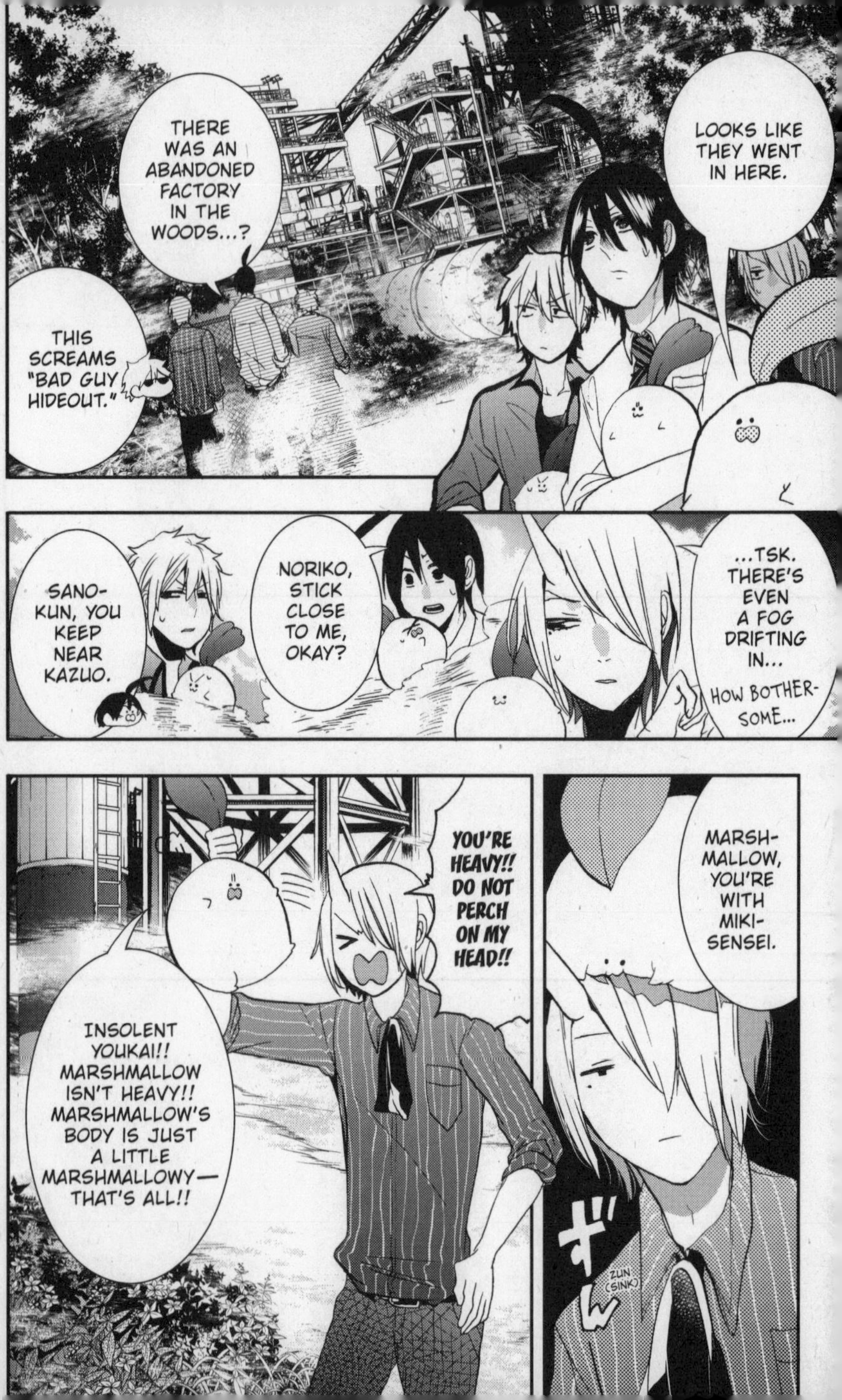
LOOKS LIKE THEY WENT IN HERE.
THERE WAS AN ABANDONED FACTORY IN THE WOODS...?
THIS SCREAMS "BAD GUY HIDEOUT."
...TSK. THERE'S EVEN A FOG DRIFTING IN...
HOW BOTHERSOME...
NORIKO, STICK CLOSE TO ME, OKAY?
SANO-KUN, YOU KEEP NEAR KAZUO.
MARSHMALLOW, YOU'RE WITH MIKI-SENSEI.
ZUN (SINK)
YOU'RE HEAVY!! DO NOT PERCH ON MY HEAD!!
INSOLENT YOUKAI!! MARSHMALLOW ISN'T HEAVY!! MARSHMALLOW'S BODY IS JUST A LITTLE MARSHMALLOWY—THAT'S ALL!!

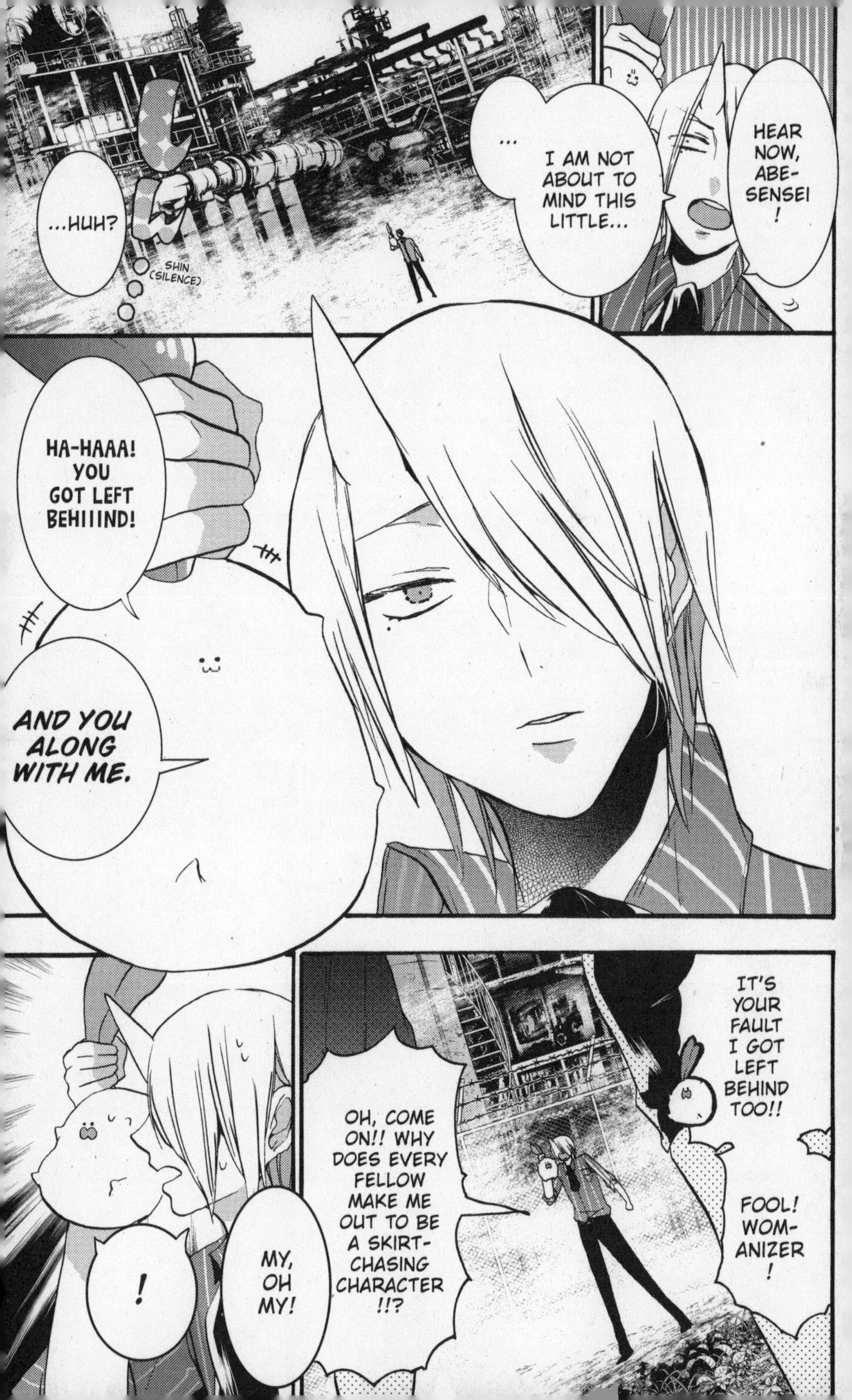
HEAR NOW, ABE-SENSEI!
I AM NOT ABOUT TO MIND THIS LITTLE...
...
...HUH?
SHIN (SILENCE)
HA-HAAA! YOU GOT LEFT BEHIIIND!
AND YOU ALONG WITH ME.
IT'S YOUR FAULT I GOT LEFT BEHIND TOO!!
FOOL! WOM-ANIZER!
OH, COME ON!! WHY DOES EVERY FELLOW MAKE ME OUT TO BE A SKIRT-CHASING CHARACTER!!?
MY, OH MY!
!

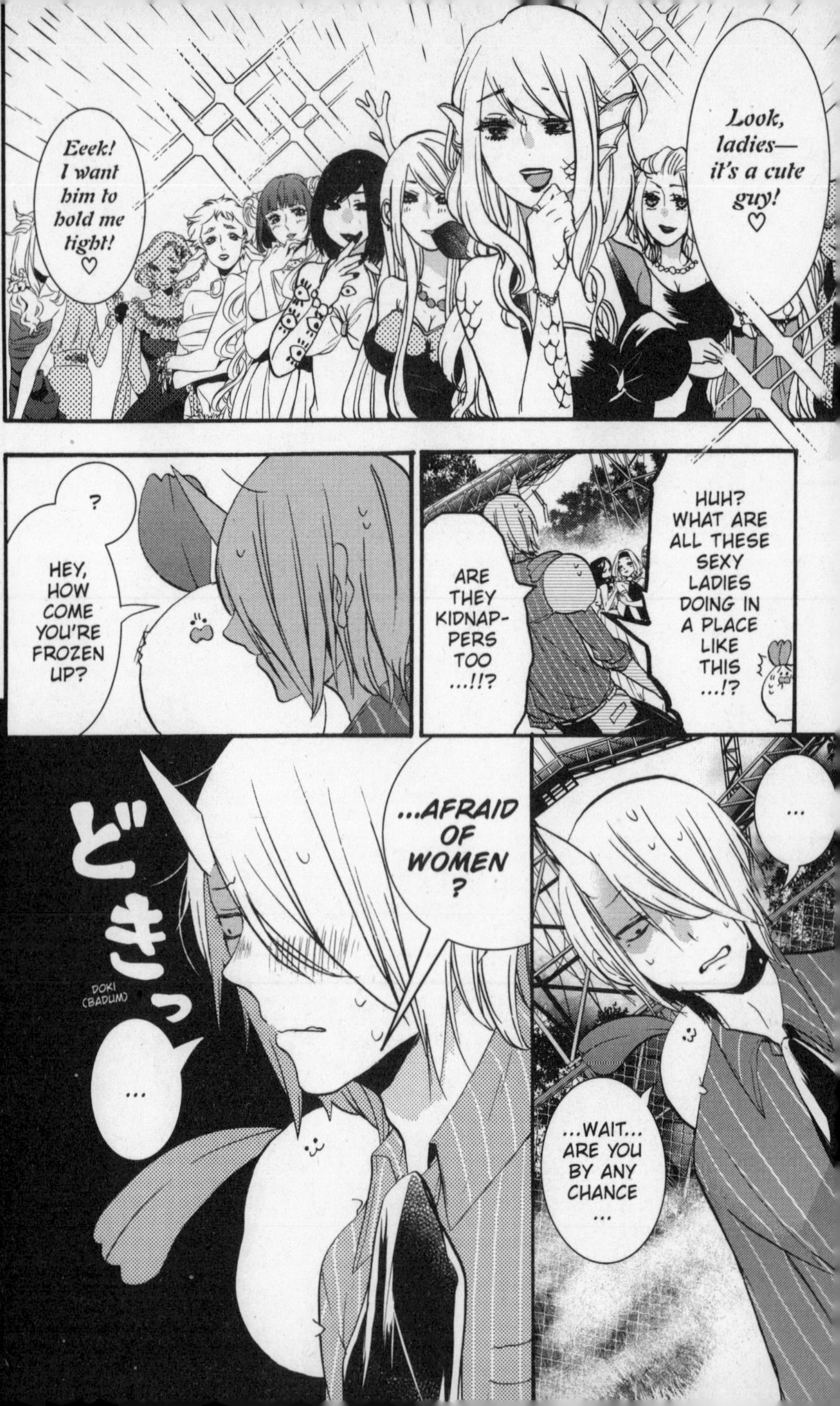
Look, ladies—it's a cute guy! ♡
Eeek! I want him to hold me tight! ♡
HUH? WHAT ARE ALL THESE SEXY LADIES DOING IN A PLACE LIKE THIS ...!?
ARE THEY KIDNAP-PERS TOO ...!!?
?
HEY, HOW COME YOU'RE FROZEN UP?
...
...WAIT... ARE YOU BY ANY CHANCE ...
...AFRAID OF WOMEN ?
どきっ
DOKI (BADUM)
...

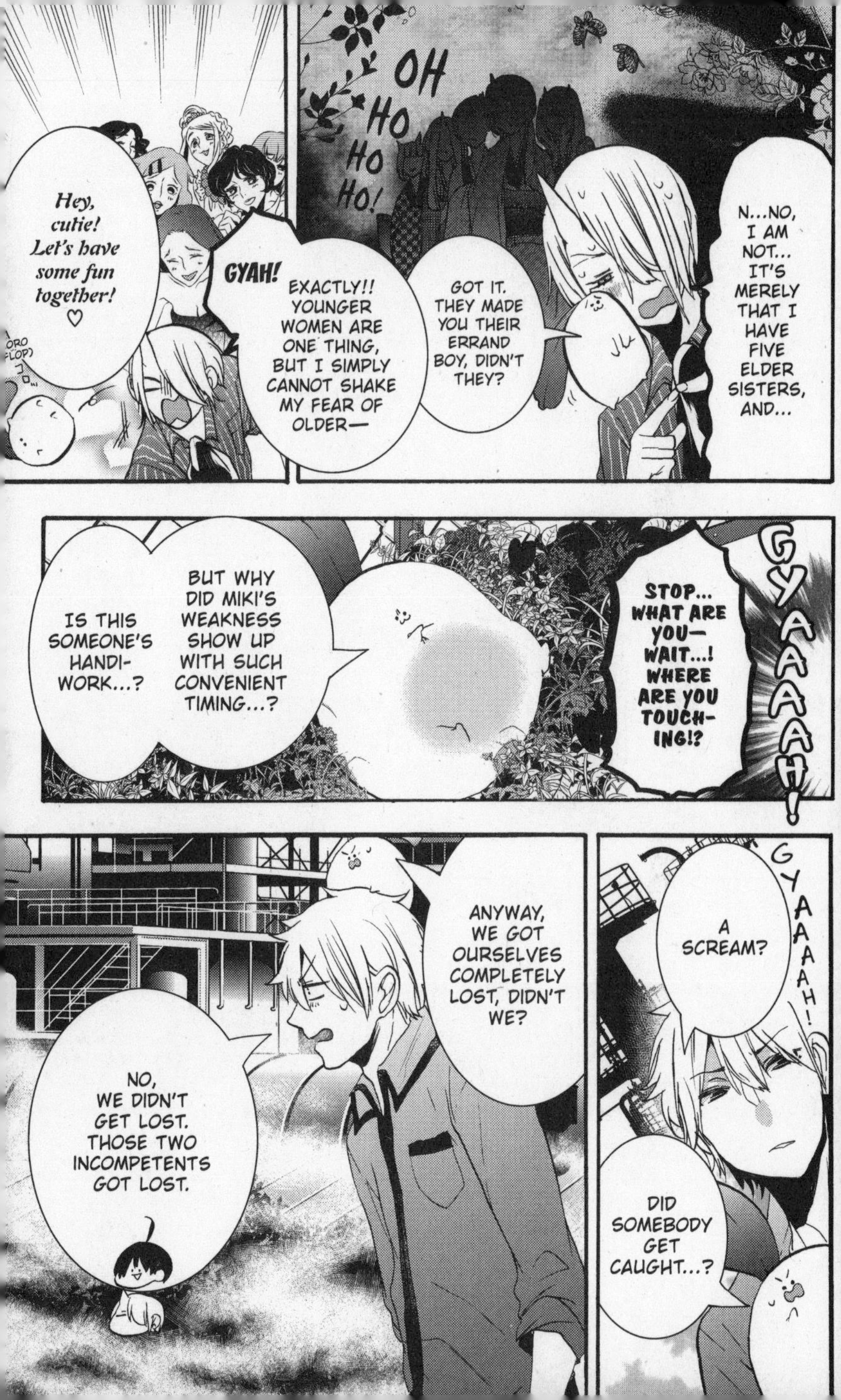
N...NO, I AM NOT... IT'S MERELY THAT I HAVE FIVE ELDER SISTERS, AND...
OH HO HO HO!
GOT IT. THEY MADE YOU THEIR ERRAND BOY, DIDN'T THEY?
EXACTLY!! YOUNGER WOMEN ARE ONE THING, BUT I SIMPLY CANNOT SHAKE MY FEAR OF OLDER—
GYAH!
Hey, cutie! Let's have some fun together! ♡
GYAAAAAH!
STOP... WHAT ARE YOU— WAIT...! WHERE ARE YOU TOUCHING!?
BUT WHY DID MIKI'S WEAKNESS SHOW UP WITH SUCH CONVENIENT TIMING...?
IS THIS SOMEONE'S HANDIWORK...?
GYAAAAAH!
A SCREAM?
DID SOMEBODY GET CAUGHT...?
ANYWAY, WE GOT OURSELVES COMPLETELY LOST, DIDN'T WE?
NO, WE DIDN'T GET LOST. THOSE TWO INCOMPETENTS GOT LOST.

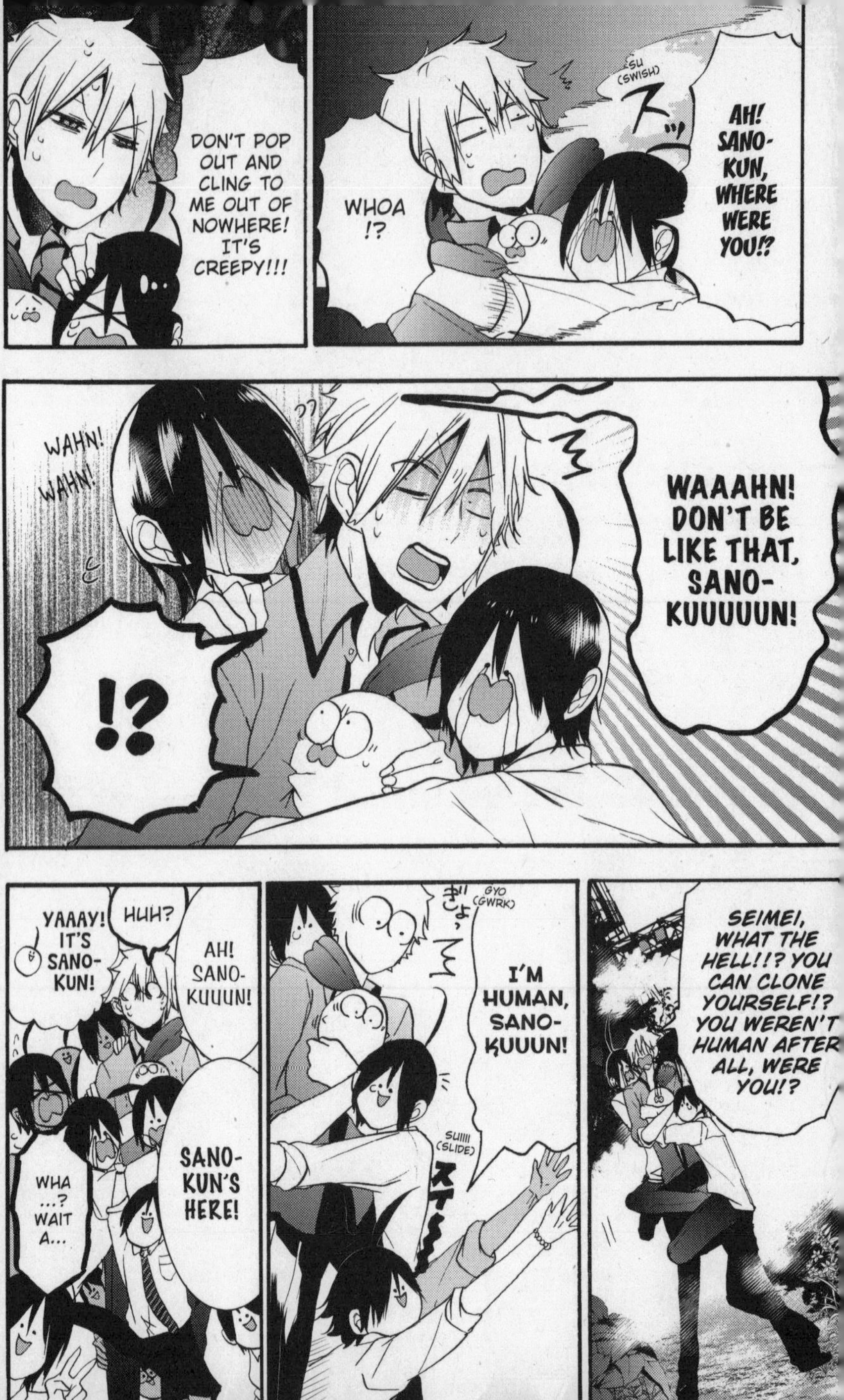
SU (SWISH)
AH! SANO-KUN, WHERE WERE YOU!?
WHOA !?
DON'T POP OUT AND CLING TO ME OUT OF NOWHERE! IT'S CREEPY!!!
WAAAHN! DON'T BE LIKE THAT, SANO-KUUUUUN!
WAHN! WAHN!
!?
SEIMEI, WHAT THE HELL!!? YOU CAN CLONE YOURSELF!? YOU WEREN'T HUMAN AFTER ALL, WERE YOU!?
GYO (GWRK)
I'M HUMAN, SANO-KUUUN!
SUIIII (SLIDE)
HUH?
AH! SANO-KUUUN!
YAAAY! IT'S SANO-KUN!
SANO-KUN'S HERE!
WHA ...? WAIT A...

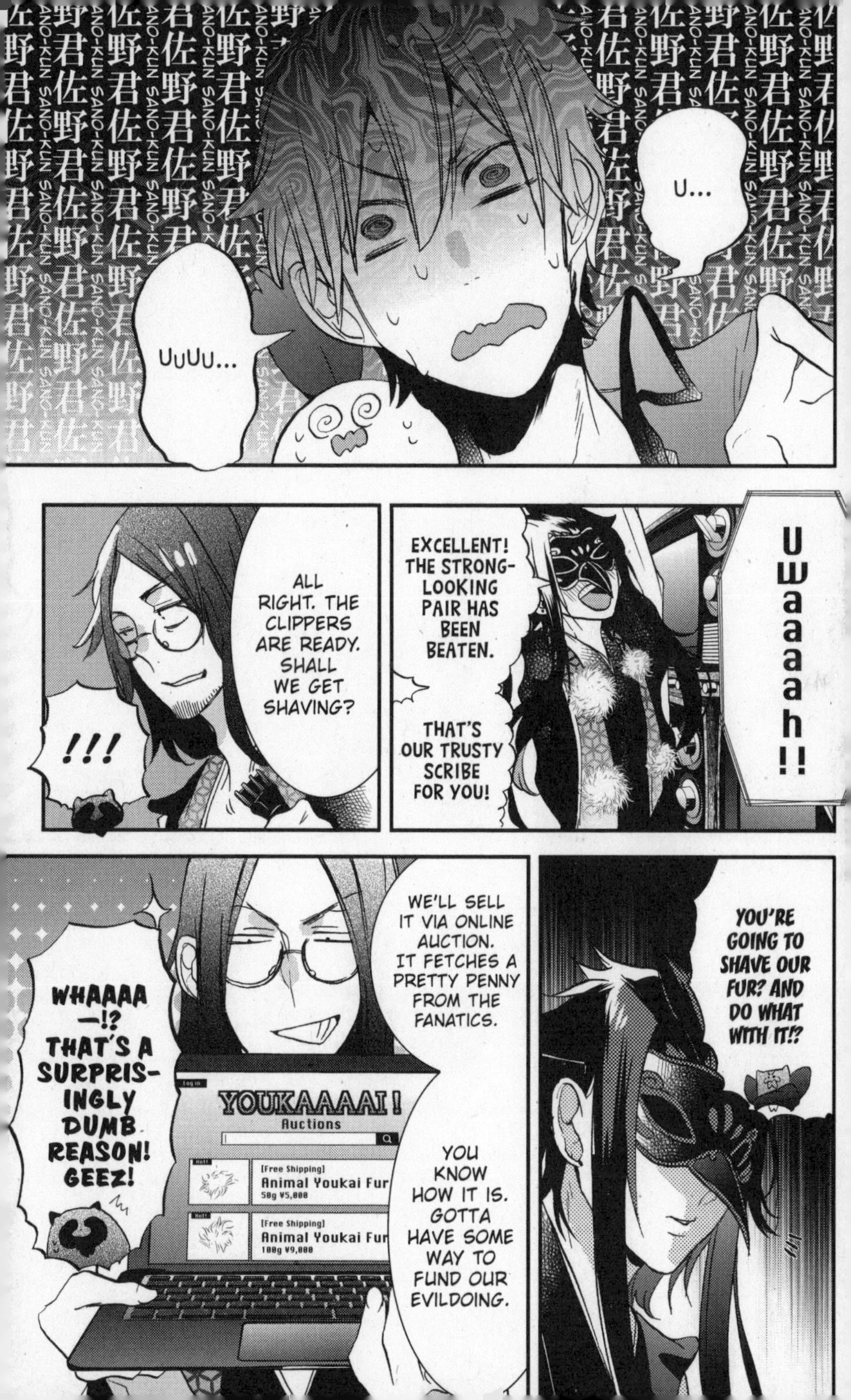

U...
UUUU...
Uwaaaah!!
EXCELLENT! THE STRONG-LOOKING PAIR HAS BEEN BEATEN.
THAT'S OUR TRUSTY SCRIBE FOR YOU!
ALL RIGHT. THE CLIPPERS ARE READY. SHALL WE GET SHAVING?
!!!
YOU'RE GOING TO SHAVE OUR FUR? AND DO WHAT WITH IT!?
WE'LL SELL IT VIA ONLINE AUCTION. IT FETCHES A PRETTY PENNY FROM THE FANATICS.
YOU KNOW HOW IT IS. GOTTA HAVE SOME WAY TO FUND OUR EVILDOING.
WHAAAA—!? THAT'S A SURPRISINGLY DUMB REASON! GEEZ!
Log in
YOUKAAAAI!
Auctions
[Free Shipping]
Animal Youkai Fur
50g ¥5,000
[Free Shipping]
Animal Youkai Fur
100g ¥9,000

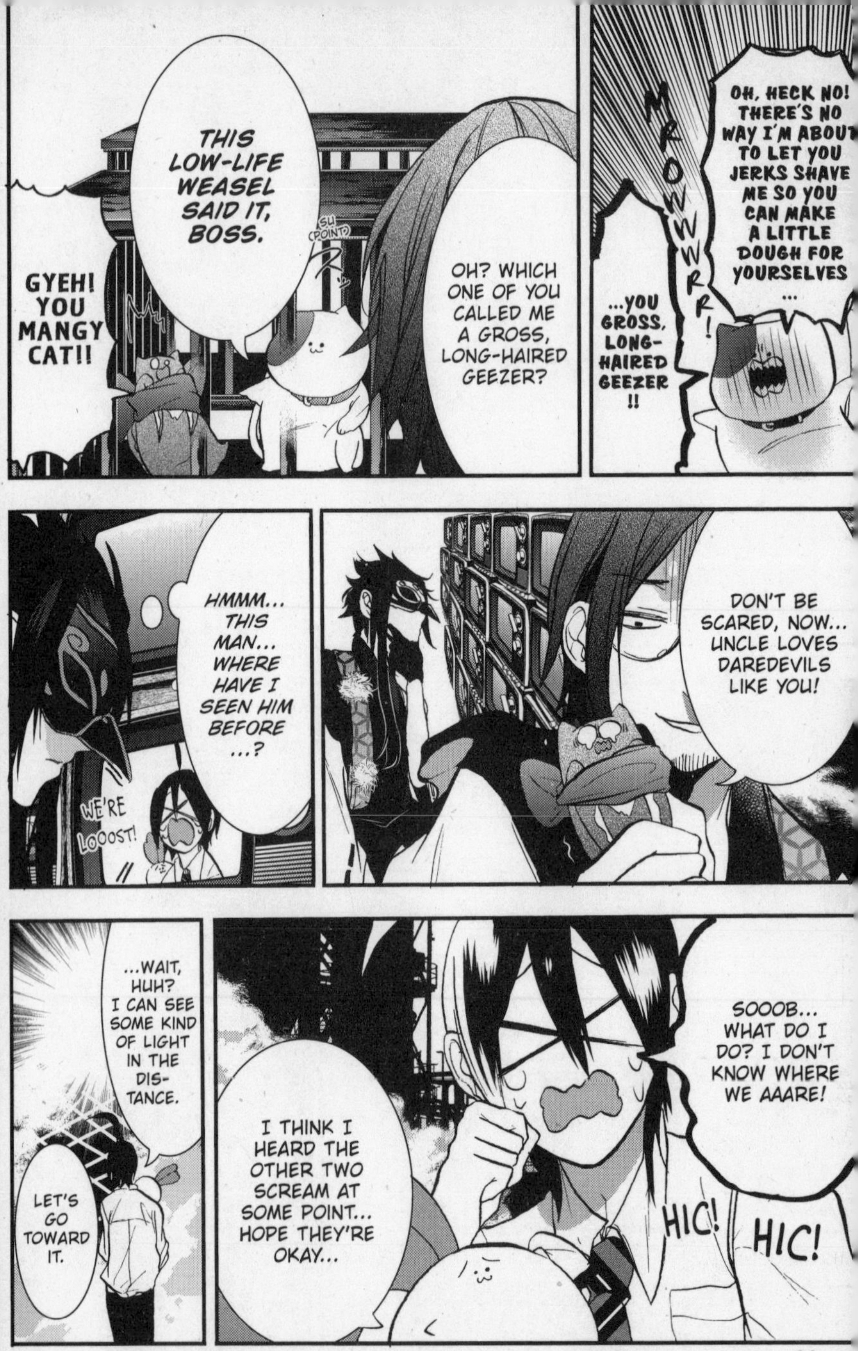
OH, HECK NO! THERE'S NO WAY I'M ABOUT TO LET YOU JERKS SHAVE ME SO YOU CAN MAKE A LITTLE DOUGH FOR YOURSELVES ...
MROWWWRR!
...YOU GROSS, LONG-HAIRED GEEZER !!
OH? WHICH ONE OF YOU CALLED ME A GROSS, LONG-HAIRED GEEZER?
THIS LOW-LIFE WEASEL SAID IT, BOSS.
SU (POINT)
GYEH! YOU MANGY CAT!!
DON'T BE SCARED, NOW... UNCLE LOVES DAREDEVILS LIKE YOU!
HMMM... THIS MAN... WHERE HAVE I SEEN HIM BEFORE ...?
WE'RE LOOOST!
SOOOB... WHAT DO I DO? I DON'T KNOW WHERE WE AAARE!
HIC!
HIC!
I THINK I HEARD THE OTHER TWO SCREAM AT SOME POINT... HOPE THEY'RE OKAY...
...WAIT, HUH? I CAN SEE SOME KIND OF LIGHT IN THE DIS-TANCE.
LET'S GO TOWARD IT.

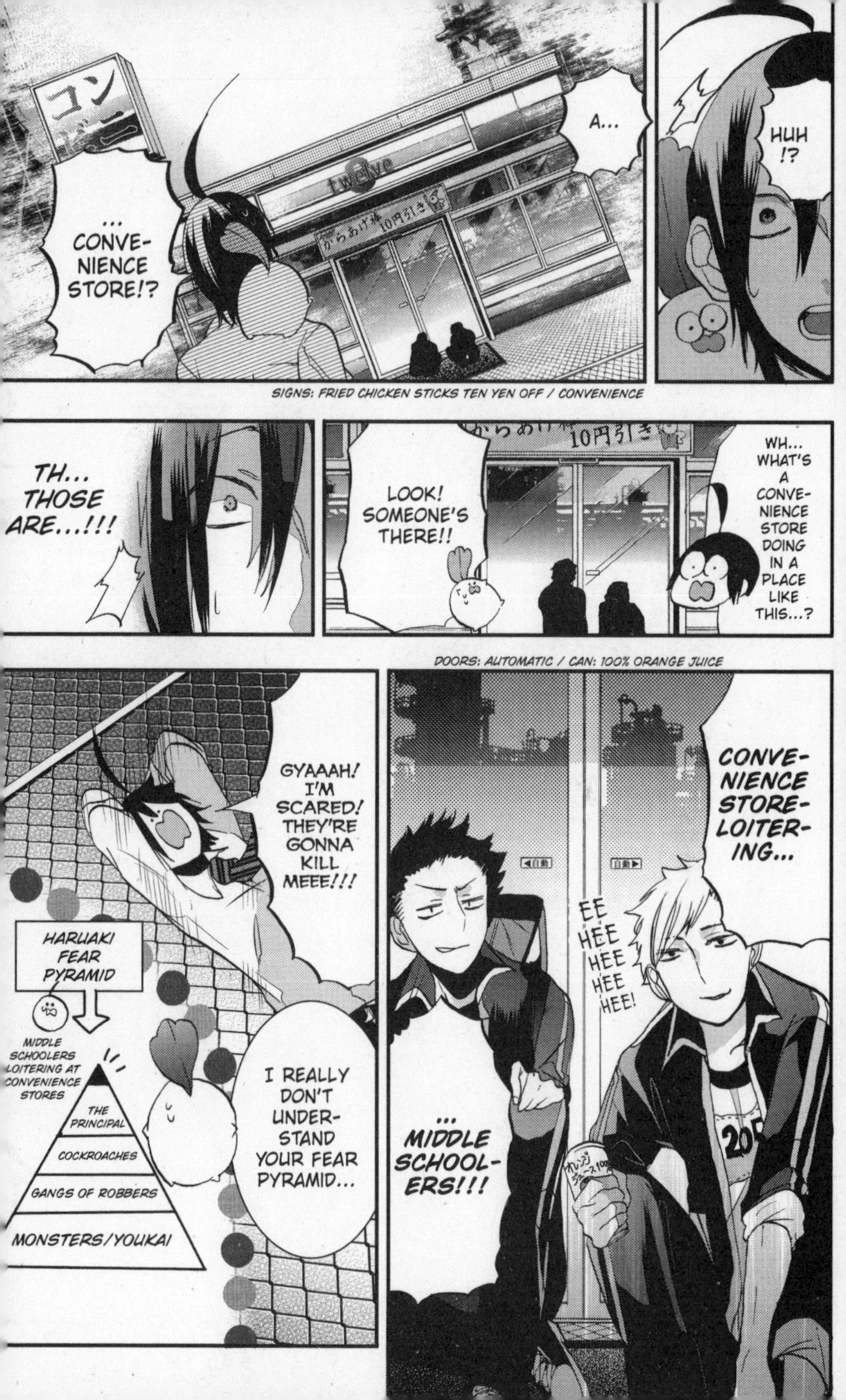
HUH!?
A...
...CONVENIENCE STORE!?
SIGNS: FRIED CHICKEN STICKS TEN YEN OFF / CONVENIENCE
WH... WHAT'S A CONVENIENCE STORE DOING IN A PLACE LIKE THIS...?
LOOK! SOMEONE'S THERE!!
TH... THOSE ARE...!!!
DOORS: AUTOMATIC / CAN: 100% ORANGE JUICE
CONVENIENCE STORE-LOITERING...
EE HEE HEE HEE HEE!
...MIDDLE SCHOOLERS!!!
GYAAAH! I'M SCARED! THEY'RE GONNA KILL MEEE!!!
HARUAKI FEAR PYRAMID
MIDDLE SCHOOLERS LOITERING AT CONVENIENCE STORES
THE PRINCIPAL
COCKROACHES
GANGS OF ROBBERS
MONSTERS/YOUKAI
I REALLY DON'T UNDERSTAND YOUR FEAR PYRAMID...

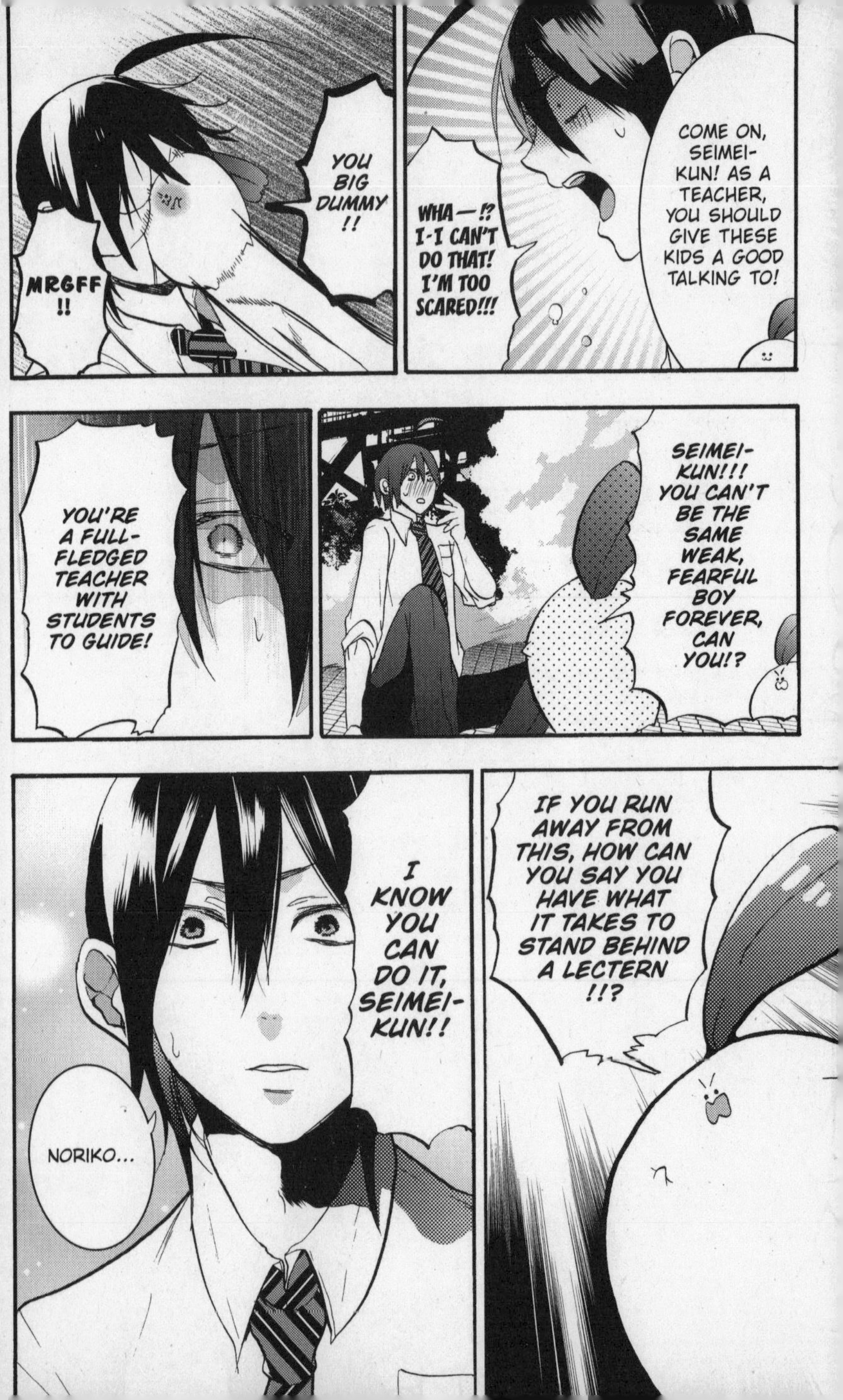
COME ON, SEIMEI-KUN! AS A TEACHER, YOU SHOULD GIVE THESE KIDS A GOOD TALKING TO!
WHA—!? I-I CAN'T DO THAT! I'M TOO SCARED!!!
YOU BIG DUMMY!!
MRGFF!!
SEIMEI-KUN!!! YOU CAN'T BE THE SAME WEAK, FEARFUL BOY FOREVER, CAN YOU!?
YOU'RE A FULL-FLEDGED TEACHER WITH STUDENTS TO GUIDE!
IF YOU RUN AWAY FROM THIS, HOW CAN YOU SAY YOU HAVE WHAT IT TAKES TO STAND BEHIND A LECTERN!!?
I KNOW YOU CAN DO IT, SEIMEI-KUN!!
NORIKO...

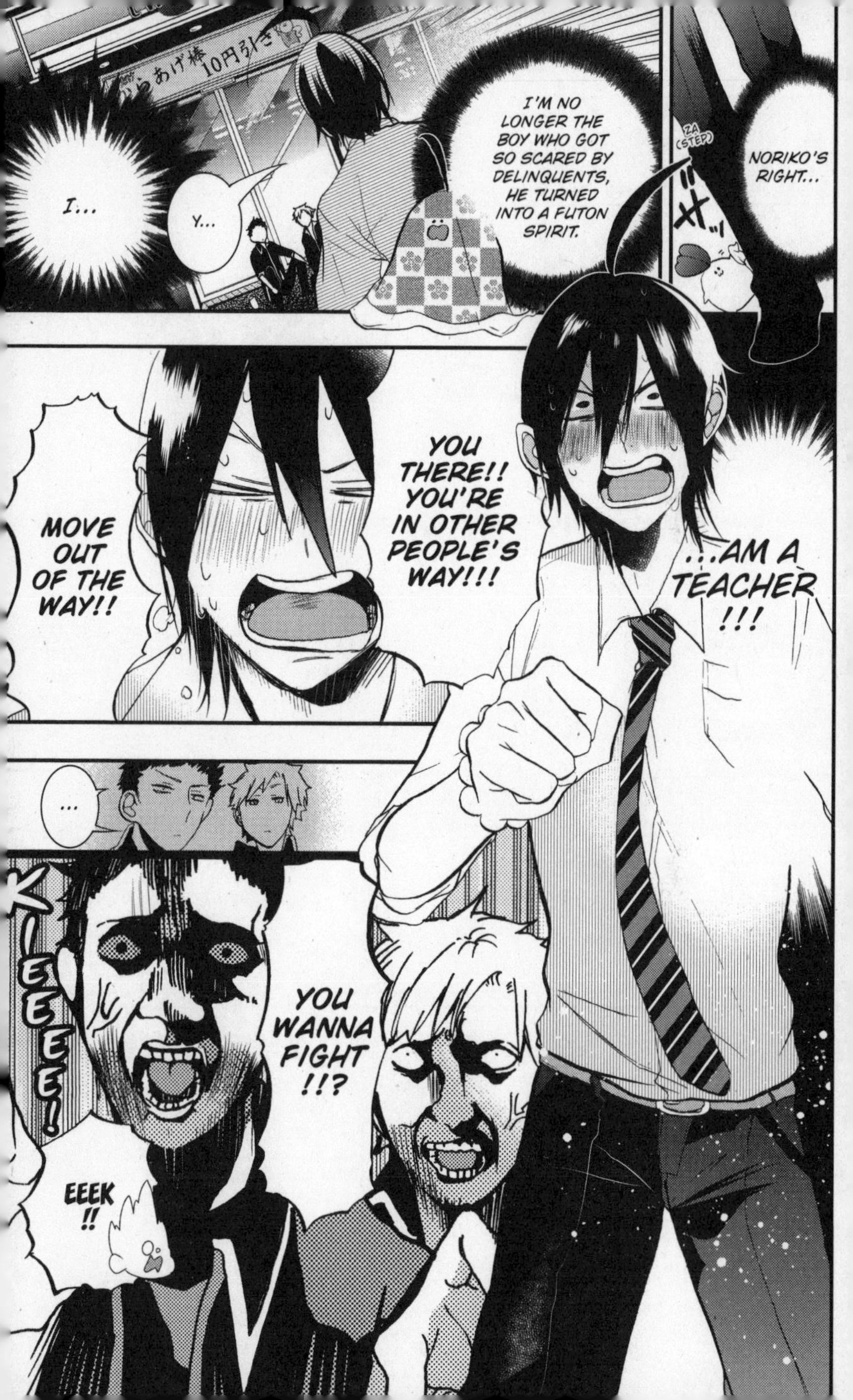
NORIKO'S RIGHT...
ZA (STEP)
I'M NO LONGER THE BOY WHO GOT SO SCARED BY DELINQUENTS, HE TURNED INTO A FUTON SPIRIT.
Y...
I...
...AM A TEACHER!!!
YOU THERE!! YOU'RE IN OTHER PEOPLE'S WAY!!!
MOVE OUT OF THE WAY!!
...
YOU WANNA FIGHT!!?
KIEEEEE!
EEEK!!

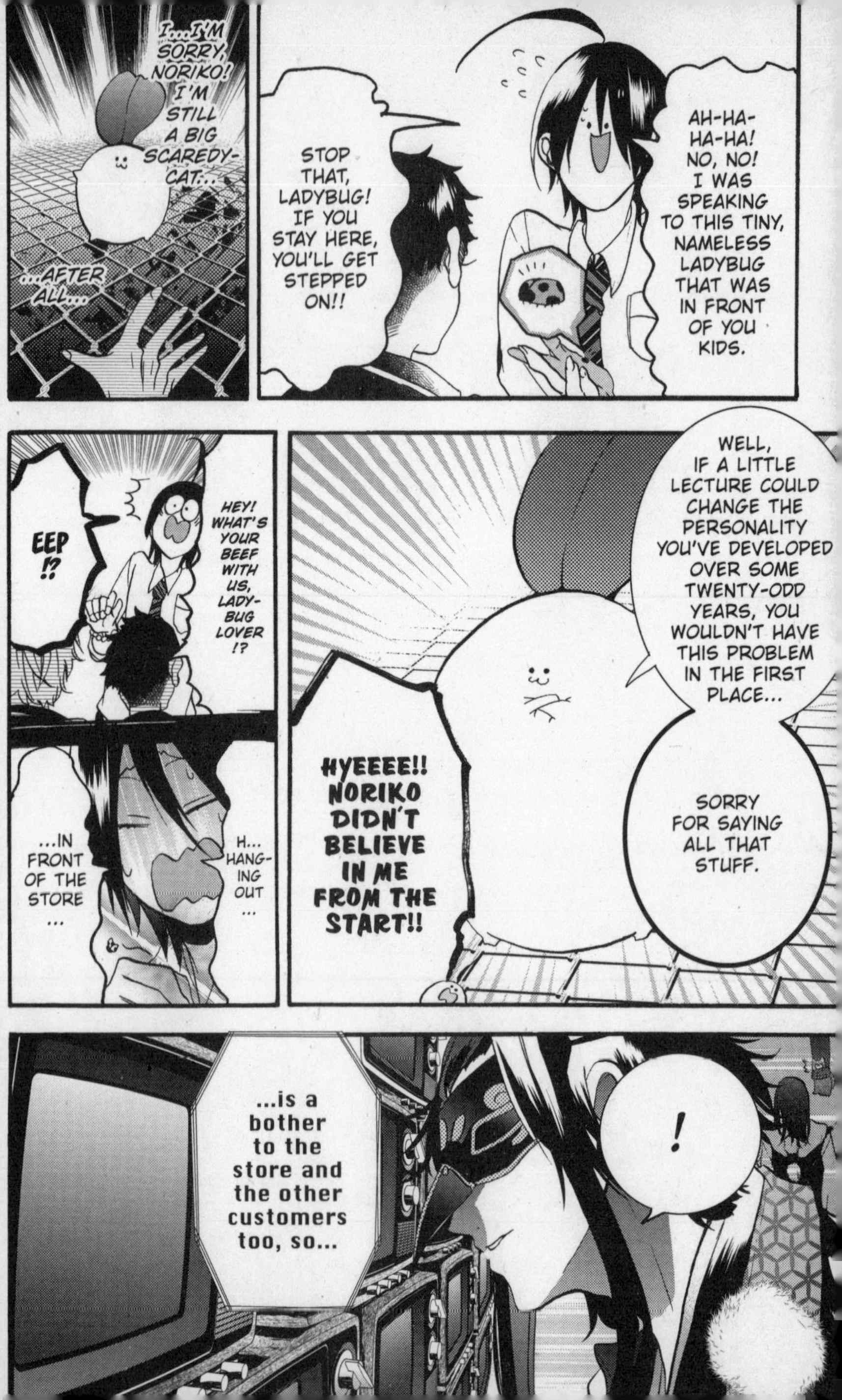
AH-HA-HA-HA! NO, NO! I WAS SPEAKING TO THIS TINY, NAMELESS LADYBUG THAT WAS IN FRONT OF YOU KIDS.
STOP THAT, LADYBUG! IF YOU STAY HERE, YOU'LL GET STEPPED ON!!
I...I'M SORRY, NORIKO! I'M STILL A BIG SCAREDY-CAT...
...AFTER ALL...
WELL, IF A LITTLE LECTURE COULD CHANGE THE PERSONALITY YOU'VE DEVELOPED OVER SOME TWENTY-ODD YEARS, YOU WOULDN'T HAVE THIS PROBLEM IN THE FIRST PLACE...
SORRY FOR SAYING ALL THAT STUFF.
HYEEEE!! NORIKO DIDN'T BELIEVE IN ME FROM THE START!!
HEY! WHAT'S YOUR BEEF WITH US, LADYBUG LOVER!?
EEP!?
H... HANGING OUT...
...IN FRONT OF THE STORE...
!
...is a bother to the store and the other customers too, so...

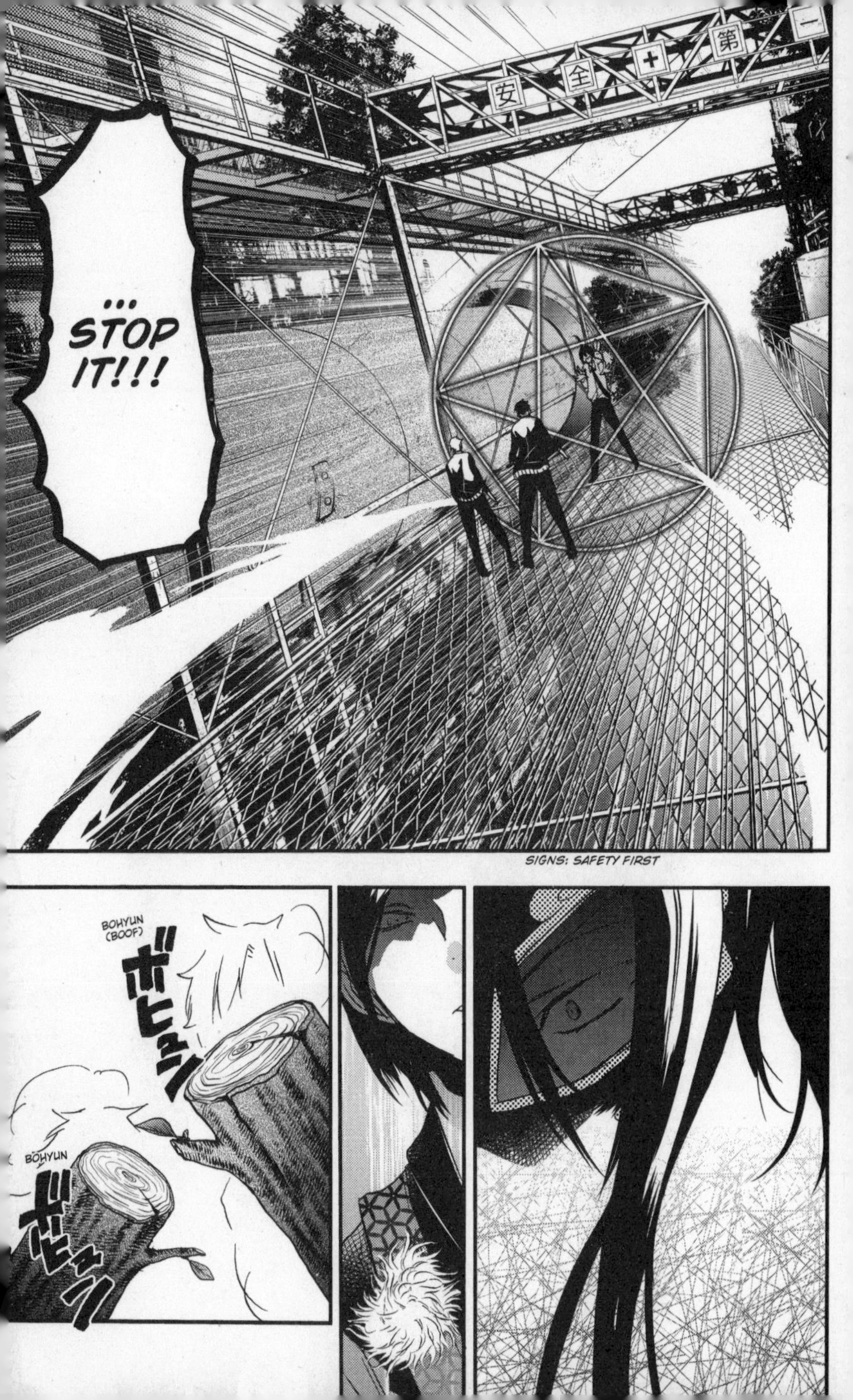
安全第一
...STOP IT!!!
SIGNS: SAFETY FIRST
BOHYUN (BOOF)
ボヒュン
BOHYUN
ボヒュン

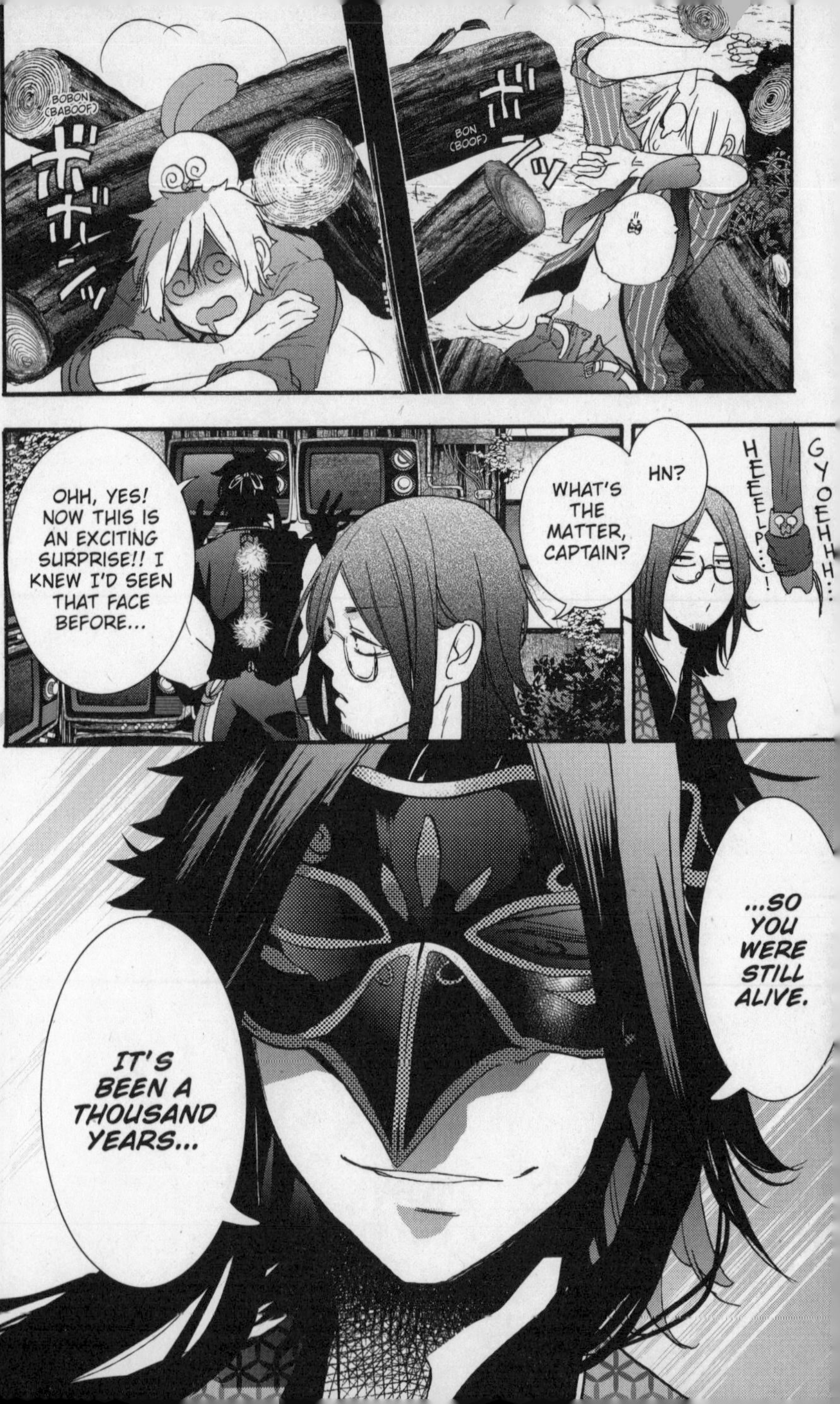
BON (BOOF)
BOBON (BABOOF)
GYOEHHH...
HEEELP...!
HN?
WHAT'S THE MATTER, CAPTAIN?
OHH, YES! NOW THIS IS AN EXCITING SURPRISE!! I KNEW I'D SEEN THAT FACE BEFORE...
...SO YOU WERE STILL ALIVE.
IT'S BEEN A THOUSAND YEARS...

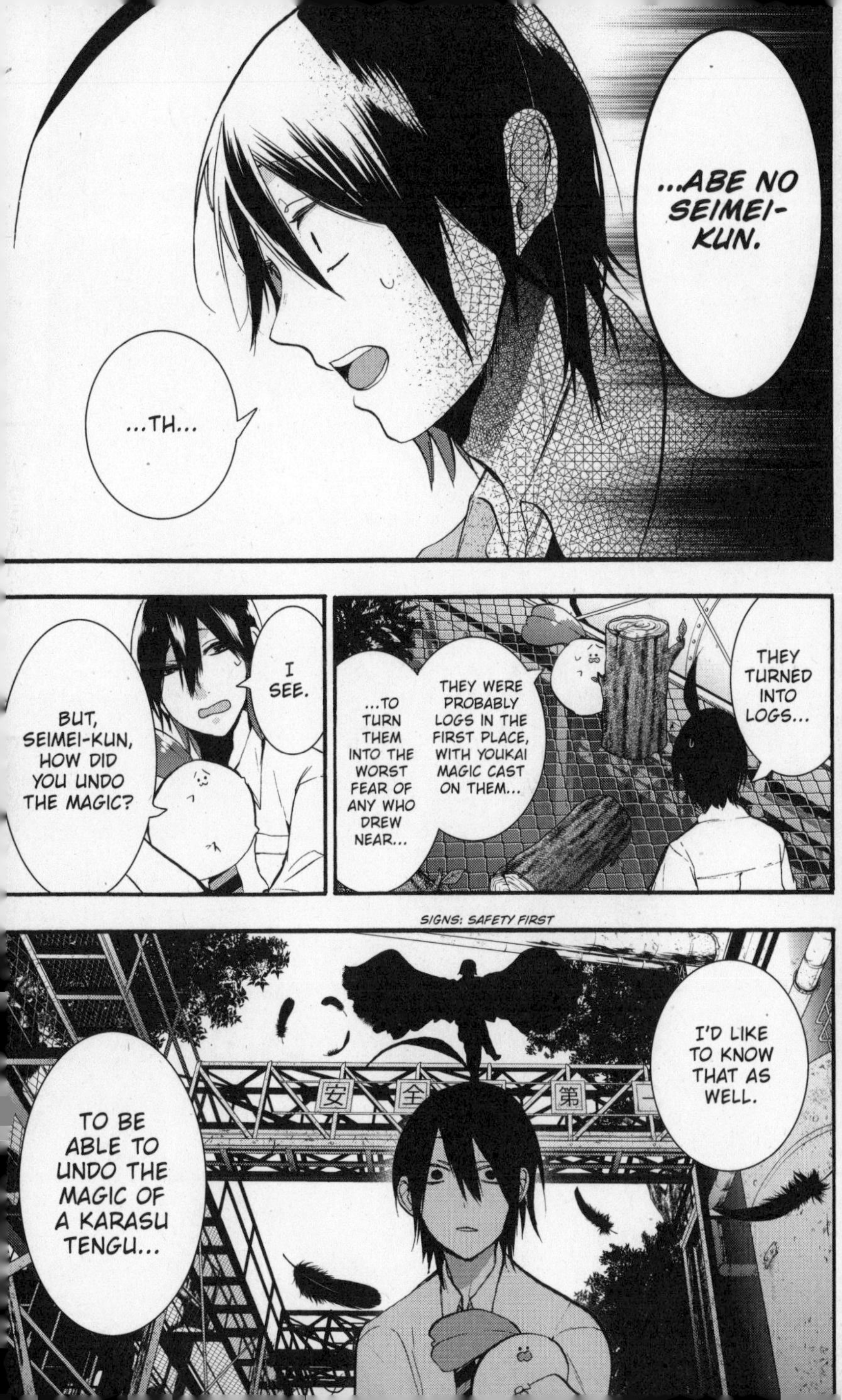
...ABE NO SEIMEI-KUN.
...TH...
THEY TURNED INTO LOGS...
THEY WERE PROBABLY LOGS IN THE FIRST PLACE, WITH YOUKAI MAGIC CAST ON THEM...
...TO TURN THEM INTO THE WORST FEAR OF ANY WHO DREW NEAR...
I SEE.
BUT, SEIMEI-KUN, HOW DID YOU UNDO THE MAGIC?
SIGNS: SAFETY FIRST
安全第一
I'D LIKE TO KNOW THAT AS WELL.
TO BE ABLE TO UNDO THE MAGIC OF A KARASU TENGU...

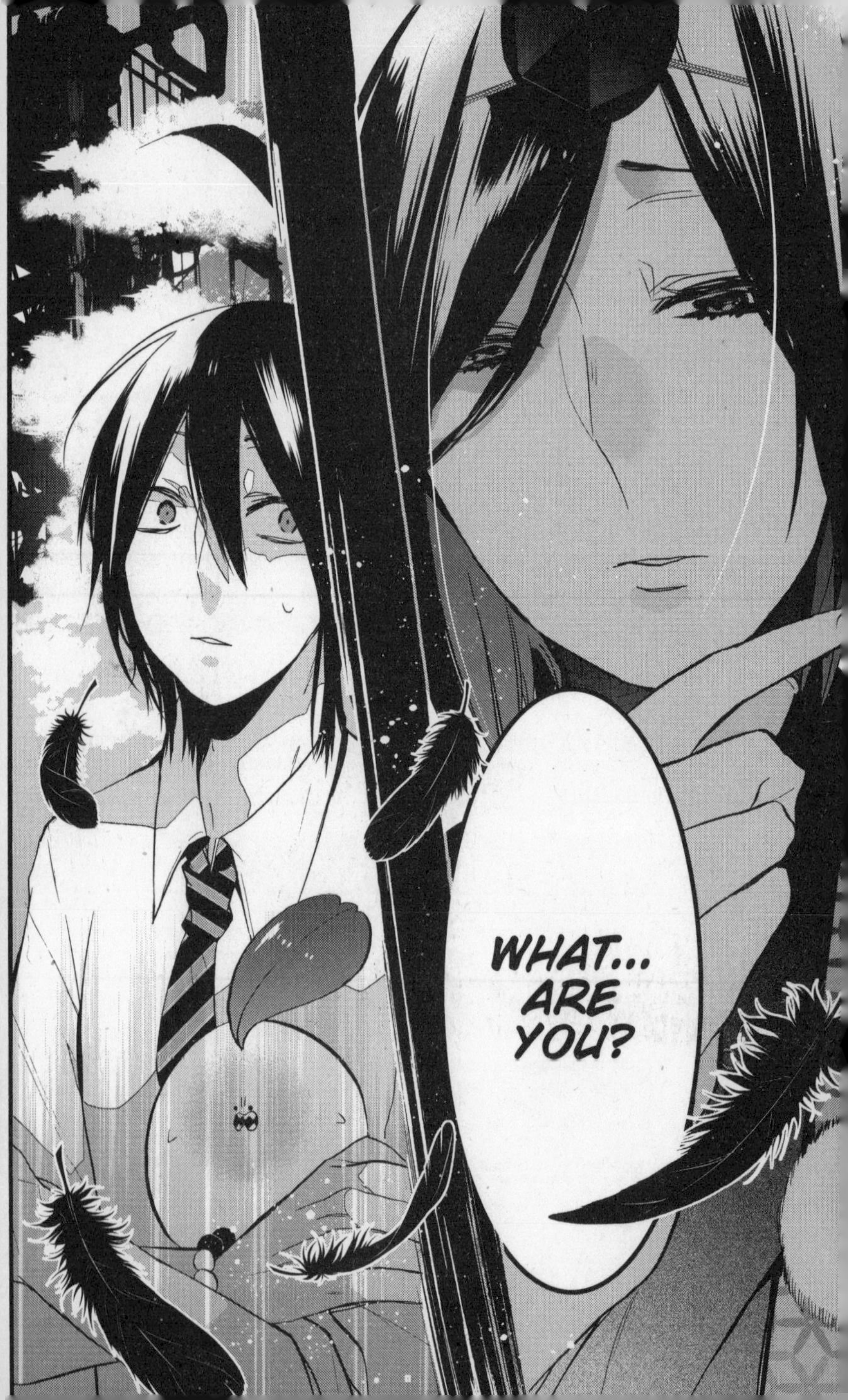
WHAT... ARE YOU?

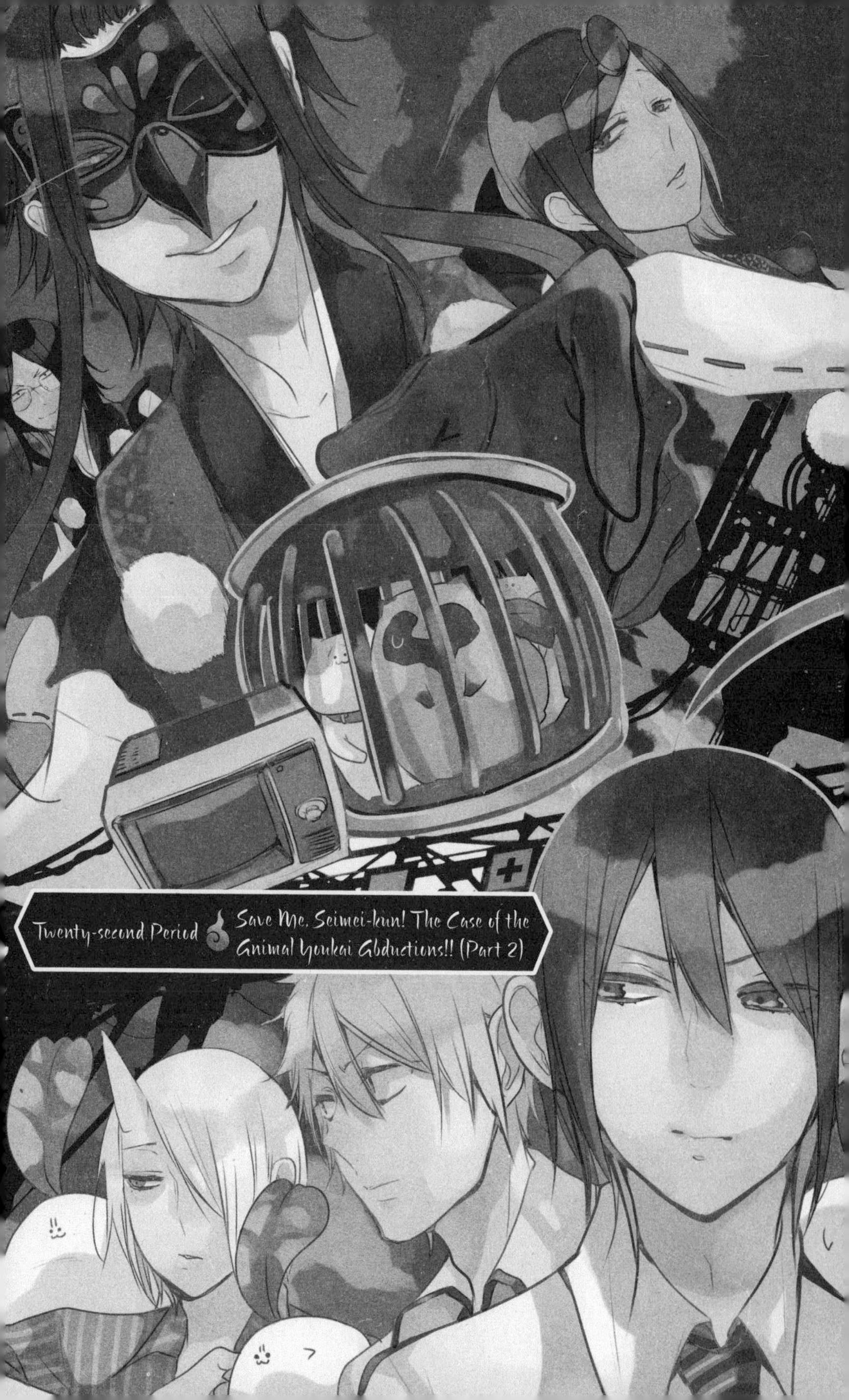

Twenty-second Period: Save Me, Seimei-kun! The Case of the Animal Youkai Abductions!! (Part 2)

A TeRRiFieD Teacher
at GHOuL School!

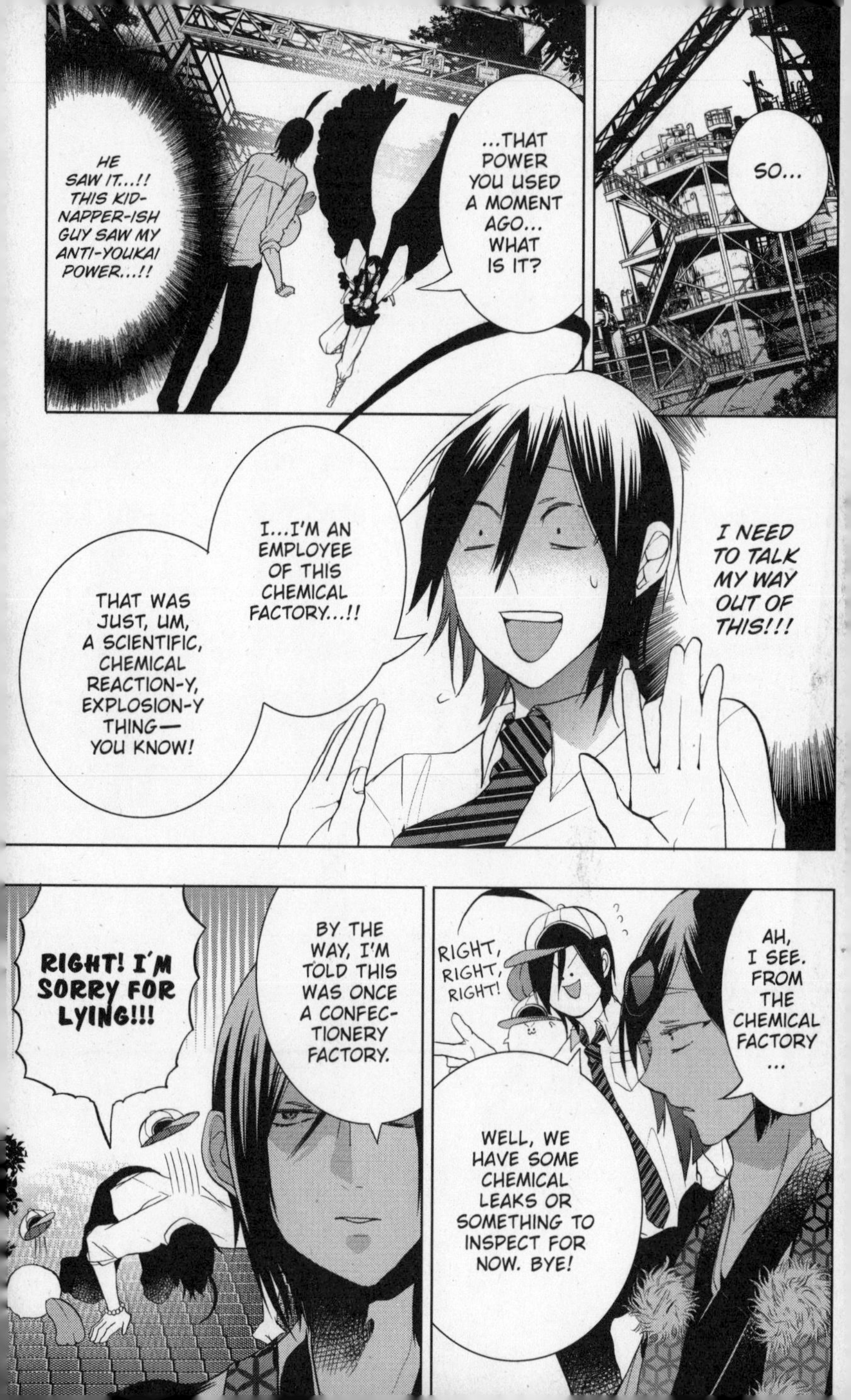
SO...
...THAT POWER YOU USED A MOMENT AGO... WHAT IS IT?
HE SAW IT...!! THIS KID-NAPPER-ISH GUY SAW MY ANTI-YOUKAI POWER...!!
I NEED TO TALK MY WAY OUT OF THIS!!!
I...I'M AN EMPLOYEE OF THIS CHEMICAL FACTORY...!!
THAT WAS JUST, UM, A SCIENTIFIC, CHEMICAL REACTION-Y, EXPLOSION-Y THING— YOU KNOW!
AH, I SEE. FROM THE CHEMICAL FACTORY...
RIGHT, RIGHT, RIGHT!
WELL, WE HAVE SOME CHEMICAL LEAKS OR SOMETHING TO INSPECT FOR NOW. BYE!
BY THE WAY, I'M TOLD THIS WAS ONCE A CONFEC-TIONERY FACTORY.
RIGHT! I'M SORRY FOR LYING!!!

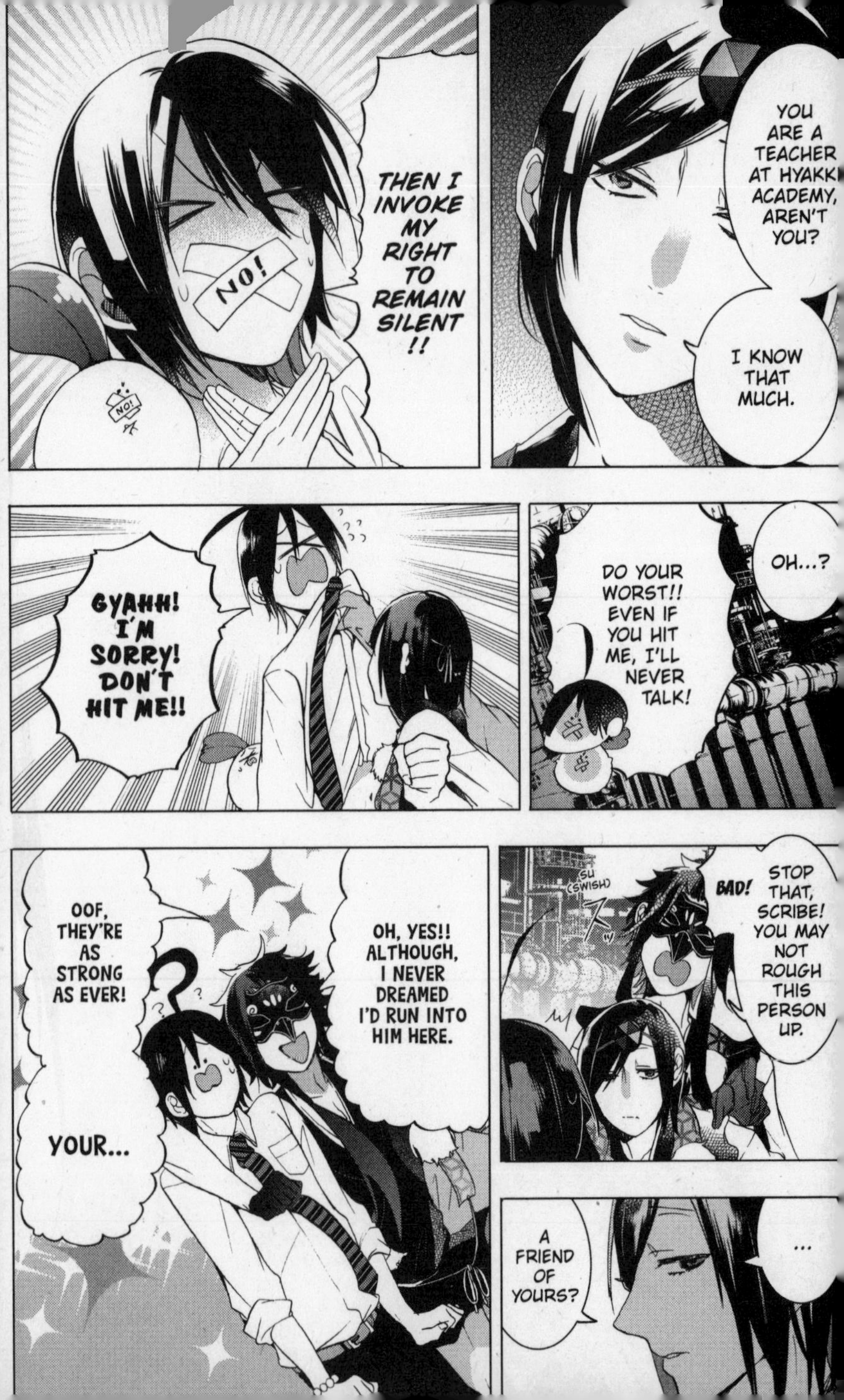
YOU ARE A TEACHER AT HYAKKI ACADEMY, AREN'T YOU?
I KNOW THAT MUCH.
THEN I INVOKE MY RIGHT TO REMAIN SILENT !!
NO!
NO!
OH...?
DO YOUR WORST!! EVEN IF YOU HIT ME, I'LL NEVER TALK!
GYAHH! I'M SORRY! DON'T HIT ME!!
STOP THAT, SCRIBE! YOU MAY NOT ROUGH THIS PERSON UP.
BAD!
SU (SWISH)
...
A FRIEND OF YOURS?
OH, YES!! ALTHOUGH, I NEVER DREAMED I'D RUN INTO HIM HERE.
OOF, THEY'RE AS STRONG AS EVER!
YOUR...

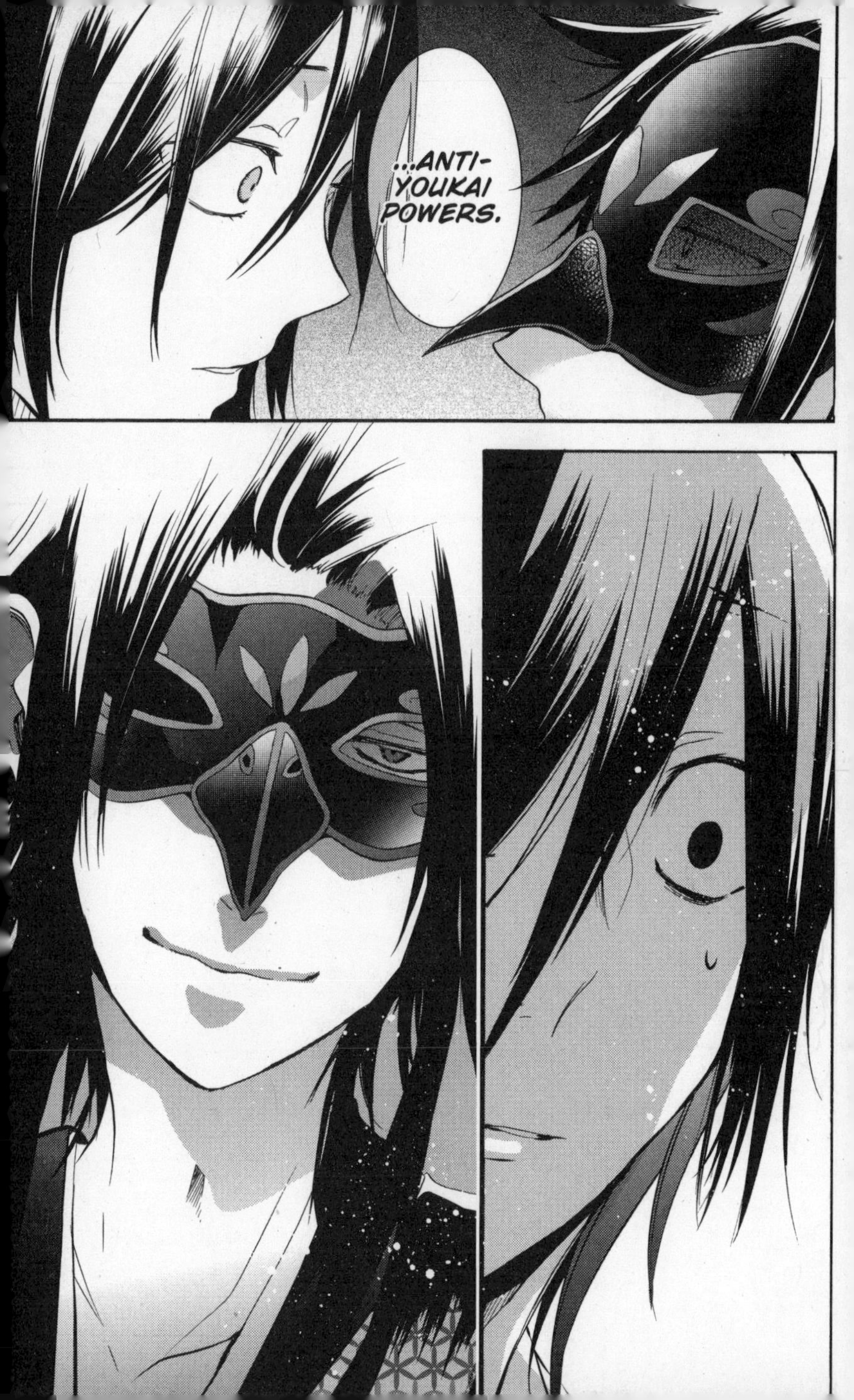
...ANTI-YOUKAI POWERS.

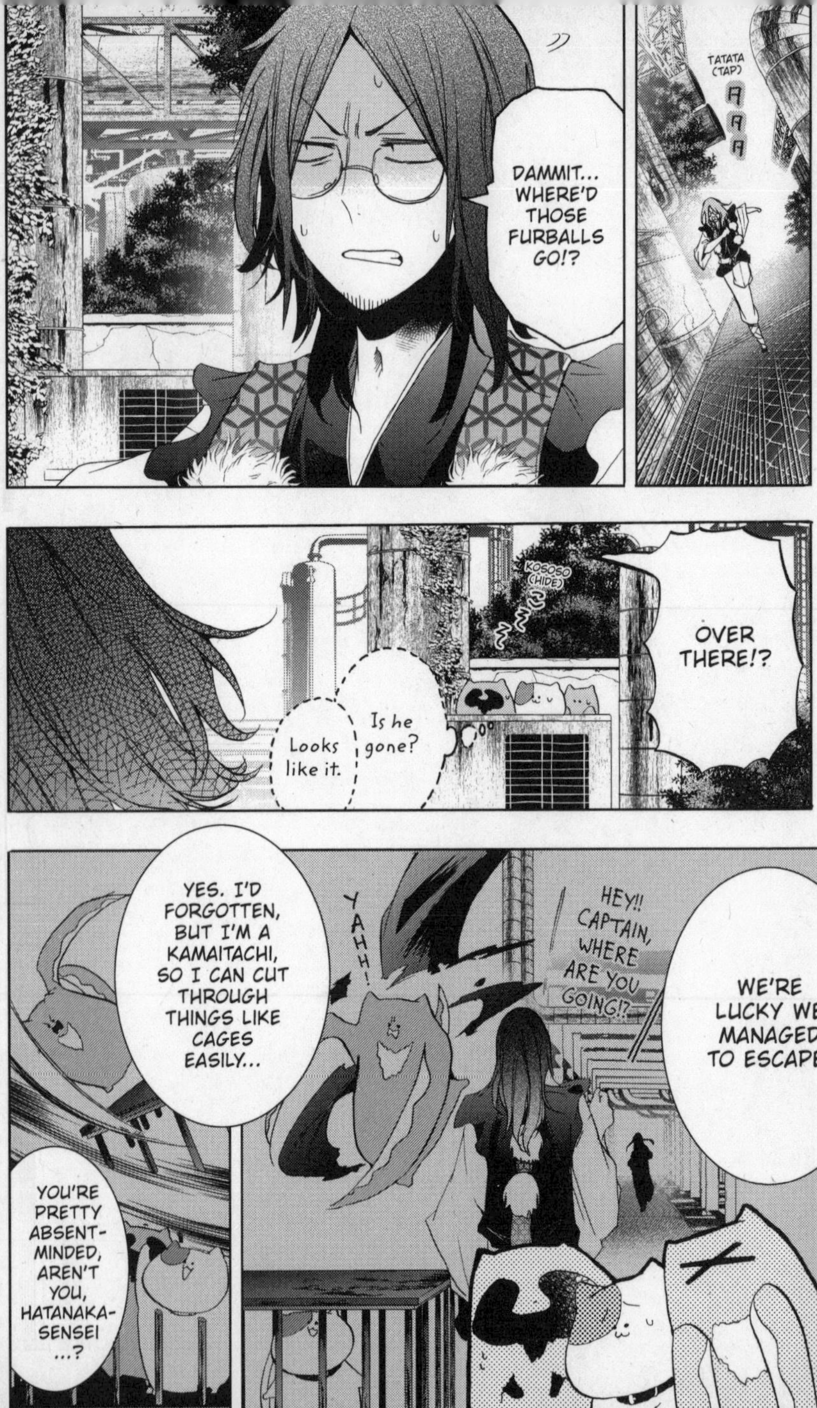
TATATA (TAP)
DAMMIT... WHERE'D THOSE FURBALLS GO!?
OVER THERE!?
KOSOSO (HIDE)
Is he gone?
Looks like it.
WE'RE LUCKY WE MANAGED TO ESCAPE.
HEY!! CAPTAIN, WHERE ARE YOU GOING!?
YAHH!
YES. I'D FORGOTTEN, BUT I'M A KAMAITACHI, SO I CAN CUT THROUGH THINGS LIKE CAGES EASILY...
YOU'RE PRETTY ABSENT-MINDED, AREN'T YOU, HATANAKA-SENSEI ...?

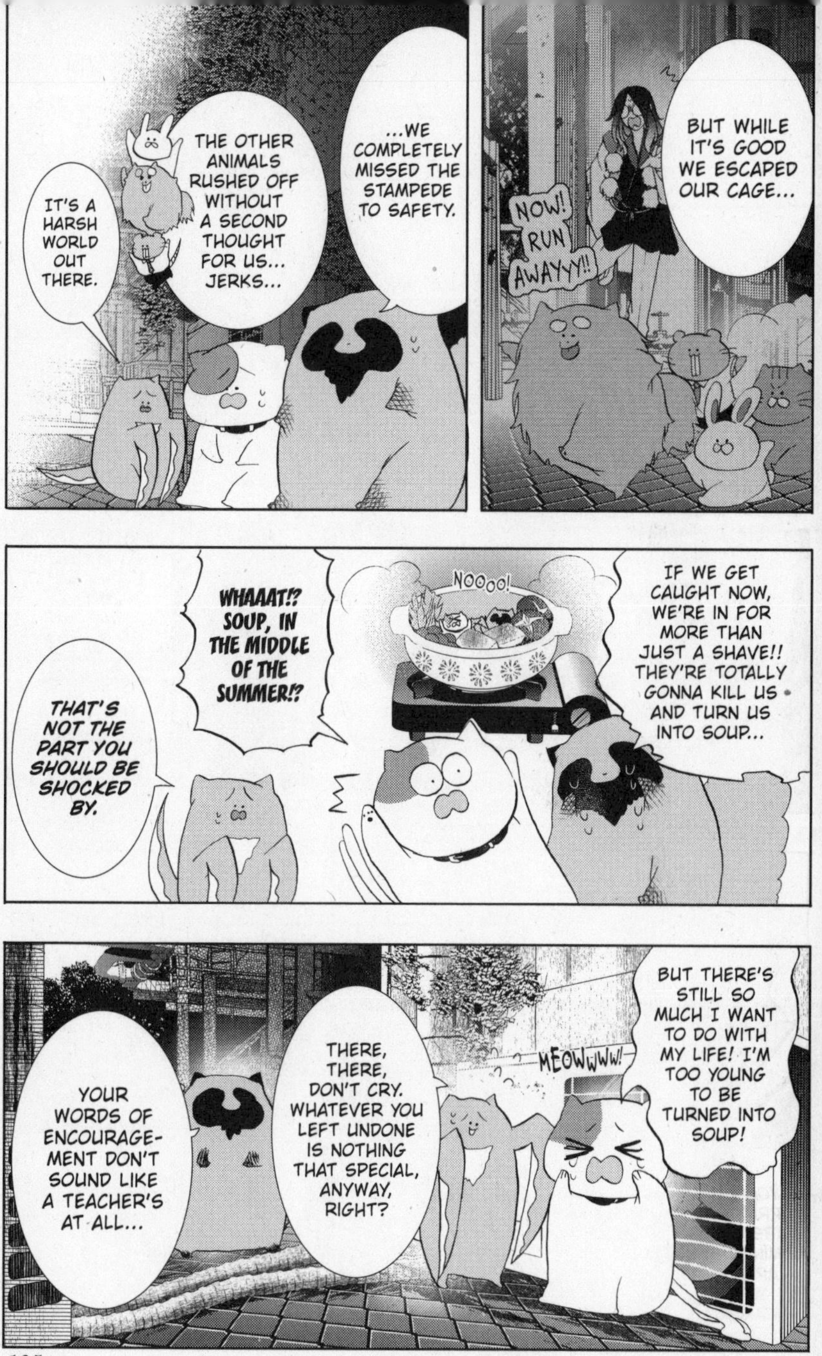
BUT WHILE IT'S GOOD WE ESCAPED OUR CAGE...
NOW! RUN AWAYYY!!
...WE COMPLETELY MISSED THE STAMPEDE TO SAFETY.
THE OTHER ANIMALS RUSHED OFF WITHOUT A SECOND THOUGHT FOR US... JERKS...
IT'S A HARSH WORLD OUT THERE.
IF WE GET CAUGHT NOW, WE'RE IN FOR MORE THAN JUST A SHAVE!! THEY'RE TOTALLY GONNA KILL US AND TURN US INTO SOUP...
NOOOO!
WHAAAT!? SOUP, IN THE MIDDLE OF THE SUMMER!?
THAT'S NOT THE PART YOU SHOULD BE SHOCKED BY.
BUT THERE'S STILL SO MUCH I WANT TO DO WITH MY LIFE! I'M TOO YOUNG TO BE TURNED INTO SOUP!
MEOWWWW!
THERE, THERE, DON'T CRY. WHATEVER YOU LEFT UNDONE IS NOTHING THAT SPECIAL, ANYWAY, RIGHT?
YOUR WORDS OF ENCOURAGE-MENT DON'T SOUND LIKE A TEACHER'S AT ALL...

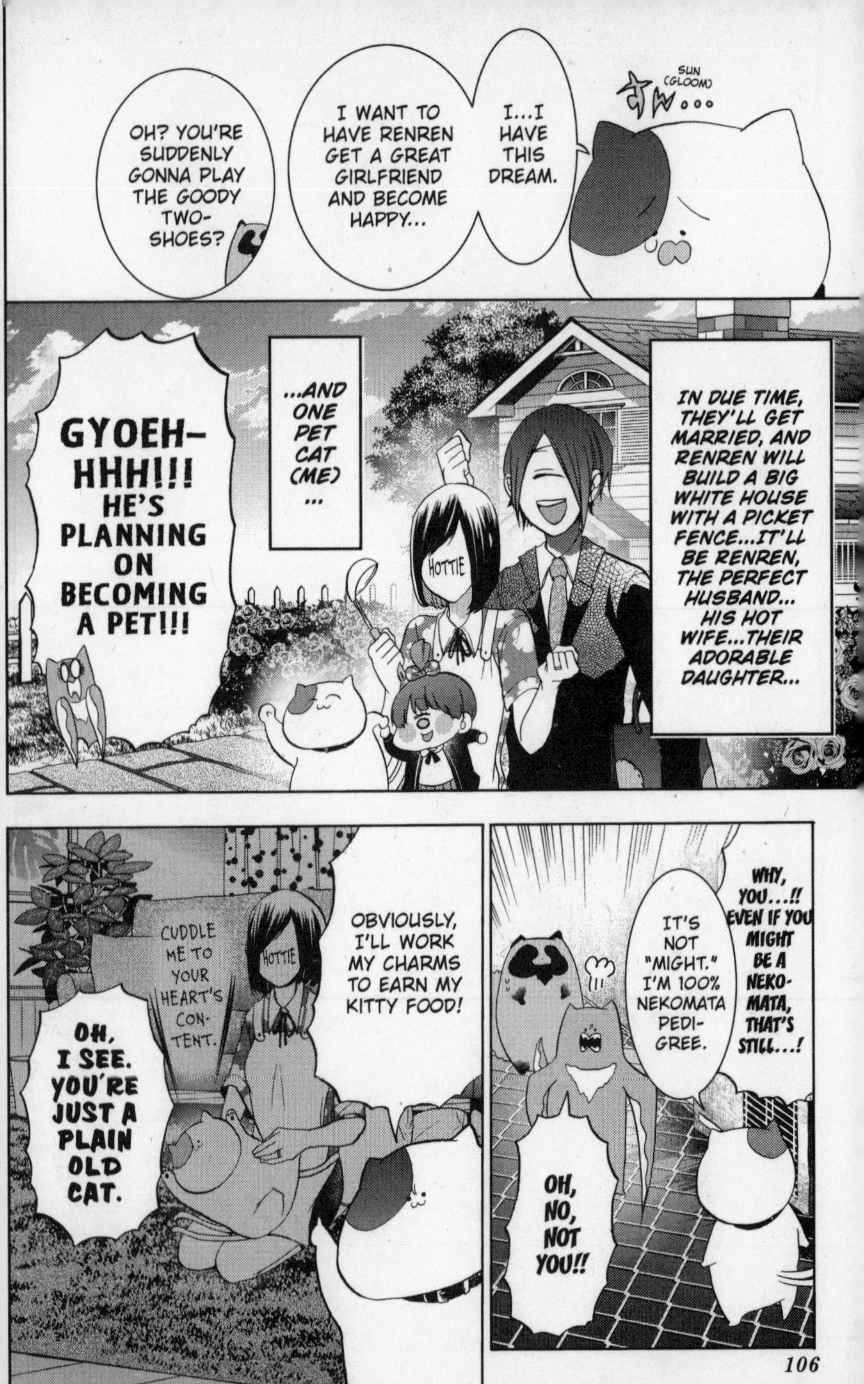

SUN (GLOOM)
I...I HAVE THIS DREAM.
I WANT TO HAVE RENREN GET A GREAT GIRLFRIEND AND BECOME HAPPY...
OH? YOU'RE SUDDENLY GONNA PLAY THE GOODY TWO-SHOES?
IN DUE TIME, THEY'LL GET MARRIED, AND RENREN WILL BUILD A BIG WHITE HOUSE WITH A PICKET FENCE...IT'LL BE RENREN, THE PERFECT HUSBAND... HIS HOT WIFE...THEIR ADORABLE DAUGHTER...
HOTTIE
...AND ONE PET CAT (ME)...
GYOEH-HHH!!! HE'S PLANNING ON BECOMING A PET!!!
WHY, YOU...!! EVEN IF YOU MIGHT BE A NEKO-MATA, THAT'S STILL...!
IT'S NOT "MIGHT." I'M 100% NEKOMATA PEDI-GREE.
OH, NO, NOT YOU!!
OBVIOUSLY, I'LL WORK MY CHARMS TO EARN MY KITTY FOOD!
HOTTIE
CUDDLE ME TO YOUR HEART'S CON-TENT.
OH, I SEE. YOU'RE JUST A PLAIN OLD CAT.

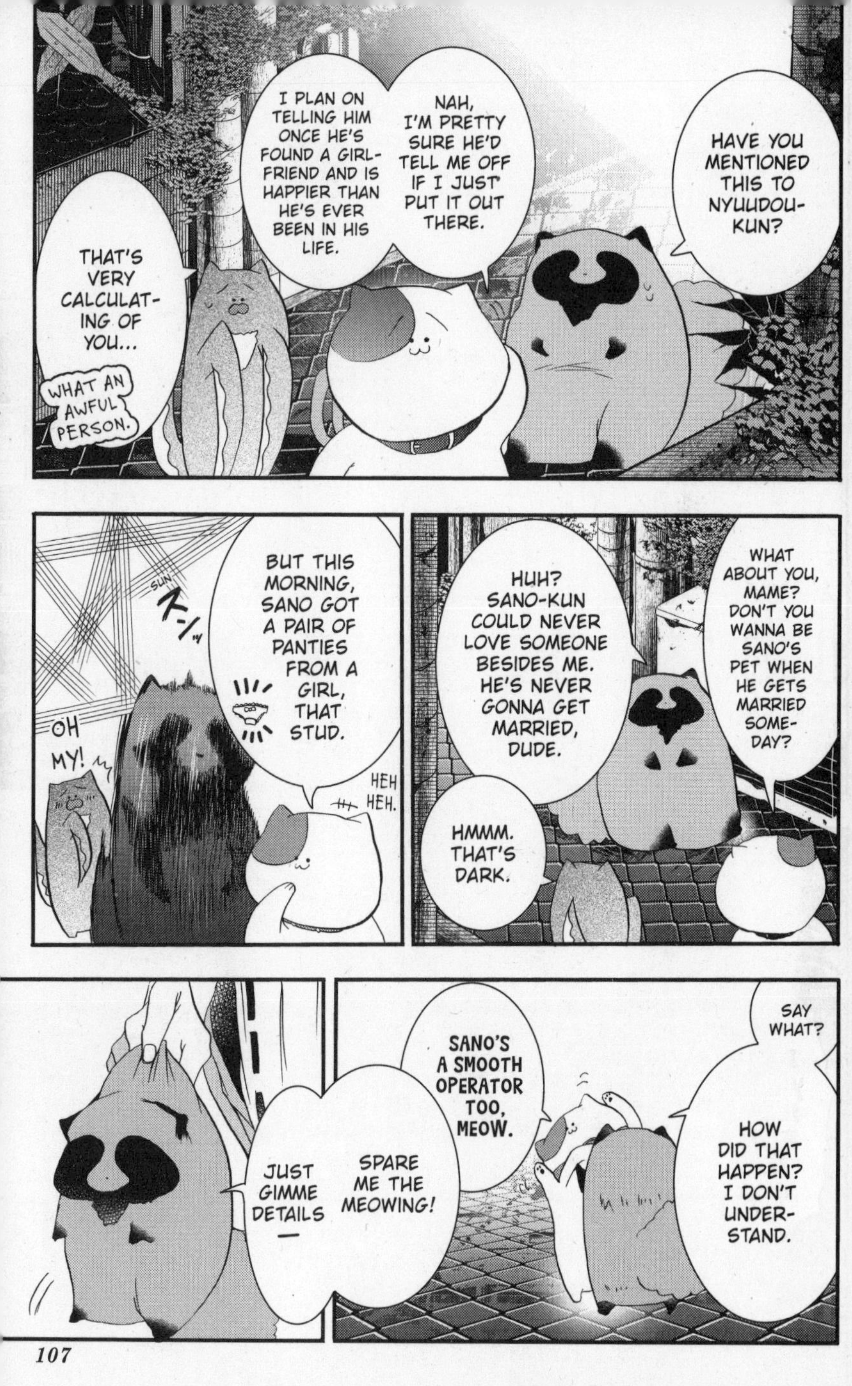
HAVE YOU MENTIONED THIS TO NYUUDOU-KUN?
NAH, I'M PRETTY SURE HE'D TELL ME OFF IF I JUST PUT IT OUT THERE.
I PLAN ON TELLING HIM ONCE HE'S FOUND A GIRLFRIEND AND IS HAPPIER THAN HE'S EVER BEEN IN HIS LIFE.
THAT'S VERY CALCULATING OF YOU...
WHAT AN AWFUL PERSON.
WHAT ABOUT YOU, MAME? DON'T YOU WANNA BE SANO'S PET WHEN HE GETS MARRIED SOMEDAY?
HUH? SANO-KUN COULD NEVER LOVE SOMEONE BESIDES ME. HE'S NEVER GONNA GET MARRIED, DUDE.
HMMM. THAT'S DARK.
BUT THIS MORNING, SANO GOT A PAIR OF PANTIES FROM A GIRL, THAT STUD.
HEH HEH.
SUN
OH MY!
SAY WHAT?
HOW DID THAT HAPPEN? I DON'T UNDERSTAND.
SANO'S A SMOOTH OPERATOR TOO, MEOW.
SPARE ME THE MEOWING!
JUST GIMME DETAILS—

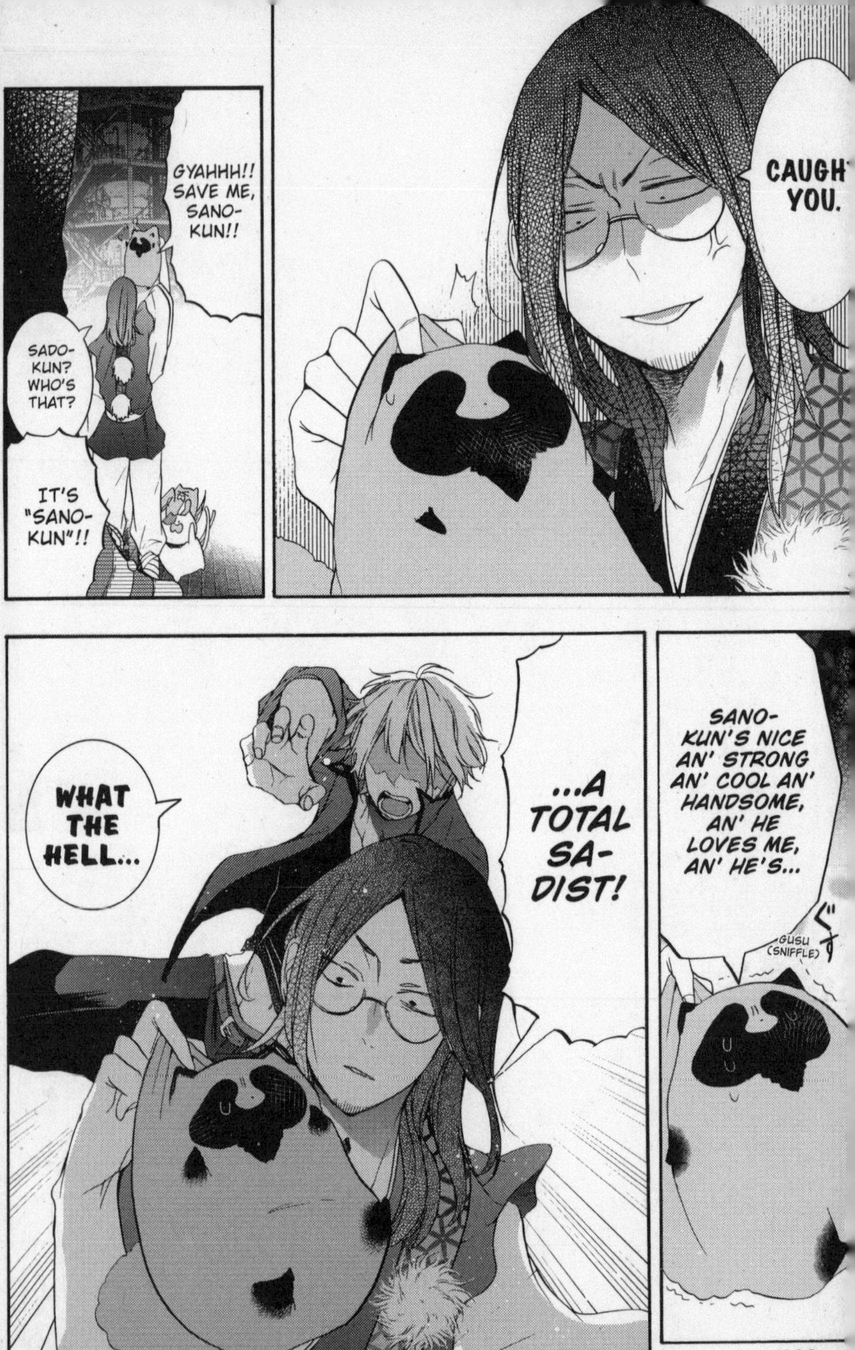
CAUGHT YOU.
GYAHHH!! SAVE ME, SANO-KUN!!
SADO-KUN? WHO'S THAT?
IT'S "SANO-KUN"!!
SANO-KUN'S NICE AN' STRONG AN' COOL AN' HANDSOME, AN' HE LOVES ME, AN' HE'S...
GUSU (SNIFFLE)
...A TOTAL SA-DIST!
WHAT THE HELL...

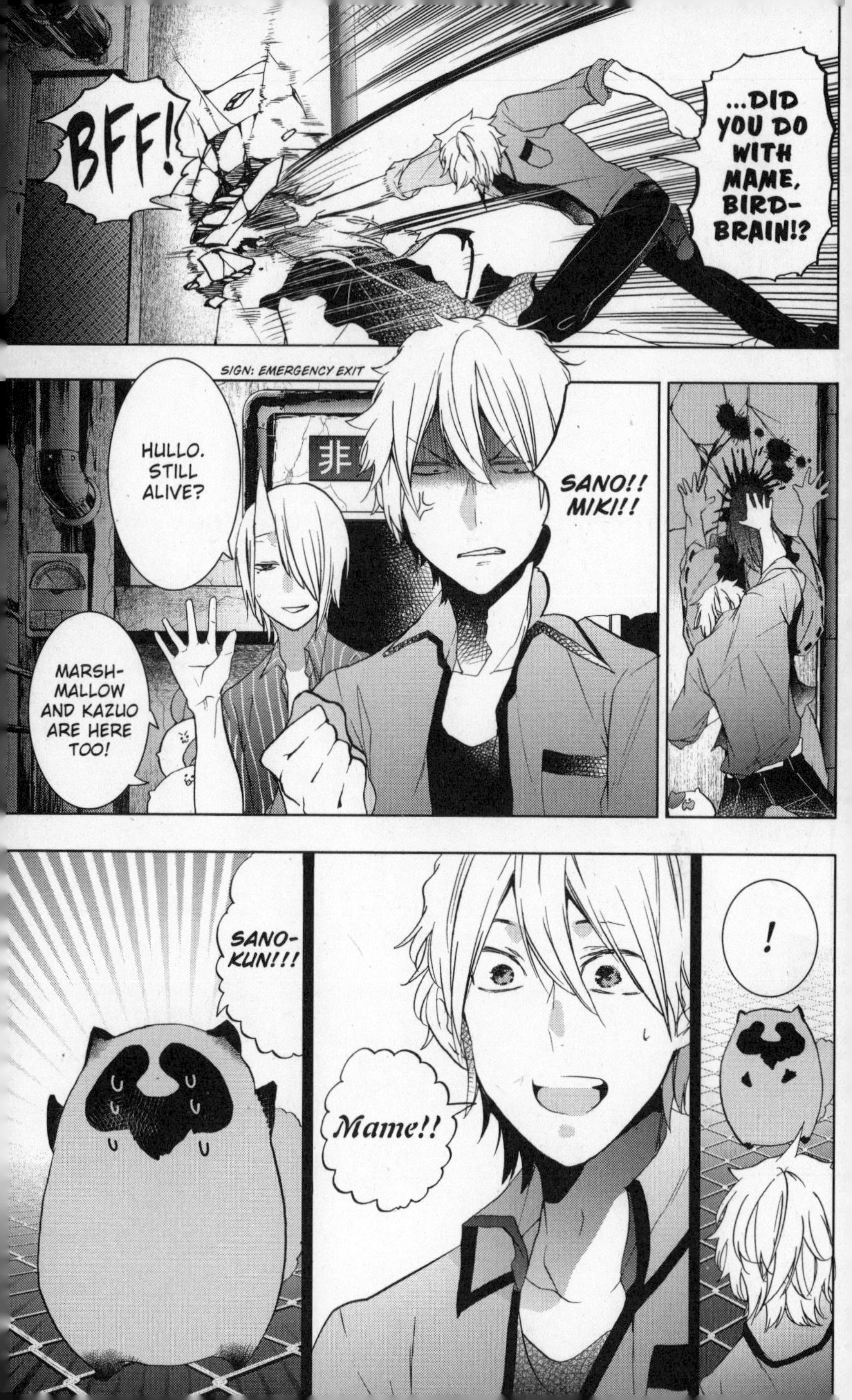
...DID YOU DO WITH MAME, BIRD-BRAIN!?
BFF!
SIGN: EMERGENCY EXIT
非
SANO!! MIKI!!
HULLO. STILL ALIVE?
MARSH-MALLOW AND KAZUO ARE HERE TOO!
!
Mame!!
SANO-KUN!!!

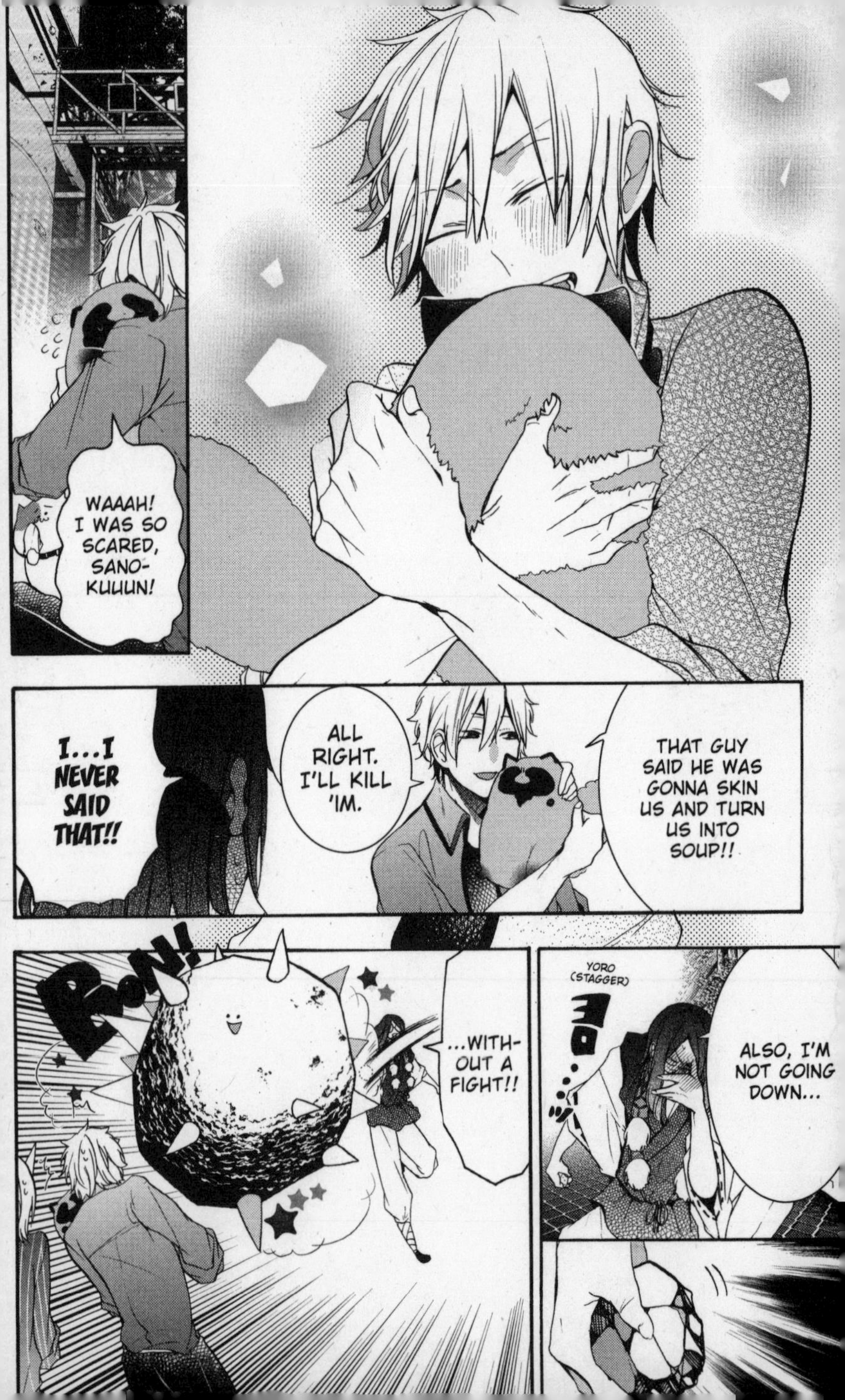
WAAAH! I WAS SO SCARED, SANO-KUUUN!
THAT GUY SAID HE WAS GONNA SKIN US AND TURN US INTO SOUP!!
ALL RIGHT. I'LL KILL 'IM.
I...I NEVER SAID THAT!!
YORO (STAGGER)
ALSO, I'M NOT GOING DOWN...
...WITH-OUT A FIGHT!!
BOOM!

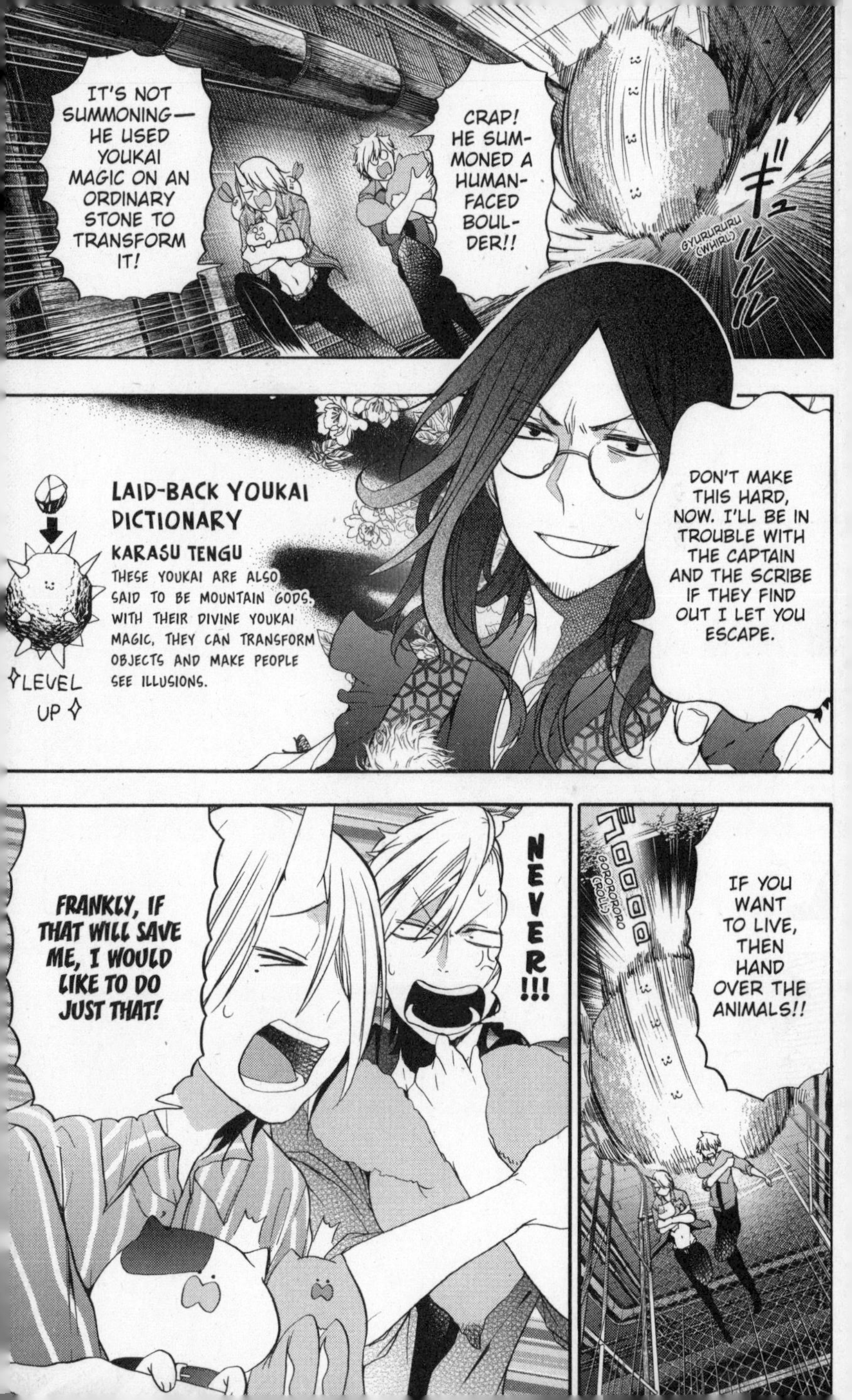
GYURURURU (WHIRL)
CRAP! HE SUMMONED A HUMAN-FACED BOULDER!!
IT'S NOT SUMMONING—HE USED YOUKAI MAGIC ON AN ORDINARY STONE TO TRANSFORM IT!
DON'T MAKE THIS HARD, NOW. I'LL BE IN TROUBLE WITH THE CAPTAIN AND THE SCRIBE IF THEY FIND OUT I LET YOU ESCAPE.
LAID-BACK YOUKAI DICTIONARY
KARASU TENGU
THESE YOUKAI ARE ALSO SAID TO BE MOUNTAIN GODS. WITH THEIR DIVINE YOUKAI MAGIC, THEY CAN TRANSFORM OBJECTS AND MAKE PEOPLE SEE ILLUSIONS.
✧LEVEL UP✧
GOROROROR (ROLL)
IF YOU WANT TO LIVE, THEN HAND OVER THE ANIMALS!!
NEVER!!!
FRANKLY, IF THAT WILL SAVE ME, I WOULD LIKE TO DO JUST THAT!

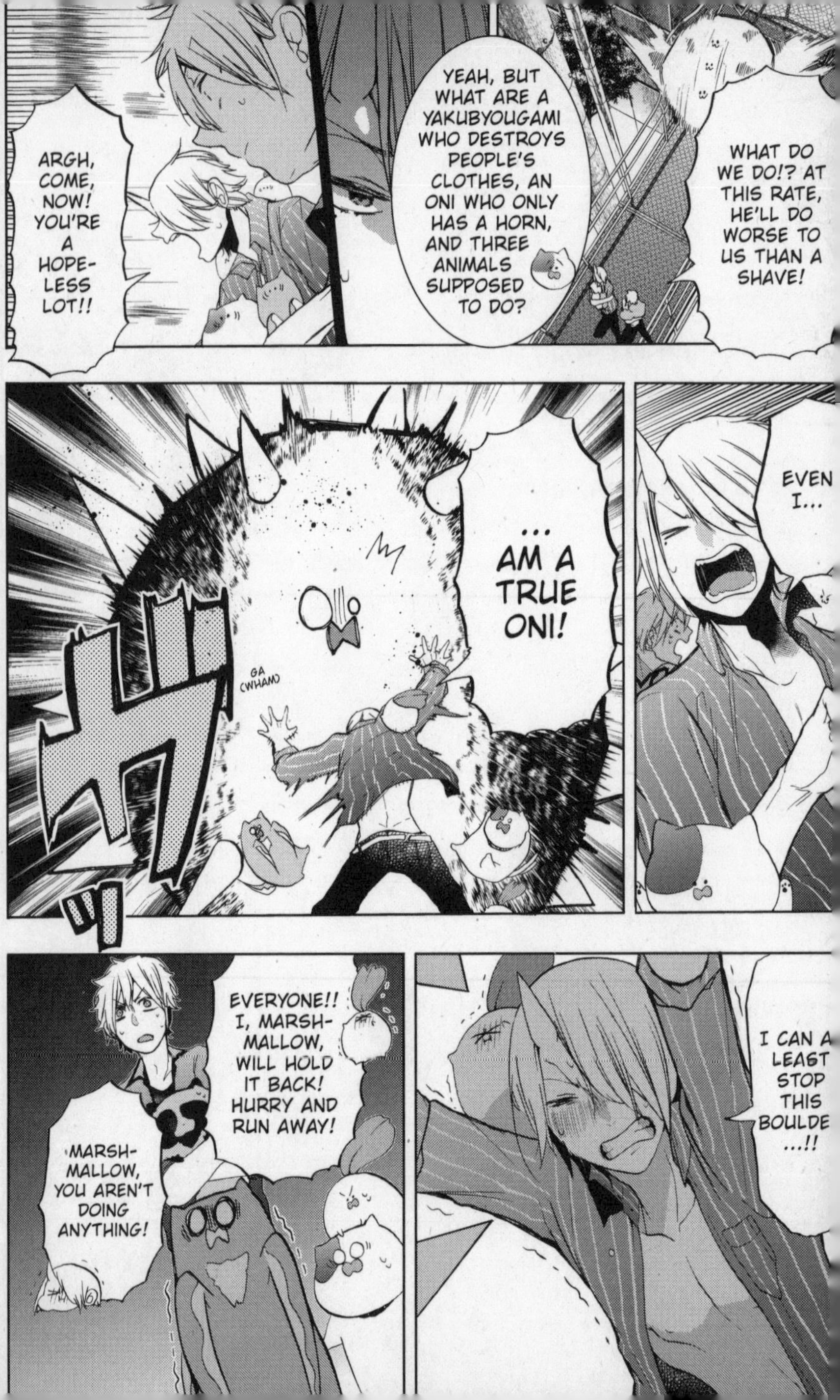
WHAT DO WE DO!? AT THIS RATE, HE'LL DO WORSE TO US THAN A SHAVE!
YEAH, BUT WHAT ARE A YAKUBYOUGAMI WHO DESTROYS PEOPLE'S CLOTHES, AN ONI WHO ONLY HAS A HORN, AND THREE ANIMALS SUPPOSED TO DO?
ARGH, COME, NOW! YOU'RE A HOPE-LESS LOT!!
EVEN I...
...AM A TRUE ONI!
GA (WHAM)
I CAN A LEAST STOP THIS BOULDE ...!!
EVERYONE!! I, MARSH-MALLOW, WILL HOLD IT BACK! HURRY AND RUN AWAY!
MARSH-MALLOW, YOU AREN'T DOING ANYTHING!

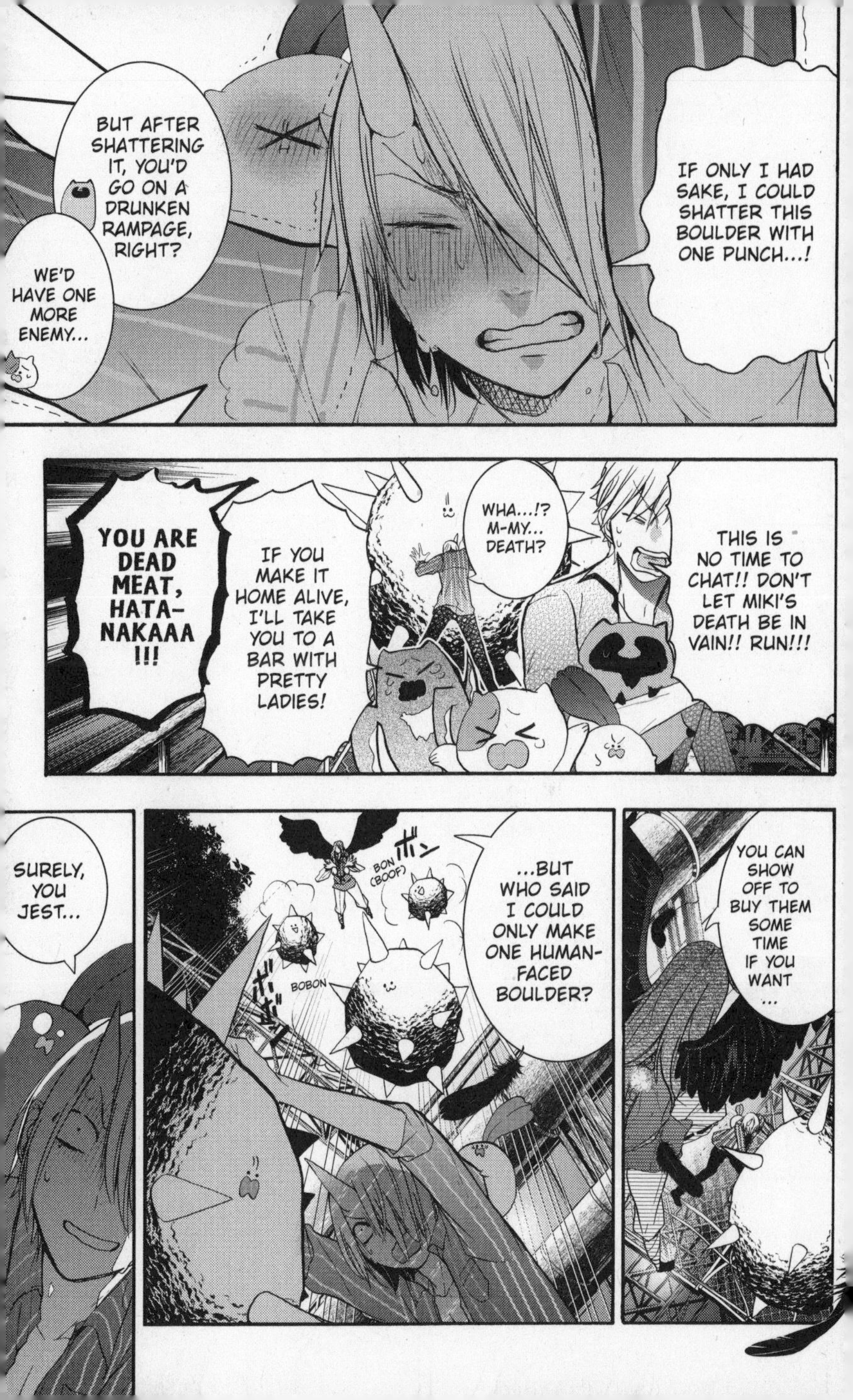
IF ONLY I HAD SAKE, I COULD SHATTER THIS BOULDER WITH ONE PUNCH...!
BUT AFTER SHATTERING IT, YOU'D GO ON A DRUNKEN RAMPAGE, RIGHT?
WE'D HAVE ONE MORE ENEMY...
THIS IS NO TIME TO CHAT!! DON'T LET MIKI'S DEATH BE IN VAIN!! RUN!!!
WHA...!? M-MY... DEATH?
IF YOU MAKE IT HOME ALIVE, I'LL TAKE YOU TO A BAR WITH PRETTY LADIES!
YOU ARE DEAD MEAT, HATA-NAKAAA!!!
YOU CAN SHOW OFF TO BUY THEM SOME TIME IF YOU WANT...
...BUT WHO SAID I COULD ONLY MAKE ONE HUMAN-FACED BOULDER?
ボン
BON (BOOF)
BOBON
SURELY, YOU JEST...

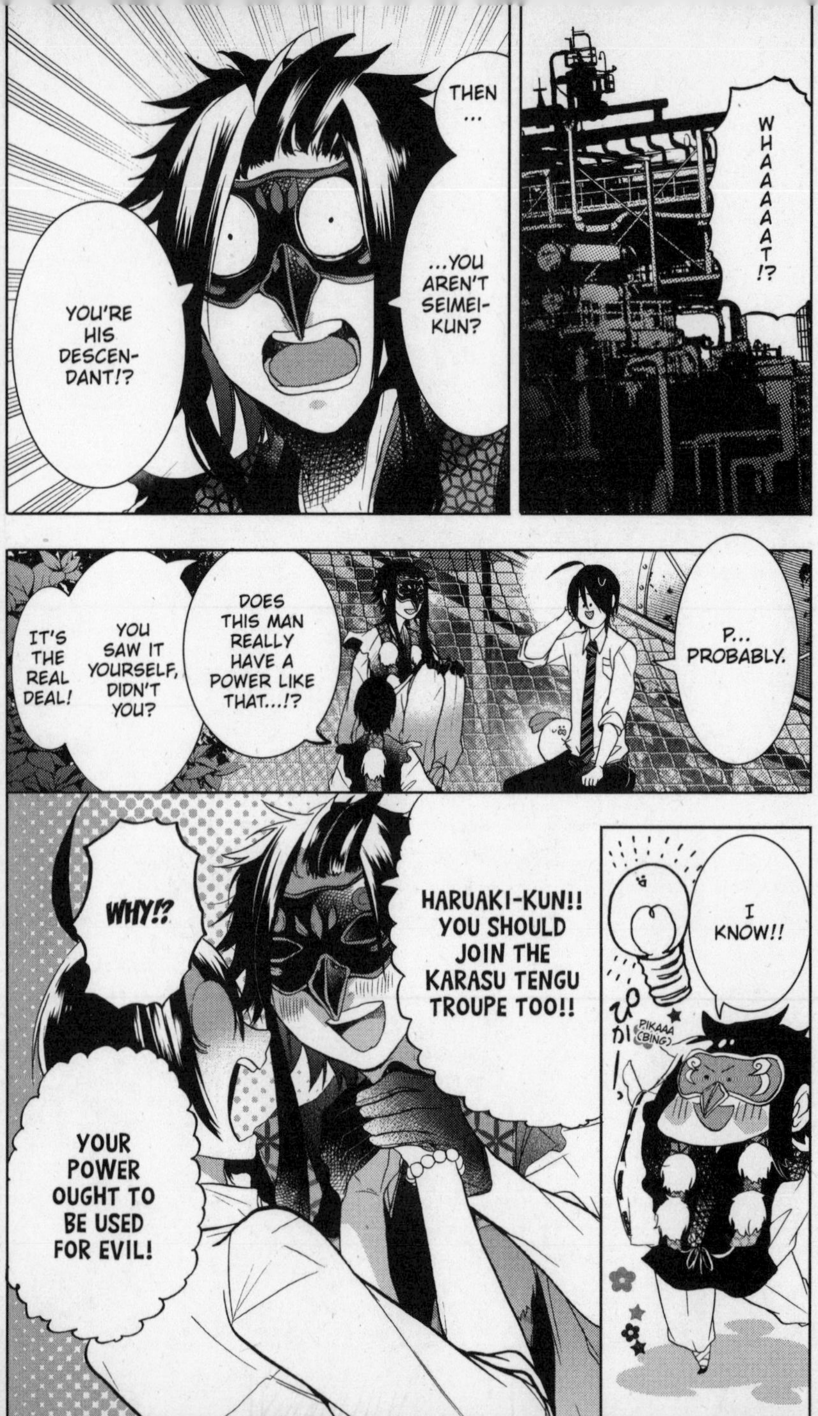
WHAAAAAAT!?
THEN...
...YOU AREN'T SEIMEI-KUN?
YOU'RE HIS DESCENDANT!?
P... PROBABLY.
DOES THIS MAN REALLY HAVE A POWER LIKE THAT...!?
YOU SAW IT YOURSELF, DIDN'T YOU?
IT'S THE REAL DEAL!
I KNOW!!
PIKAAA (BING)
HARUAKI-KUN!! YOU SHOULD JOIN THE KARASU TENGU TROUPE TOO!!
WHY!?
YOUR POWER OUGHT TO BE USED FOR EVIL!

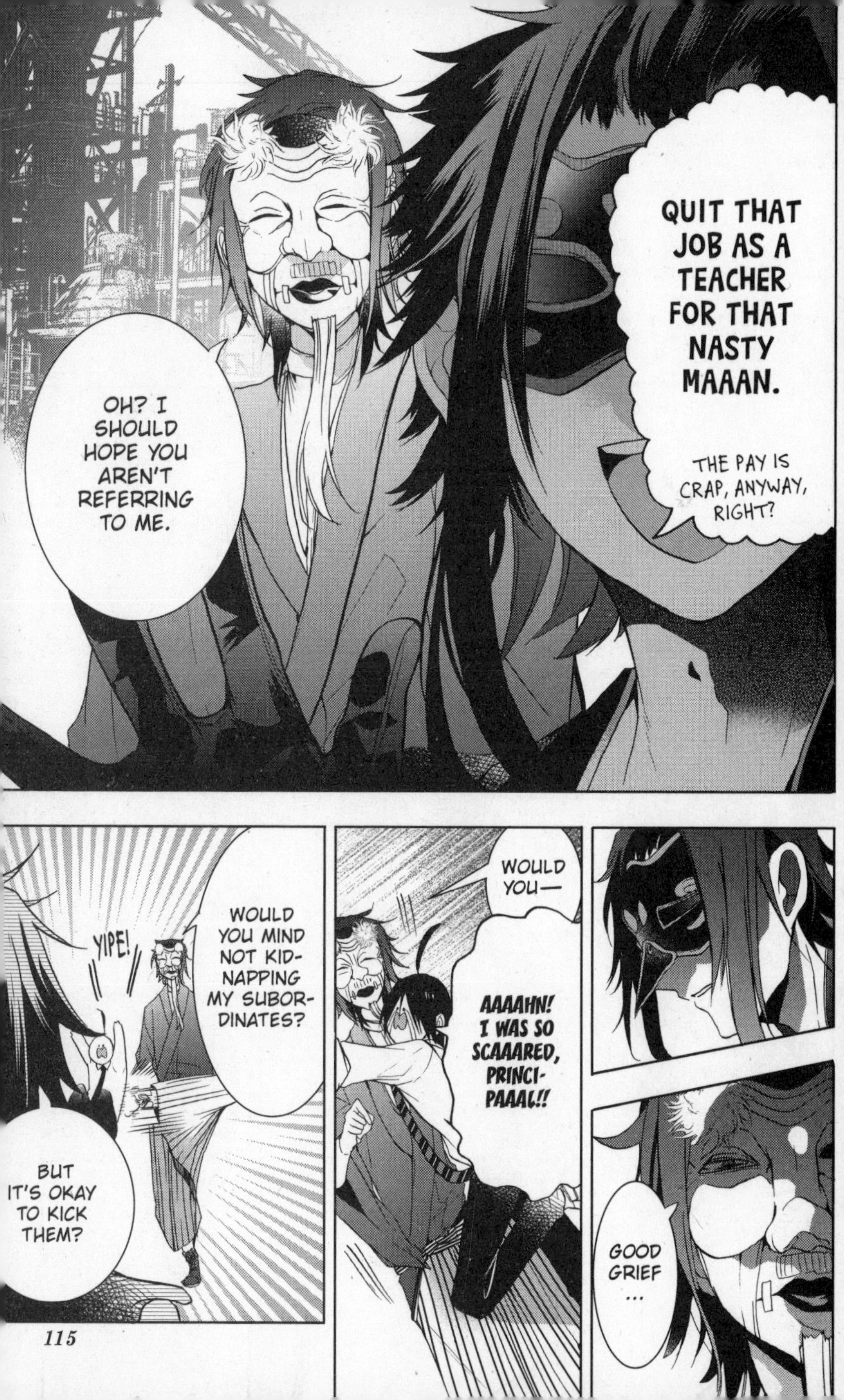
QUIT THAT JOB AS A TEACHER FOR THAT NASTY MAAAN.
THE PAY IS CRAP, ANYWAY, RIGHT?
OH? I SHOULD HOPE YOU AREN'T REFERRING TO ME.
GOOD GRIEF ...
WOULD YOU—
AAAAHN! I WAS SO SCAAARED, PRINCI-PAAAL!!
WOULD YOU MIND NOT KID-NAPPING MY SUBOR-DINATES?
YIPE!
BUT IT'S OKAY TO KICK THEM?

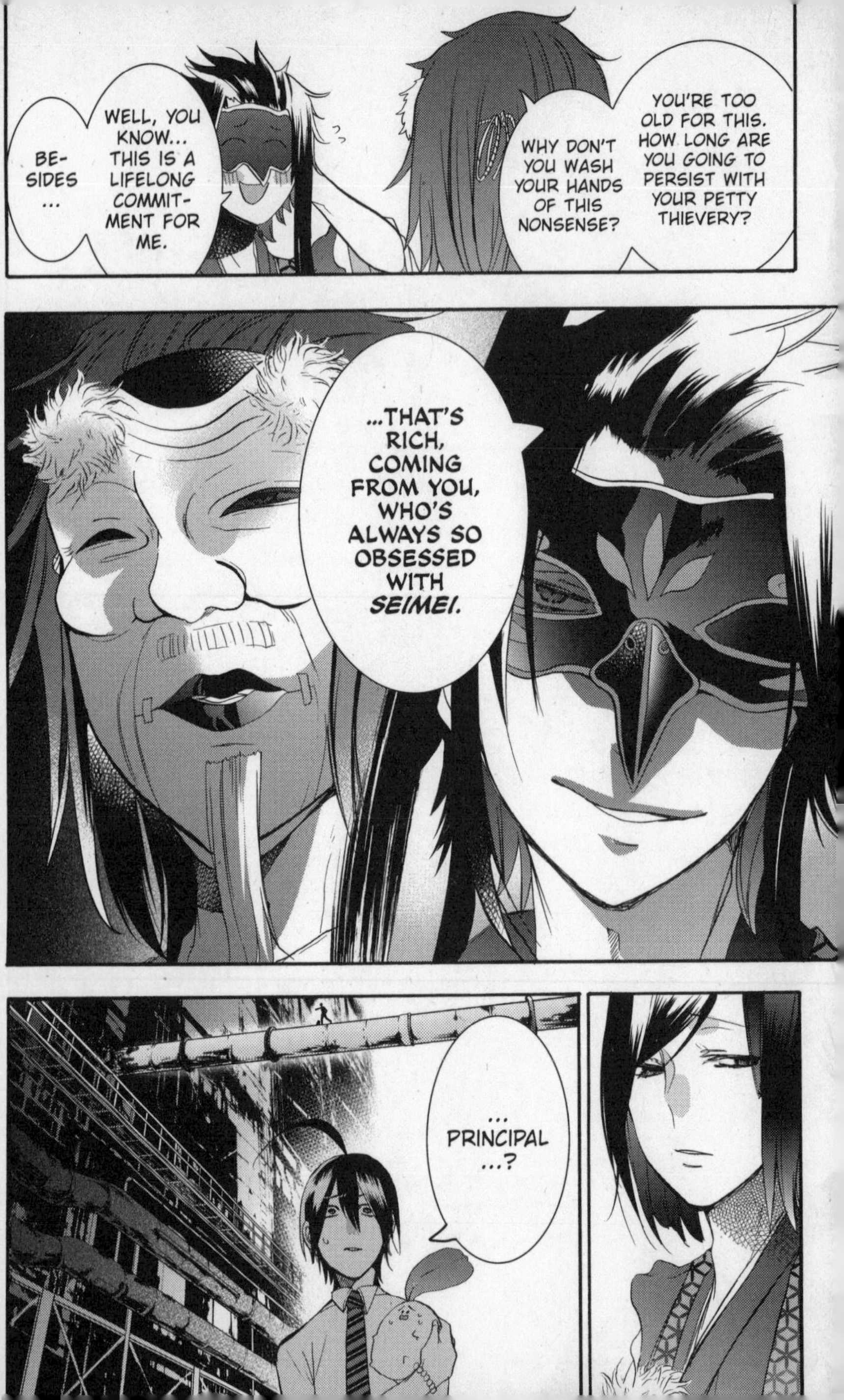
YOU'RE TOO OLD FOR THIS. HOW LONG ARE YOU GOING TO PERSIST WITH YOUR PETTY THIEVERY?
WHY DON'T YOU WASH YOUR HANDS OF THIS NONSENSE?
WELL, YOU KNOW... THIS IS A LIFELONG COMMIT-MENT FOR ME.
BE-SIDES...
...THAT'S RICH, COMING FROM YOU, WHO'S ALWAYS SO OBSESSED WITH *SEIMEI*.
...PRINCIPAL...?

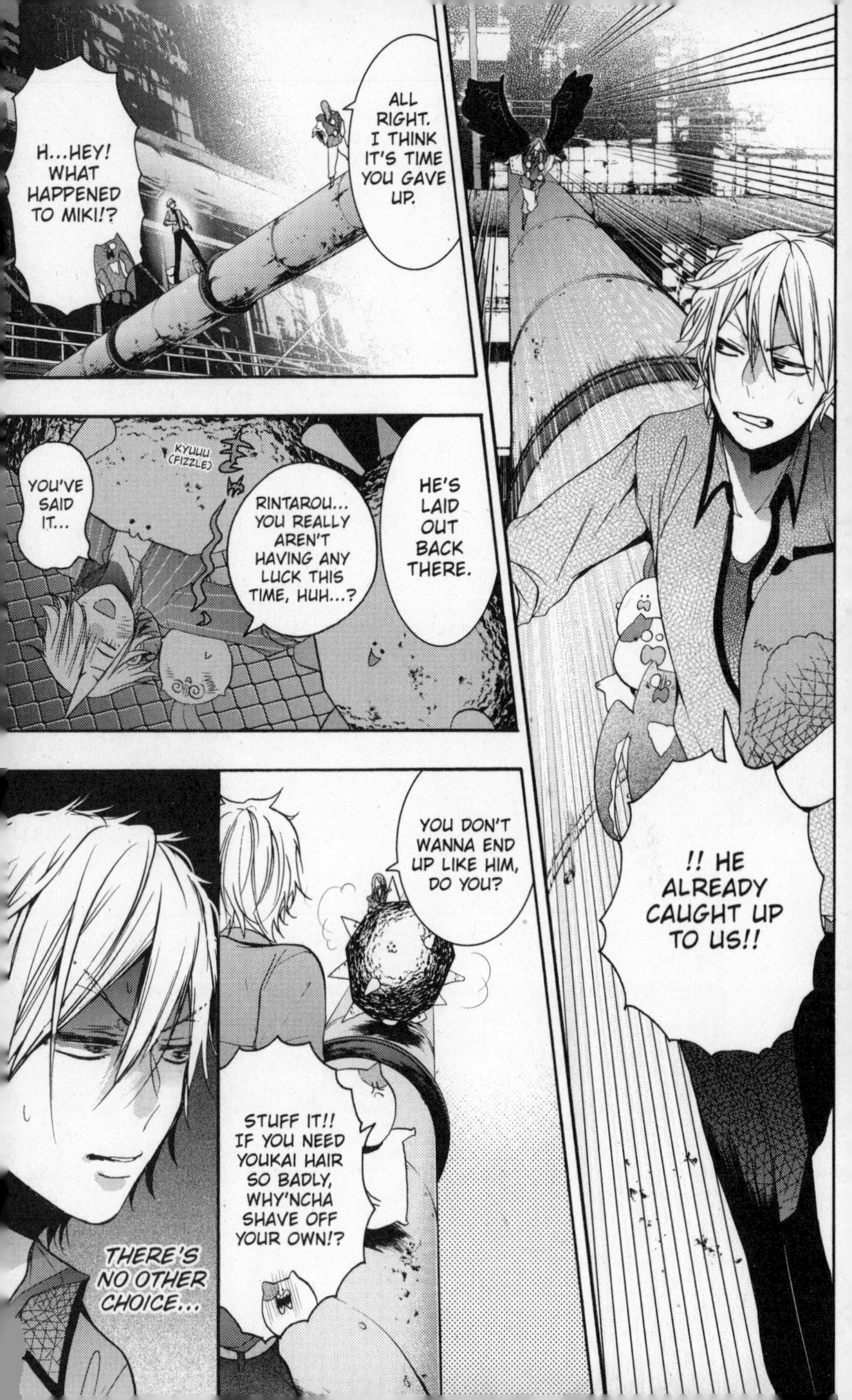
!! HE ALREADY CAUGHT UP TO US!!
ALL RIGHT. I THINK IT'S TIME YOU GAVE UP.
H...HEY! WHAT HAPPENED TO MIKI!?
HE'S LAID OUT BACK THERE.
KYUUU (FIZZLE)
RINTAROU... YOU REALLY AREN'T HAVING ANY LUCK THIS TIME, HUH...?
YOU'VE SAID IT...
YOU DON'T WANNA END UP LIKE HIM, DO YOU?
STUFF IT!! IF YOU NEED YOUKAI HAIR SO BADLY, WHY'NCHA SHAVE OFF YOUR OWN!?
THERE'S NO OTHER CHOICE...

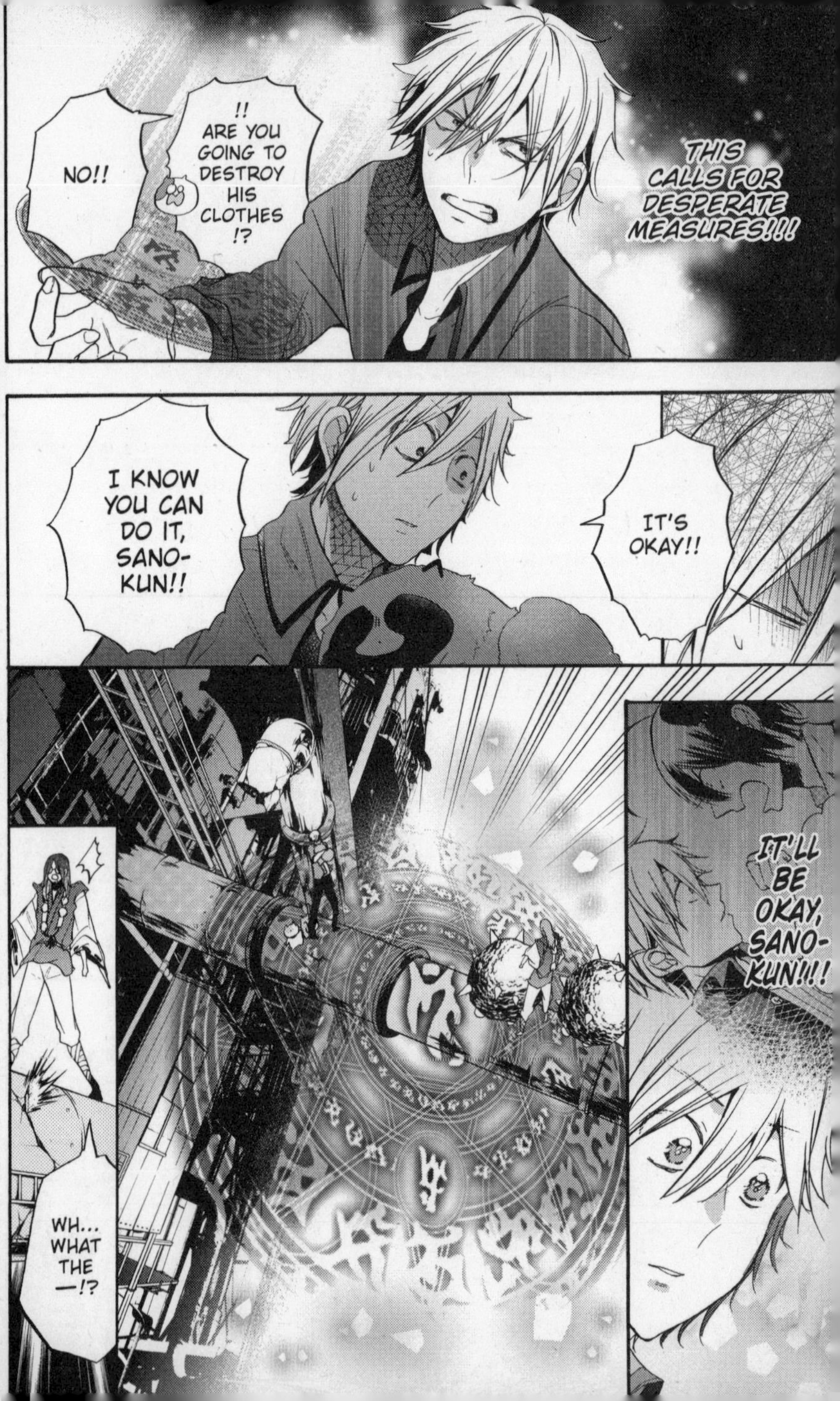
THIS CALLS FOR DESPERATE MEASURES!!!
!! ARE YOU GOING TO DESTROY HIS CLOTHES !?
NO!!
IT'S OKAY!!
I KNOW YOU CAN DO IT, SANO-KUN!!
IT'LL BE OKAY, SANO-KUN!!!
WH... WHAT THE—!?

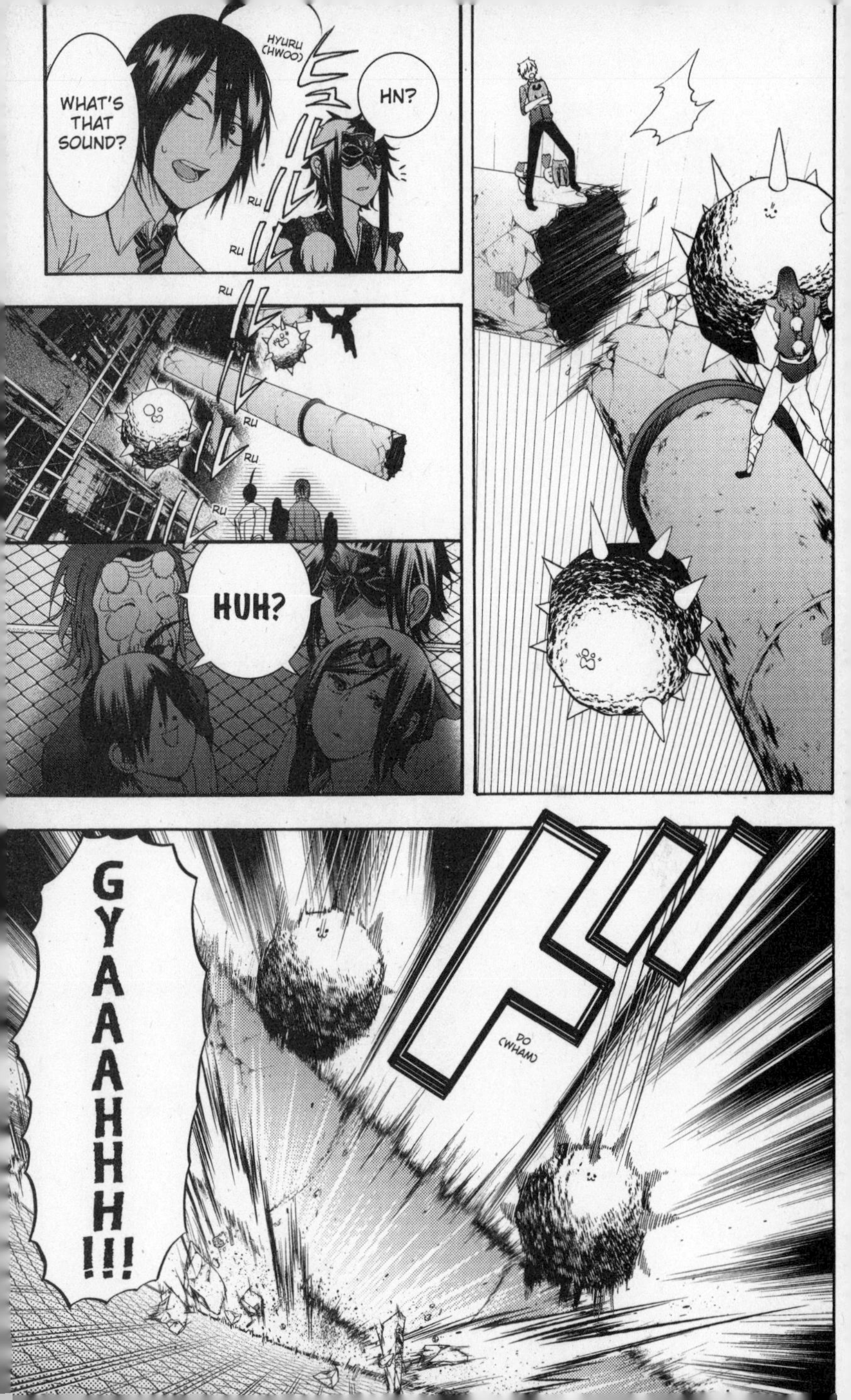
HYURU (HWOO)
HN?
WHAT'S THAT SOUND?
RU
RU
RU
RU
RU
RU
HUH?
DO (WHAM)
GYAAAHHH!!!

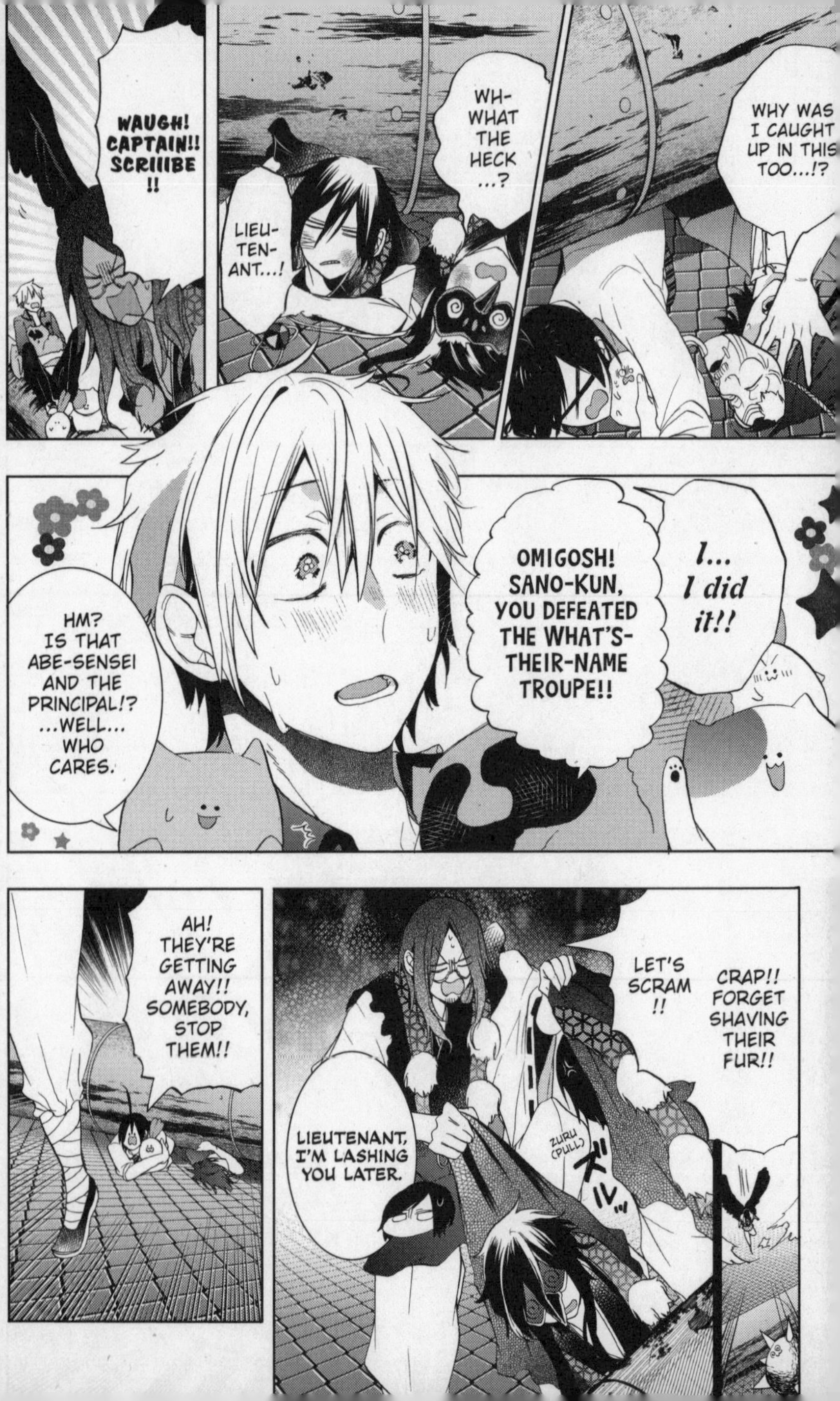
WHY WAS I CAUGHT UP IN THIS TOO...!?
WH- WHAT THE HECK ...?
LIEU- TEN- ANT...!
WAUGH! CAPTAIN!! SCRIIIBE !!
I... I did it!!
OMIGOSH! SANO-KUN, YOU DEFEATED THE WHAT'S-THEIR-NAME TROUPE!!
HM? IS THAT ABE-SENSEI AND THE PRINCIPAL!? ...WELL... WHO CARES.
CRAP!! FORGET SHAVING THEIR FUR!!
LET'S SCRAM !!
ZURU (PULL)
LIEUTENANT, I'M LASHING YOU LATER.
AH! THEY'RE GETTING AWAY!! SOMEBODY, STOP THEM!!

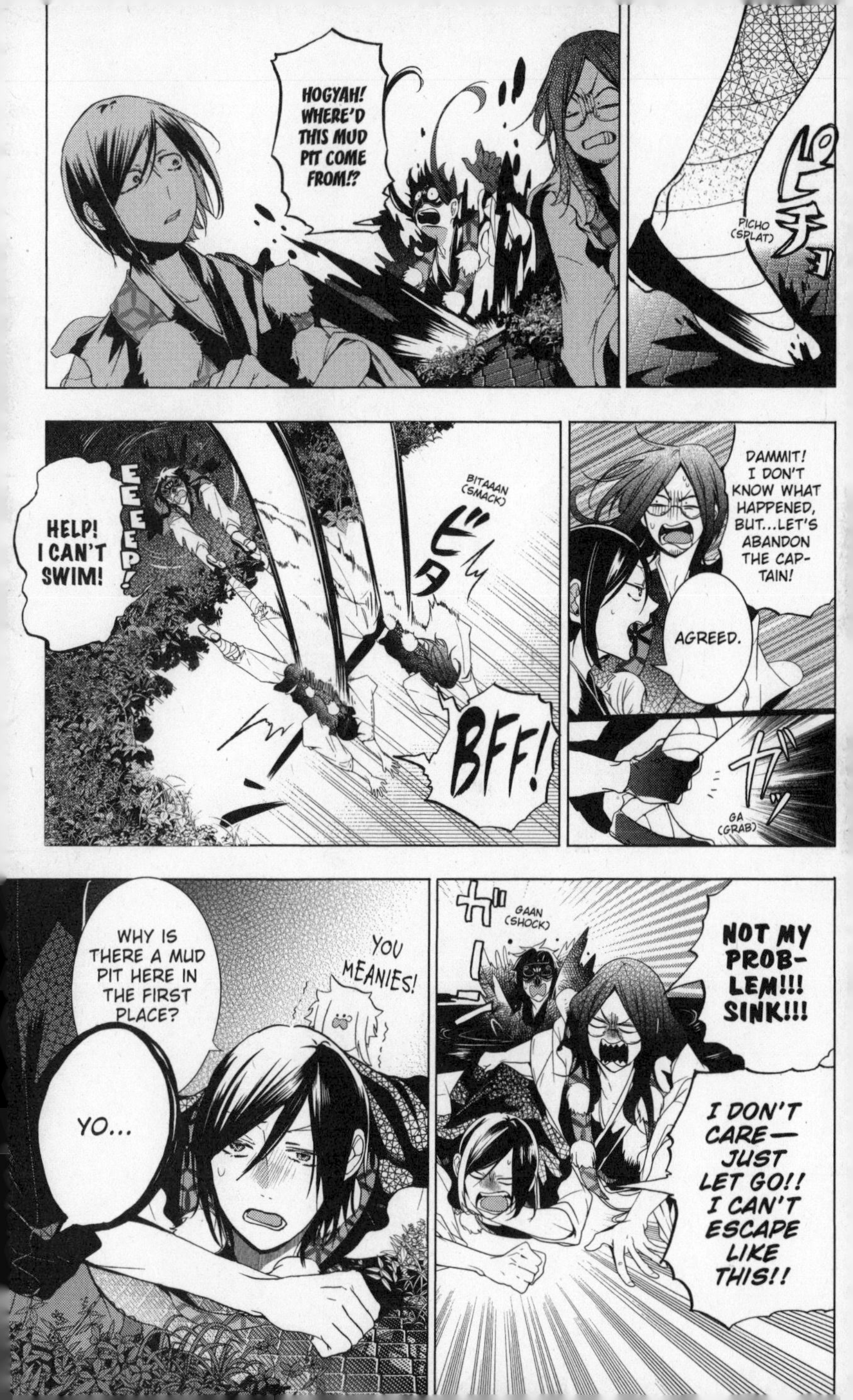
PICHO (SPLAT)
HOGYAH! WHERE'D THIS MUD PIT COME FROM!?
DAMMIT! I DON'T KNOW WHAT HAPPENED, BUT...LET'S ABANDON THE CAPTAIN!
AGREED.
GA (GRAB)
BITAAAN (SMACK)
EEEEP!
HELP! I CAN'T SWIM!
BFF!
GAAN (SHOCK)
NOT MY PROBLEM!!! SINK!!!
I DON'T CARE—JUST LET GO!! I CAN'T ESCAPE LIKE THIS!!
YOU MEANIES!
WHY IS THERE A MUD PIT HERE IN THE FIRST PLACE?
YO...

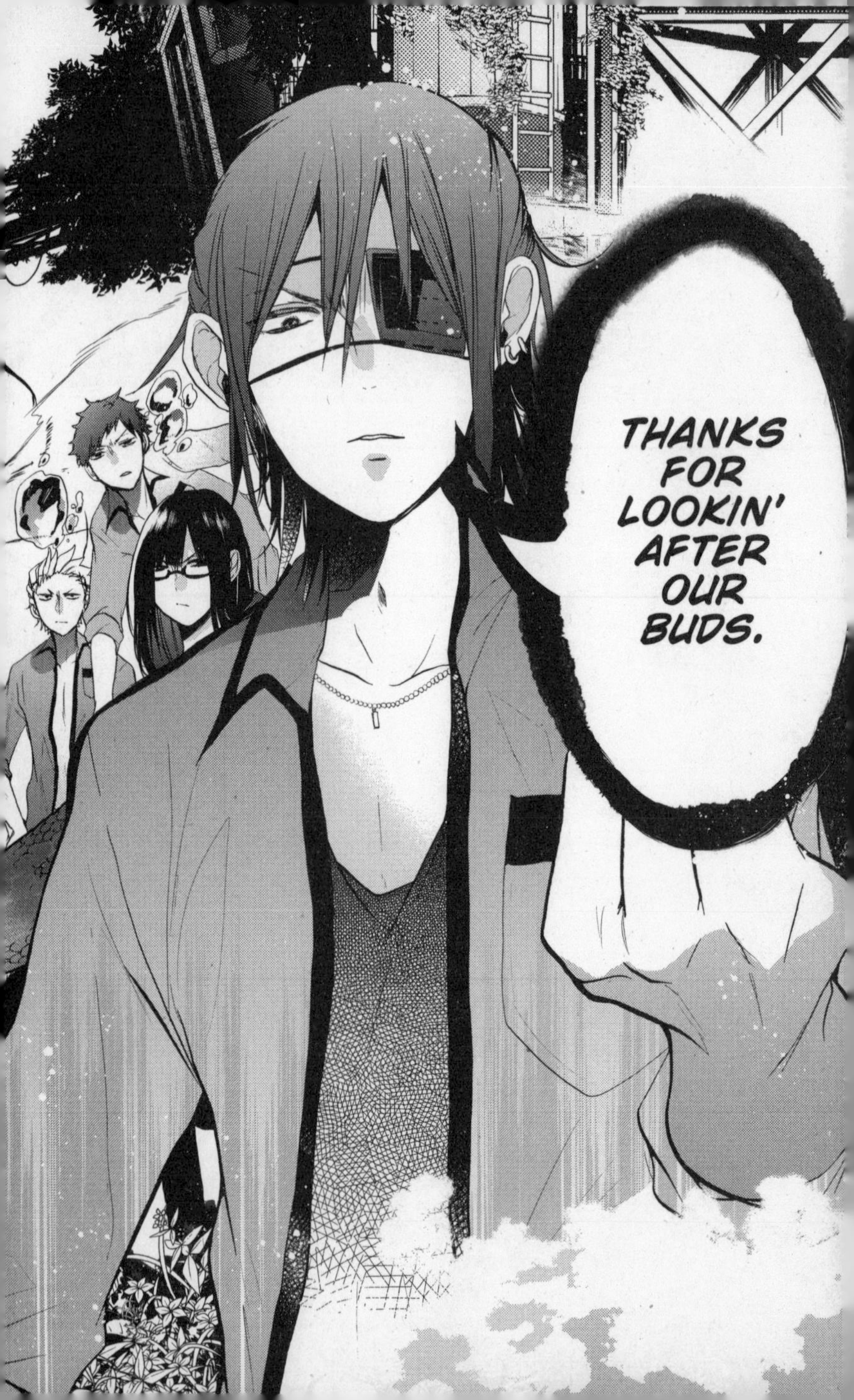
THANKS FOR LOOKIN' AFTER OUR BUDS.

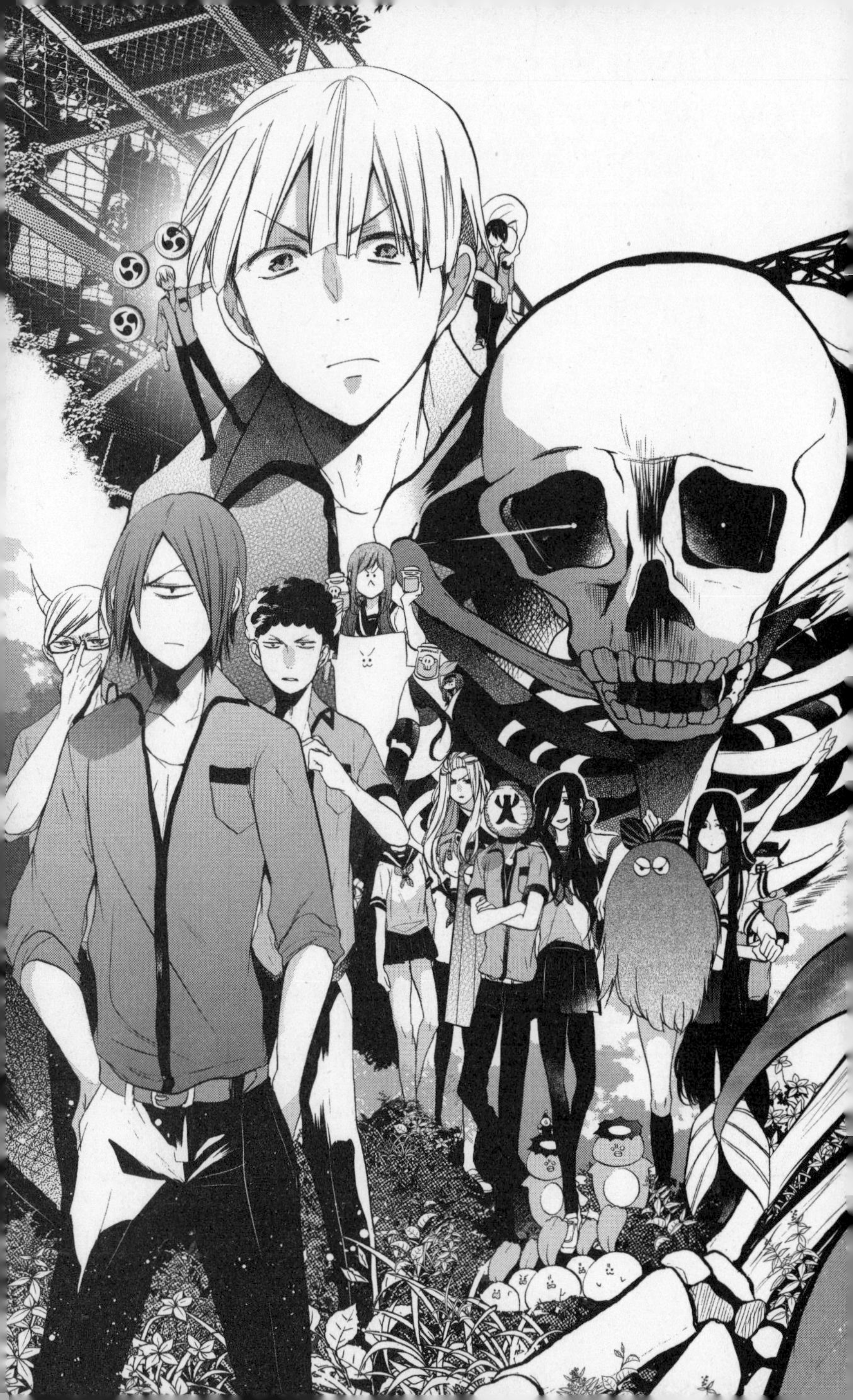

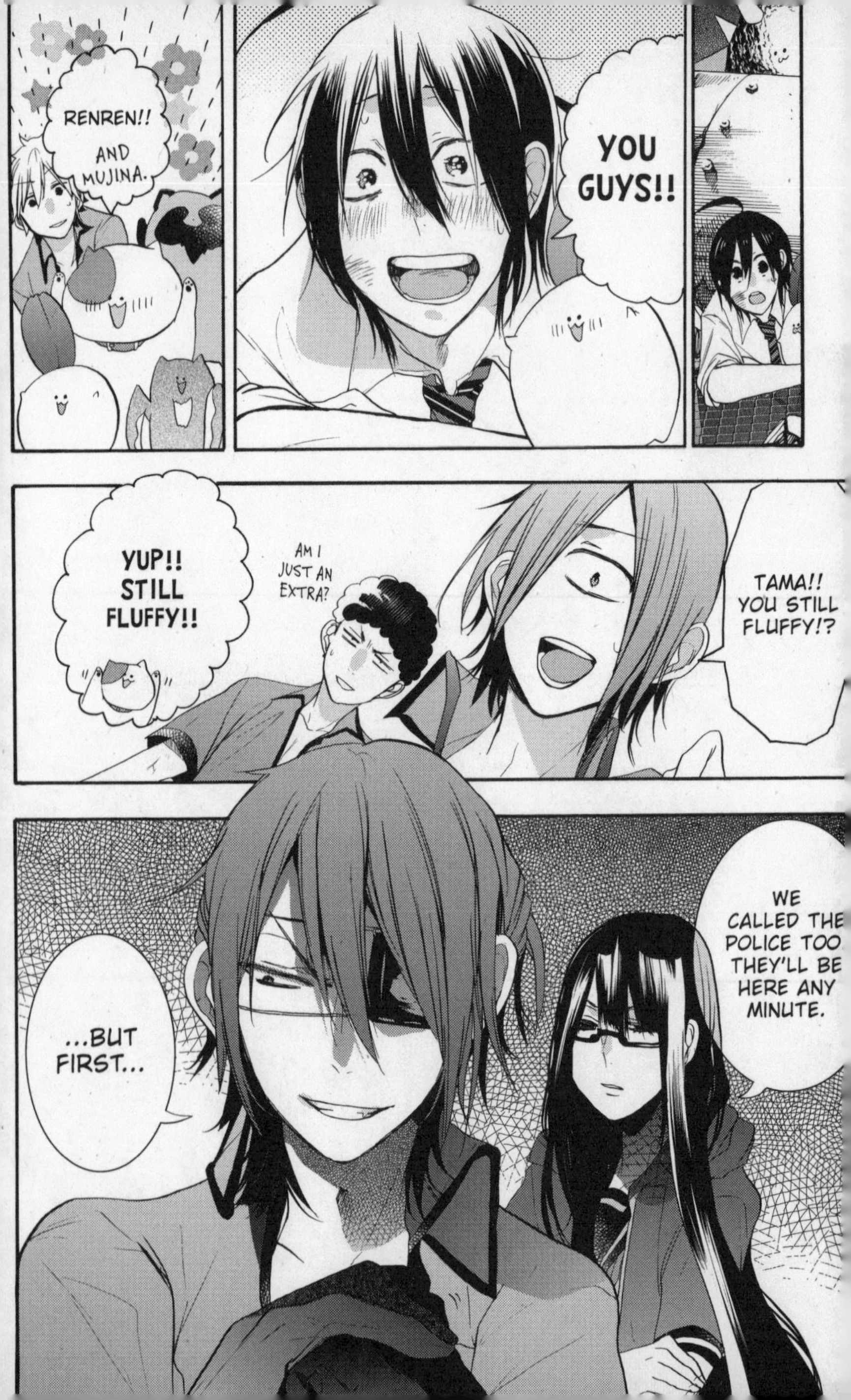
YOU GUYS!!
RENREN!! AND MUJINA.
TAMA!! YOU STILL FLUFFY!?
AM I JUST AN EXTRA?
YUP!! STILL FLUFFY!!
WE CALLED THE POLICE TOO. THEY'LL BE HERE ANY MINUTE.
...BUT FIRST...

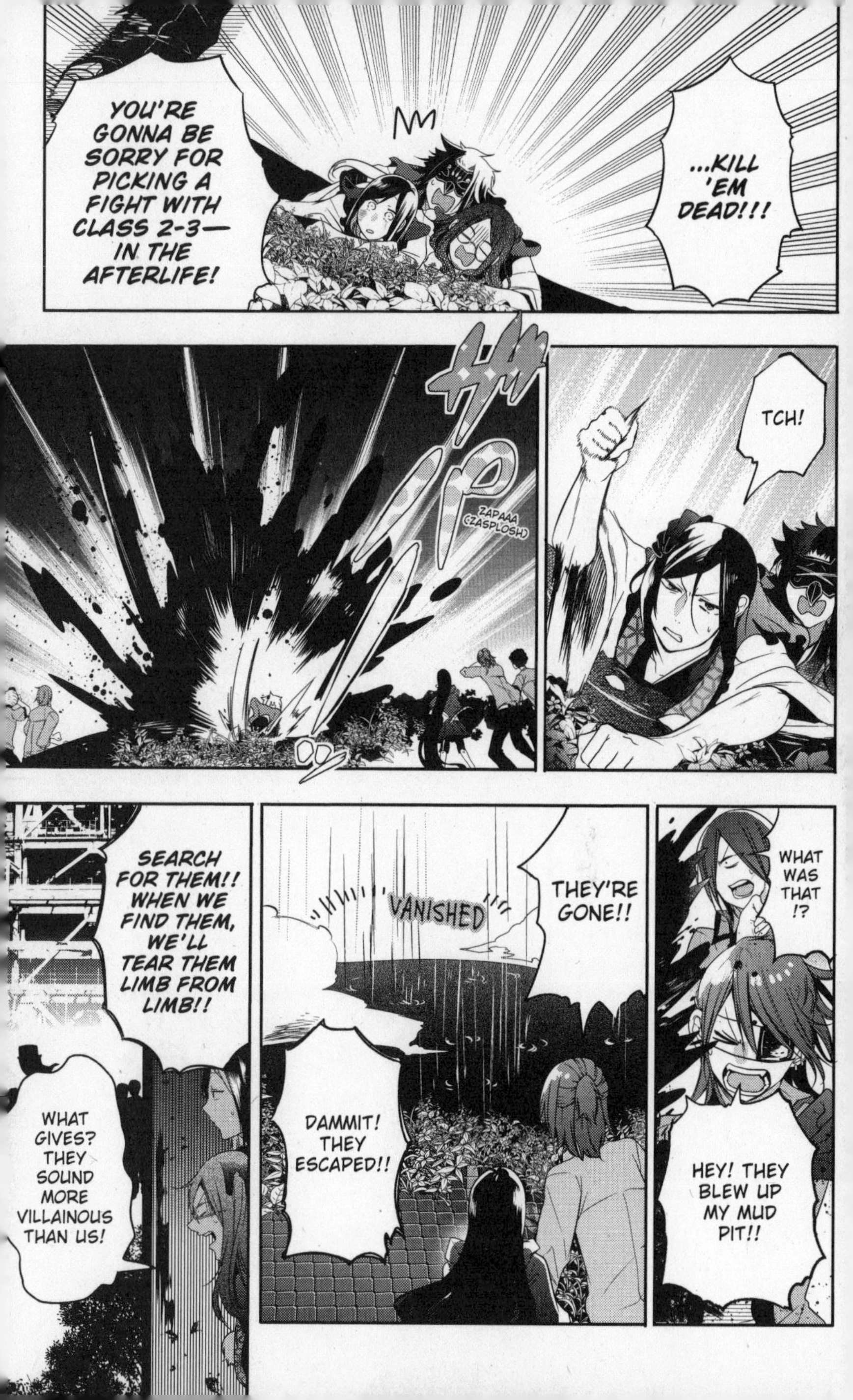
...KILL 'EM DEAD!!!
YOU'RE GONNA BE SORRY FOR PICKING A FIGHT WITH CLASS 2-3— IN THE AFTERLIFE!
TCH!
ZAPAAA (ZASPLOSH)
WHAT WAS THAT!?
HEY! THEY BLEW UP MY MUD PIT!!
THEY'RE GONE!!
VANISHED
DAMMIT! THEY ESCAPED!!
SEARCH FOR THEM!! WHEN WE FIND THEM, WE'LL TEAR THEM LIMB FROM LIMB!!
WHAT GIVES? THEY SOUND MORE VILLAINOUS THAN US!

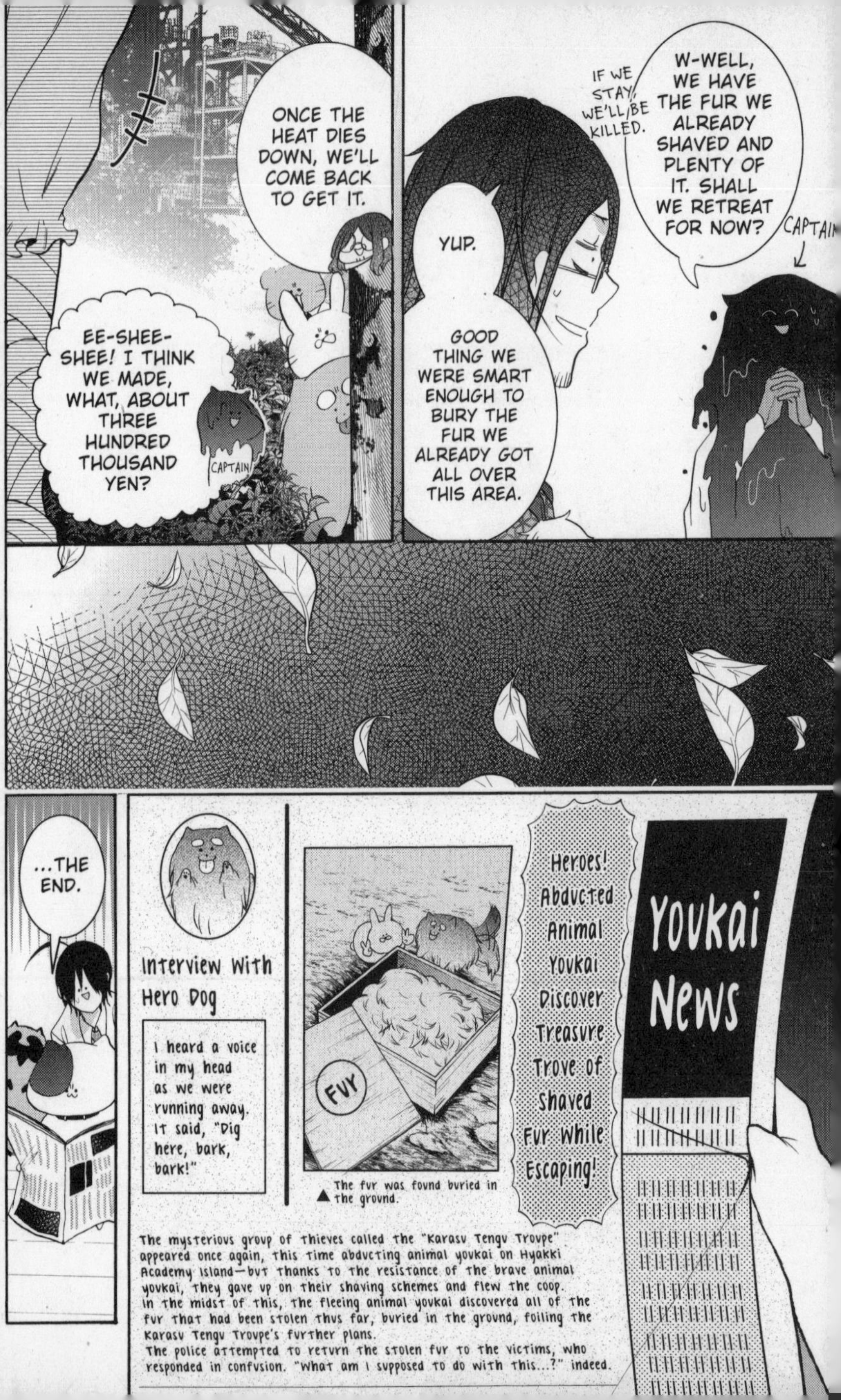
IF WE STAY, WE'LL BE KILLED.
W-WELL, WE HAVE THE FUR WE ALREADY SHAVED AND PLENTY OF IT. SHALL WE RETREAT FOR NOW?
CAPTAIN
YUP.
GOOD THING WE WERE SMART ENOUGH TO BURY THE FUR WE ALREADY GOT ALL OVER THIS AREA.
ONCE THE HEAT DIES DOWN, WE'LL COME BACK TO GET IT.
EE-SHEE-SHEE! I THINK WE MADE, WHAT, ABOUT THREE HUNDRED THOUSAND YEN?
CAPTAIN
Youkai News
Heroes! Abducted Animal Youkai Discover Treasure Trove of Shaved Fur While Escaping!
Fur
▲ The fur was found buried in the ground.
Interview With Hero Dog
I heard a voice in my head as we were running away. It said, "Dig here, bark, bark!"
The mysterious group of thieves called the "Karasu Tengu Troupe" appeared once again, this time abducting animal youkai on Hyakki Academy Island—but thanks to the resistance of the brave animal youkai, they gave up on their shaving schemes and flew the coop.
In the midst of this, the fleeing animal youkai discovered all of the fur that had been stolen thus far, buried in the ground, foiling the Karasu Tengu Troupe's further plans.
The police attempted to return the stolen fur to the victims, who responded in confusion. "What am I supposed to do with this...?" indeed.
...THE END.

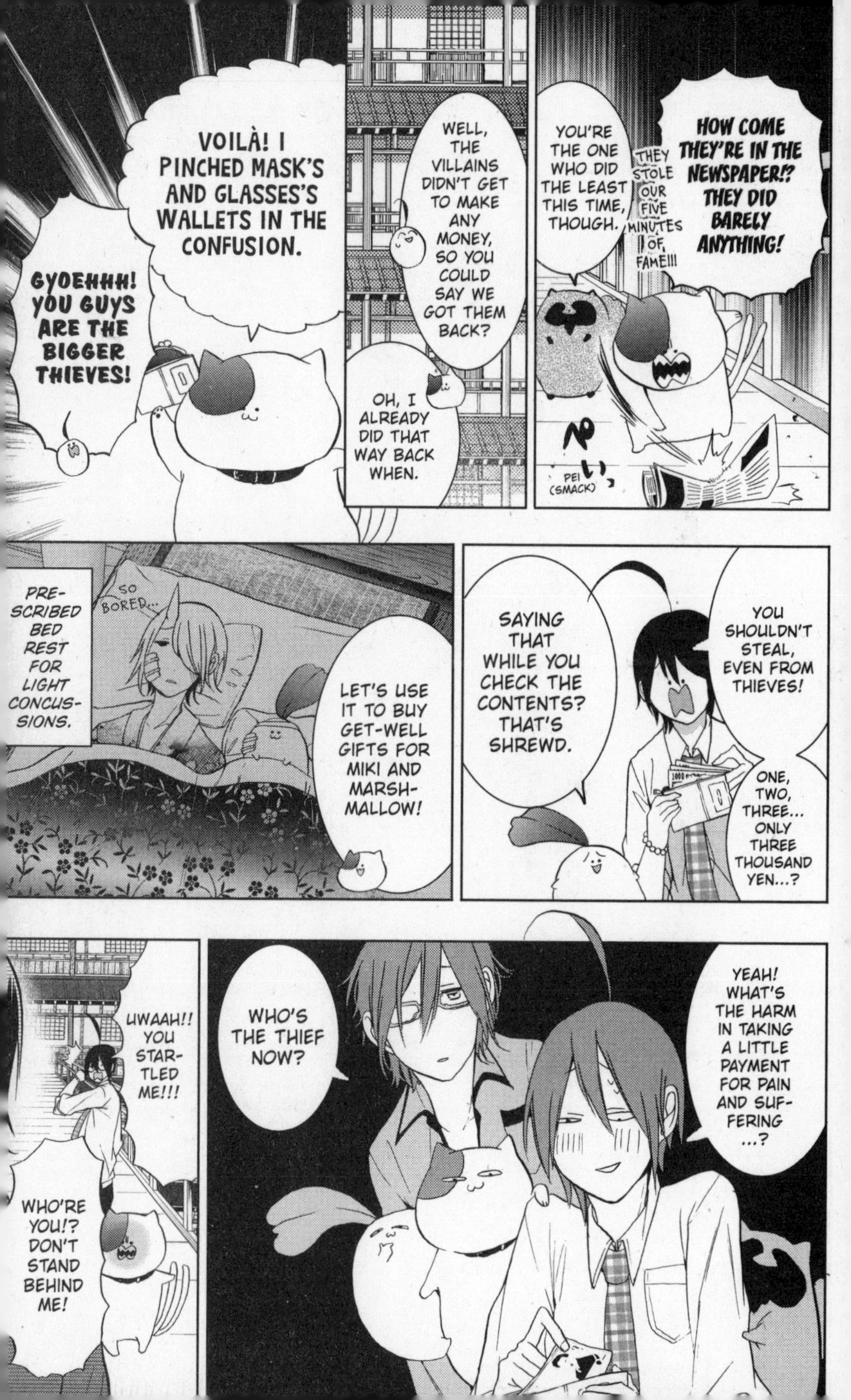
HOW COME THEY'RE IN THE NEWSPAPER!? THEY DID BARELY ANYTHING!
THEY STOLE OUR FIVE MINUTES OF FAME!!!
YOU'RE THE ONE WHO DID THE LEAST THIS TIME, THOUGH.
PEI (SMACK)
WELL, THE VILLAINS DIDN'T GET TO MAKE ANY MONEY, SO YOU COULD SAY WE GOT THEM BACK?
OH, I ALREADY DID THAT WAY BACK WHEN.
VOILÀ! I PINCHED MASK'S AND GLASSES'S WALLETS IN THE CONFUSION.
GYOEHHH! YOU GUYS ARE THE BIGGER THIEVES!
YOU SHOULDN'T STEAL, EVEN FROM THIEVES!
ONE, TWO, THREE... ONLY THREE THOUSAND YEN...?
SAYING THAT WHILE YOU CHECK THE CONTENTS? THAT'S SHREWD.
PRE-SCRIBED BED REST FOR LIGHT CONCUS-SIONS.
SO BORED...
LET'S USE IT TO BUY GET-WELL GIFTS FOR MIKI AND MARSH-MALLOW!
YEAH! WHAT'S THE HARM IN TAKING A LITTLE PAYMENT FOR PAIN AND SUF-FERING ...?
WHO'S THE THIEF NOW?
UWAAH!! YOU STAR-TLED ME!!!
WHO'RE YOU!? DON'T STAND BEHIND ME!

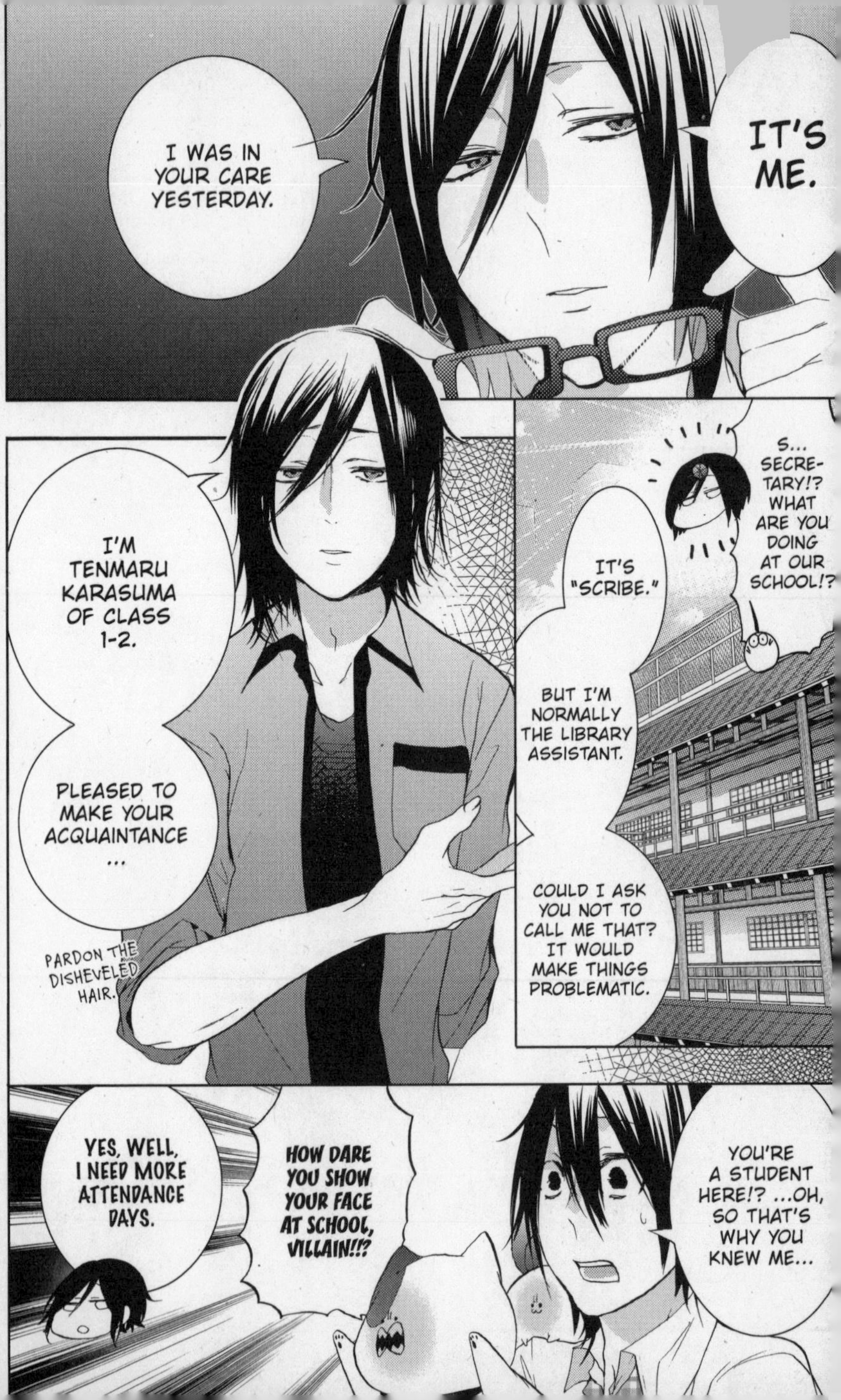
IT'S ME.
I WAS IN YOUR CARE YESTERDAY.
S... SECRETARY!? WHAT ARE YOU DOING AT OUR SCHOOL!?
IT'S "SCRIBE."
BUT I'M NORMALLY THE LIBRARY ASSISTANT.
COULD I ASK YOU NOT TO CALL ME THAT? IT WOULD MAKE THINGS PROBLEMATIC.
I'M TENMARU KARASUMA OF CLASS 1-2.
PLEASED TO MAKE YOUR ACQUAINTANCE ...
PARDON THE DISHEVELED HAIR.
YOU'RE A STUDENT HERE!? ...OH, SO THAT'S WHY YOU KNEW ME...
HOW DARE YOU SHOW YOUR FACE AT SCHOOL, VILLAIN!!?
YES, WELL, I NEED MORE ATTENDANCE DAYS.

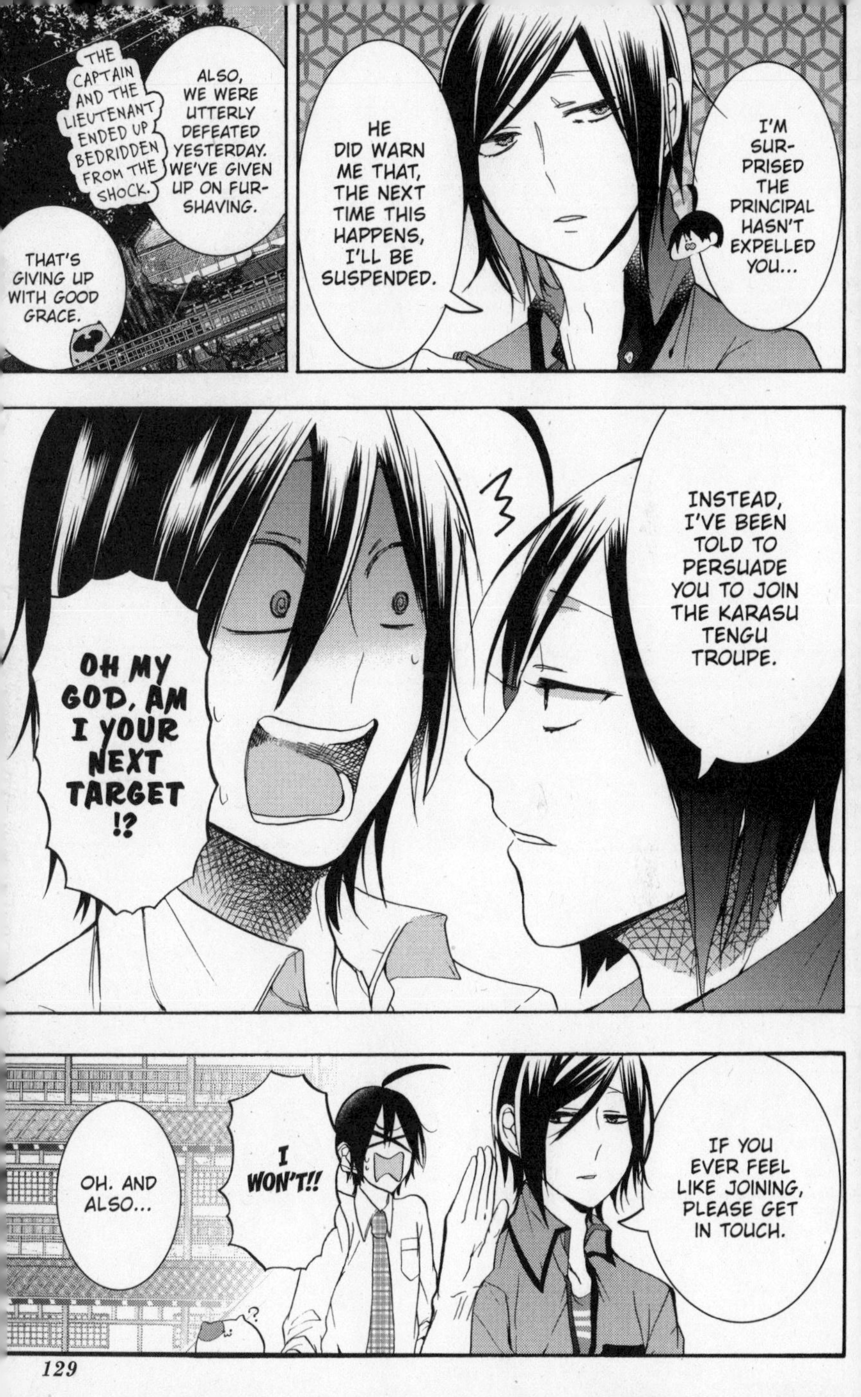
I'M SUR-PRISED THE PRINCIPAL HASN'T EXPELLED YOU...
HE DID WARN ME THAT, THE NEXT TIME THIS HAPPENS, I'LL BE SUSPENDED.
ALSO, WE WERE UTTERLY DEFEATED YESTERDAY. WE'VE GIVEN UP ON FUR-SHAVING.
THE CAPTAIN AND THE LIEUTENANT ENDED UP BEDRIDDEN FROM THE SHOCK.
THAT'S GIVING UP WITH GOOD GRACE.
INSTEAD, I'VE BEEN TOLD TO PERSUADE YOU TO JOIN THE KARASU TENGU TROUPE.
OH MY GOD, AM I YOUR NEXT TARGET !?
IF YOU EVER FEEL LIKE JOINING, PLEASE GET IN TOUCH.
I WON'T!!
OH. AND ALSO...

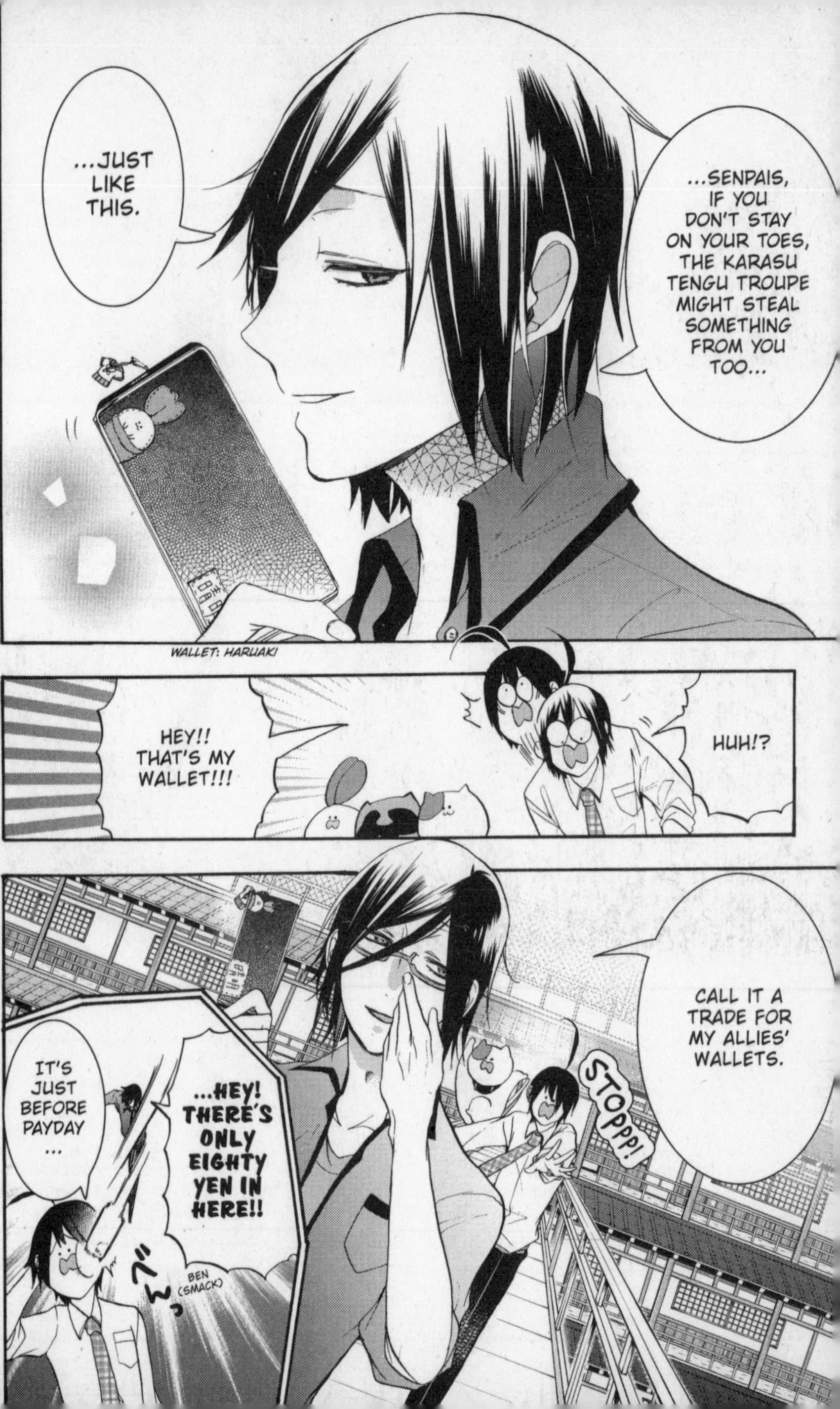
...SENPAIS, IF YOU DON'T STAY ON YOUR TOES, THE KARASU TENGU TROUPE MIGHT STEAL SOMETHING FROM YOU TOO...
...JUST LIKE THIS.
WALLET: HARUAKI
HUH!?
HEY!! THAT'S MY WALLET!!!
CALL IT A TRADE FOR MY ALLIES' WALLETS.
STOPPP!
...HEY! THERE'S ONLY EIGHTY YEN IN HERE!!
IT'S JUST BEFORE PAYDAY ...
べんっ
BEN (SMACK)

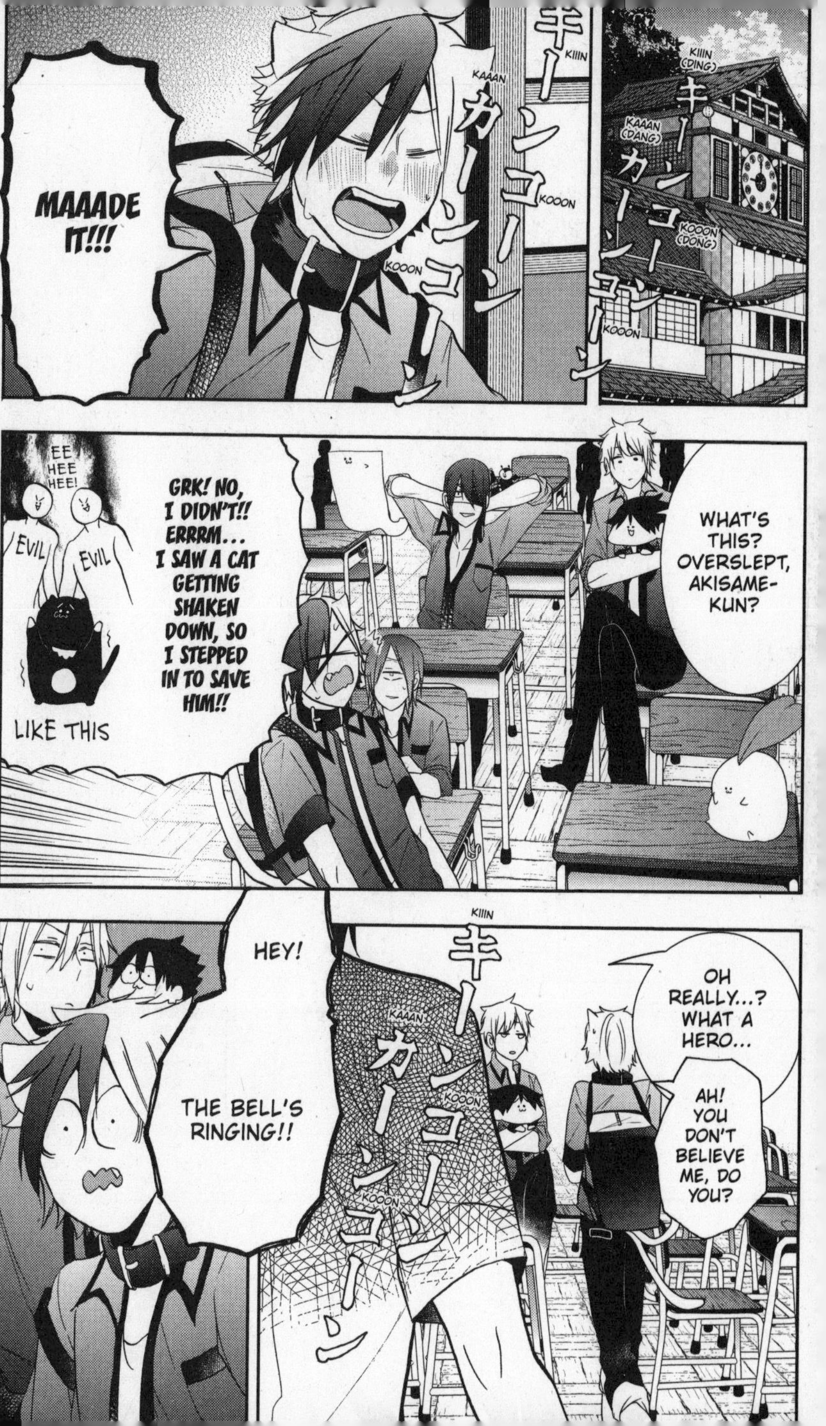
KIIIN (DING)
KAAAN (DANG)
KOOON (DONG)
KOOON
KIIIN
KAAAN
KOOON
KOOON
MAAADE IT!!!
WHAT'S THIS? OVERSLEPT, AKISAME-KUN?
GRK! NO, I DIDN'T!! ERRRM... I SAW A CAT GETTING SHAKEN DOWN, SO I STEPPED IN TO SAVE HIM!!
EE HEE HEE!
EVIL
EVIL
LIKE THIS
KIIIN
OH REALLY...? WHAT A HERO...
AH! YOU DON'T BELIEVE ME, DO YOU?
KAAAN
KOOON
KOOON
HEY!
THE BELL'S RINGING!!

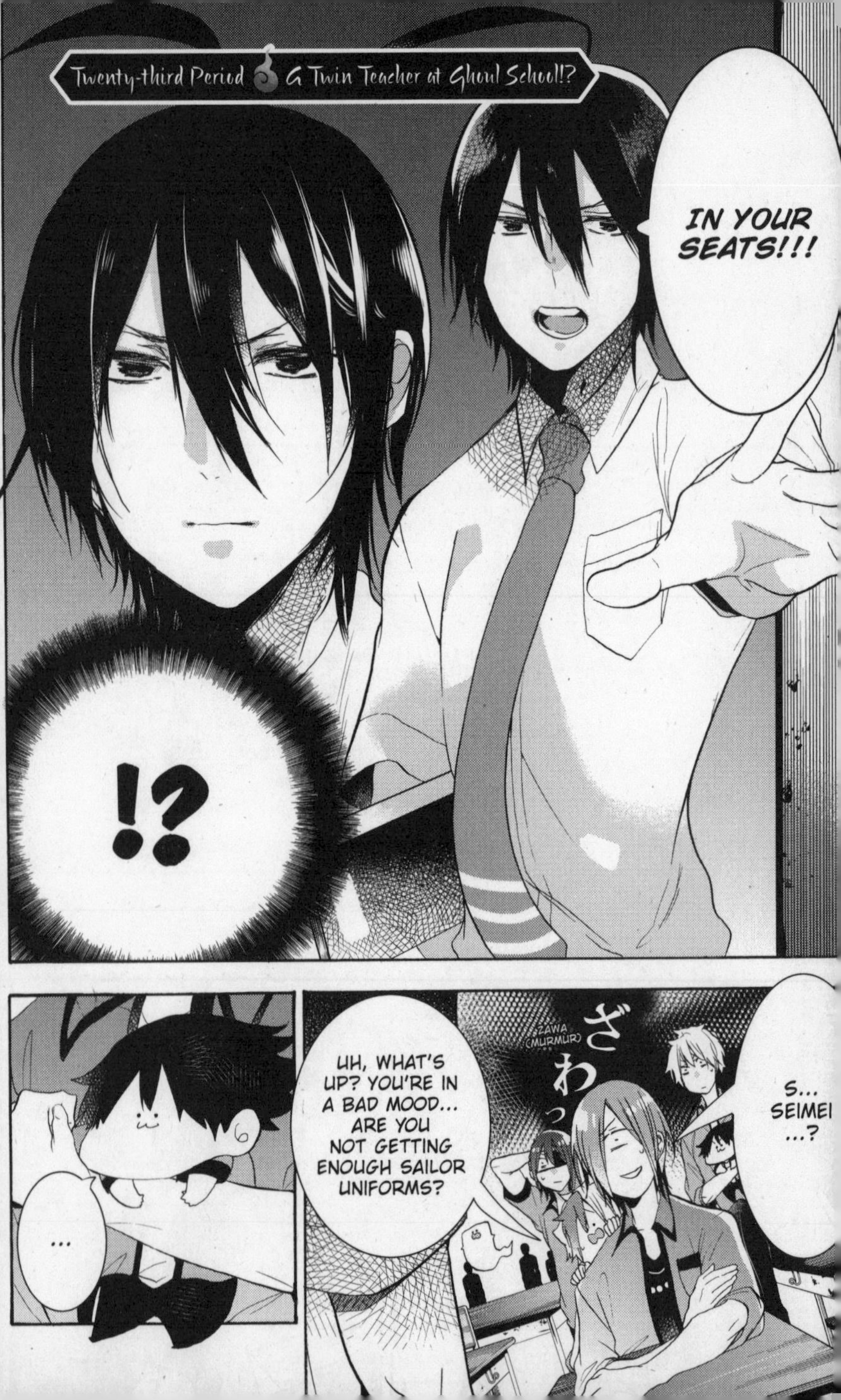
Twenty-third Period
A Twin Teacher at Ghoul School!?
IN YOUR SEATS!!!
!?
S... SEIMEI ...?
ざわっ
ZAWA (MURMUR)
UH, WHAT'S UP? YOU'RE IN A BAD MOOD... ARE YOU NOT GETTING ENOUGH SAILOR UNIFORMS?
...

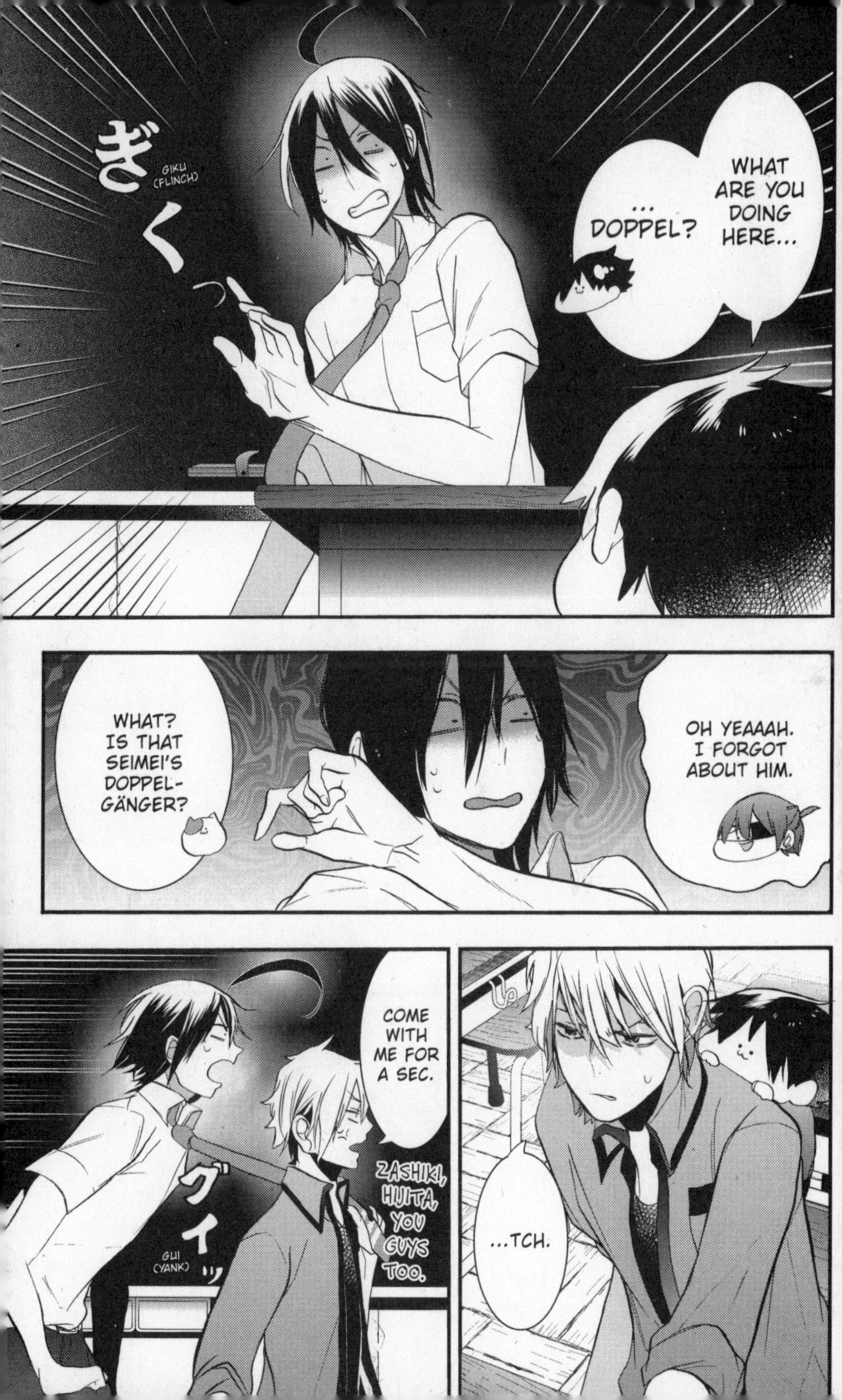
WHAT ARE YOU DOING HERE...
...DOPPEL?
ぎく
GIKU (FLINCH)
OH YEAAAH. I FORGOT ABOUT HIM.
WHAT? IS THAT SEIMEI'S DOPPEL-GÄNGER?
...TCH.
COME WITH ME FOR A SEC.
ZASHIKI, HIJITA, YOU GUYS TOO.
グイッ
GUI (YANK)

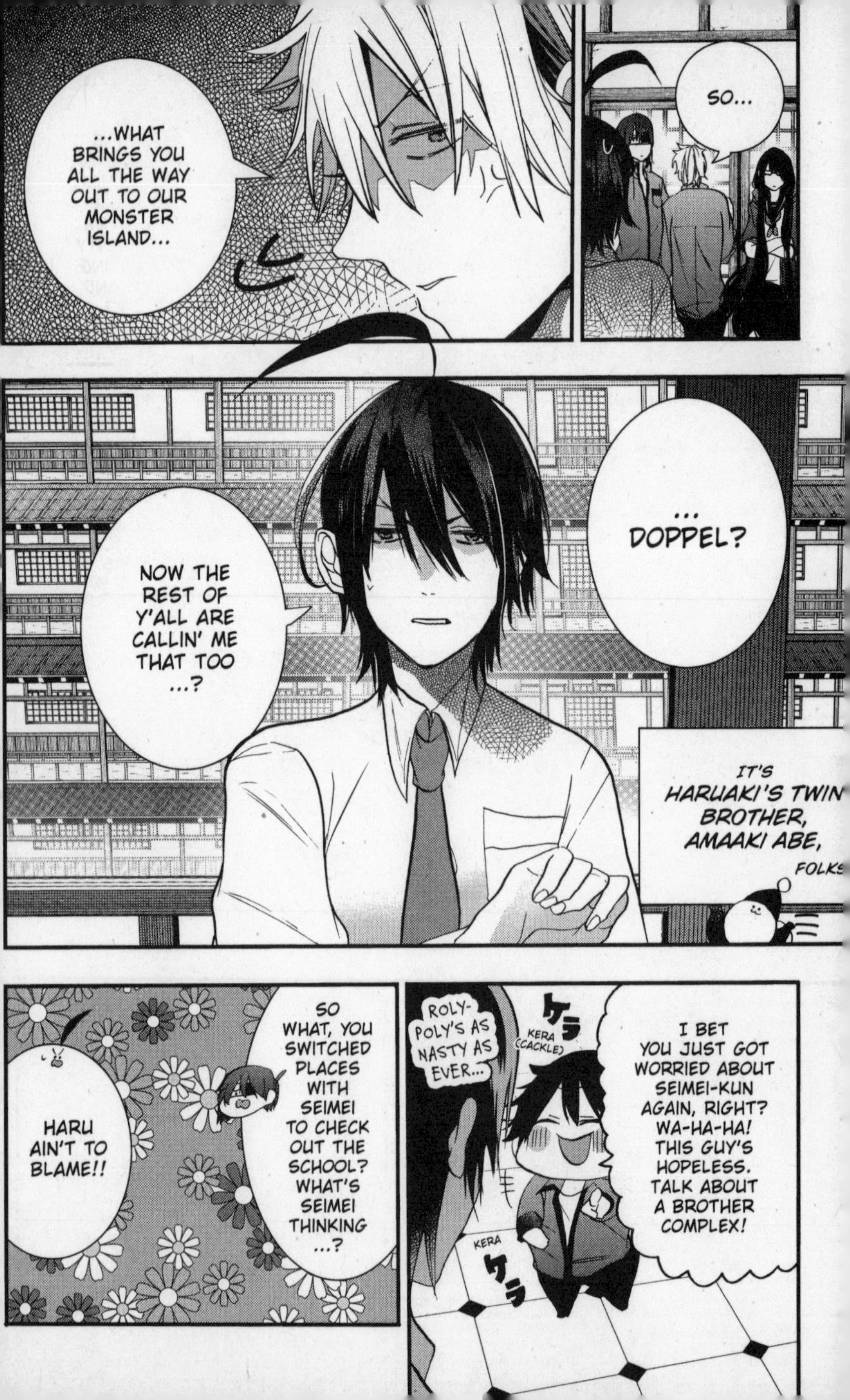
SO...
...WHAT BRINGS YOU ALL THE WAY OUT TO OUR MONSTER ISLAND...
... DOPPEL?
NOW THE REST OF Y'ALL ARE CALLIN' ME THAT TOO ...?
IT'S HARUAKI'S TWIN BROTHER, AMAAKI ABE, FOLKS
I BET YOU JUST GOT WORRIED ABOUT SEIMEI-KUN AGAIN, RIGHT? WA-HA-HA! THIS GUY'S HOPELESS. TALK ABOUT A BROTHER COMPLEX!
ケラ KERA (CACKLE)
ROLY-POLY'S AS NASTY AS EVER...
KERA ケラ
SO WHAT, YOU SWITCHED PLACES WITH SEIMEI TO CHECK OUT THE SCHOOL? WHAT'S SEIMEI THINKING ...?
HARU AIN'T TO BLAME!!

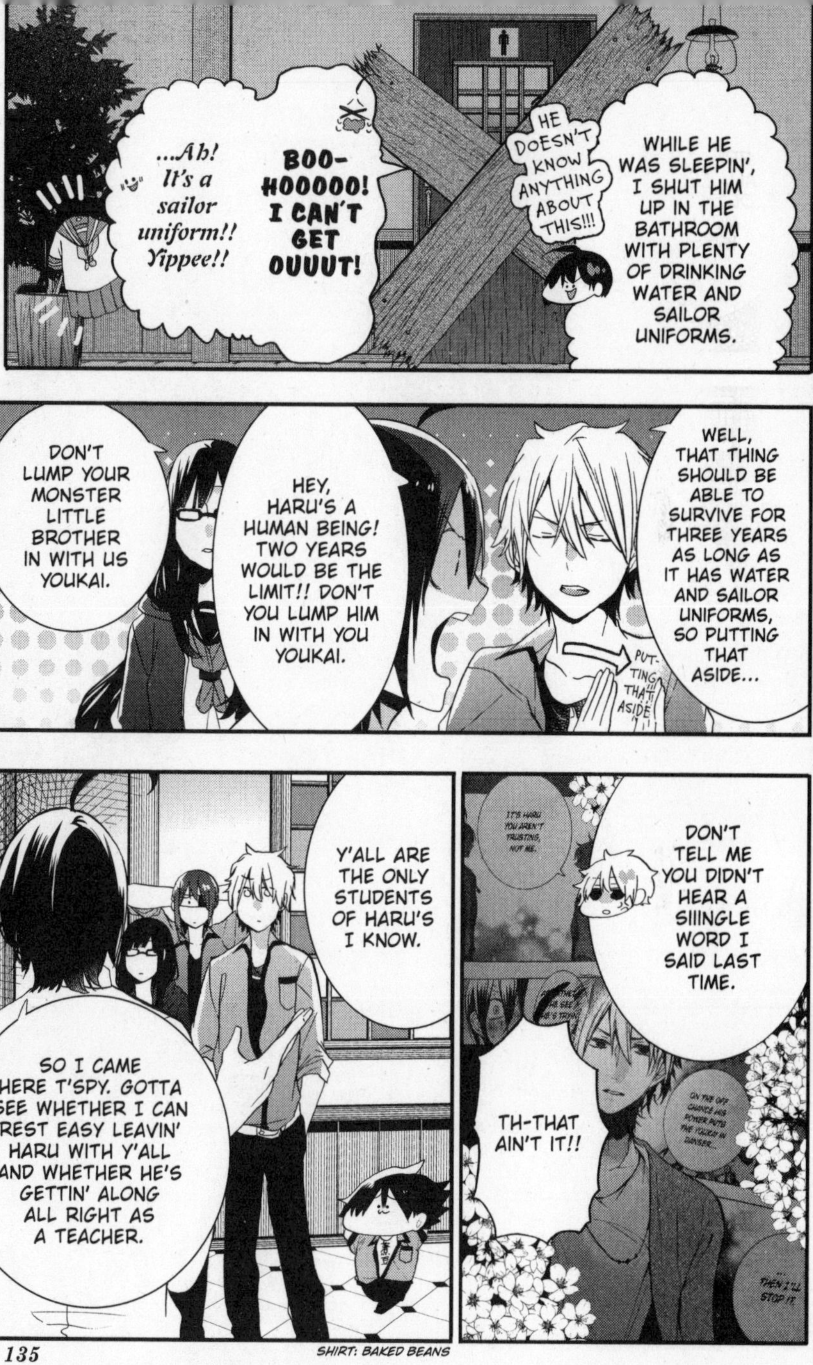
WHILE HE WAS SLEEPIN', I SHUT HIM UP IN THE BATHROOM WITH PLENTY OF DRINKING WATER AND SAILOR UNIFORMS.
HE DOESN'T KNOW ANYTHING ABOUT THIS!!!
BOO-HOOOOO! I CAN'T GET OUUUT!
...Ah! It's a sailor uniform!! Yippee!!
WELL, THAT THING SHOULD BE ABLE TO SURVIVE FOR THREE YEARS AS LONG AS IT HAS WATER AND SAILOR UNIFORMS, SO PUTTING THAT ASIDE...
PUTTING THAT ASIDE
HEY, HARU'S A HUMAN BEING! TWO YEARS WOULD BE THE LIMIT!! DON'T YOU LUMP HIM IN WITH YOU YOUKAI.
DON'T LUMP YOUR MONSTER LITTLE BROTHER IN WITH US YOUKAI.
DON'T TELL ME YOU DIDN'T HEAR A SIIINGLE WORD I SAID LAST TIME.
IT'S HARU YOU AREN'T TRUSTING, NOT ME.
TH-THAT AIN'T IT!!
ON THE OFF CHANCE HIS POWER PUTS THE YOUKAI IN DANGER...
...THEN I'LL STOP IT.
Y'ALL ARE THE ONLY STUDENTS OF HARU'S I KNOW.
SO I CAME HERE T'SPY. GOTTA SEE WHETHER I CAN REST EASY LEAVIN' HARU WITH Y'ALL AND WHETHER HE'S GETTIN' ALONG ALL RIGHT AS A TEACHER.

SHIRT: BAKED BEANS

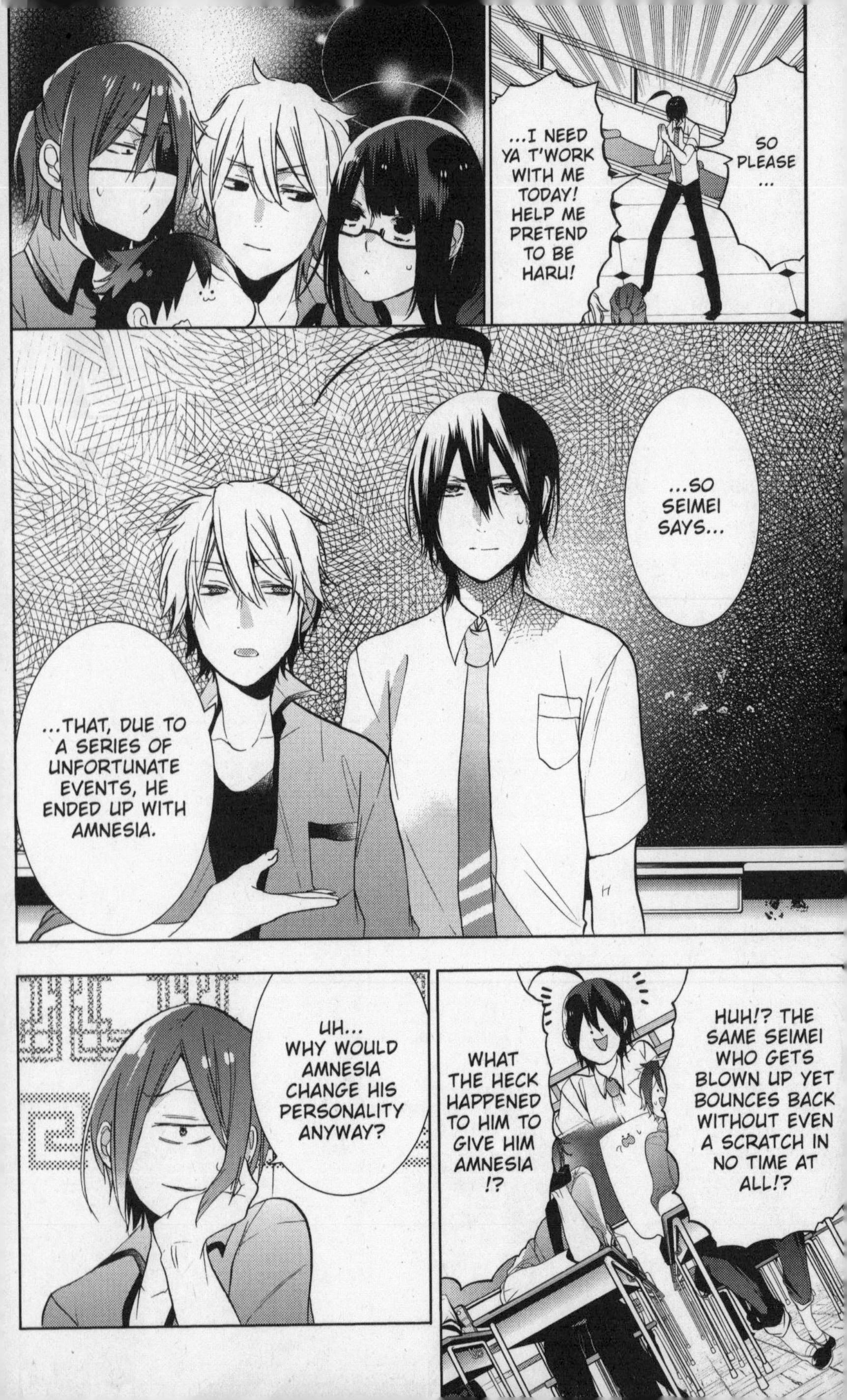
SO PLEASE ...
...I NEED YA T'WORK WITH ME TODAY! HELP ME PRETEND TO BE HARU!
...SO SEIMEI SAYS...
...THAT, DUE TO A SERIES OF UNFORTUNATE EVENTS, HE ENDED UP WITH AMNESIA.
HUH!? THE SAME SEIMEI WHO GETS BLOWN UP YET BOUNCES BACK WITHOUT EVEN A SCRATCH IN NO TIME AT ALL!?
WHAT THE HECK HAPPENED TO HIM TO GIVE HIM AMNESIA !?
UH... WHY WOULD AMNESIA CHANGE HIS PERSONALITY ANYWAY?

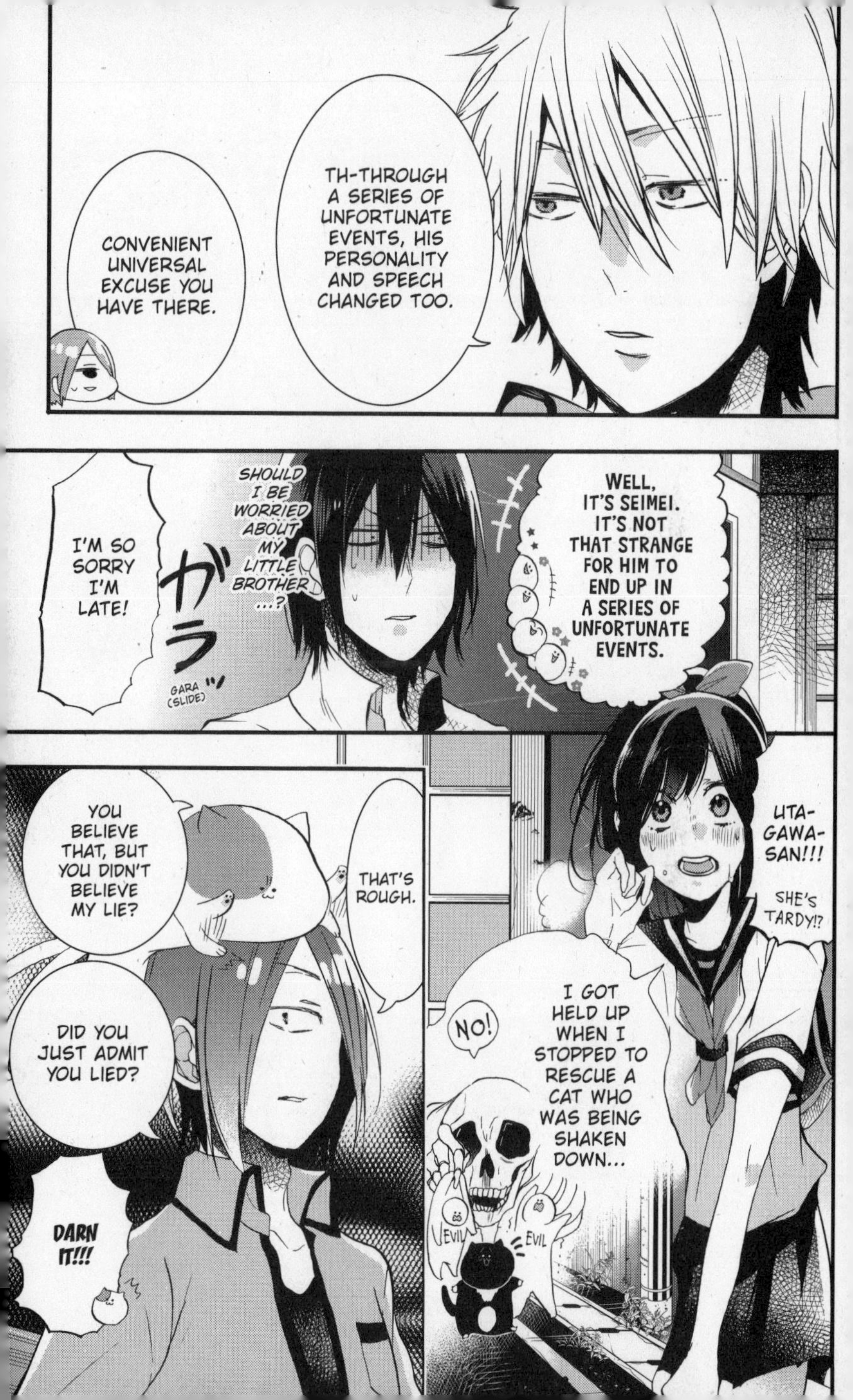
TH-THROUGH A SERIES OF UNFORTUNATE EVENTS, HIS PERSONALITY AND SPEECH CHANGED TOO.
CONVENIENT UNIVERSAL EXCUSE YOU HAVE THERE.
WELL, IT'S SEIMEI. IT'S NOT THAT STRANGE FOR HIM TO END UP IN A SERIES OF UNFORTUNATE EVENTS.
SHOULD I BE WORRIED ABOUT MY LITTLE BROTHER ...?
GARA (SLIDE)
I'M SO SORRY I'M LATE!
UTA-GAWA-SAN!!!
SHE'S TARDY!?
I GOT HELD UP WHEN I STOPPED TO RESCUE A CAT WHO WAS BEING SHAKEN DOWN...
NO!
EVIL
EVIL
THAT'S ROUGH.
YOU BELIEVE THAT, BUT YOU DIDN'T BELIEVE MY LIE?
DID YOU JUST ADMIT YOU LIED?
DARN IT!!!

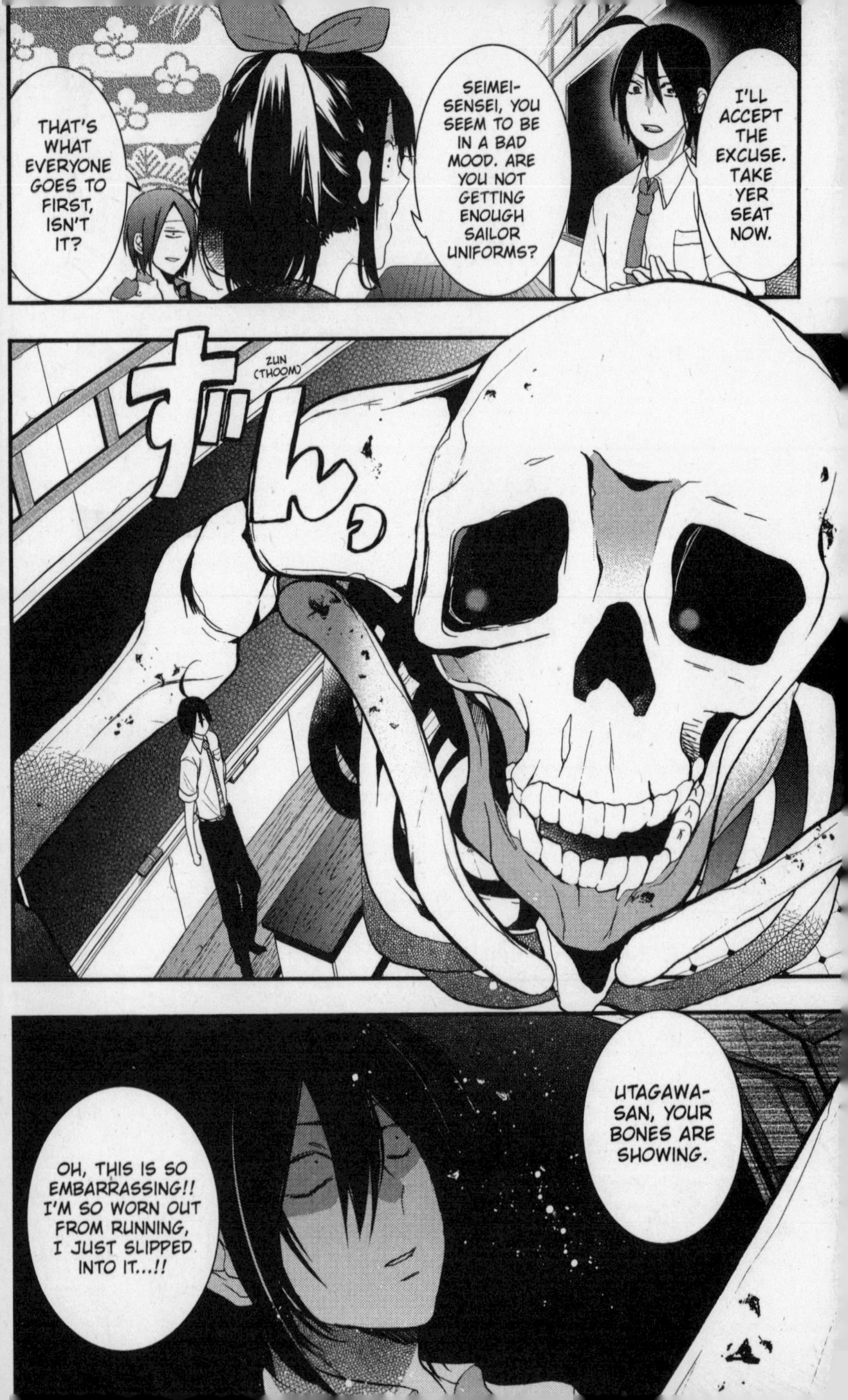
I'LL ACCEPT THE EXCUSE. TAKE YER SEAT NOW.
SEIMEI-SENSEI, YOU SEEM TO BE IN A BAD MOOD. ARE YOU NOT GETTING ENOUGH SAILOR UNIFORMS?
THAT'S WHAT EVERYONE GOES TO FIRST, ISN'T IT?
ずんっ
ZUN (THOOM)
UTAGAWA-SAN, YOUR BONES ARE SHOWING.
OH, THIS IS SO EMBARRASSING!! I'M SO WORN OUT FROM RUNNING, I JUST SLIPPED INTO IT...!!

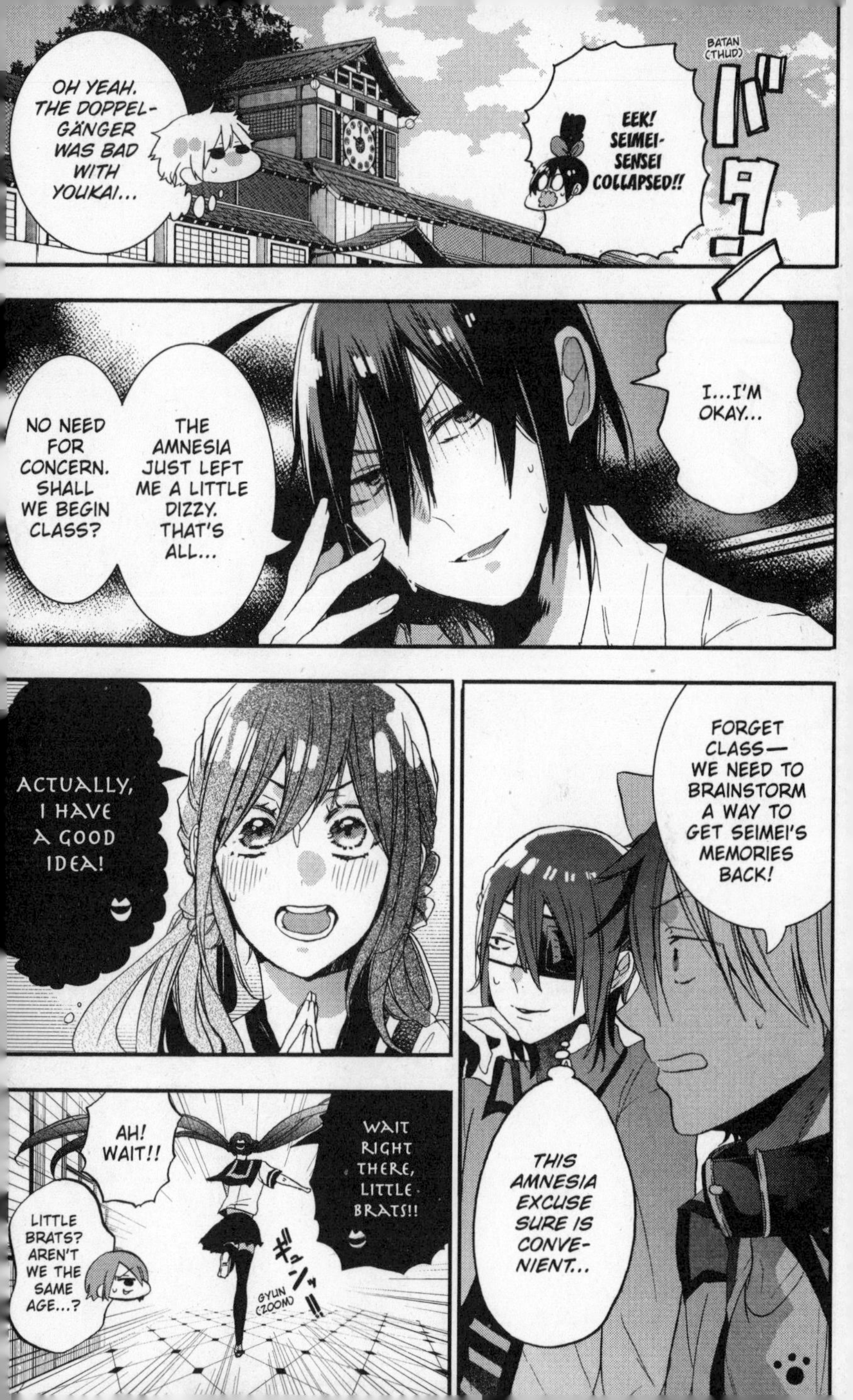
BATAN (THUD)
EEK! SEIMEI-SENSEI COLLAPSED!!
OH YEAH. THE DOPPELGÄNGER WAS BAD WITH YOUKAI...
I...I'M OKAY...
THE AMNESIA JUST LEFT ME A LITTLE DIZZY. THAT'S ALL...
NO NEED FOR CONCERN. SHALL WE BEGIN CLASS?
FORGET CLASS—WE NEED TO BRAINSTORM A WAY TO GET SEIMEI'S MEMORIES BACK!
THIS AMNESIA EXCUSE SURE IS CONVENIENT...
ACTUALLY, I HAVE A GOOD IDEA!
WAIT RIGHT THERE, LITTLE BRATS!!
GYUN (ZOOM)
AH! WAIT!!
LITTLE BRATS? AREN'T WE THE SAME AGE...?

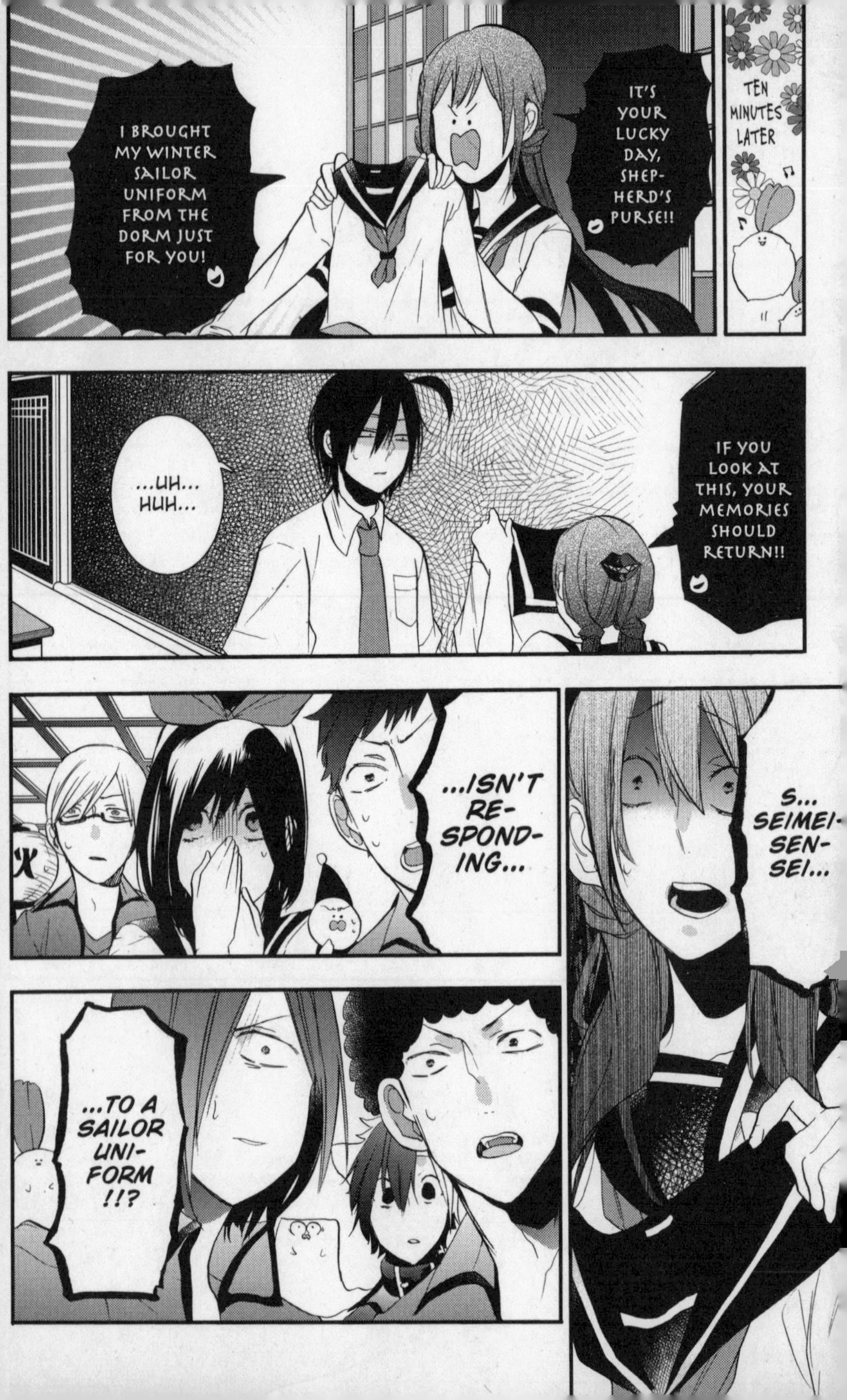
TEN MINUTES LATER
IT'S YOUR LUCKY DAY, SHEP-HERD'S PURSE!!
I BROUGHT MY WINTER SAILOR UNIFORM FROM THE DORM JUST FOR YOU!
IF YOU LOOK AT THIS, YOUR MEMORIES SHOULD RETURN!!
...UH... HUH...
S... SEIMEI-SEN-SEI...
...ISN'T RE-SPOND-ING...
...TO A SAILOR UNI-FORM!!?

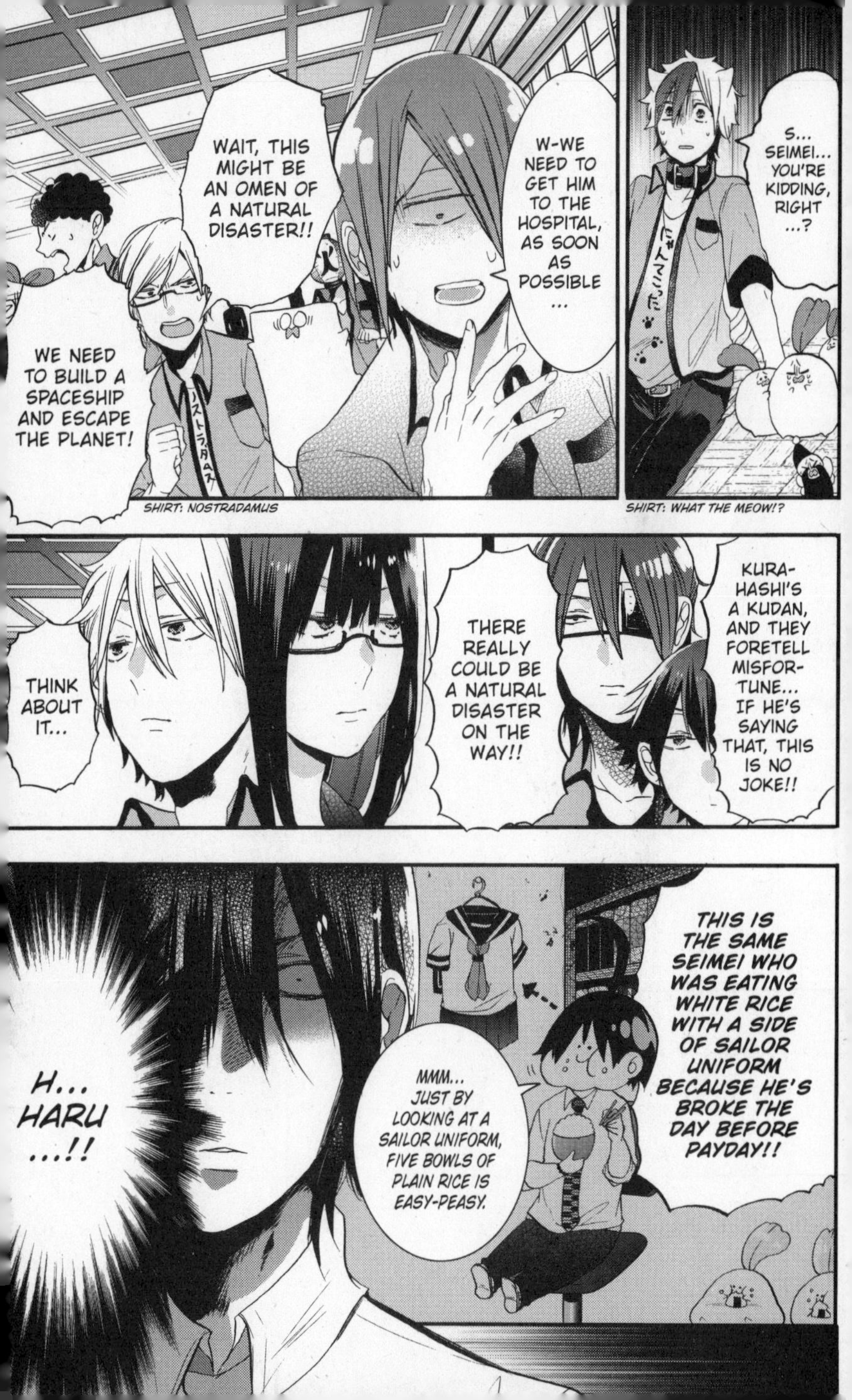
S... SEIMEI... YOU'RE KIDDING, RIGHT ...?
SHIRT: WHAT THE MEOW!?
W-WE NEED TO GET HIM TO THE HOSPITAL, AS SOON AS POSSIBLE ...
WAIT, THIS MIGHT BE AN OMEN OF A NATURAL DISASTER!!
WE NEED TO BUILD A SPACESHIP AND ESCAPE THE PLANET!
SHIRT: NOSTRADAMUS
KURA-HASHI'S A KUDAN, AND THEY FORETELL MISFOR-TUNE... IF HE'S SAYING THAT, THIS IS NO JOKE!!
THERE REALLY COULD BE A NATURAL DISASTER ON THE WAY!!
THINK ABOUT IT...
THIS IS THE SAME SEIMEI WHO WAS EATING WHITE RICE WITH A SIDE OF SAILOR UNIFORM BECAUSE HE'S BROKE THE DAY BEFORE PAYDAY!!
MMM... JUST BY LOOKING AT A SAILOR UNIFORM, FIVE BOWLS OF PLAIN RICE IS EASY-PEASY.
H... HARU ...!!

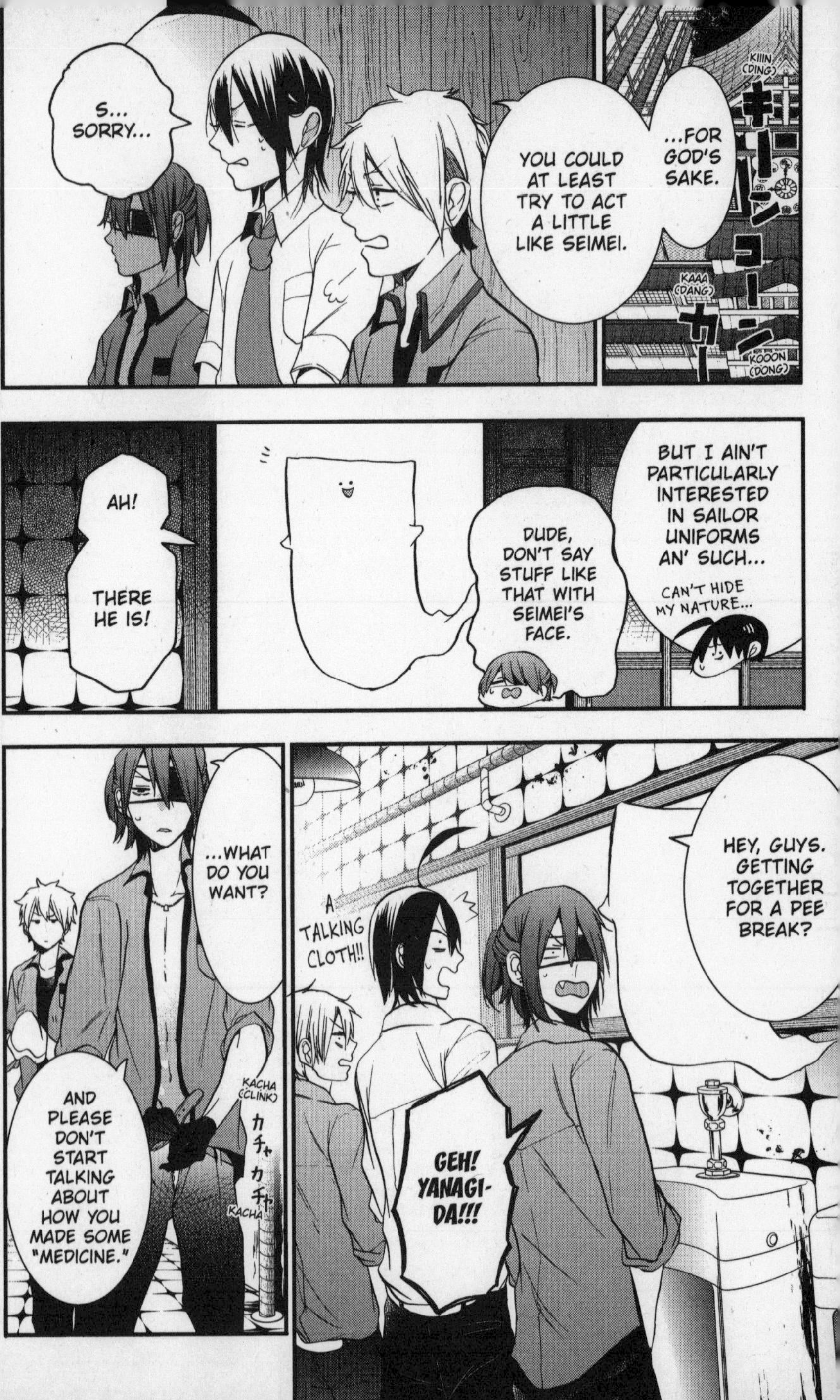
KIIN (DING)
KAAA (DANG)
KOOON (DONG)
...FOR GOD'S SAKE.
YOU COULD AT LEAST TRY TO ACT A LITTLE LIKE SEIMEI.
S... SORRY...
BUT I AIN'T PARTICULARLY INTERESTED IN SAILOR UNIFORMS AN' SUCH...
CAN'T HIDE MY NATURE...
DUDE, DON'T SAY STUFF LIKE THAT WITH SEIMEI'S FACE.
AH!
THERE HE IS!
HEY, GUYS. GETTING TOGETHER FOR A PEE BREAK?
A TALKING CLOTH!!
GEH! YANAGI-DA!!!
...WHAT DO YOU WANT?
KACHA (CLINK) KACHA
AND PLEASE DON'T START TALKING ABOUT HOW YOU MADE SOME "MEDICINE."

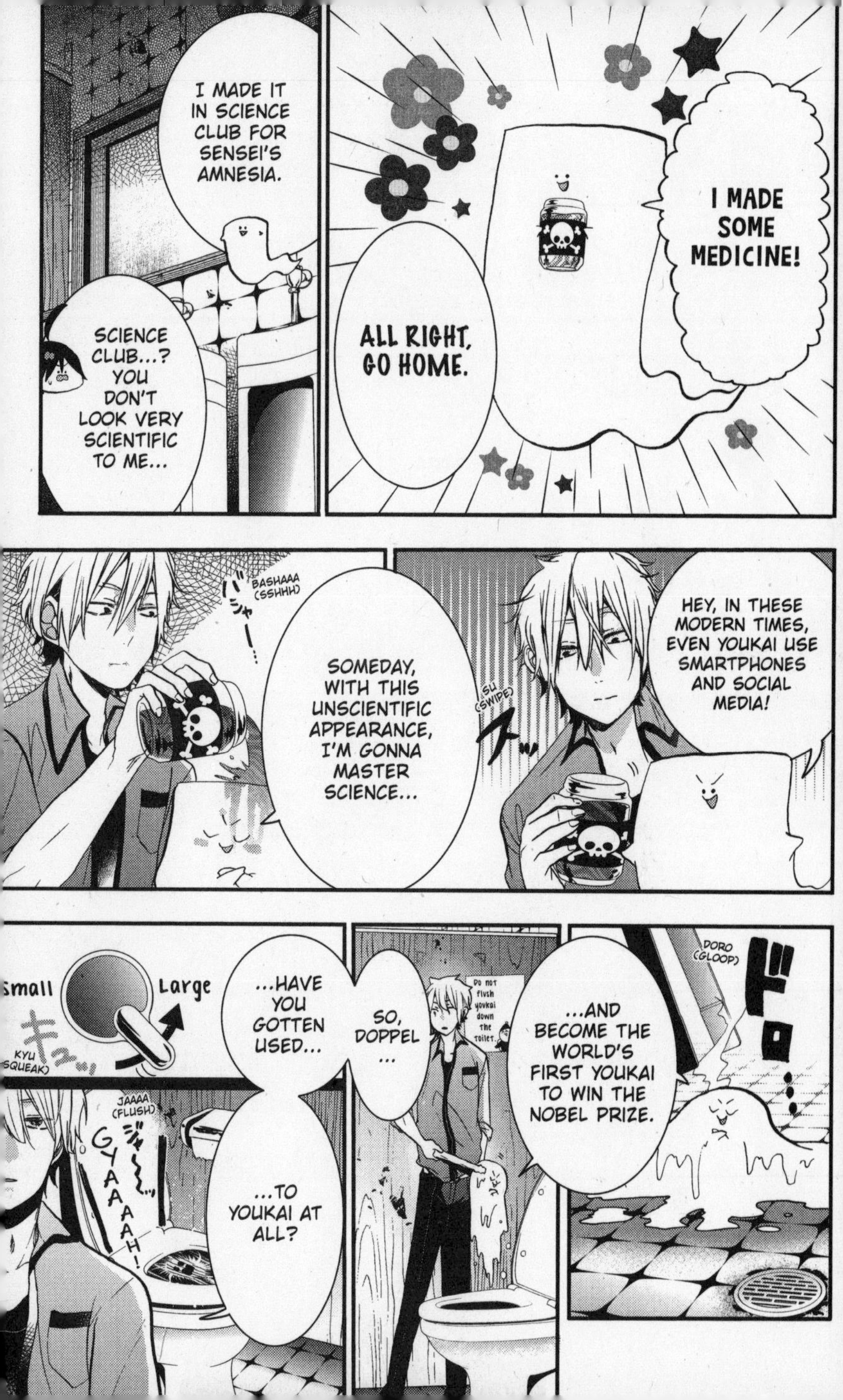
I MADE SOME MEDICINE!
ALL RIGHT, GO HOME.
I MADE IT IN SCIENCE CLUB FOR SENSEI'S AMNESIA.
SCIENCE CLUB...? YOU DON'T LOOK VERY SCIENTIFIC TO ME...
HEY, IN THESE MODERN TIMES, EVEN YOUKAI USE SMARTPHONES AND SOCIAL MEDIA!
SU (SWIPE)
SOMEDAY, WITH THIS UNSCIENTIFIC APPEARANCE, I'M GONNA MASTER SCIENCE...
BASHAAA (SSHHH)
DORO (GLOOP)
...AND BECOME THE WORLD'S FIRST YOUKAI TO WIN THE NOBEL PRIZE.
Do not flush youkai down the toilet.
SO, DOPPEL...
...HAVE YOU GOTTEN USED...
...TO YOUKAI AT ALL?
Small
Large
KYU (SQUEAK)
JAAAA (FLUSH)
GYAAAAAH!

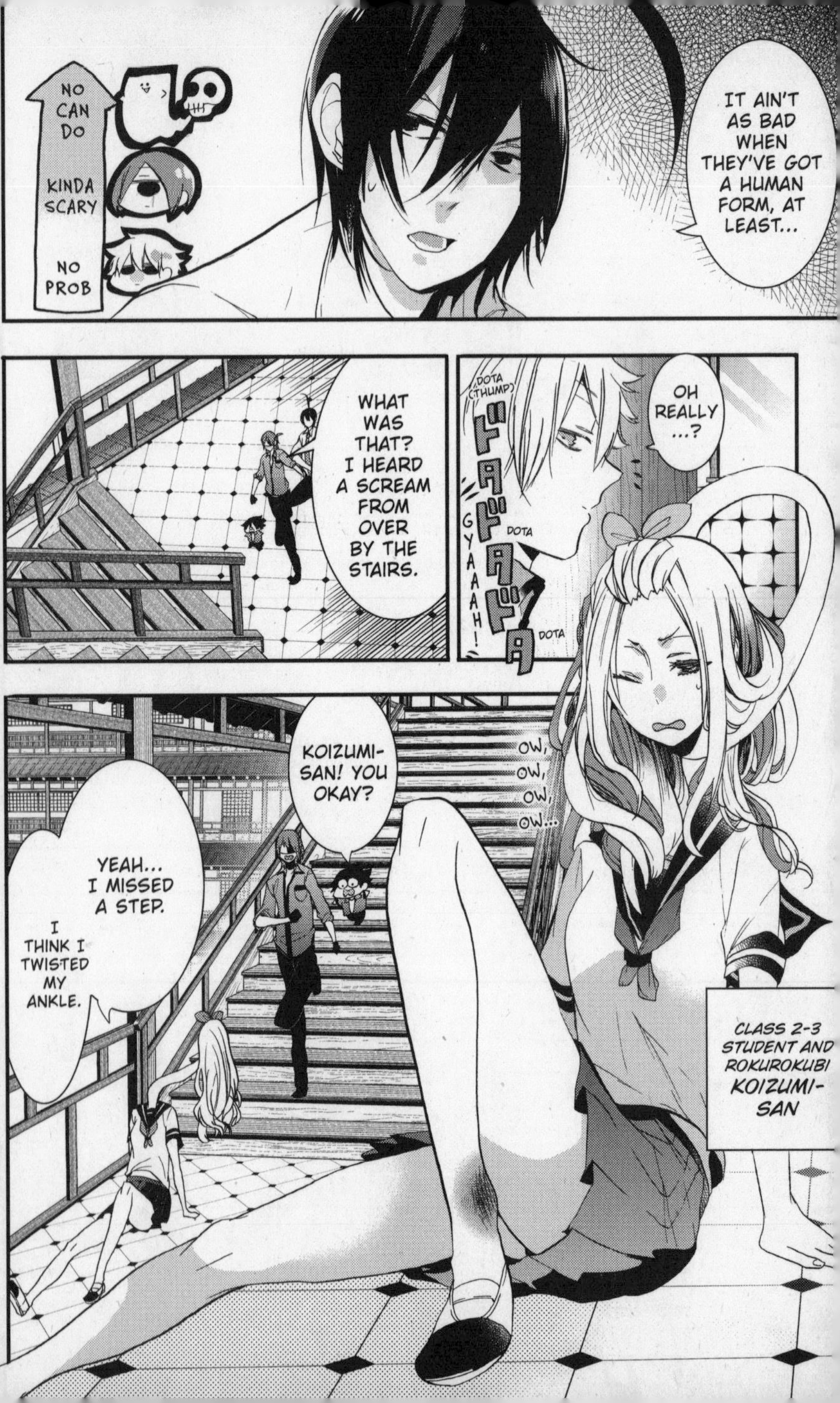
IT AIN'T AS BAD WHEN THEY'VE GOT A HUMAN FORM, AT LEAST...
NO CAN DO
KINDA SCARY
NO PROB
OH REALLY ...?
DOTA (THUMP)
GYAAAAH!
DOTA
DOTA
WHAT WAS THAT? I HEARD A SCREAM FROM OVER BY THE STAIRS.
OW, OW, OW, OW...
KOIZUMI-SAN! YOU OKAY?
CLASS 2-3 STUDENT AND ROKUROKUBI KOIZUMI-SAN
YEAH... I MISSED A STEP.
I THINK I TWISTED MY ANKLE.

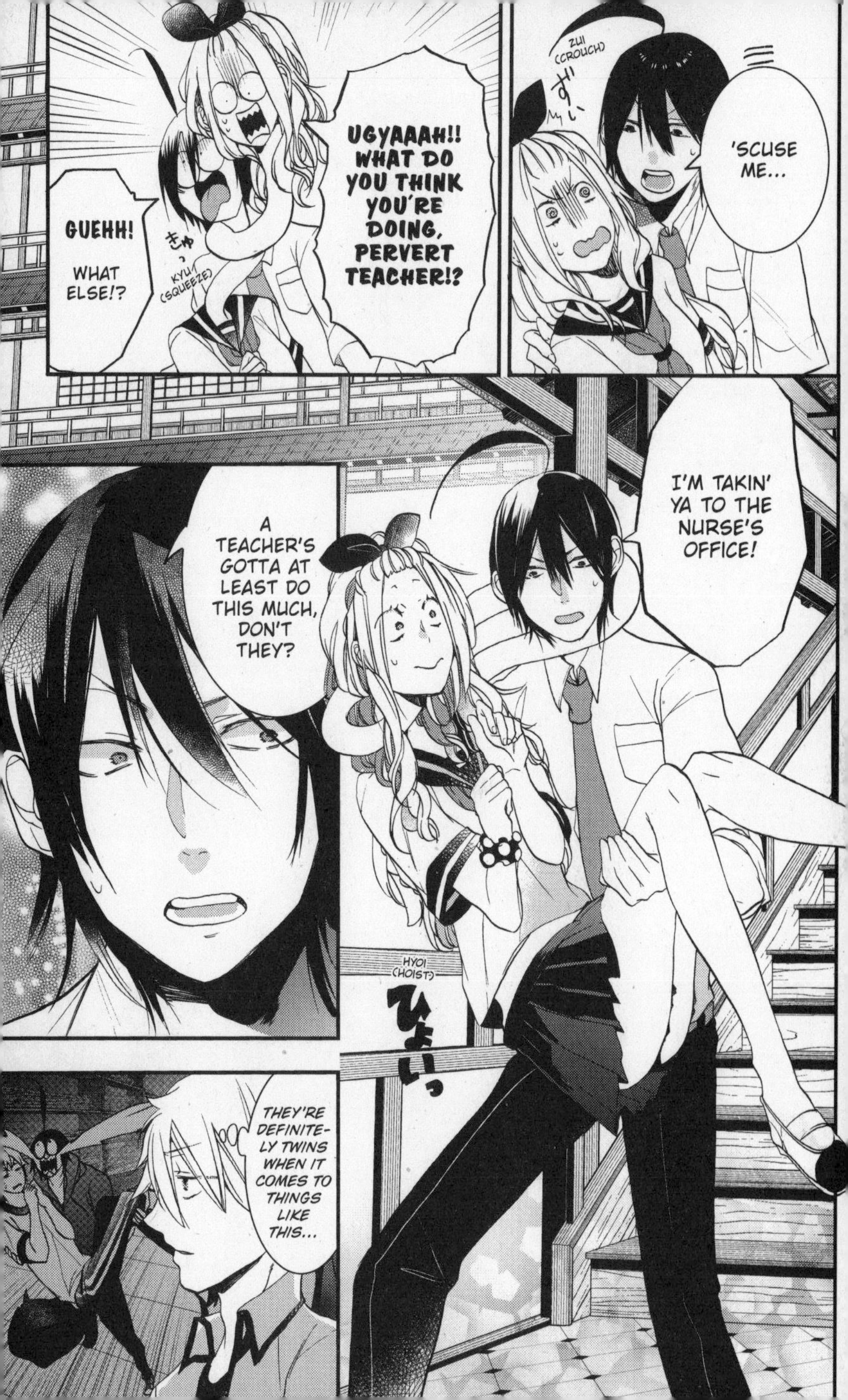
ZUI (CROUCH)
ずい
'SCUSE ME...
UGYAAAH!! WHAT DO YOU THINK YOU'RE DOING, PERVERT TEACHER!?
GUEHH!
WHAT ELSE!?
KYU (SQUEEZE)
きゅっ
I'M TAKIN' YA TO THE NURSE'S OFFICE!
HYOI (HOIST)
ひょいっ
A TEACHER'S GOTTA AT LEAST DO THIS MUCH, DON'T THEY?
THEY'RE DEFINITE-LY TWINS WHEN IT COMES TO THINGS LIKE THIS...

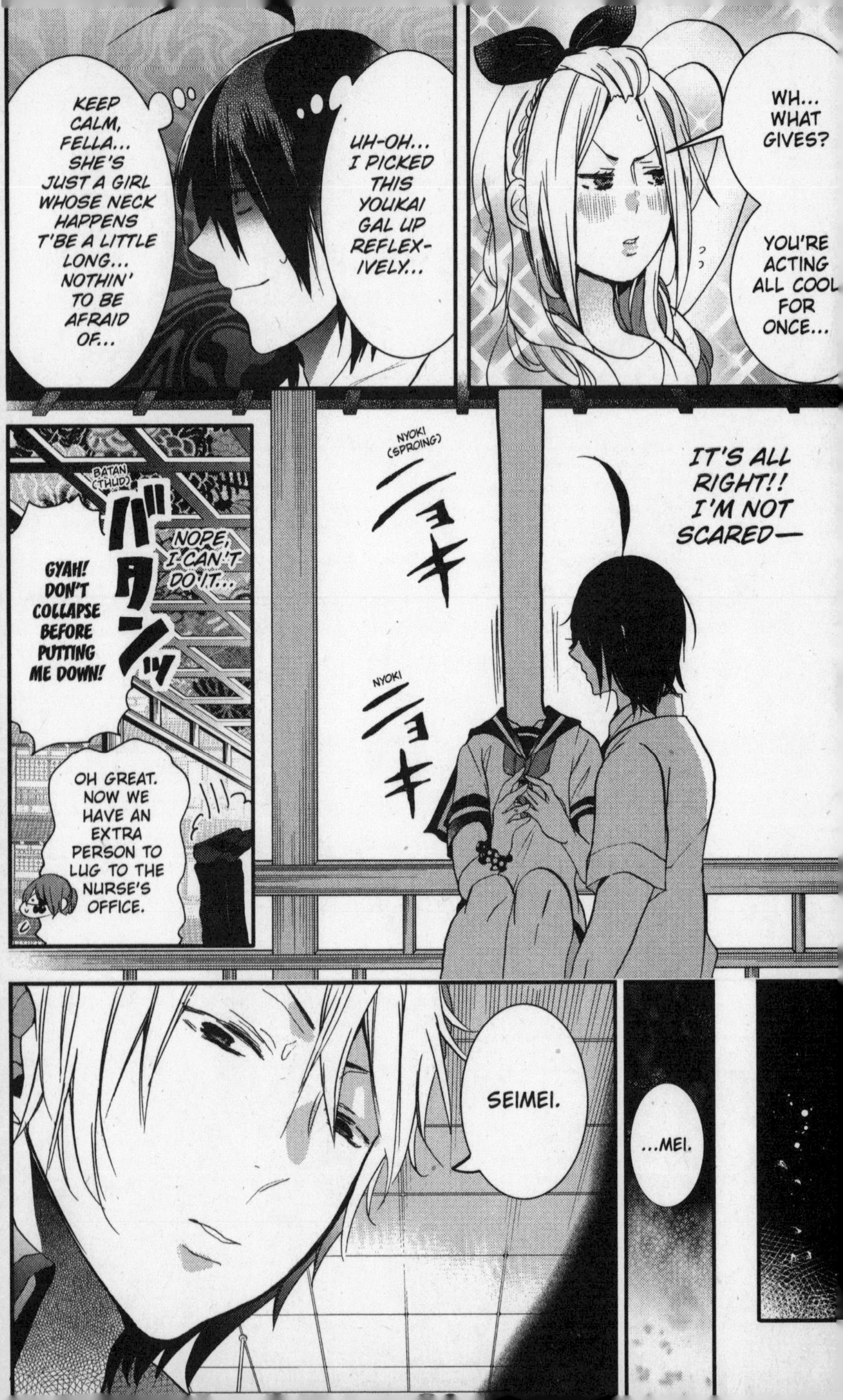
WH... WHAT GIVES?
YOU'RE ACTING ALL COOL FOR ONCE...
UH-OH... I PICKED THIS YOUKAI GAL UP REFLEX-IVELY...
KEEP CALM, FELLA... SHE'S JUST A GIRL WHOSE NECK HAPPENS T'BE A LITTLE LONG... NOTHIN' TO BE AFRAID OF...
IT'S ALL RIGHT!! I'M NOT SCARED—
NYOKI (SPROING)
ニョキ
NYOKI
ニョキ
BATAN (THUD)
バターンッ
NOPE, I CAN'T DO IT...
GYAH! DON'T COLLAPSE BEFORE PUTTING ME DOWN!
OH GREAT. NOW WE HAVE AN EXTRA PERSON TO LUG TO THE NURSE'S OFFICE.
...MEI.
SEIMEI.

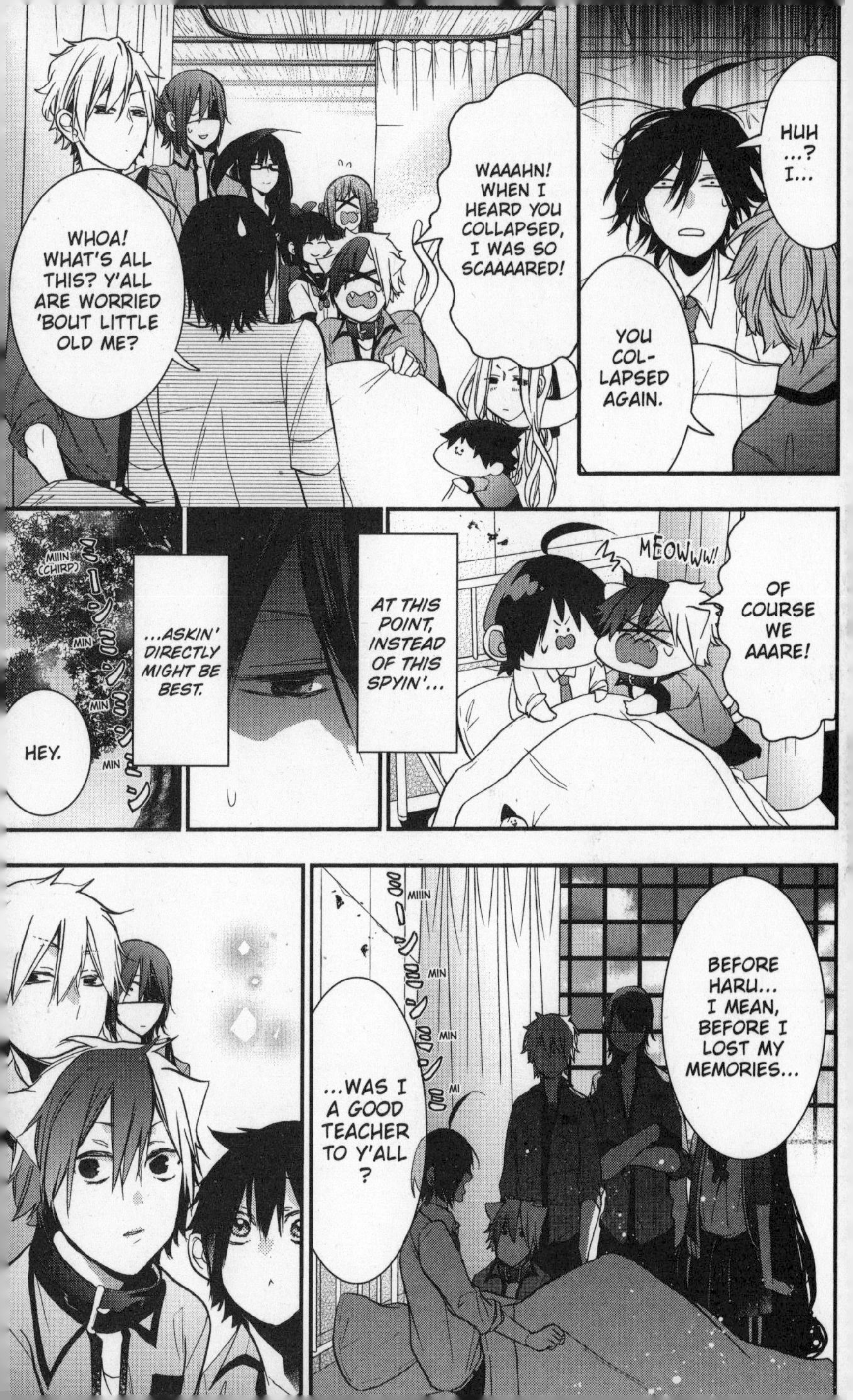
HUH ...? I...
YOU COL-LAPSED AGAIN.
WAAAHN! WHEN I HEARD YOU COLLAPSED, I WAS SO SCAAAARED!
WHOA! WHAT'S ALL THIS? Y'ALL ARE WORRIED 'BOUT LITTLE OLD ME?
MEOWWW!
OF COURSE WE AAARE!
AT THIS POINT, INSTEAD OF THIS SPYIN'...
...ASKIN' DIRECTLY MIGHT BE BEST.
MIIIN (CHIRP)
MIN
MIN
MIN
HEY.
MIIIN
MIN
MIN
MI
BEFORE HARU... I MEAN, BEFORE I LOST MY MEMORIES...
...WAS I A GOOD TEACHER TO Y'ALL?

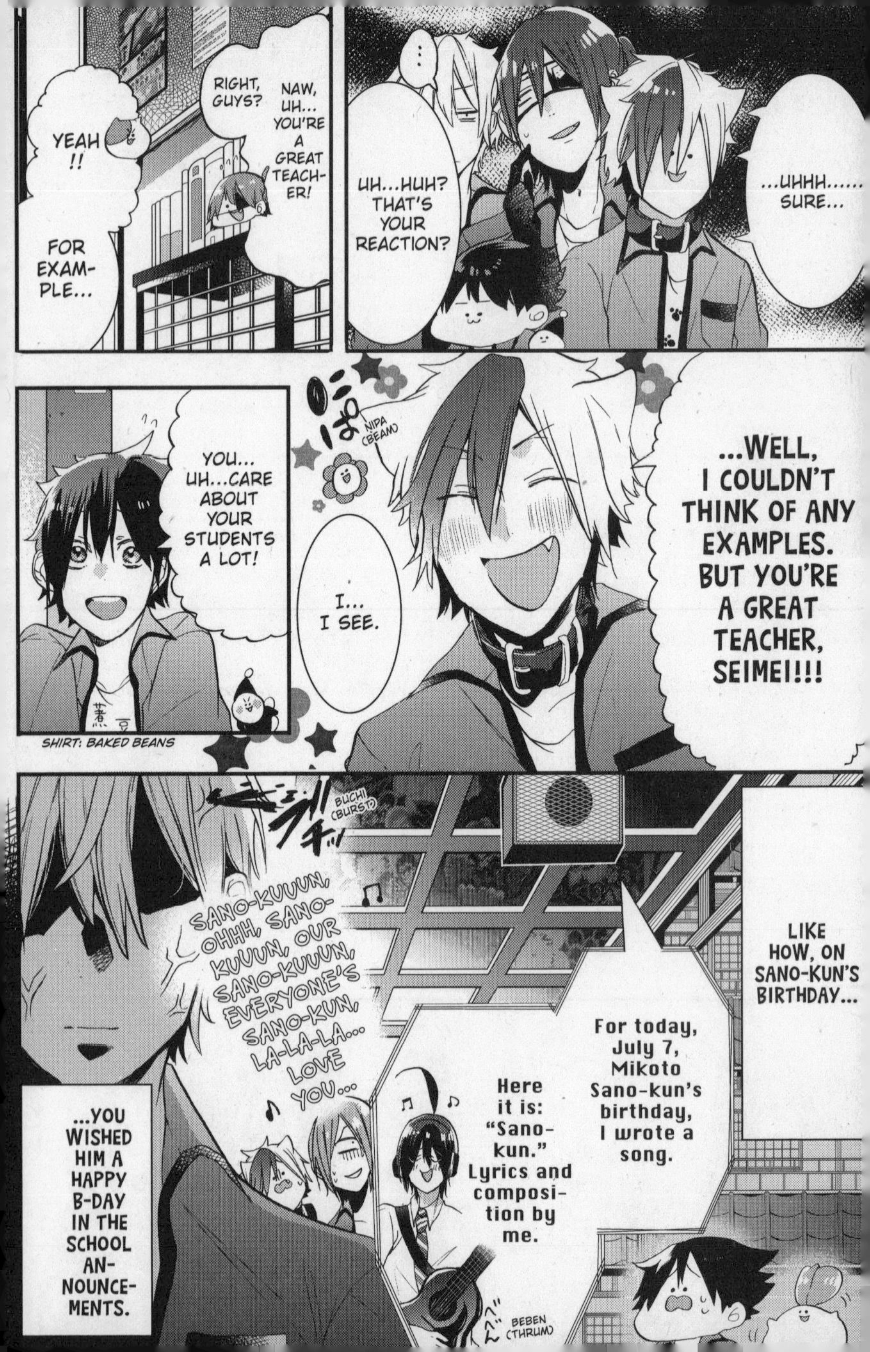
...UHHH...... SURE...
...
UH...HUH? THAT'S YOUR REACTION?
NAW, UH... YOU'RE A GREAT TEACHER!
RIGHT, GUYS?
YEAH!!
FOR EXAMPLE...
...WELL, I COULDN'T THINK OF ANY EXAMPLES. BUT YOU'RE A GREAT TEACHER, SEIMEI!!!
NIPA (BEAM)
I... I SEE.
YOU... UH...CARE ABOUT YOUR STUDENTS A LOT!
SHIRT: BAKED BEANS
LIKE HOW, ON SANO-KUN'S BIRTHDAY...
BUCHI (BURST)
For today, July 7, Mikoto Sano-kun's birthday, I wrote a song.
Here it is: "Sano-kun." Lyrics and composition by me.
SANO-KUUUN, OHHH, SANO-KUUUN, OUR SANO-KUUUN, EVERYONE'S SANO-KUN, LA-LA-LA... LOVE YOU...
...YOU WISHED HIM A HAPPY B-DAY IN THE SCHOOL ANNOUNCEMENTS.
BEBEN (THRUM)

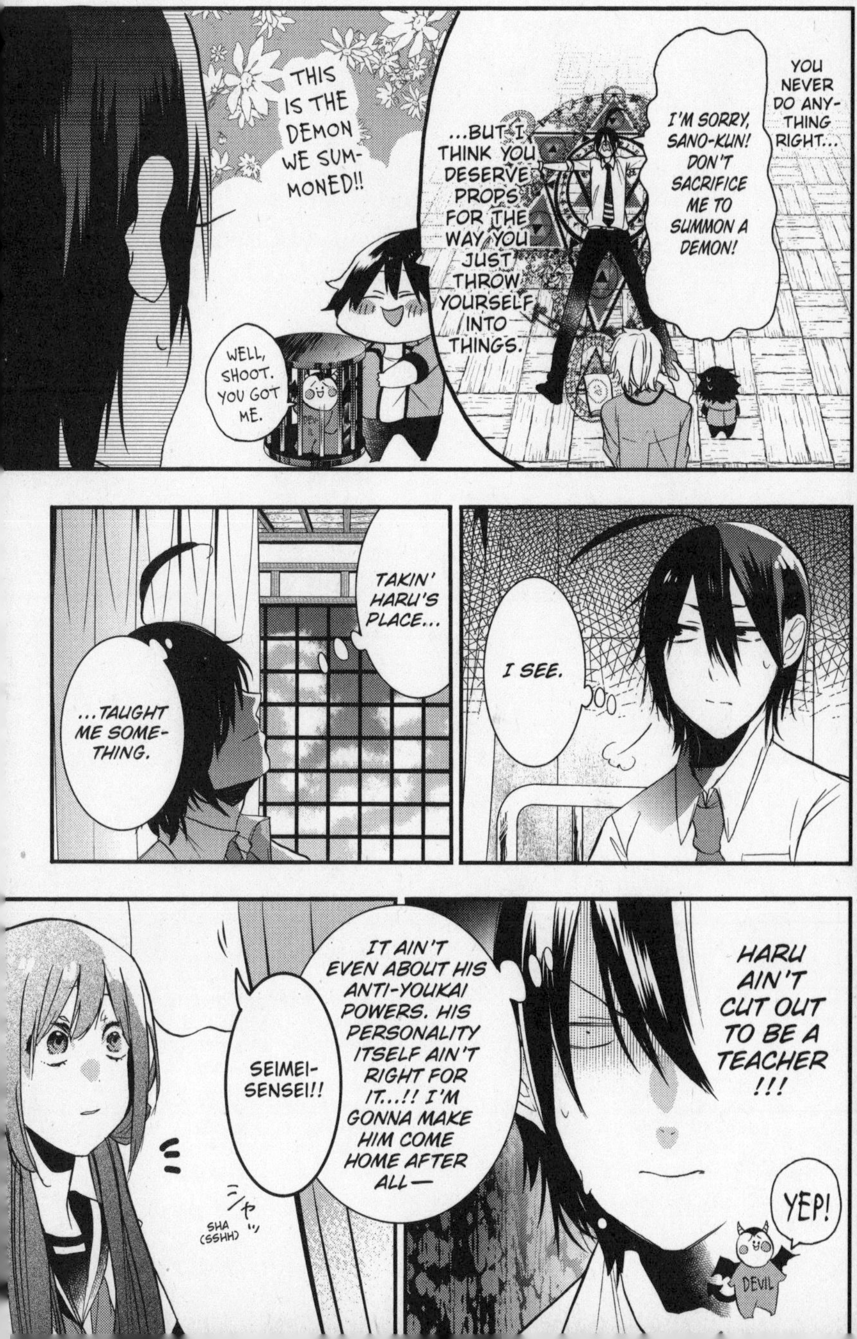
YOU NEVER DO ANYTHING RIGHT...
I'M SORRY, SANO-KUN! DON'T SACRIFICE ME TO SUMMON A DEMON!
...BUT I THINK YOU DESERVE PROPS FOR THE WAY YOU JUST THROW YOURSELF INTO THINGS.
THIS IS THE DEMON WE SUMMONED!!
WELL, SHOOT. YOU GOT ME.
DEVIL
I SEE.
TAKIN' HARU'S PLACE...
...TAUGHT ME SOMETHING.
HARU AIN'T CUT OUT TO BE A TEACHER!!!
YEP!
DEVIL
IT AIN'T EVEN ABOUT HIS ANTI-YOUKAI POWERS. HIS PERSONALITY ITSELF AIN'T RIGHT FOR IT...!! I'M GONNA MAKE HIM COME HOME AFTER ALL—
SEIMEI-SENSEI!!
SHA (SSHH)

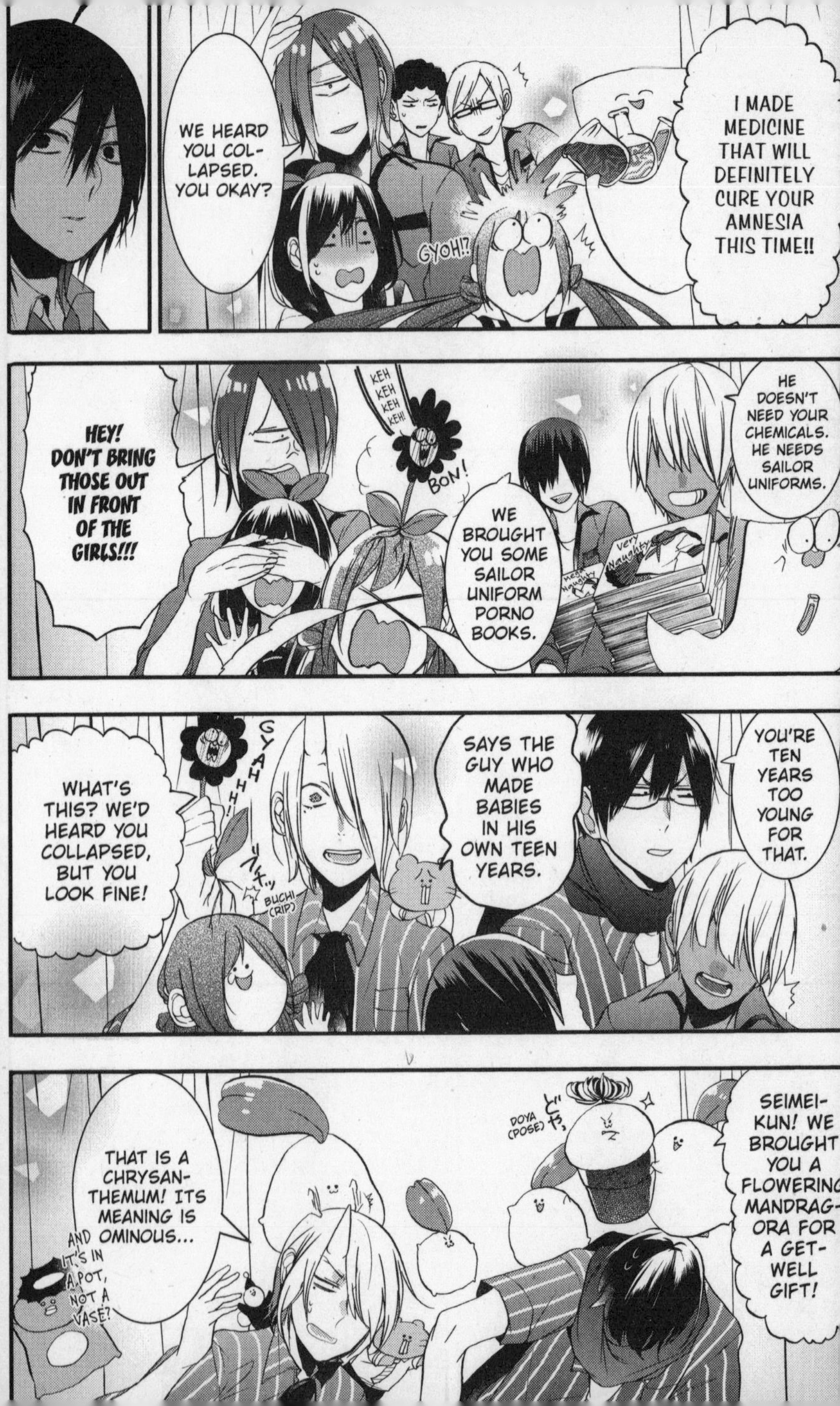
I MADE MEDICINE THAT WILL DEFINITELY CURE YOUR AMNESIA THIS TIME!!
GYOH!?
WE HEARD YOU COL-LAPSED. YOU OKAY?
HE DOESN'T NEED YOUR CHEMICALS. HE NEEDS SAILOR UNIFORMS.
Very Naughty
WE BROUGHT YOU SOME SAILOR UNIFORM PORNO BOOKS.
BON!
KEH KEH KEH KEH!
HEY! DON'T BRING THOSE OUT IN FRONT OF THE GIRLS!!!
YOU'RE TEN YEARS TOO YOUNG FOR THAT.
SAYS THE GUY WHO MADE BABIES IN HIS OWN TEEN YEARS.
GYAHH!
BUCHI (RIP)
WHAT'S THIS? WE'D HEARD YOU COLLAPSED, BUT YOU LOOK FINE!
SEIMEI-KUN! WE BROUGHT YOU A FLOWERING MANDRAGORA FOR A GET-WELL GIFT!
DOYA (POSE)
THAT IS A CHRYSANTHEMUM! ITS MEANING IS OMINOUS...
AND IT'S IN A POT, NOT A VASE?

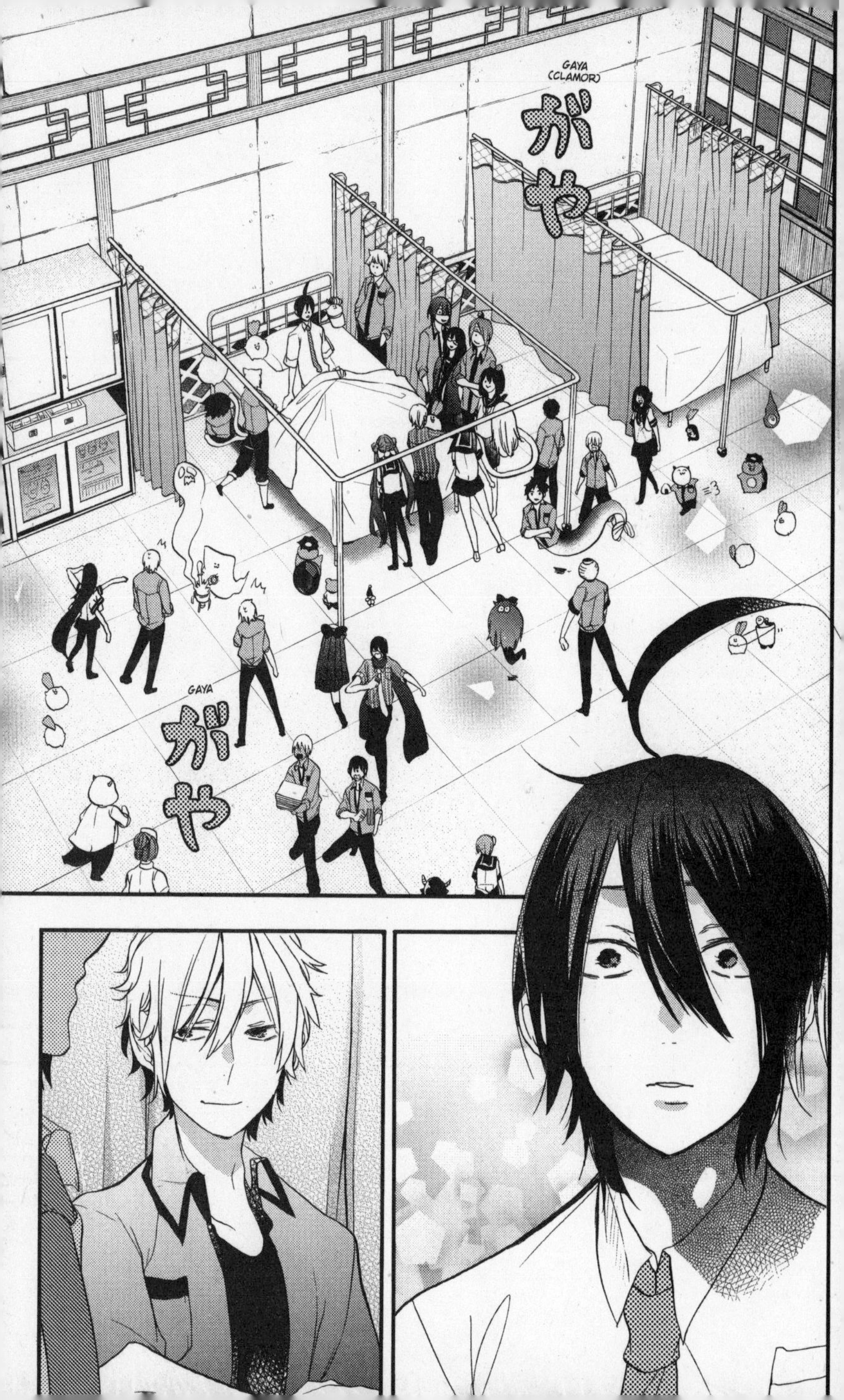
GAYA (CLAMOR)
がや
GAYA
がや

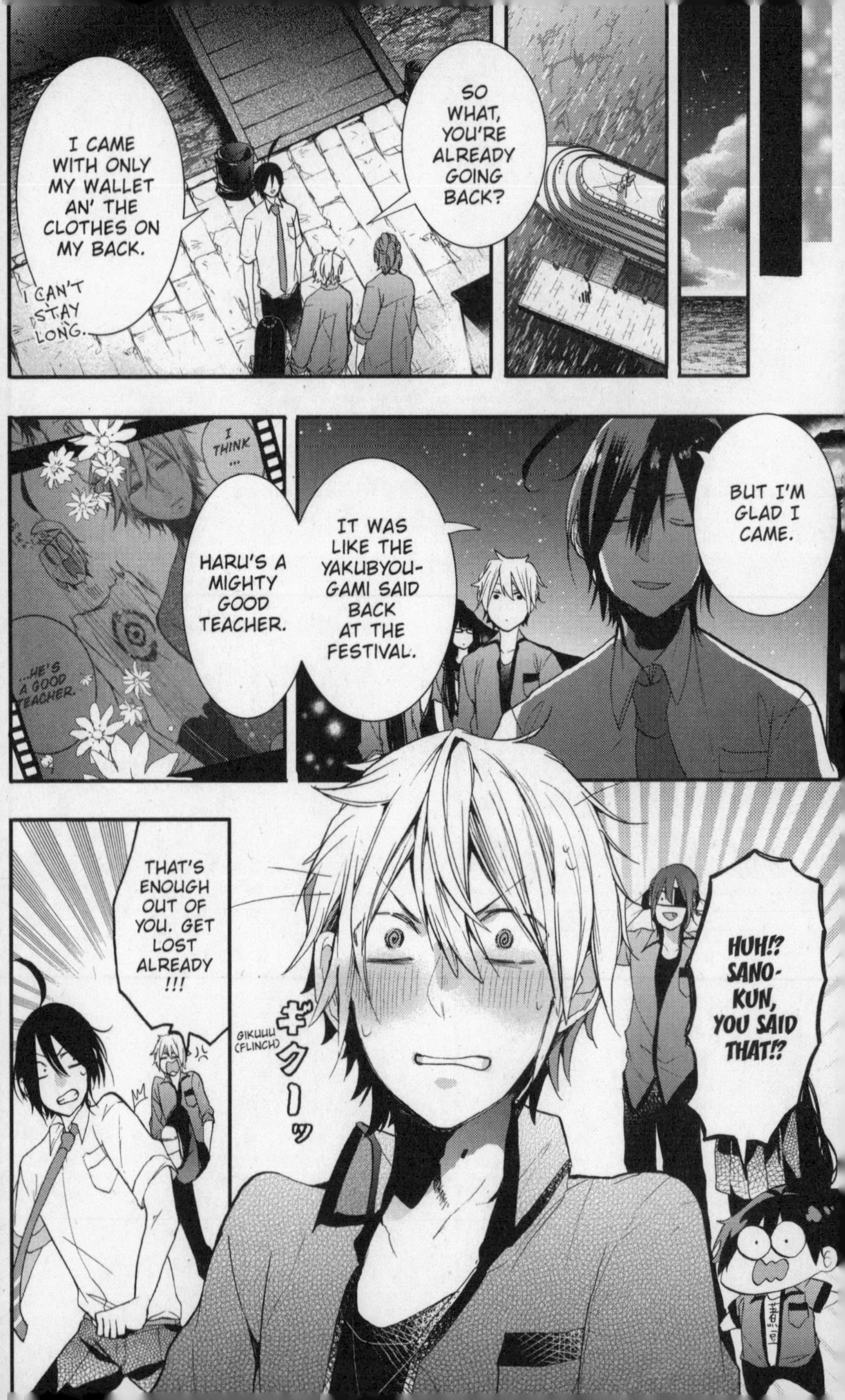
SO WHAT, YOU'RE ALREADY GOING BACK?
I CAME WITH ONLY MY WALLET AN' THE CLOTHES ON MY BACK.
I CAN'T STAY LONG.
BUT I'M GLAD I CAME.
IT WAS LIKE THE YAKUBYOU-GAMI SAID BACK AT THE FESTIVAL.
HARU'S A MIGHTY GOOD TEACHER.
I THINK...
...HE'S A GOOD TEACHER.
HUH!? SANO-KUN, YOU SAID THAT!?
ギクーッ
GIKUUU (FLINCH)
THAT'S ENOUGH OUT OF YOU. GET LOST ALREADY!!!

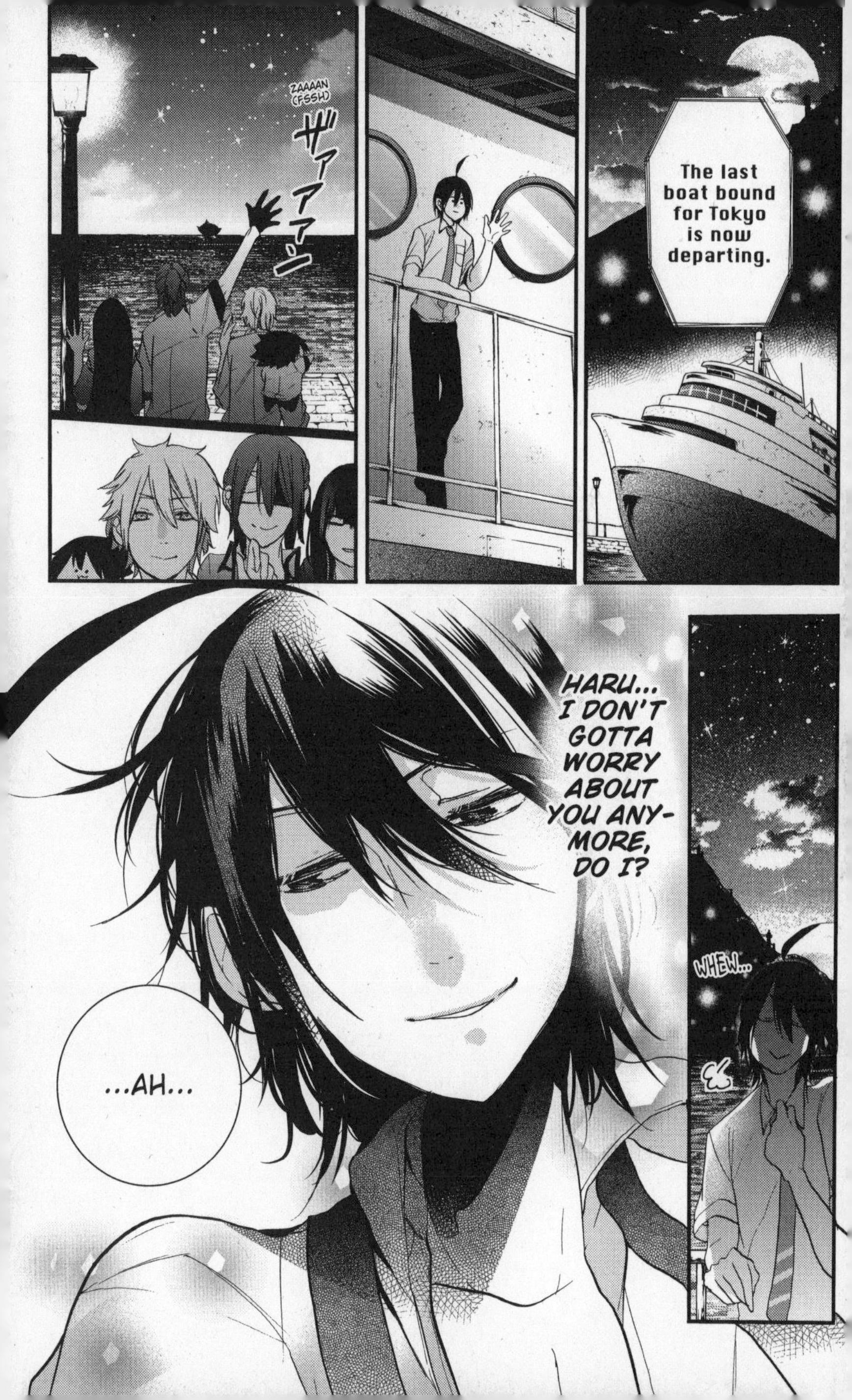
The last boat bound for Tokyo is now departing.
ZAAAAN (FSSH)
WHEW...
HARU... I DON'T GOTTA WORRY ABOUT YOU ANY-MORE, DO I?
...AH...

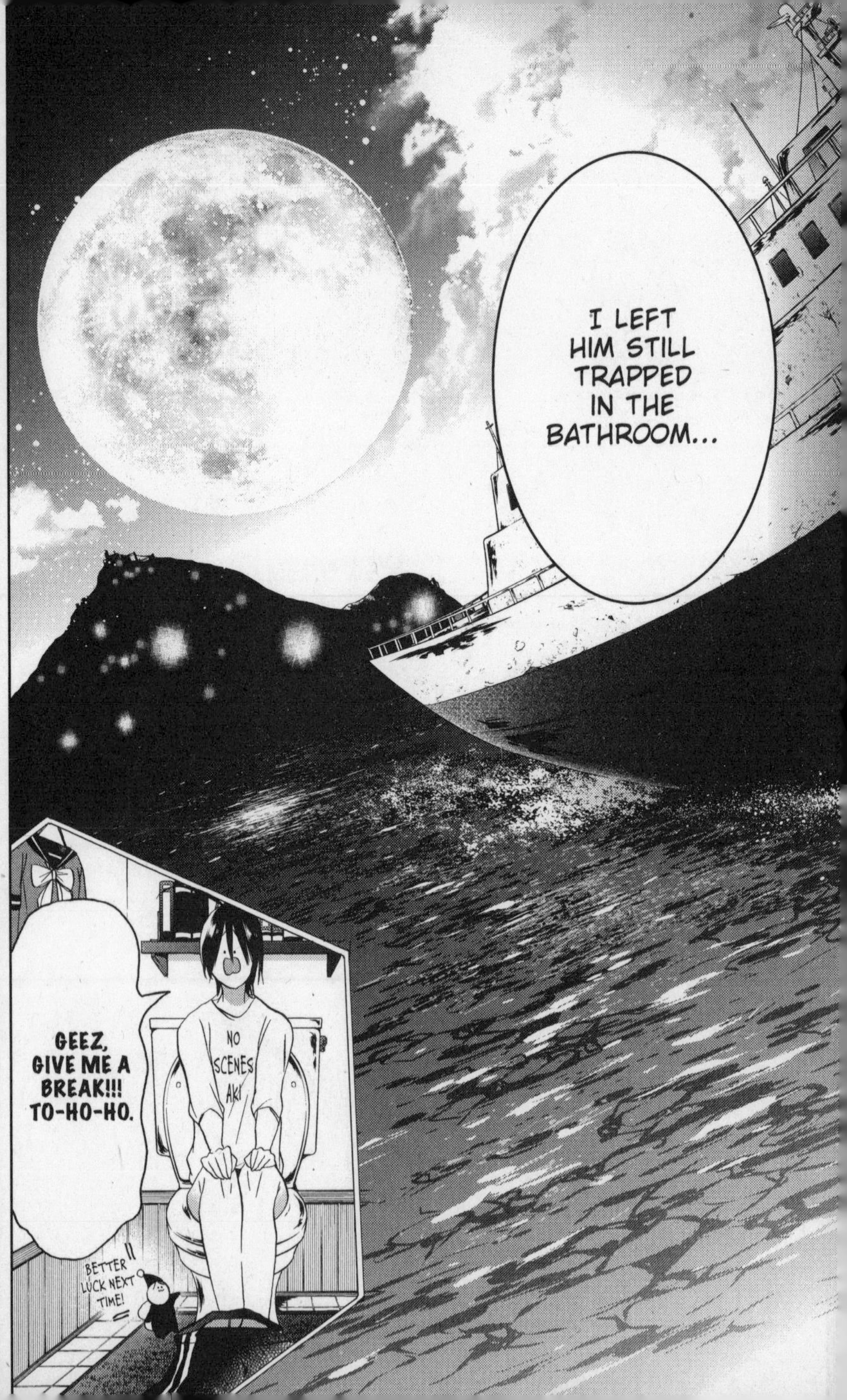
I LEFT HIM STILL TRAPPED IN THE BATHROOM...
NO SCENES AKI
GEEZ, GIVE ME A BREAK!!! TO-HO-HO.
BETTER LUCK NEXT TIME!

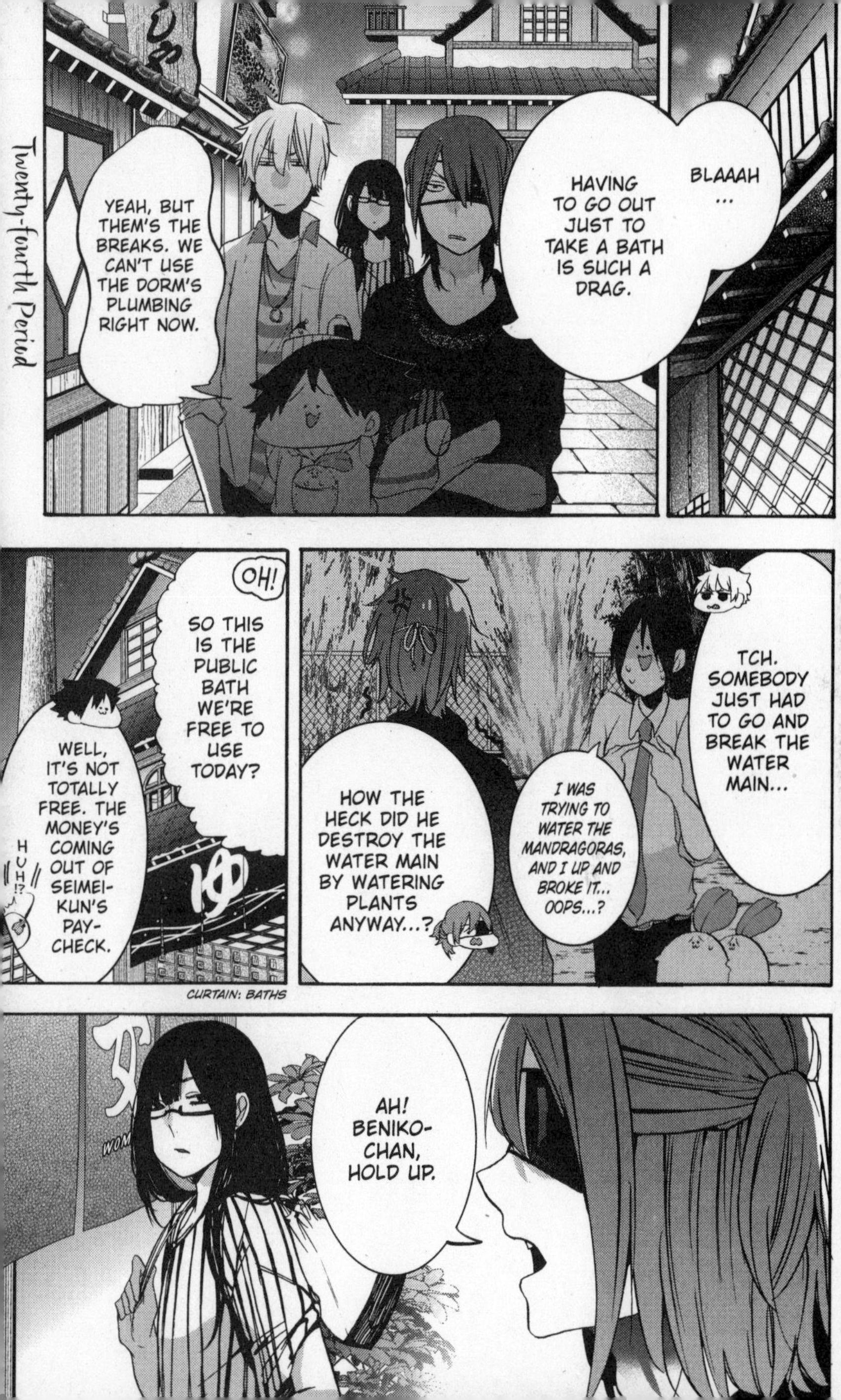
BLAAAH ...
HAVING TO GO OUT JUST TO TAKE A BATH IS SUCH A DRAG.
YEAH, BUT THEM'S THE BREAKS. WE CAN'T USE THE DORM'S PLUMBING RIGHT NOW.
TCH. SOMEBODY JUST HAD TO GO AND BREAK THE WATER MAIN...
I WAS TRYING TO WATER THE MANDRAGORAS, AND I UP AND BROKE IT... OOPS...?
HOW THE HECK DID HE DESTROY THE WATER MAIN BY WATERING PLANTS ANYWAY...?
OH!
SO THIS IS THE PUBLIC BATH WE'RE FREE TO USE TODAY?
WELL, IT'S NOT TOTALLY FREE. THE MONEY'S COMING OUT OF SEIMEI-KUN'S PAYCHECK.
HUH!?
AH! BENIKO-CHAN, HOLD UP.

CURTAIN: BATHS

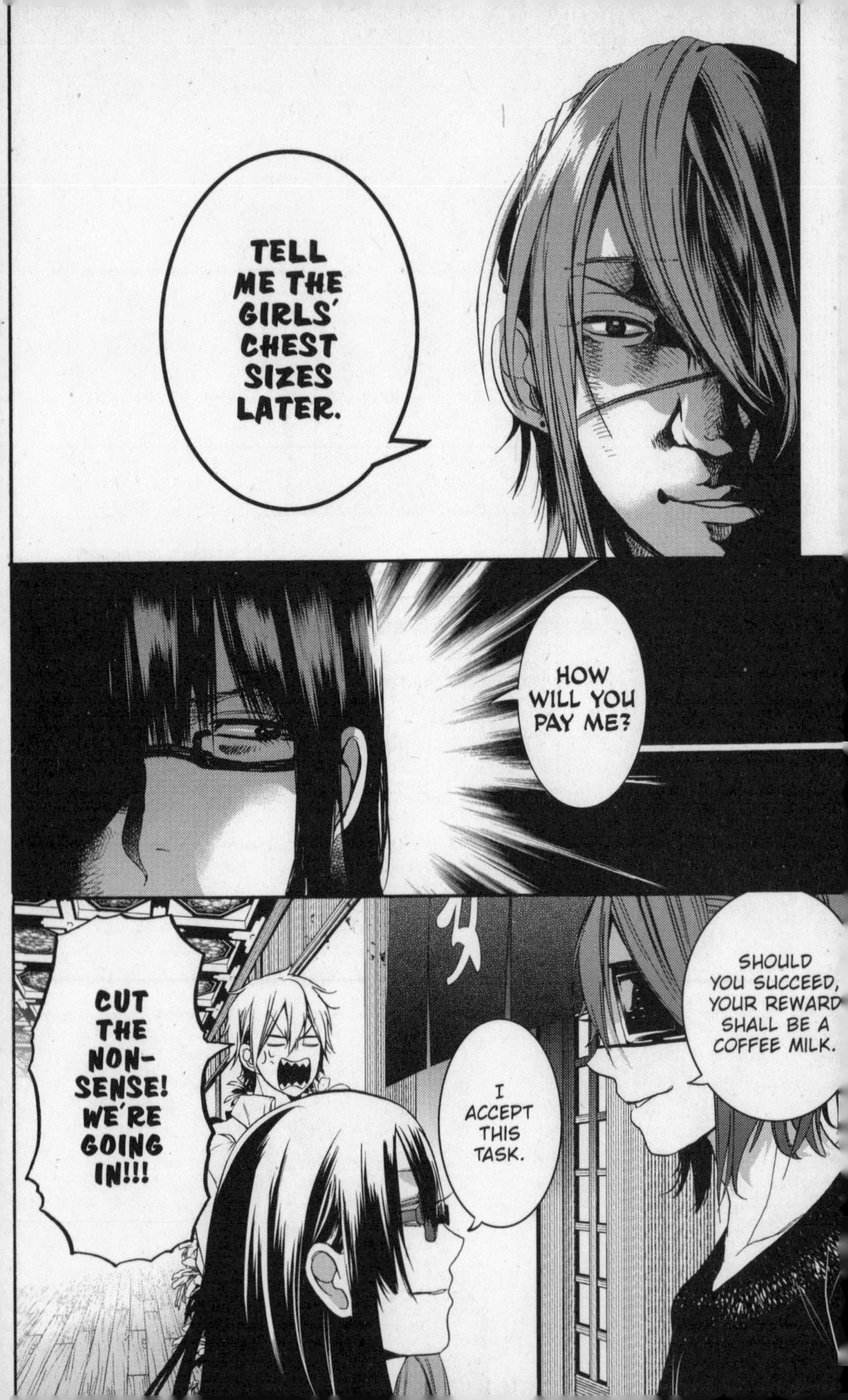
TELL ME THE GIRLS' CHEST SIZES LATER.
HOW WILL YOU PAY ME?
SHOULD YOU SUCCEED, YOUR REWARD SHALL BE A COFFEE MILK.
I ACCEPT THIS TASK.
CUT THE NON-SENSE! WE'RE GOING IN!!!

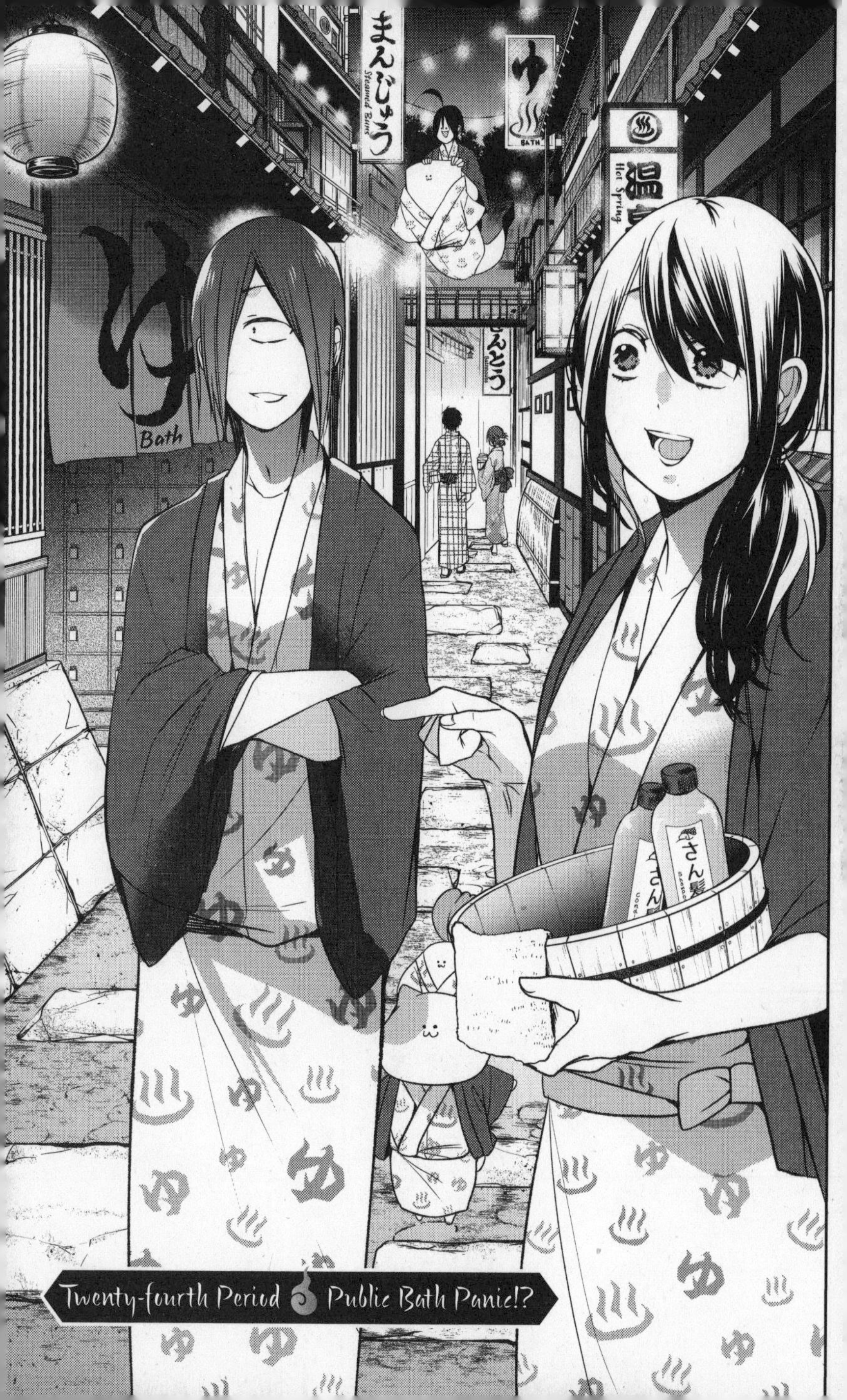
まんじゅう
Steamed Buns
ゆ
BATH
Hot Spring
ゆ
Bath
Twenty-fourth Period
Public Bath Panic!?

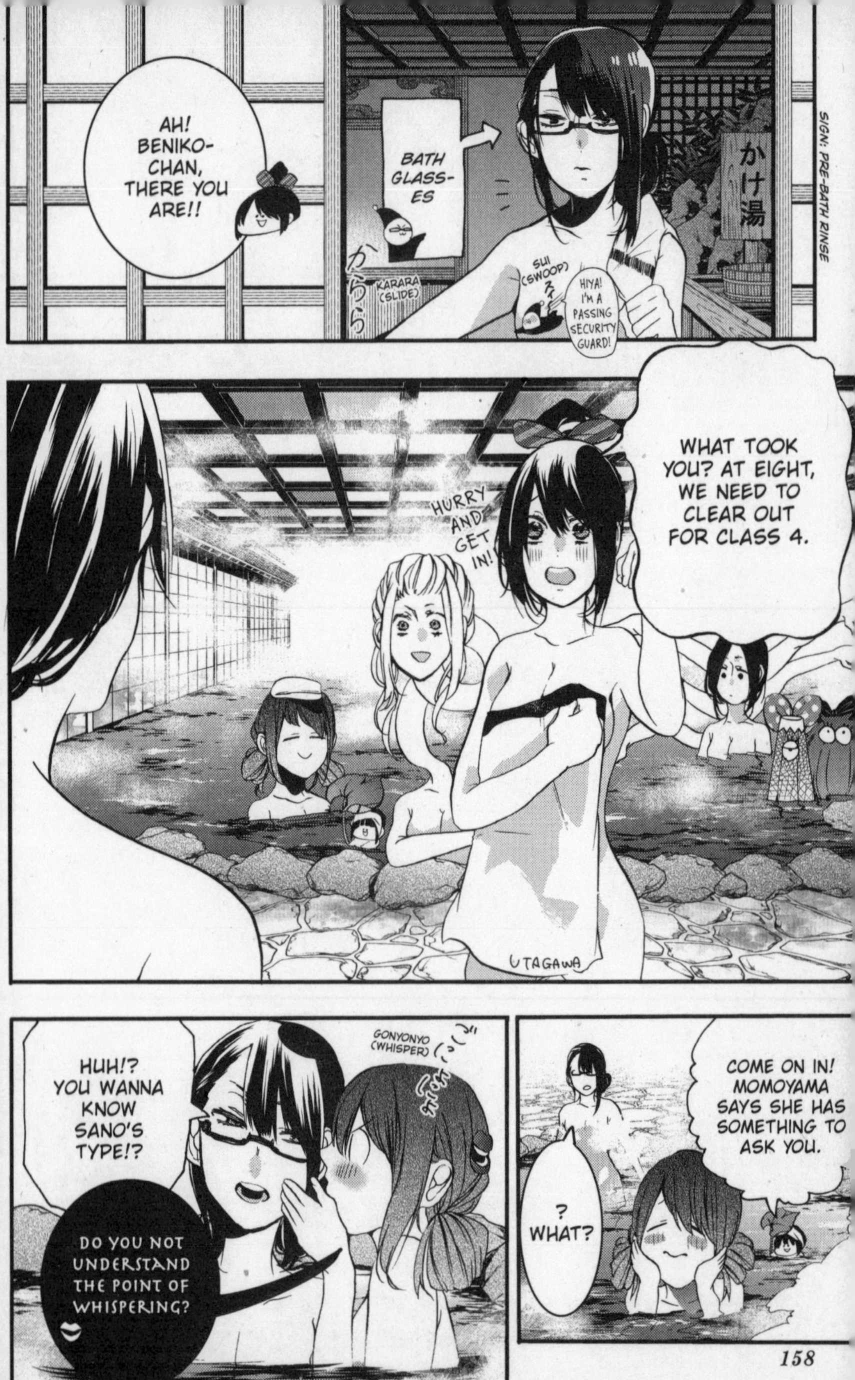
かけ湯
SIGN: PRE-BATH RINSE
BATH GLASS-ES
からら
KARARA (SLIDE)
SUI (SWOOP)
HIYA! I'M A PASSING SECURITY GUARD!
AH! BENIKO-CHAN, THERE YOU ARE!!
WHAT TOOK YOU? AT EIGHT, WE NEED TO CLEAR OUT FOR CLASS 4.
HURRY AND GET IN!
UTAGAWA
COME ON IN! MOMOYAMA SAYS SHE HAS SOMETHING TO ASK YOU.
? WHAT?
GONYONYO (WHISPER)
HUH!? YOU WANNA KNOW SANO'S TYPE!?
DO YOU NOT UNDERSTAND THE POINT OF WHISPERING?

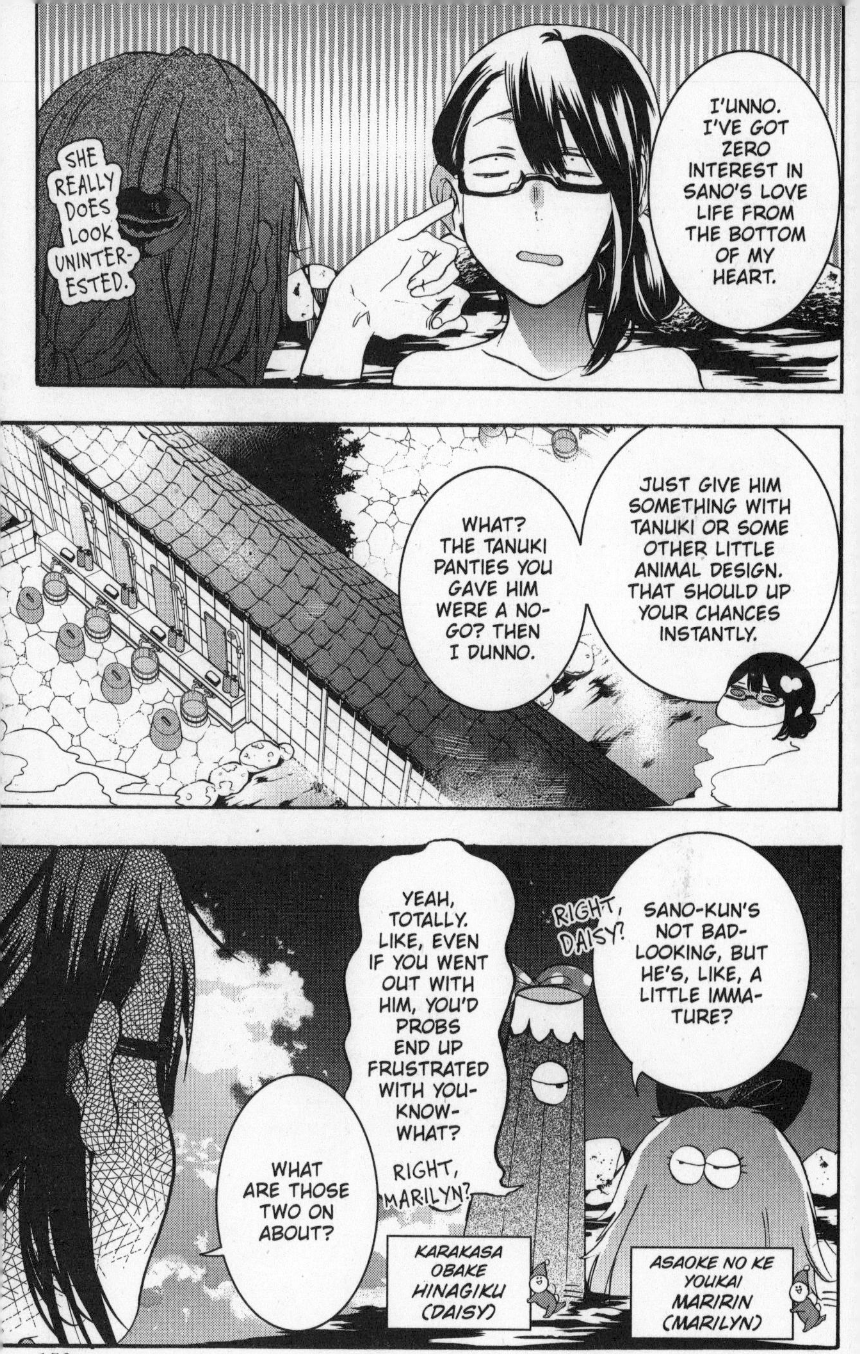
I'UNNO. I'VE GOT ZERO INTEREST IN SANO'S LOVE LIFE FROM THE BOTTOM OF MY HEART.
SHE REALLY DOES LOOK UNINTER-ESTED.
JUST GIVE HIM SOMETHING WITH TANUKI OR SOME OTHER LITTLE ANIMAL DESIGN. THAT SHOULD UP YOUR CHANCES INSTANTLY.
WHAT? THE TANUKI PANTIES YOU GAVE HIM WERE A NO-GO? THEN I DUNNO.
SANO-KUN'S NOT BAD-LOOKING, BUT HE'S, LIKE, A LITTLE IMMA-TURE?
RIGHT, DAISY?
YEAH, TOTALLY. LIKE, EVEN IF YOU WENT OUT WITH HIM, YOU'D PROBS END UP FRUSTRATED WITH YOU-KNOW-WHAT?
RIGHT, MARILYN?
ASAOKE NO KE YOUKAI MARIRIN (MARILYN)
KARAKASA OBAKE HINAGIKU (DAISY)
WHAT ARE THOSE TWO ON ABOUT?

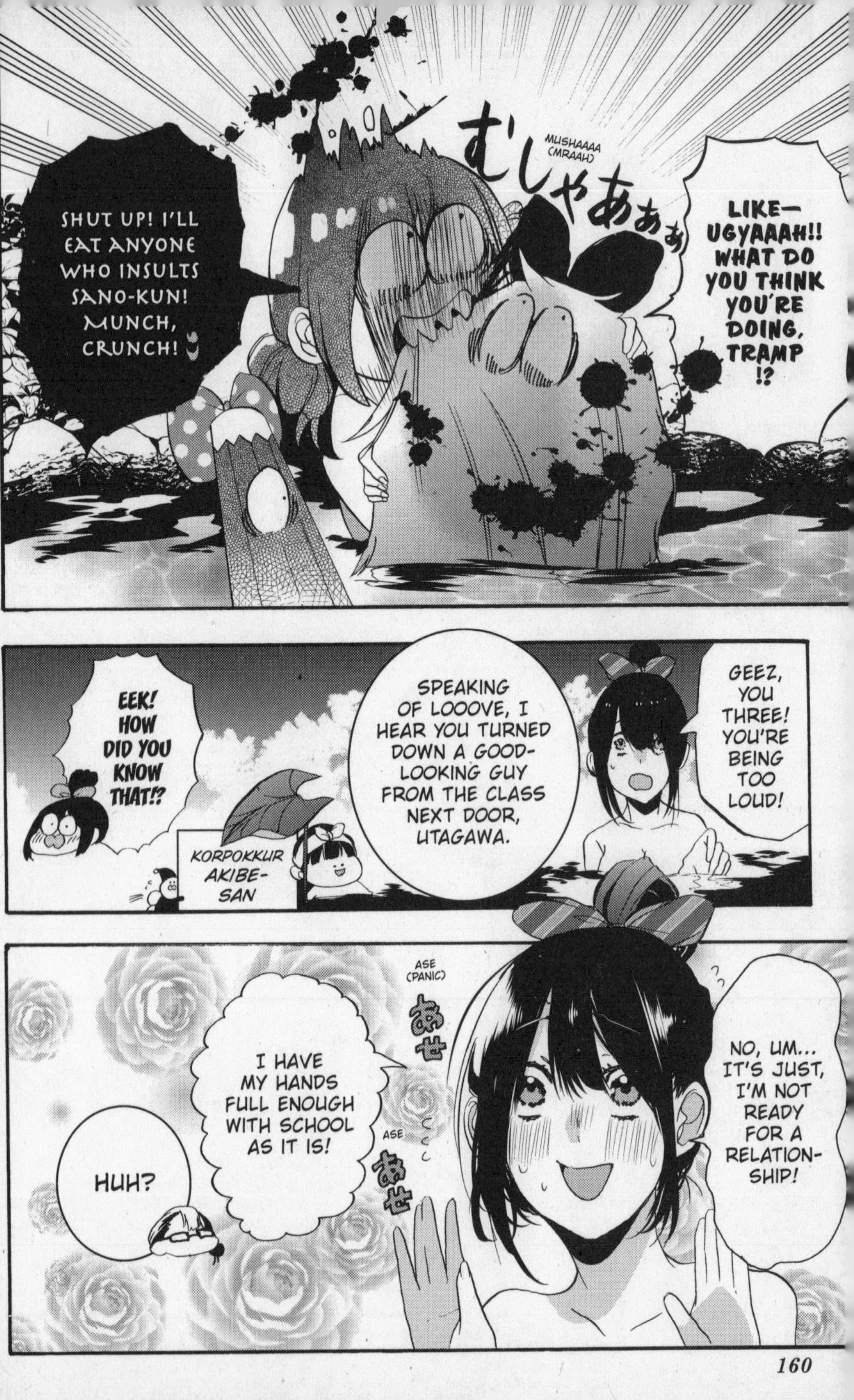
LIKE—UGYAAAH!! WHAT DO YOU THINK YOU'RE DOING, TRAMP!?
むしゃあぁぁ
MUSHAAAA (MRAAH)
SHUT UP! I'LL EAT ANYONE WHO INSULTS SANO-KUN! MUNCH, CRUNCH!
GEEZ, YOU THREE! YOU'RE BEING TOO LOUD!
SPEAKING OF LOOOVE, I HEAR YOU TURNED DOWN A GOOD-LOOKING GUY FROM THE CLASS NEXT DOOR, UTAGAWA.
KORPOKKUR AKIBE-SAN
EEK! HOW DID YOU KNOW THAT!?
NO, UM... IT'S JUST, I'M NOT READY FOR A RELATION-SHIP!
あせ
ASE (PANIC)
あせ
ASE
I HAVE MY HANDS FULL ENOUGH WITH SCHOOL AS IT IS!
HUH?

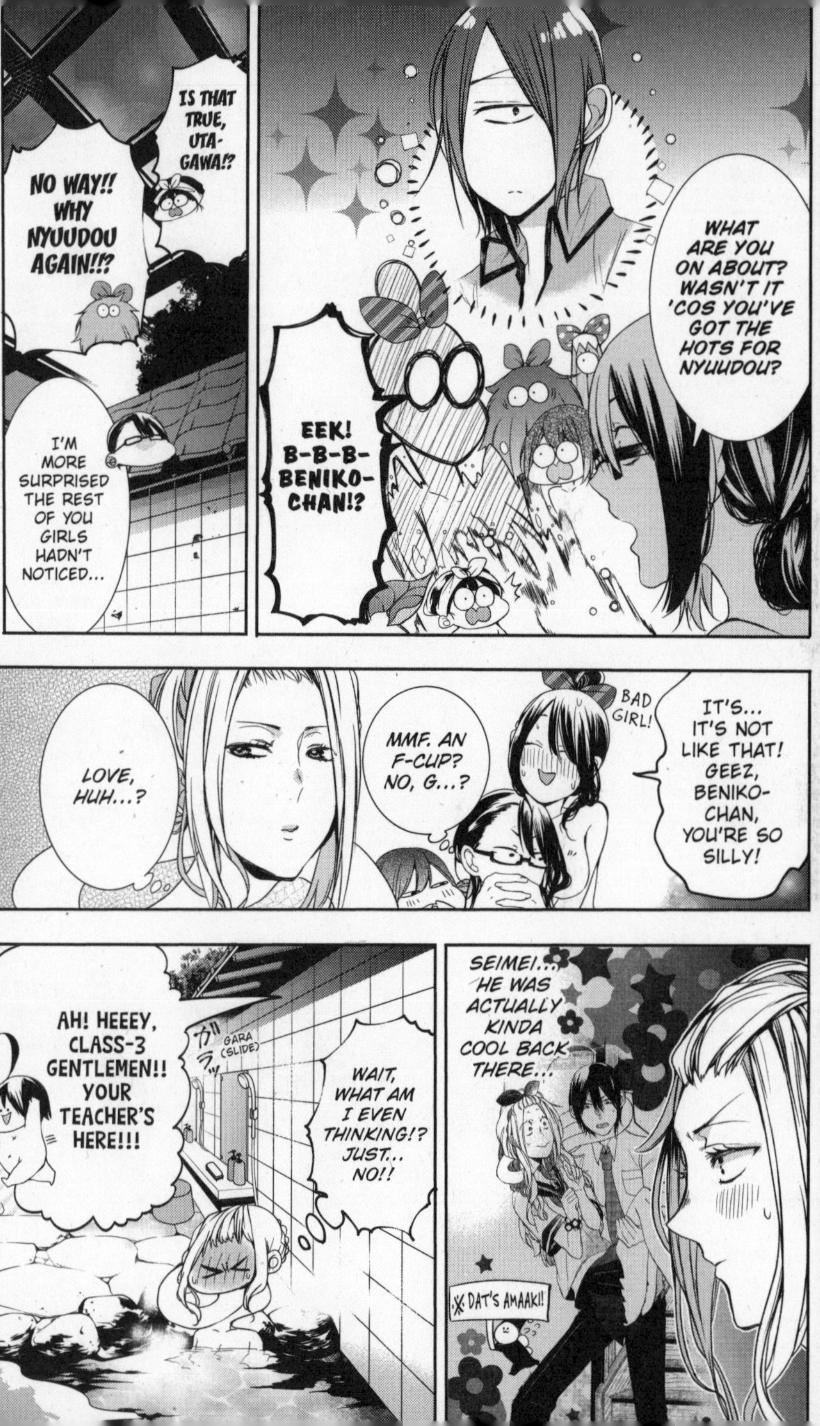
WHAT ARE YOU ON ABOUT? WASN'T IT 'COS YOU'VE GOT THE HOTS FOR NYUUDOU?
EEK! B-B-B-BENIKO-CHAN!?
IS THAT TRUE, UTA-GAWA!?
NO WAY!! WHY NYUUDOU AGAIN!!?
I'M MORE SURPRISED THE REST OF YOU GIRLS HADN'T NOTICED...
IT'S... IT'S NOT LIKE THAT! GEEZ, BENIKO-CHAN, YOU'RE SO SILLY!
BAD GIRL!
MMF. AN F-CUP? NO, G...?
LOVE, HUH...?
SEIMEI... HE WAS ACTUALLY KINDA COOL BACK THERE...
※ DAT'S AMAAKI!
WAIT, WHAT AM I EVEN THINKING!? JUST... NO!!
GARA (SLIDE)
AH! HEEEY, CLASS-3 GENTLEMEN!! YOUR TEACHER'S HERE!!!

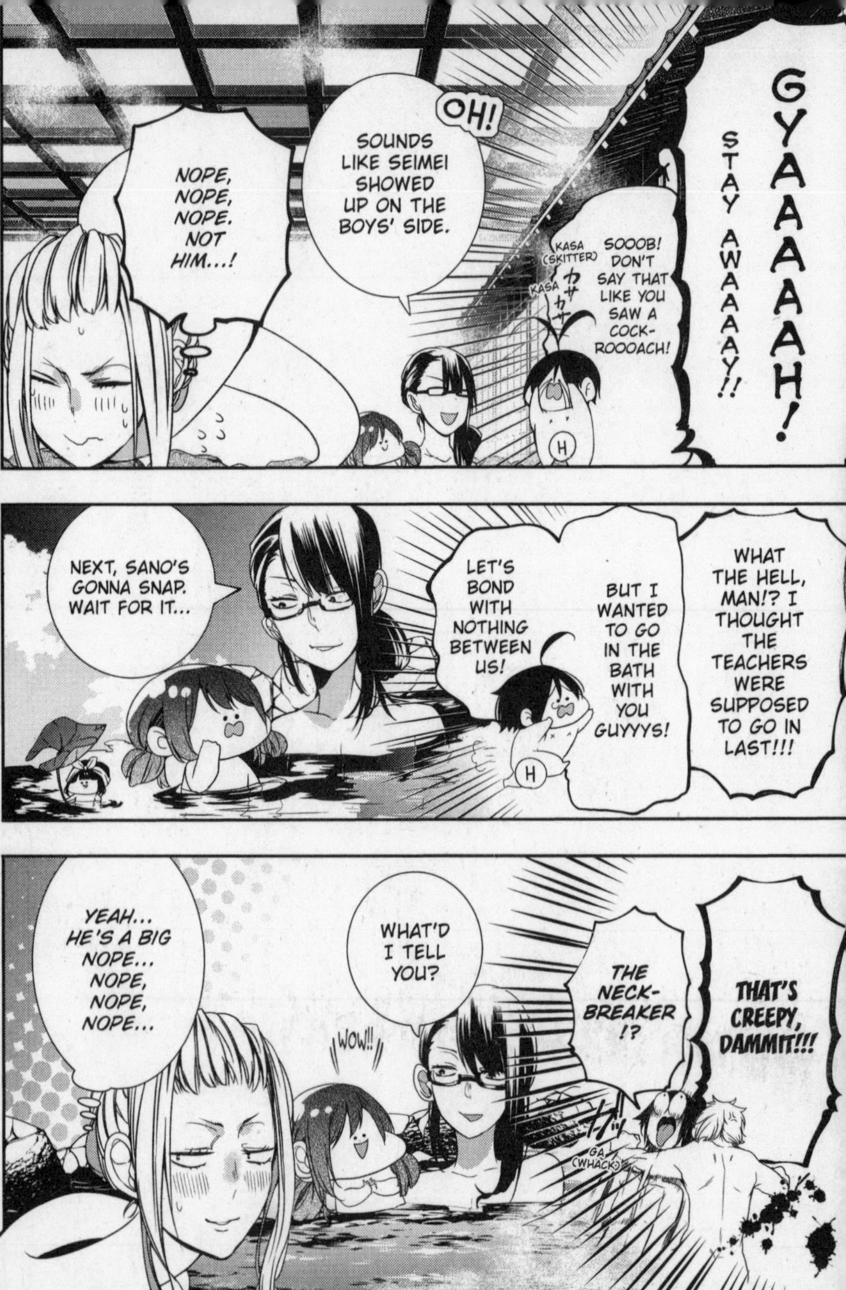
GYAAAAAH!
STAY AWAAAAAY!!
SOOOB! DON'T SAY THAT LIKE YOU SAW A COCK-ROOOOACH!
KASA (SKITTER) KASA
OH!
SOUNDS LIKE SEIMEI SHOWED UP ON THE BOYS' SIDE.
NOPE, NOPE, NOPE. NOT HIM...!
WHAT THE HELL, MAN!? I THOUGHT THE TEACHERS WERE SUPPOSED TO GO IN LAST!!!
BUT I WANTED TO GO IN THE BATH WITH YOU GUYYYS!
LET'S BOND WITH NOTHING BETWEEN US!
NEXT, SANO'S GONNA SNAP. WAIT FOR IT...
THAT'S CREEPY, DAMMIT!!!
THE NECK-BREAKER!?
GA (WHACK)
WHAT'D I TELL YOU?
WOW!!
YEAH... HE'S A BIG NOPE... NOPE, NOPE, NOPE...

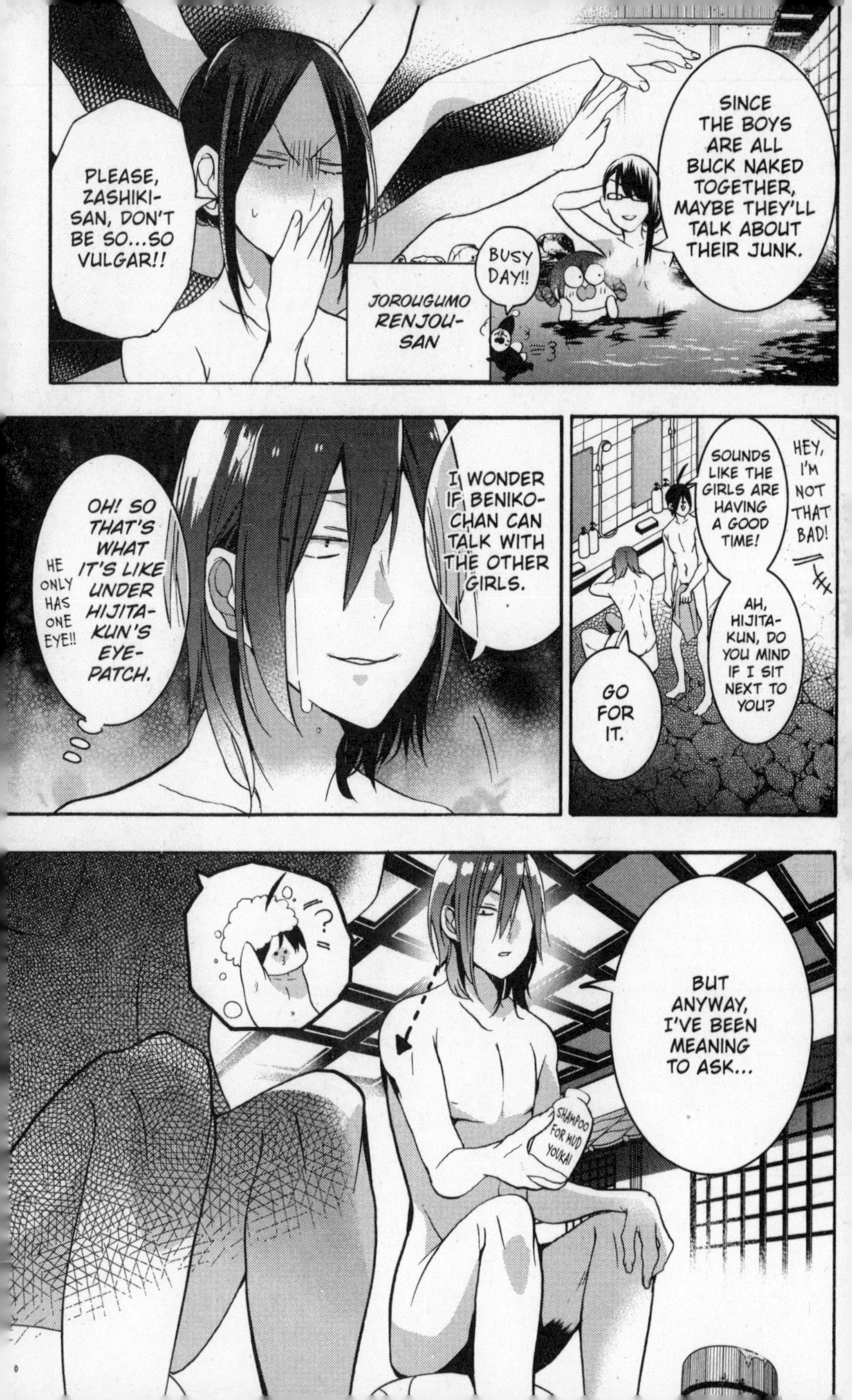
SINCE THE BOYS ARE ALL BUCK NAKED TOGETHER, MAYBE THEY'LL TALK ABOUT THEIR JUNK.
BUSY DAY!!
JOROUGUMO RENJOU-SAN
PLEASE, ZASHIKI-SAN, DON'T BE SO...SO VULGAR!!
HEY, I'M NOT THAT BAD!
SOUNDS LIKE THE GIRLS ARE HAVING A GOOD TIME!
AH, HIJITA-KUN, DO YOU MIND IF I SIT NEXT TO YOU?
GO FOR IT.
I WONDER IF BENIKO-CHAN CAN TALK WITH THE OTHER GIRLS.
OH! SO THAT'S WHAT IT'S LIKE UNDER HIJITA-KUN'S EYE-PATCH.
HE ONLY HAS ONE EYE!!
BUT ANYWAY, I'VE BEEN MEANING TO ASK...
SHAMPOO FOR MUD YOUKAI
!?

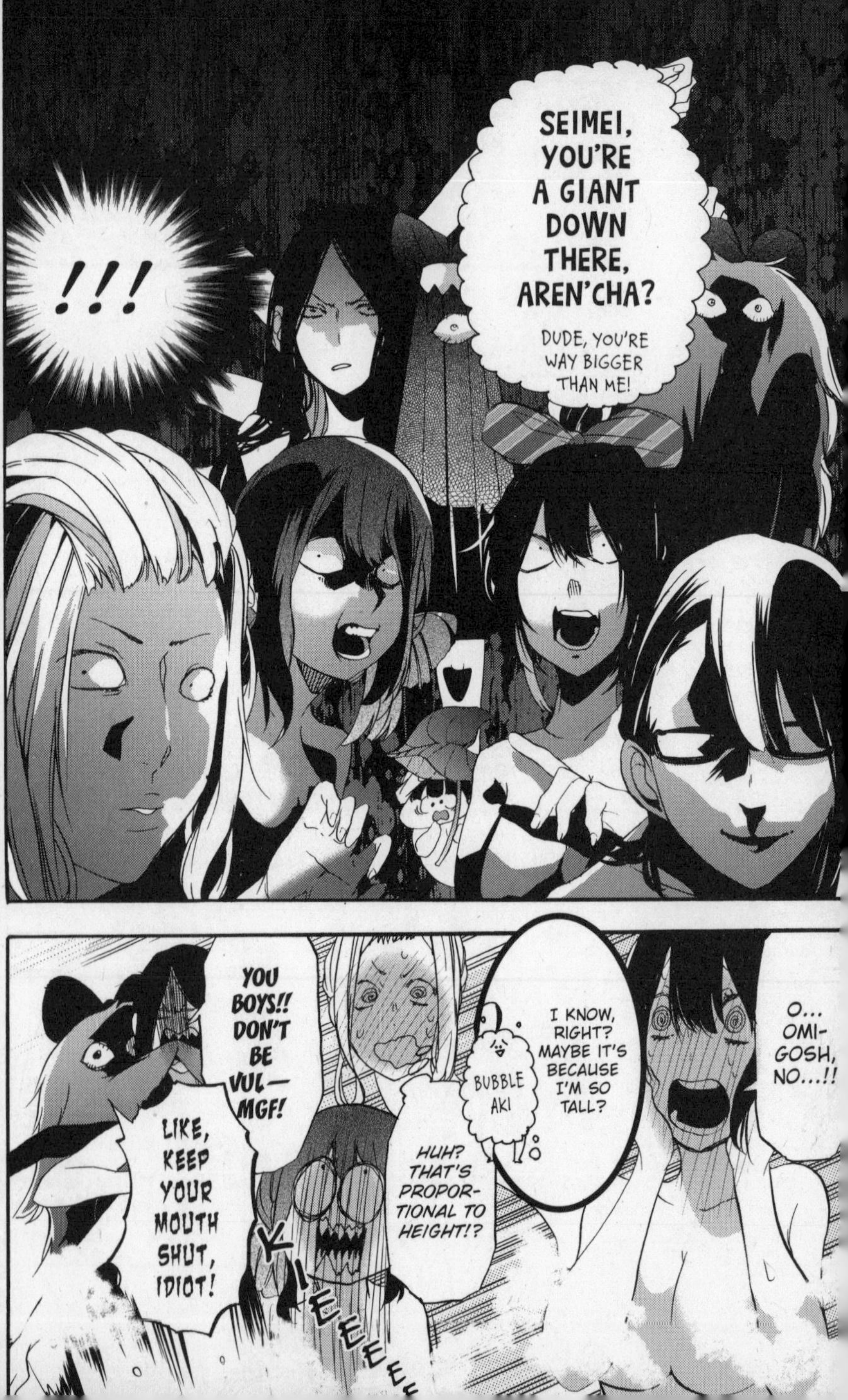
SEIMEI, YOU'RE A GIANT DOWN THERE, AREN'CHA?
DUDE, YOU'RE WAY BIGGER THAN ME!
!!!
O... OMI-GOSH, NO...!!
I KNOW, RIGHT? MAYBE IT'S BECAUSE I'M SO TALL?
BUBBLE AKI
HUH? THAT'S PROPORTIONAL TO HEIGHT!?
YOU BOYS!! DON'T BE VUL—MGF!
LIKE, KEEP YOUR MOUTH SHUT, IDIOT!
KIEEEEE

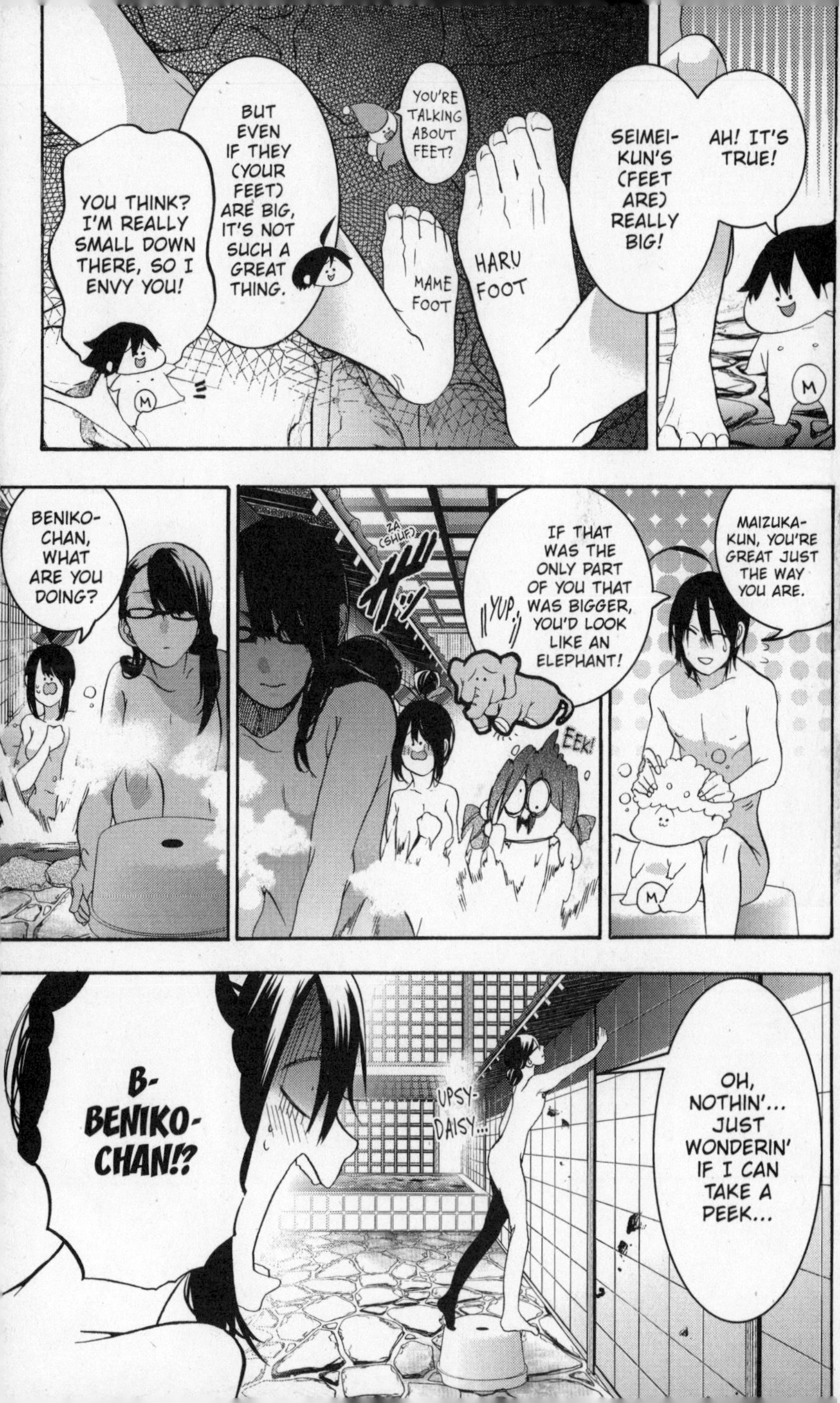
AH! IT'S TRUE!
SEIMEI-KUN'S (FEET ARE) REALLY BIG!
YOU'RE TALKING ABOUT FEET?
HARU FOOT
MAME FOOT
BUT EVEN IF THEY (YOUR FEET) ARE BIG, IT'S NOT SUCH A GREAT THING.
YOU THINK? I'M REALLY SMALL DOWN THERE, SO I ENVY YOU!
MAIZUKA-KUN, YOU'RE GREAT JUST THE WAY YOU ARE.
IF THAT WAS THE ONLY PART OF YOU THAT WAS BIGGER, YOU'D LOOK LIKE AN ELEPHANT!
YUP.
EEK!
ZA (SHUF)
BENIKO-CHAN, WHAT ARE YOU DOING?
OH, NOTHIN'... JUST WONDERIN' IF I CAN TAKE A PEEK...
UPSY-DAISY...
B-BENIKO-CHAN!?

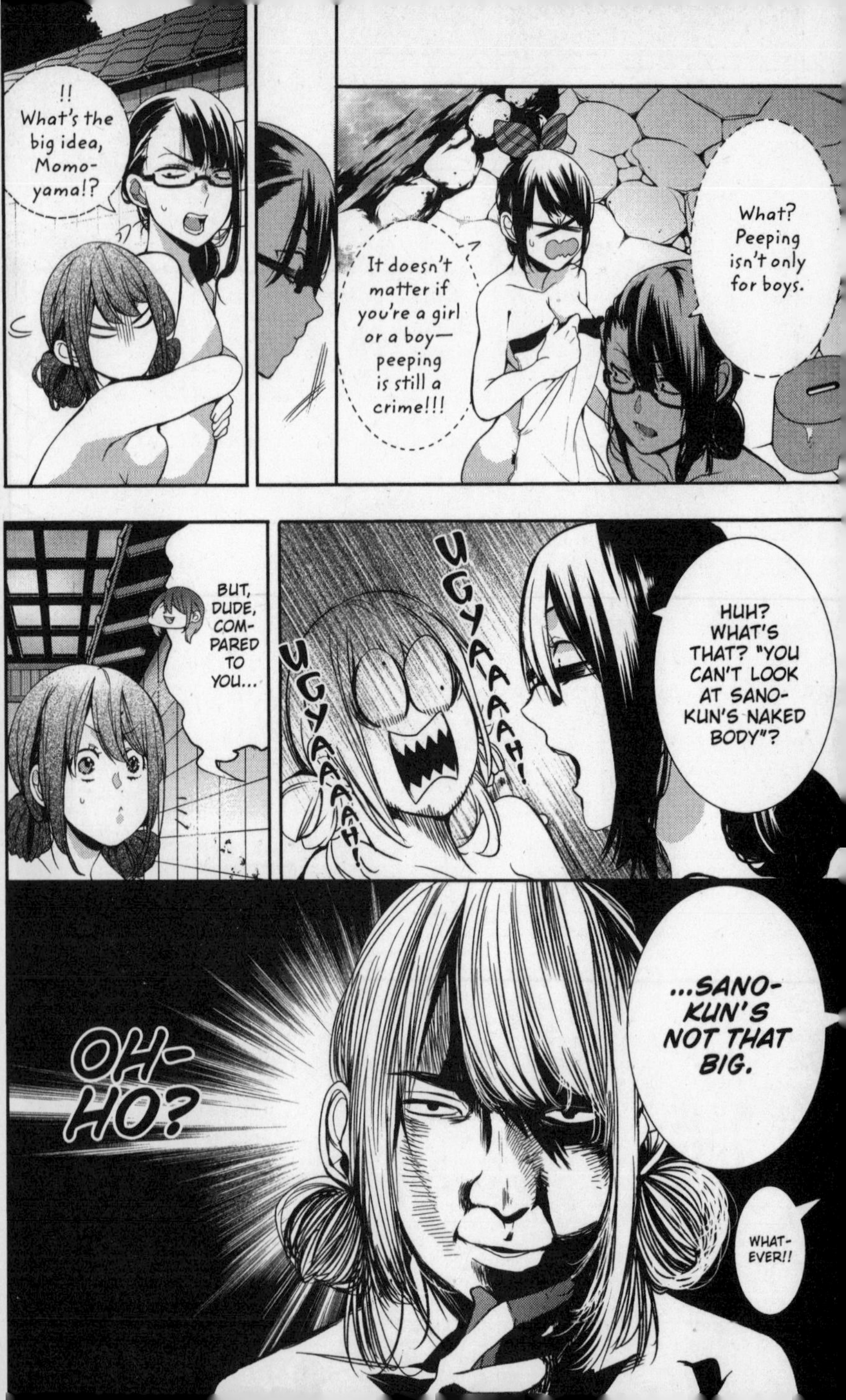
What? Peeping isn't only for boys.
It doesn't matter if you're a girl or a boy—peeping is still a crime!!!
!! What's the big idea, Momo-yama!?
HUH? WHAT'S THAT? "YOU CAN'T LOOK AT SANO-KUN'S NAKED BODY"?
UGYAAAAAH!
UGYAAAAAH!
BUT, DUDE, COMPARED TO YOU...
...SANO-KUN'S NOT THAT BIG.
WHAT-EVER!!
OH-HO?

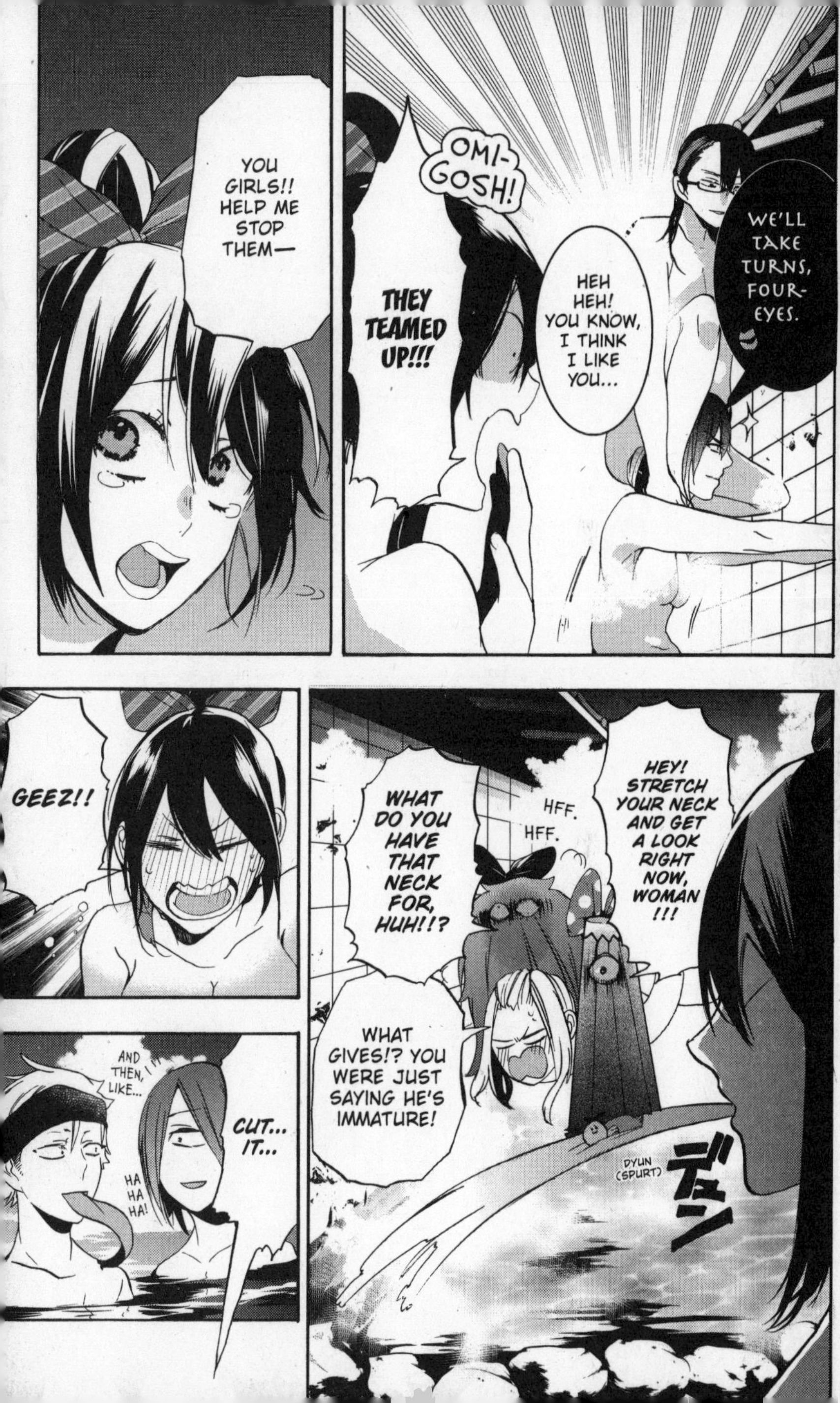

WE'LL TAKE TURNS, FOUR-EYES.
HEH HEH! YOU KNOW, I THINK I LIKE YOU...
OMI-GOSH!
THEY TEAMED UP!!!
YOU GIRLS!! HELP ME STOP THEM—
HEY! STRETCH YOUR NECK AND GET A LOOK RIGHT NOW, WOMAN!!!
WHAT DO YOU HAVE THAT NECK FOR, HUH!!?
HFF. HFF.
WHAT GIVES!? YOU WERE JUST SAYING HE'S IMMATURE!
デュン
DYUN (SPURT)
GEEZ!!
AND THEN, LIKE...
CUT... IT...
HA HA HA!

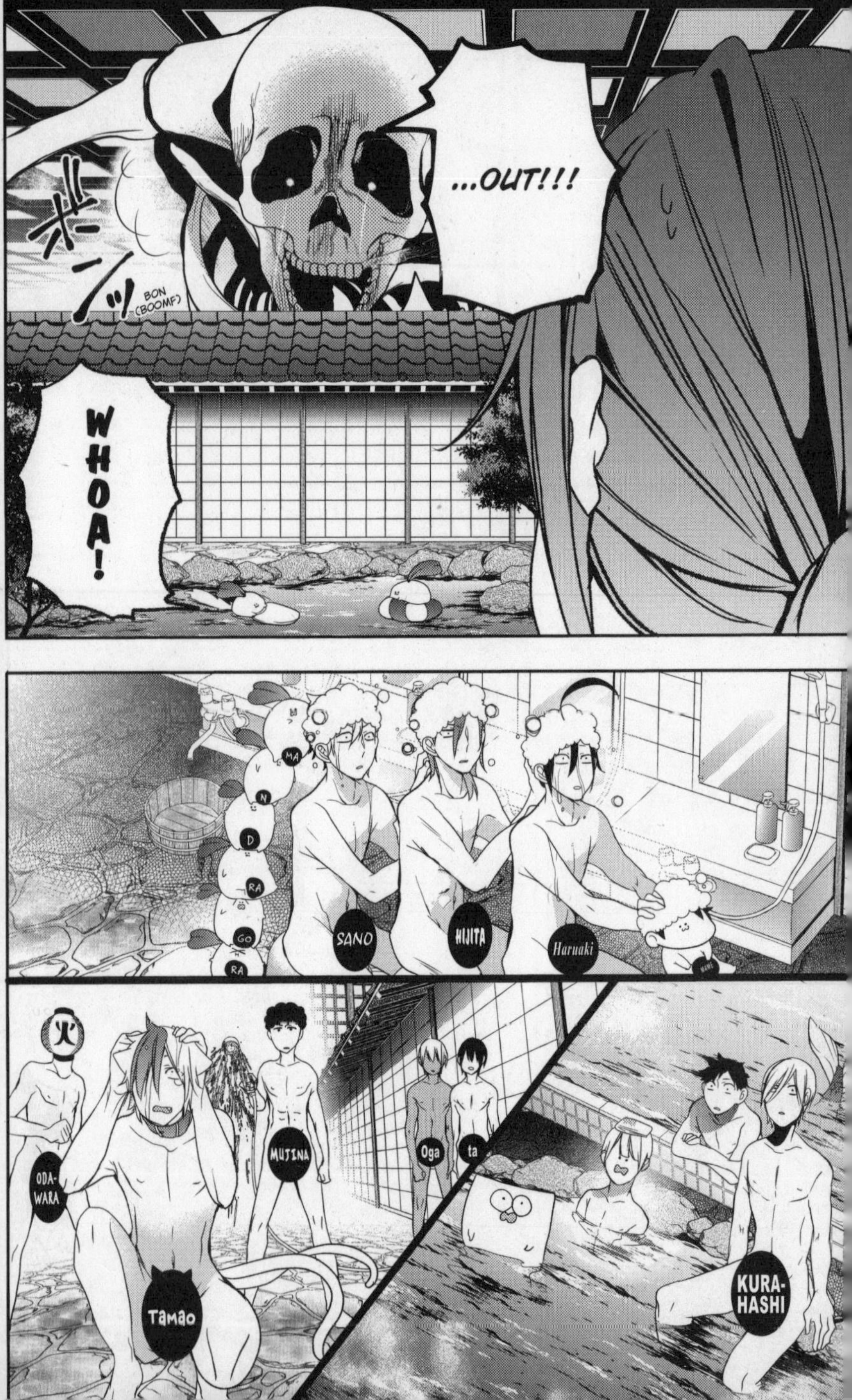
...OUT!!!
WHOA!
BON (BOOMF)
Haruaki
MAME
HIJITA
SANO
MA N D RA GO RA
KURA-HASHI
Oga ta
MUJINA
Tamao
ODA-WARA

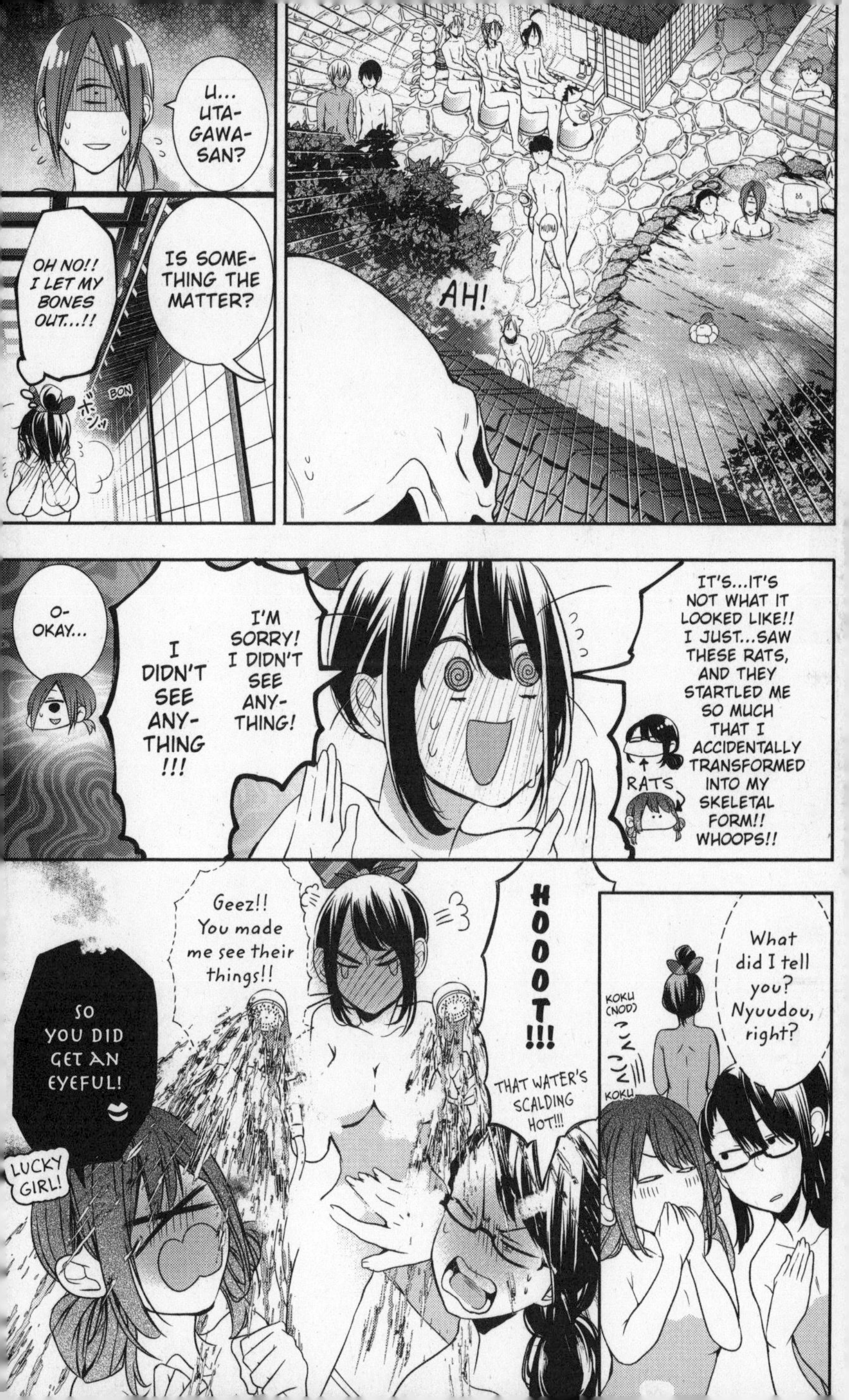
AH!
U... UTA-GAWA-SAN?
IS SOME-THING THE MATTER?
OH NO!! I LET MY BONES OUT...!!
BON
IT'S...IT'S NOT WHAT IT LOOKED LIKE!! I JUST...SAW THESE RATS, AND THEY STARTLED ME SO MUCH THAT I ACCIDENTALLY TRANSFORMED INTO MY SKELETAL FORM!! WHOOPS!!
RATS
I'M SORRY! I DIDN'T SEE ANY-THING!
I DIDN'T SEE ANY-THING!!!
O-OKAY...
What did I tell you? Nyuudou, right?
KOKU (NOD)
KOKU
HOOOT!!!
Geez!! You made me see their things!!
THAT WATER'S SCALDING HOT!!!
SO YOU DID GET AN EYEFUL!
LUCKY GIRL!

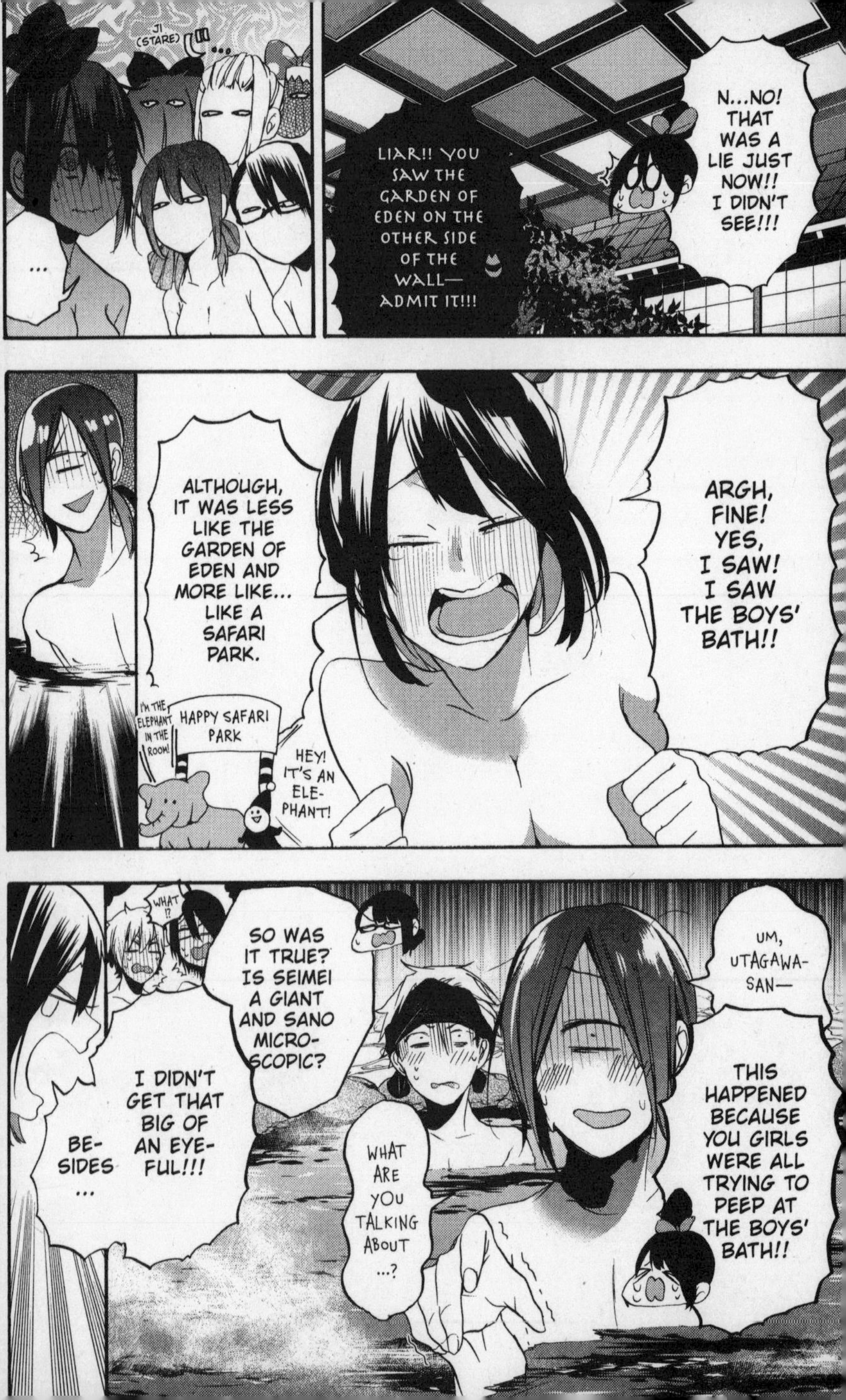
N...NO! THAT WAS A LIE JUST NOW!! I DIDN'T SEE!!!
LIAR!! YOU SAW THE GARDEN OF EDEN ON THE OTHER SIDE OF THE WALL—ADMIT IT!!!
JI (STARE)
...
...
ARGH, FINE! YES, I SAW! I SAW THE BOYS' BATH!!
ALTHOUGH, IT WAS LESS LIKE THE GARDEN OF EDEN AND MORE LIKE... LIKE A SAFARI PARK.
HEY! IT'S AN ELE-PHANT!
HAPPY SAFARI PARK
I'M THE ELEPHANT IN THE ROOM!
UM, UTAGAWA-SAN—
THIS HAPPENED BECAUSE YOU GIRLS WERE ALL TRYING TO PEEP AT THE BOYS' BATH!!
WHAT ARE YOU TALKING ABOUT ...?
SO WAS IT TRUE? IS SEIMEI A GIANT AND SANO MICRO-SCOPIC?
WHAT !?
I DIDN'T GET THAT BIG OF AN EYE-FUL!!!
BE-SIDES ...

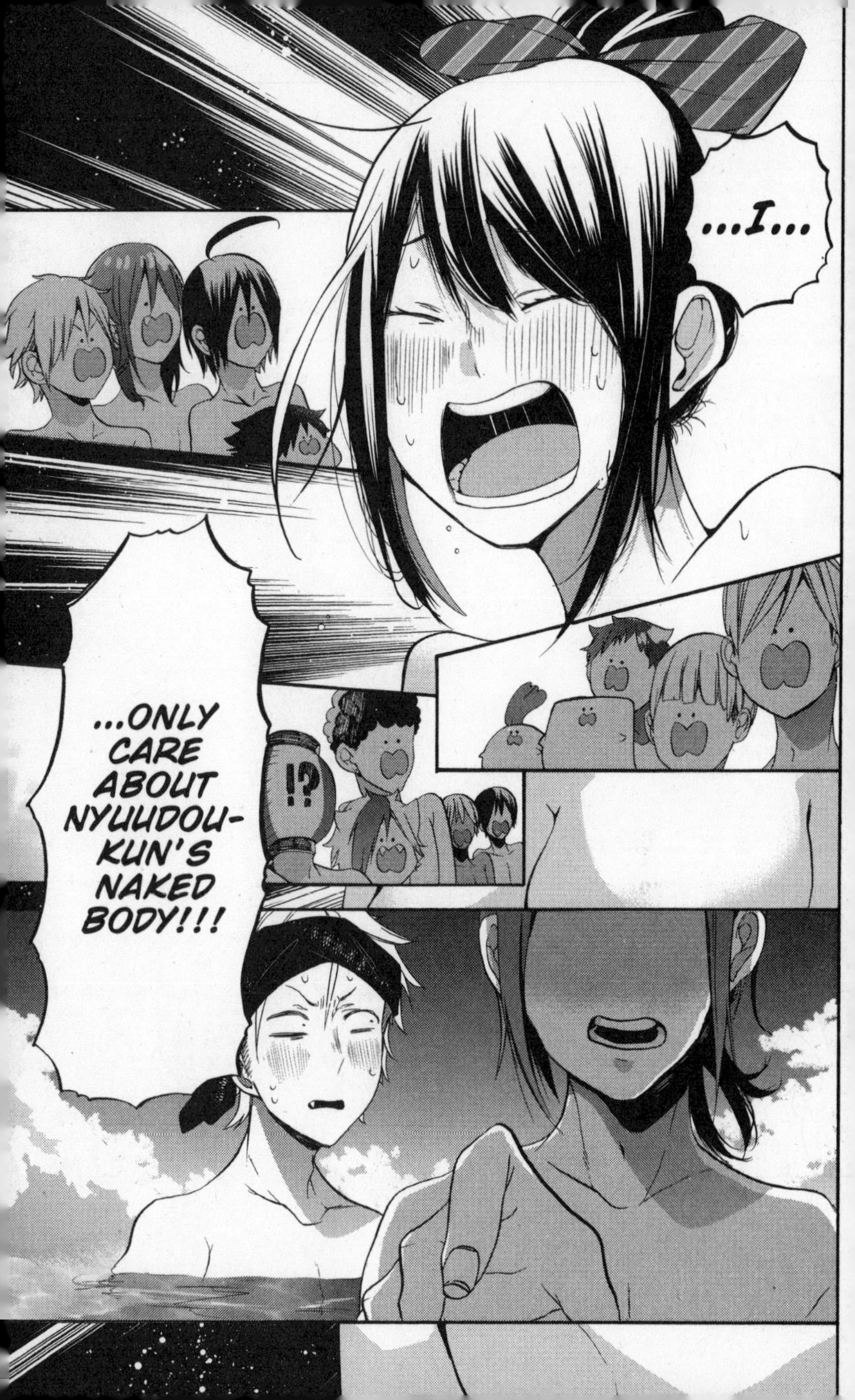
...I...
...ONLY CARE ABOUT NYUUDOU-KUN'S NAKED BODY!!!
!?

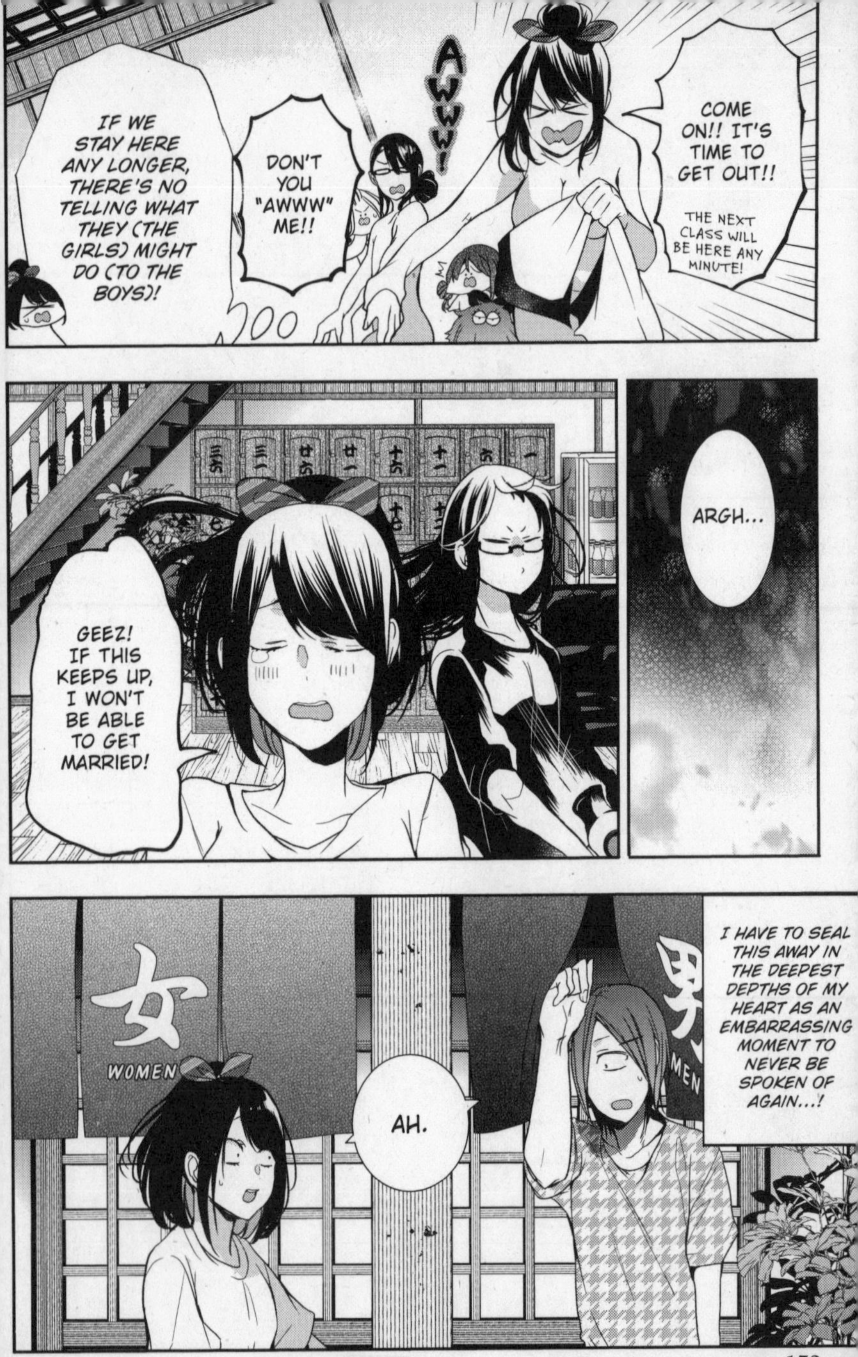
COME ON!! IT'S TIME TO GET OUT!!
THE NEXT CLASS WILL BE HERE ANY MINUTE!
AWWW!
DON'T YOU "AWWW" ME!!
IF WE STAY HERE ANY LONGER, THERE'S NO TELLING WHAT THEY (THE GIRLS) MIGHT DO (TO THE BOYS)!
ARGH...
GEEZ! IF THIS KEEPS UP, I WON'T BE ABLE TO GET MARRIED!
I HAVE TO SEAL THIS AWAY IN THE DEEPEST DEPTHS OF MY HEART AS AN EMBARRASSING MOMENT TO NEVER BE SPOKEN OF AGAIN...!
男
MEN
AH.
女
WOMEN

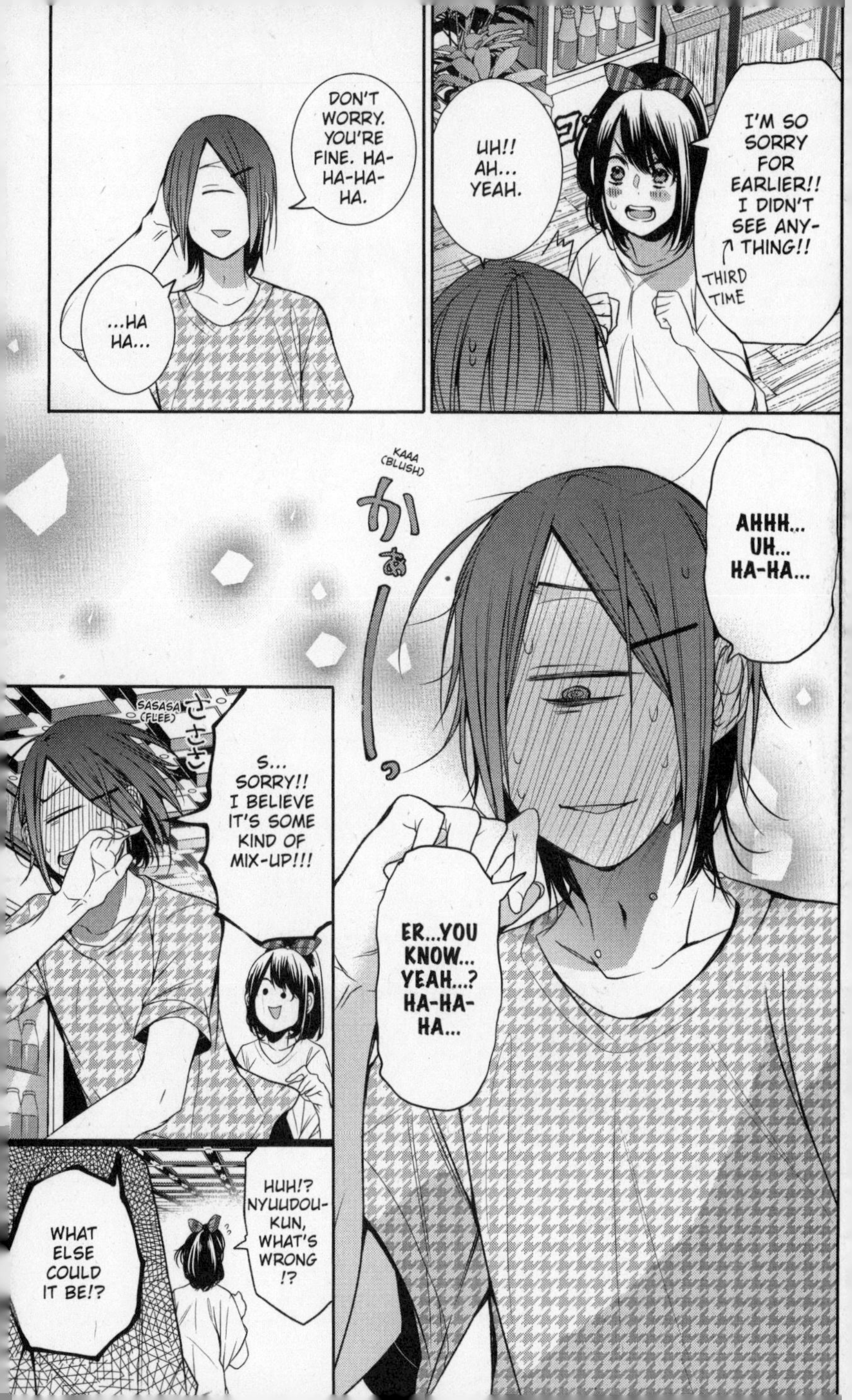

I'M SO SORRY FOR EARLIER!! I DIDN'T SEE ANYTHING!!
THIRD TIME
UH!! AH... YEAH.
DON'T WORRY. YOU'RE FINE. HA-HA-HA-HA.
...HA HA...
KAAA (BLUSH)
AHHH... UH... HA-HA...
ER...YOU KNOW... YEAH...? HA-HA-HA...
SASASA (FLEE)
S... SORRY!! I BELIEVE IT'S SOME KIND OF MIX-UP!!!
HUH!? NYUUDOU-KUN, WHAT'S WRONG!?
WHAT ELSE COULD IT BE!?

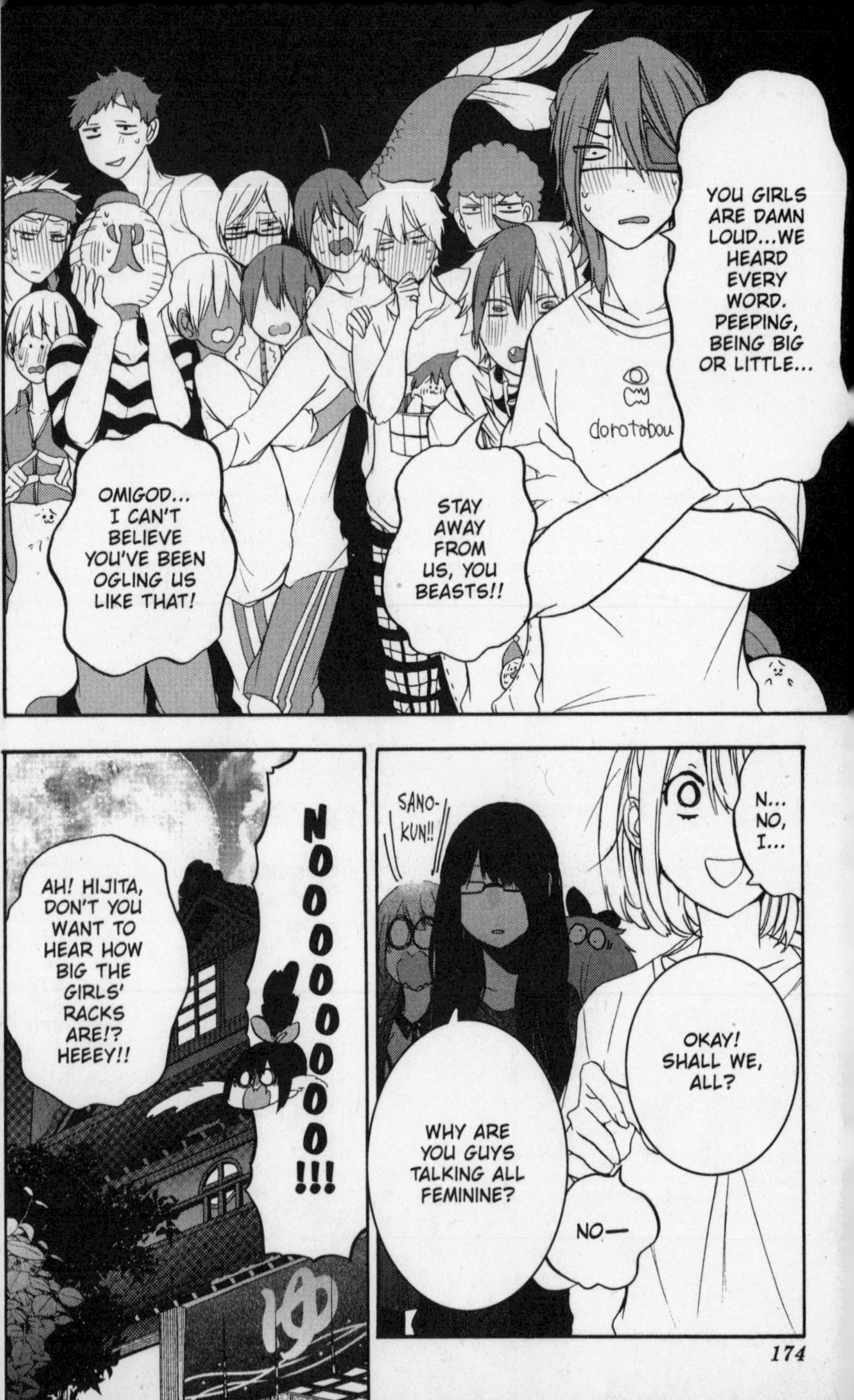
YOU GIRLS ARE DAMN LOUD...WE HEARD EVERY WORD. PEEPING, BEING BIG OR LITTLE...
dorotabou
STAY AWAY FROM US, YOU BEASTS!!
OMIGOD... I CAN'T BELIEVE YOU'VE BEEN OGLING US LIKE THAT!
N... NO, I...
SANO-KUN!!
OKAY! SHALL WE, ALL?
WHY ARE YOU GUYS TALKING ALL FEMININE?
NO—
AH! HIJITA, DON'T YOU WANT TO HEAR HOW BIG THE GIRLS' RACKS ARE!? HEEEY!!
NOOOOOOOOOOO!!!

HOMEROOM: BONUS PAGES!

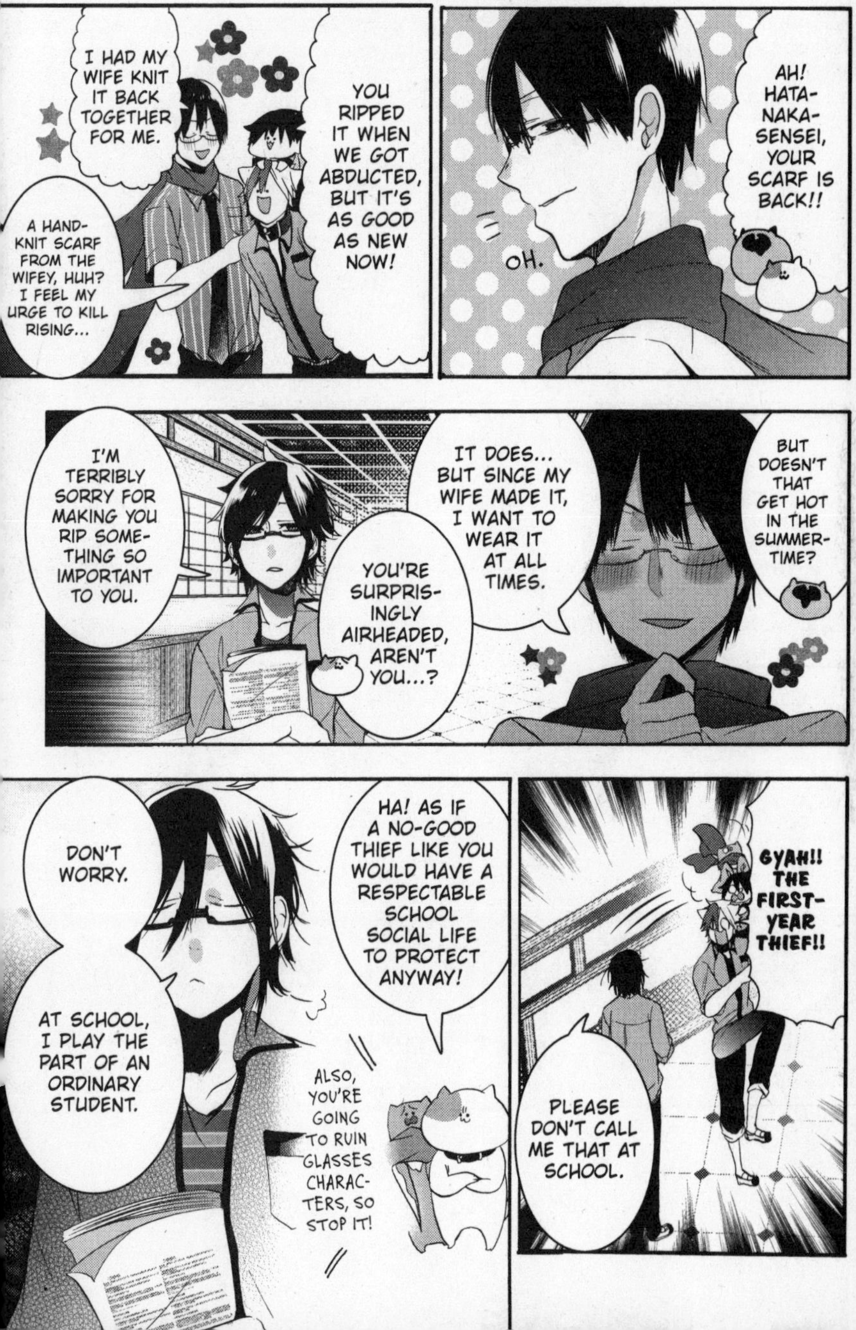
AH! HATA-NAKA-SENSEI, YOUR SCARF IS BACK!!
OH.
YOU RIPPED IT WHEN WE GOT ABDUCTED, BUT IT'S AS GOOD AS NEW NOW!
I HAD MY WIFE KNIT IT BACK TOGETHER FOR ME.
A HAND-KNIT SCARF FROM THE WIFEY, HUH? I FEEL MY URGE TO KILL RISING...
BUT DOESN'T THAT GET HOT IN THE SUMMER-TIME?
IT DOES... BUT SINCE MY WIFE MADE IT, I WANT TO WEAR IT AT ALL TIMES.
YOU'RE SURPRIS-INGLY AIRHEADED, AREN'T YOU...?
I'M TERRIBLY SORRY FOR MAKING YOU RIP SOME-THING SO IMPORTANT TO YOU.
GYAH!! THE FIRST-YEAR THIEF!!
PLEASE DON'T CALL ME THAT AT SCHOOL.
HA! AS IF A NO-GOOD THIEF LIKE YOU WOULD HAVE A RESPECTABLE SCHOOL SOCIAL LIFE TO PROTECT ANYWAY!
DON'T WORRY.
AT SCHOOL, I PLAY THE PART OF AN ORDINARY STUDENT.
ALSO, YOU'RE GOING TO RUIN GLASSES CHARAC-TERS, SO STOP IT!

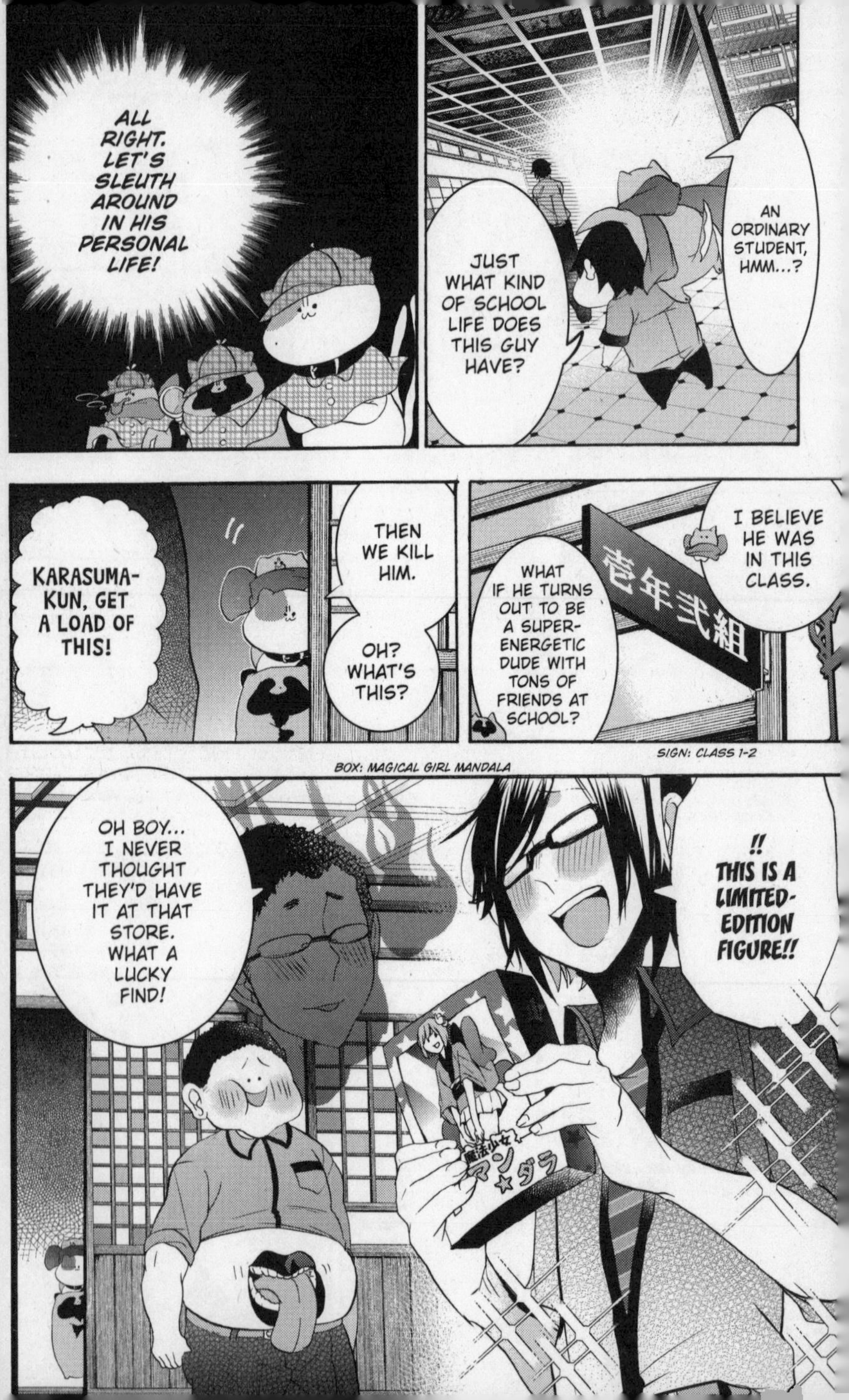
AN ORDINARY STUDENT, HMM...?
JUST WHAT KIND OF SCHOOL LIFE DOES THIS GUY HAVE?
ALL RIGHT. LET'S SLEUTH AROUND IN HIS PERSONAL LIFE!
I BELIEVE HE WAS IN THIS CLASS.
壱年弐組
WHAT IF HE TURNS OUT TO BE A SUPER-ENERGETIC DUDE WITH TONS OF FRIENDS AT SCHOOL?
SIGN: CLASS 1-2
THEN WE KILL HIM.
OH? WHAT'S THIS?
KARASUMA-KUN, GET A LOAD OF THIS!
BOX: MAGICAL GIRL MANDALA
!! THIS IS A LIMITED-EDITION FIGURE!!
魔法少女マンダラ
OH BOY... I NEVER THOUGHT THEY'D HAVE IT AT THAT STORE. WHAT A LUCKY FIND!

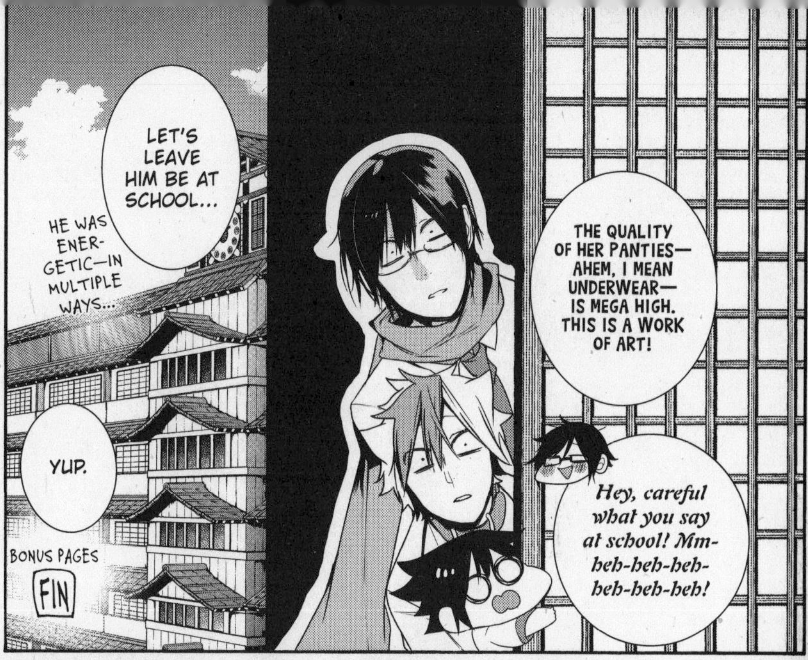
THE QUALITY OF HER PANTIES—AHEM, I MEAN UNDERWEAR—IS MEGA HIGH. THIS IS A WORK OF ART!
Hey, careful what you say at school! Mm-heh-heh-heh-heh-heh-heh-heh!
LET'S LEAVE HIM BE AT SCHOOL...
HE WAS ENER-GETIC—IN MULTIPLE WAYS...
YUP.
BONUS PAGES
FIN

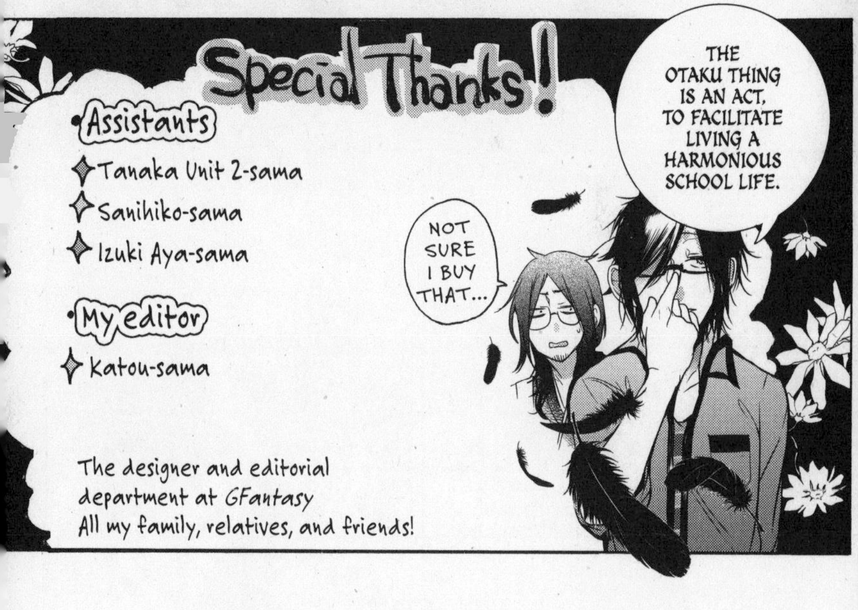
THE OTAKU THING IS AN ACT, TO FACILITATE LIVING A HARMONIOUS SCHOOL LIFE.
Special Thanks!
•Assistants
Tanaka Unit 2-sama
Sanihiko-sama
Izuki Aya-sama
•My editor
Katou-sama
The designer and editorial department at GFantasy
All my family, relatives, and friends!
NOT SURE I BUY THAT...

A Terrified Teacher at Ghoul School!
Volume 5 coming December 2018!

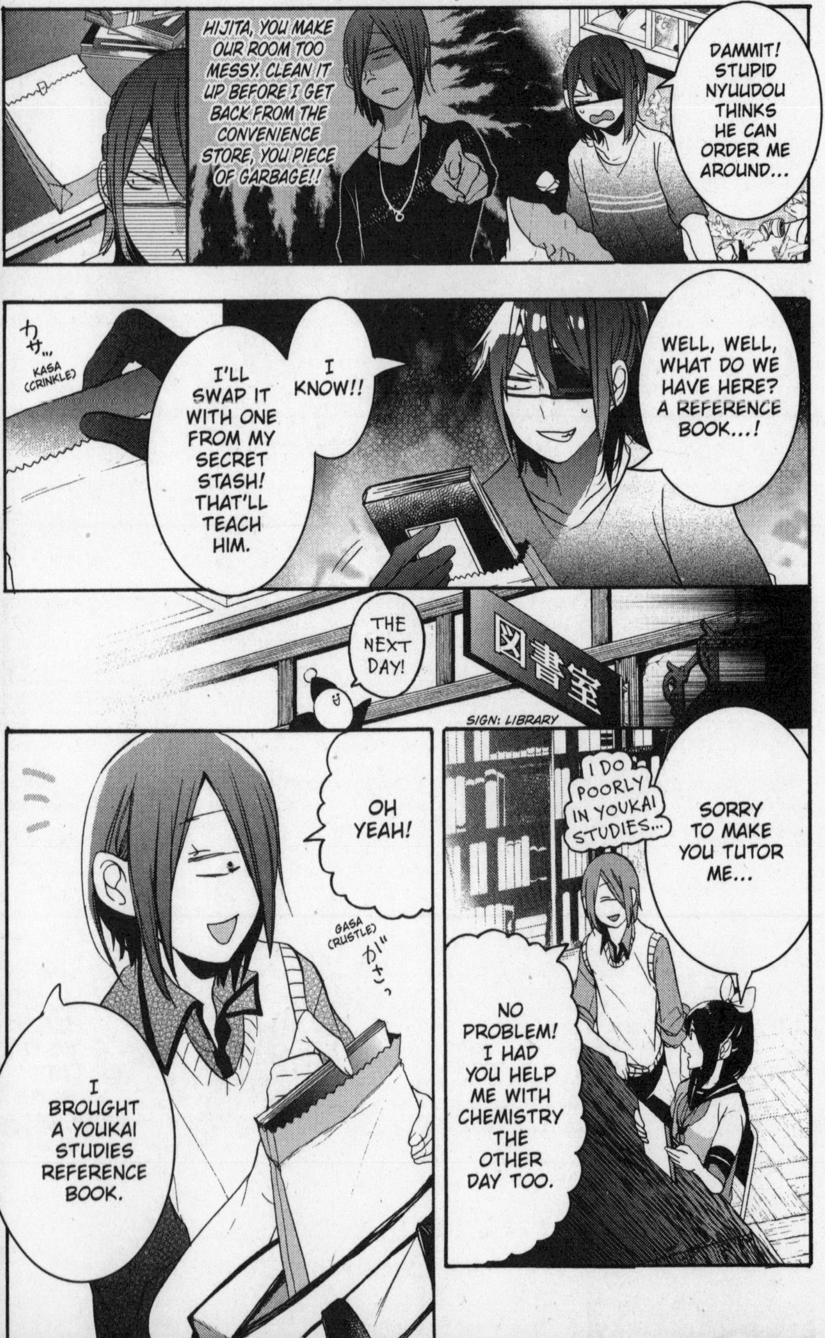
DAMMIT! STUPID NYUUDOU THINKS HE CAN ORDER ME AROUND...
HIJITA, YOU MAKE OUR ROOM TOO MESSY. CLEAN IT UP BEFORE I GET BACK FROM THE CONVENIENCE STORE, YOU PIECE OF GARBAGE!!
WELL, WELL, WHAT DO WE HAVE HERE? A REFERENCE BOOK...!
I KNOW!!
I'LL SWAP IT WITH ONE FROM MY SECRET STASH! THAT'LL TEACH HIM.
カサ…
KASA (CRINKLE)
図書室
THE NEXT DAY!
SIGN: LIBRARY
SORRY TO MAKE YOU TUTOR ME...
I DO POORLY IN YOUKAI STUDIES...
NO PROBLEM! I HAD YOU HELP ME WITH CHEMISTRY THE OTHER DAY TOO.
OH YEAH!
GASA (RUSTLE)
がさっ
I BROUGHT A YOUKAI STUDIES REFERENCE BOOK.

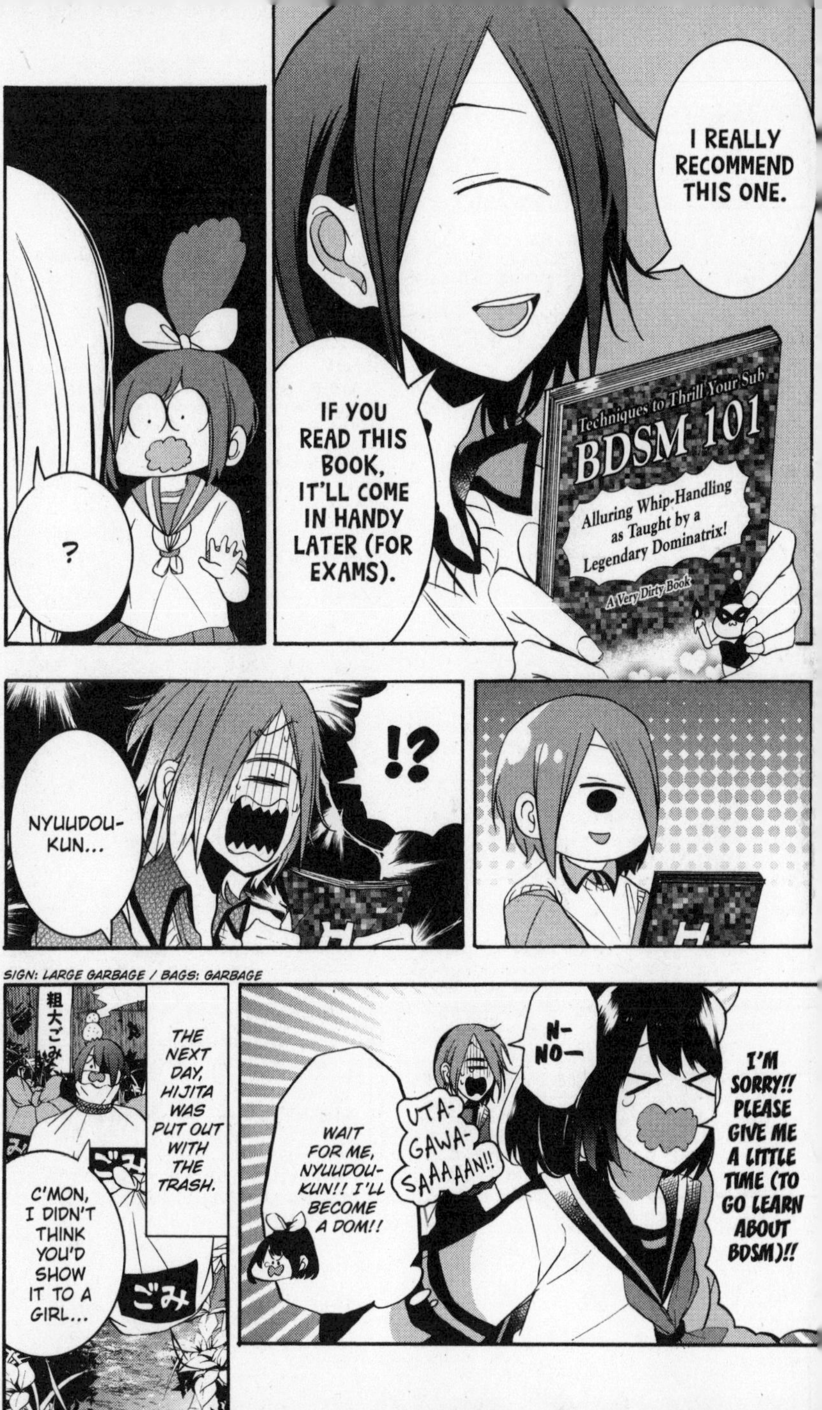
I REALLY RECOMMEND THIS ONE.
IF YOU READ THIS BOOK, IT'LL COME IN HANDY LATER (FOR EXAMS).
Techniques to Thrill Your Sub
BDSM 101
Alluring Whip-Handling as Taught by a Legendary Dominatrix!
A Very Dirty Book
?
!?
NYUUDOU-KUN...
SIGN: LARGE GARBAGE / BAGS: GARBAGE
N-NO—
I'M SORRY!! PLEASE GIVE ME A LITTLE TIME (TO GO LEARN ABOUT BDSM)!!
UTA-GAWA-SAAAAAN!!
WAIT FOR ME, NYUUDOU-KUN!! I'LL BECOME A DOM!!
粗大ごみ
THE NEXT DAY, HIJITA WAS PUT OUT WITH THE TRASH.
C'MON, I DIDN'T THINK YOU'D SHOW IT TO A GIRL...
ごみ

Translation Notes

Common Honorifics

no honorific: Indicates familiarity or closeness; if used without permission or reason, addressing someone in this manner would constitute an insult.

-san: The Japanese equivalent of Mr./Mrs./Miss. If a situation calls for politeness, this is the fail-safe honorific.

-sama: Conveys great respect; may also indicate that the social status of the speaker is lower than that of the addressee.

-kun: Used most often when referring to boys, this indicates affection or familiarity. Occasionally used by older men among their peers, but it may also be used by anyone referring to a person of lower standing.

-chan: An affectionate honorific indicating familiarity used mostly in reference to girls; also used in reference to cute persons or animals of either gender.

-senpai: A suffix used to address upperclassmen or more experienced coworkers.

-sensei: A respectful term for teachers, artists, or high-level professionals.

PAGE 1
Chuu is the Japanese onomatopoeia for a mouse's squeak.

PAGE 6
Hatanaka-sensei's given name, **Izuna**, comes from the name of the common weasel (corresponding to his *youkai* type).

PAGE 25
The **Battle of Sekigahara** (1600) was a decisive battle fought by an eastern army led by Ieyasu Tokugawa and a western army led by Mitsunari Ishida; Tokugawa's side won, gaining control of the territory belonging to the losing side. This was the beginning of the Tokugawa shogunate.

PAGE 27
Nure-onna (lit. "wet/soaked woman") has the body of a snake, the head of a woman, the tongue of a snake, and long, black hair. She haunts shores and rivers, washing her hair in the water. She might disguise herself as a woman with a bundled-up baby to lure human prey.

PAGE 30
In the original Japanese, the Ogata twins remark that Haruaki didn't scare away any thieves (*dorobou*) but did scare a *dorotabou* (Hijita's *youkai* type). Haruaki then calls Hijita Dorotabou-kun and corrects himself to Dorotabou-kun (swapping the *bou* character in *dorotabou* for the *bou* character in *dorobou*).

PAGE 35
Raijin is the god of lightning, with an *oni*-like appearance and drums upon his back that he beats to create thunder and lightning. **Fuujin** is the god of wind, with an *oni*-like appearance and a sack of wind thrown over his shoulder. Both are fearsome troublemakers, but they can also be protectors and have statues at the entrances to many shrines and temples in Japan. Technically, they are *kami* (gods), and **Takamagahara** is the dwelling place of the gods.

The **Edo period** (1603–1867), also known as the Tokugawa period, was a period of growth and stabilization under the rule of the Tokugawa shogunate following the turbulent Warring States period.

PAGE 36
Nurikabe (lit. "plaster wall") is a large wall *youkai* that blocks the path of travelers. Sometimes, it's even invisible.

PAGE 43
In Japanese, the name for **tag** is *oni gokko*—the *oni* game. So *youkai* playing tag would be kind of meta...

PAGE 45
The **yakubyougami** is a god of pestilence.

PAGE 48
The **futakuchi-onna** (lit. "two-mouthed woman") is a *youkai* who looks like a human woman but with a second mouth on the back of her head and long hair that can move like tentacles to feed her voracious second mouth. In some stories, she is a woman who feeds only her own children but not her stepchild and is cursed in revenge; in others, she is a woman who seems to rarely eat, but her secret mouth actually eats twice as much.

PAGE 51
Kappa are a very well-known type of *youkai* in Japan that often appear in ponds and rivers. They're notorious tricksters and can be rendered helpless by spilling the water that rests in the "dish" on their head.

PAGE 54
Yanagida is an *itton-momen* (flying bolt of cloth), so **itton-curtain** is a play on his *youkai* name.

PAGE 67
Tanuki are transforming raccoon dogs; Mame is a type of *tanuki*, the *mame-danuki*.

PAGE 70
The boys say they want to make **sekihan**, a red rice dish eaten on joyous occasions, to celebrate Sano's, uh, becoming a man.

PAGE 82
The **karasu tengu** are *tengu* (lit. "heavenly dog"/goblins) *youkai* with human bodies, wings upon their backs, and bird heads (*karasu* means "crow"), who wear monk's robes. *Tengu* are known for kidnapping people and being very proud. (A long nose like a *tengu*'s is a visual symbol for pride or haughtiness.) They're also more like minor gods than other trickster *youkai*.

PAGE 97
Abe no Seimei (921 to 1005) was a diviner for the imperial court said to have all kinds of supernatural powers, like Haruaki's.

PAGE 104
The **kamaitachi** is a weasel *youkai* with sickle-like claws.

PAGE 106
The **nekomata** is a mischievous two-tailed cat that walks on its hind legs.

PAGE 108
Here, the lieutenant of the Karasu Tengu Troupe mishears "Sano" as **sado**, which means "sadist" in Japanese.

PAGE 141
The **kudan** is a cow *youkai* that foretells the future.

PAGE 144
Koizumi is a **rokurokubi**. This *youkai*, usually a woman, looks and acts like a normal human in the day, but after going to bed at night, her neck stretches and looks for prey. In the morning, her body goes back to normal. She might have red marks or similar evidence of her true nature on her neck.

PAGE 159
The **asaoke no ke** is a hair *youkai*. The **karakasa obake** is a paper umbrella monster with one leg.

Hinagiku is the Japanese name for daisies.

PAGE 160
The **korpokkur** are a race of tiny people in Ainu folklore. They live under butterbur leaves, thus the leaf Akibe holds over herself.

PAGE 161
An **F-cup** in Japan corresponds to a DD-cup in the USA, and a G-cup to a DDD- or E-cup.

PAGE 163
The **jorougumo** (lit. "entangling bride" or, alternatively, "woman spider") is a large spider *youkai* who can shape-shift into a beautiful woman to lure in human prey.

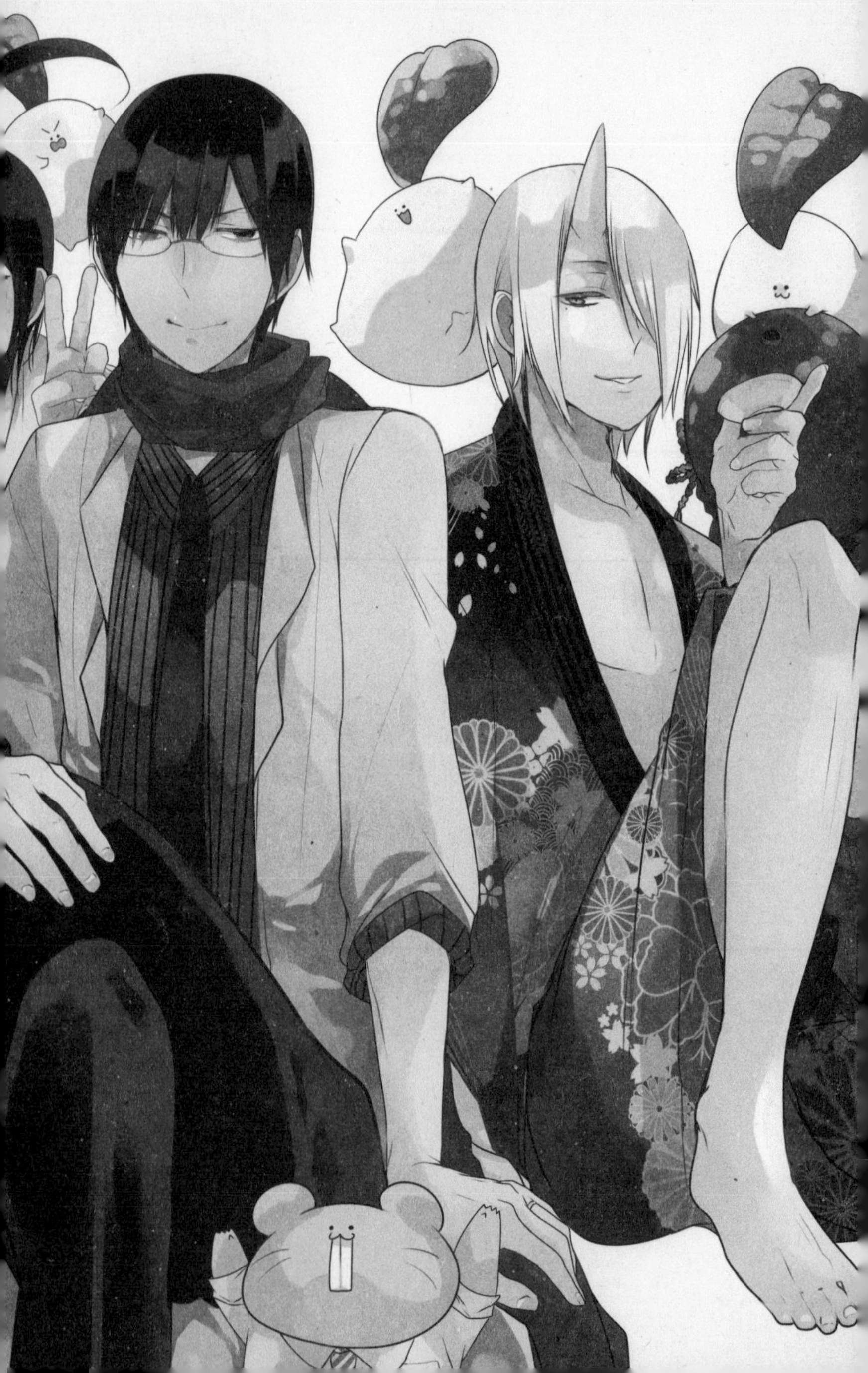

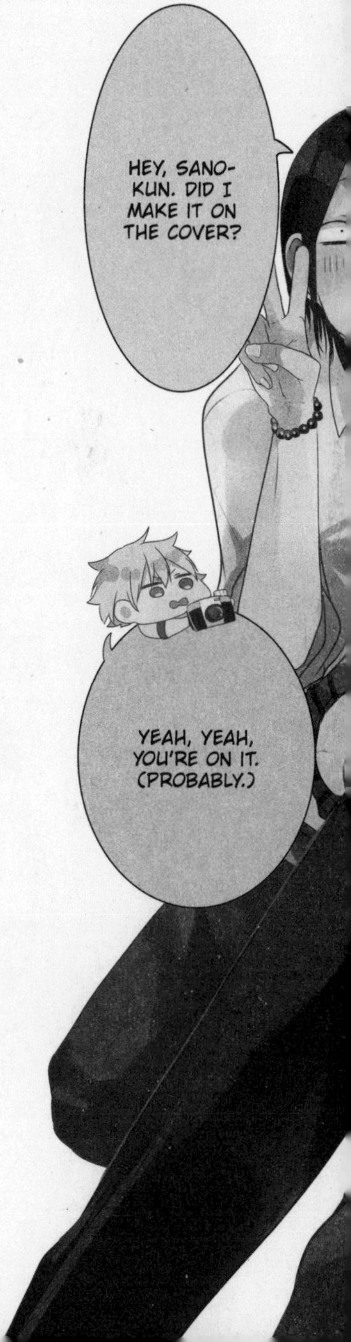
HEY, SANO-KUN. DID I MAKE IT ON THE COVER?
YEAH, YEAH, YOU'RE ON IT. (PROBABLY.)

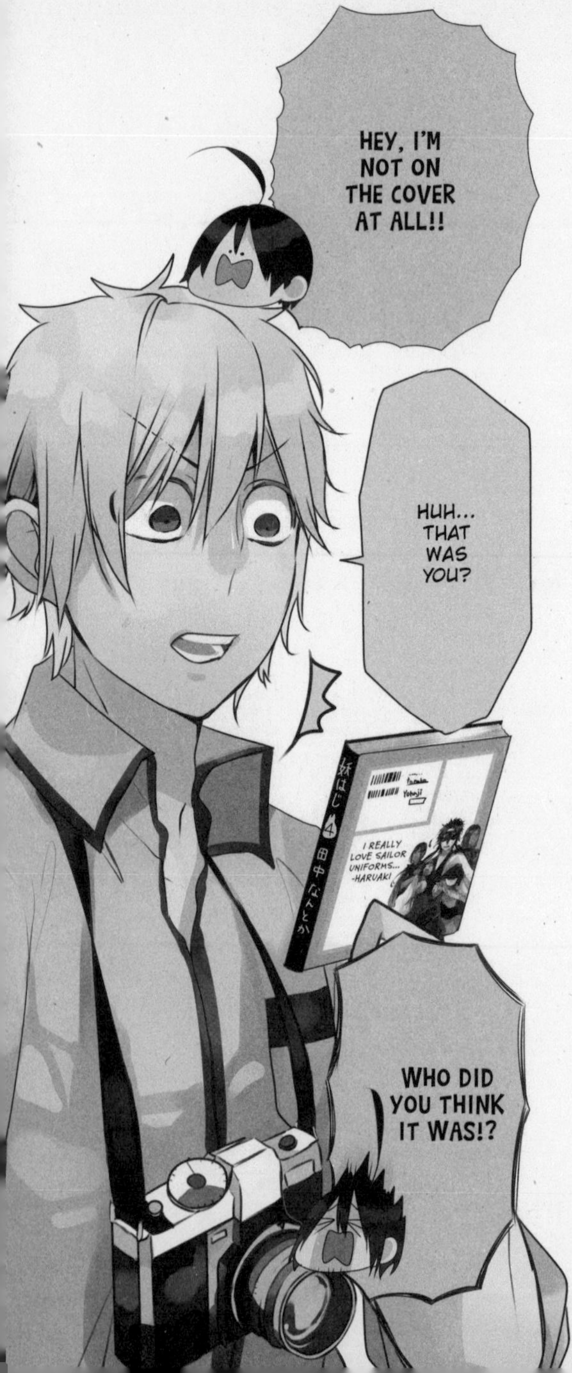
HEY, I'M NOT ON THE COVER AT ALL!!
HUH... THAT WAS YOU?
妖はじ 4 田中なんとか
I REALLY LOVE SAILOR UNIFORMS... -HARUAKI
WHO DID YOU THINK IT WAS!?

SPINE: GHOUL SCHOOL 4 — MAI TANAKA

A Terrified Teacher at Ghoul School!

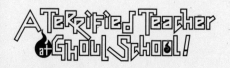

FINAL FANTASY
ファイナルファンタジー　ロスト・ストレンジャー
LOST STRANGER

Keep up with the latest chapters in the simul-pub version! Available now worldwide wherever e-books are sold!

For more information, visit www.yenpress.com

Yen Press

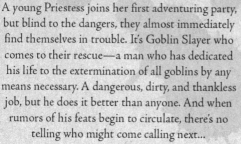

Karino Takatsu, creator of **SERVANT x SERVICE**, presents:

My Monster Girl's Too Cool For You

Burning adoration melts her heart...literally!

In a world where *youkai* and humans attend school together, a boy named Atsushi Fukuzumi falls for snow *youkai* Muku Shiroishi. Fukuzumi's passionate feelings melt Muku's heart...and the rest of her?! The first volume of an interspecies romantic comedy you're sure to fall head over heels for is now available!!

YenPress.com

Read new installments of this series every month at the same time as Japan!

CHAPTERS AVAILABLE NOW AT E-TAILERS EVERYWHERE!

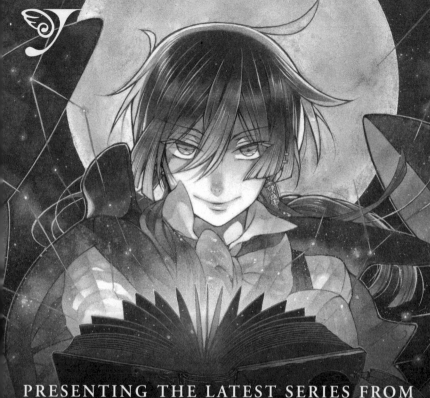

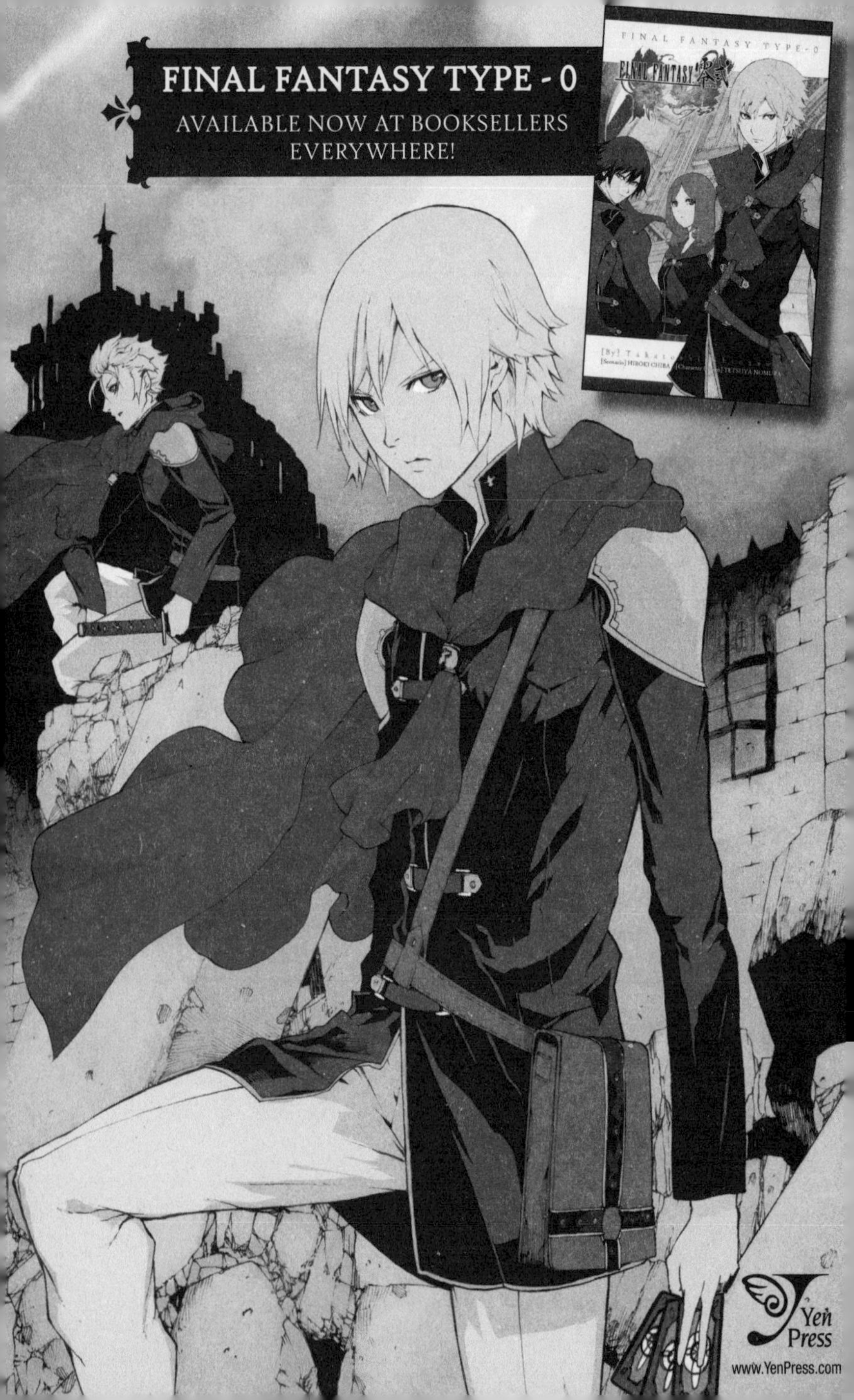

FINAL FANTASY 零式
TYPE-0™

FINAL FANTASY TYPE-0
©2012 Takatoshi Shiozawa / SQUARE ENIX
©2011 SQUARE ENIX CO.,LTD.
All Rights Reserved.

Art: TAKATOSHI SHIOZAWA
Character Design: TETSUYA NOMURA
Scenario: HIROKI CHIBA

The cadets of Akademeia's Class Zero are legends, with strength and magic unrivaled, and crimson capes symbolizing the great Vermilion Bird of the Dominion. But will their elite training be enough to keep them alive when a war breaks out and the Class Zero cadets find themselves at the front and center of a bloody political battlefield?!

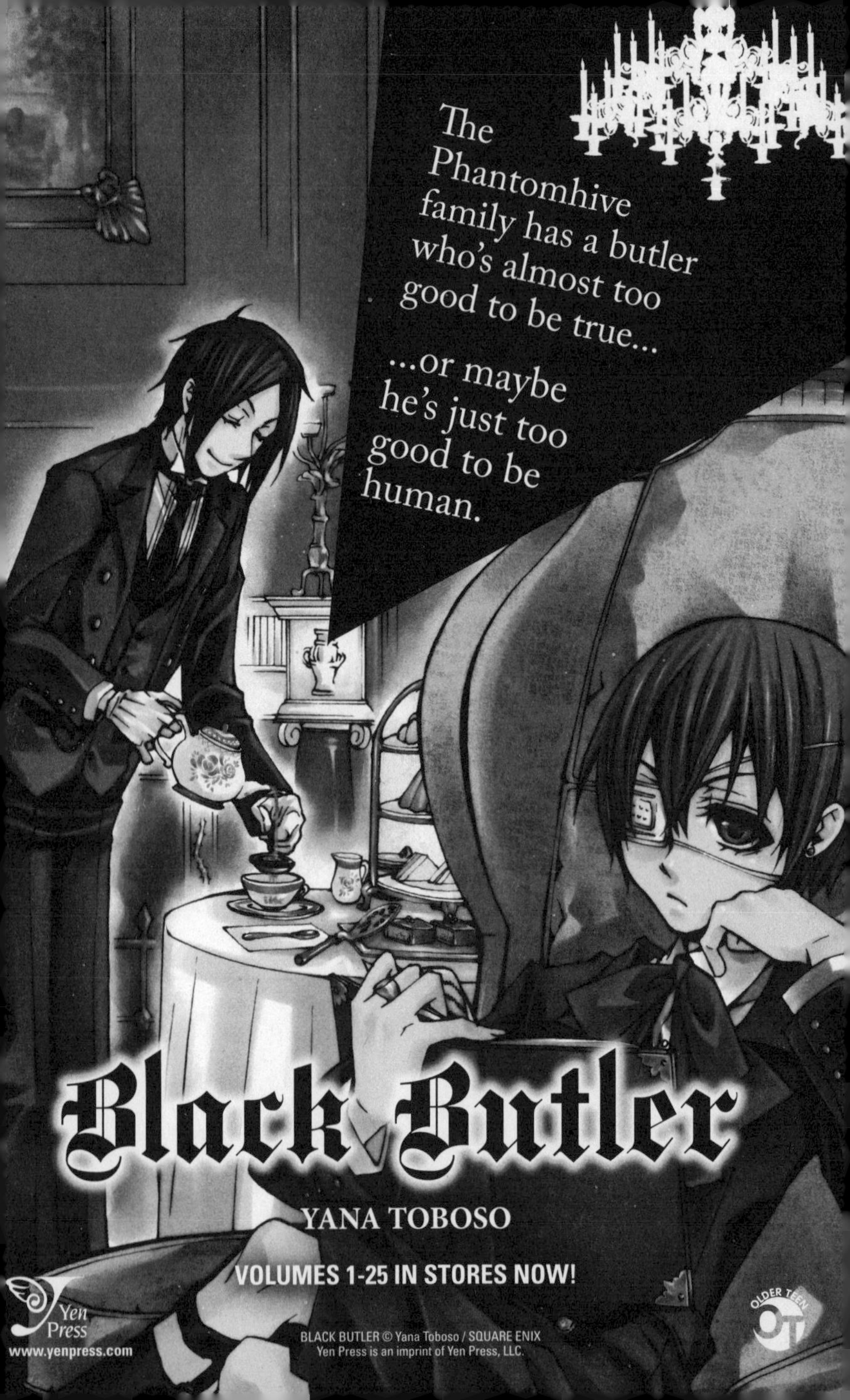
The Phantomhive family has a butler who's almost too good to be true...
...or maybe he's just too good to be human.
Black Butler
YANA TOBOSO
VOLUMES 1-25 IN STORES NOW!
Yen Press
www.yenpress.com
BLACK BUTLER © Yana Toboso / SQUARE ENIX
Yen Press is an imprint of Yen Press, LLC.
OLDER TEEN
OT

MURDERER
IN THE STREETS, KILLER
IN THE SHEETS!

A TERRIFI[ed] at GHOUL School!

Mai Tanaka

🔥 **Translation: AMANDA HALEY**
🔥 **Lettering: LYS BLAKESLEE**

This book is a work of fiction. Names, characters, places, and incidents are the product of the author's imagination or are used fictitiously. Any resemblance to actual events, locales, or persons, living or dead, is coincidental.

YOKAI GAKKO NO SENSEI HAJIMEMASHITA! Vol. 4 © 2016 Mai Tanaka/ SQUARE ENIX CO., LTD. First published in Japan in 2016 by SQUARE ENIX CO., LTD. English translation rights arranged with SQUARE ENIX CO., LTD. and Yen Press, LLC through Tuttle-Mori Agency, Inc., Tokyo.

English translation © 2018 by SQUARE ENIX CO., LTD.

Yen Press
1290 Avenue of the Americas
New York, NY 10104

Visit us at yenpress.com
facebook.com/yenpress
twitter.com/yenpress
yenpress.tumblr.com
instagram.com/yenpress

First Yen Pres[s]
September 2[0]

Yen Press is
of Yen Press,
The Yen Pres[s]
and logo are
trademarks [of]
Yen Press, LL[C].

The publisher is not responsible for websites (or their content) that are not owned by the publisher.

Library of Congress Control Number:
2017954141

ISBNs: 978-0-316-44729-4
(paperback)
[978-0-3]16-44730-0
(ebook)

[1]4 3 2 1

WOR

[U]nited States
[of] America